PRAISE FO

"Eric Brown's *Helix* is a classic concept—a built world to dwarf Rama and Ringworld—a setting for a hugely imaginative adventure. *Helix* is the very DNA of true SF. This is the rediscovery of wonder."
Stephen Baxter

"He is a masterful storyteller. Eric Brown is often lauded as the next big thing in science fiction and you can see why..."
Strange Horizons

"Eric Brown is *the* name to watch in SF."
Peter F. Hamilton

"SF infused with a cosmopolitan and literary sensibility... accomplished and affecting."
Paul J. McAuley

"*Helix* is essentially a romp—a gloriously old-fashioned slice of science fiction... What gives the novel a unique spin is its intertwining parallel plots. It's smart, fun, page-turning stuff, with an engaging cast and plenty of twists... A hugely entertaining read."
SFX Magazine

"*Kéthani*'s beauty is in its simplicity—by never attempting to aim above its height, it attains a kind of self-contained allure that is almost impossible to ignore. This is surely one of Brown's breakthrough stories, an achievement that highlights the extensive talents of an author destined, like his characters, for something far greater."
SciFi Now

"There is always something strikingly probable about the futures that Eric Brown writes... No matter how dark the future that Eric Brown imagines, the hope of redemption is always present. No matter how alien the world he describes, there is always something hauntingly familiar about the situations that unfold there."
Tony Ballantyne

"Eric Brown joins the ranks of Graham Joyce, Christopher Priest and Robert Holdstock as a master fabulist."
Paul di Filippo

"*Helix* is equal parts adventure, drama and wonder. Sometimes they work alone, providing a raw dose of science fiction. Other times, Brown uses them in concert to spin an irresistible blend that pulls the narrative along almost faster than you can keep up. However it's served, *Helix* is a delightful read and is an excellent reminder of why we read science fiction: it's fun!"
SF Signal

"Classic science-fiction components and a general reverence for science make this tale of intergalactic travel a worthy, occasionally awe-inspiring read... Brown's spectacular creativity creates a constantly compelling read... a memorable addition to the genre."
Kirkus Reviews

"Brown concentrates on stunning landscapes and in the way he conveys the conflicting points of view between races... No matter how familiar each character becomes, they continue to appear completely alien when viewed through the opposing set of eyes. Brown has a casual and unpretentious style and... the accessibility, the tenderness between characters and more importantly the scale of wonder involved are what makes this highly enjoyable escapism."
Interzone

Also by Eric Brown

Novels
Xenopath
Necropath
Cosmopath
Kéthani
Helix
New York Dreams
New York Blues
New York Nights
Penumbra
Engineman
Meridian Days

Novellas
Starship Fall
Starship Summer
Revenge
The Extraordinary Voyage of Jules Verne
Approaching Omega
A Writer's Life

Collections
Threshold Shift
The Fall of Tartarus
Deep Future
Parallax View (with Keith Brooke)
Blue Shifting
The Time-Lapsed Man

As Editor
The Mammoth Book of New Jules Verne Adventures (with Mike Ashley)

First published 2010 by Solaris
an imprint of Rebellion Publishing Ltd,
Riverside House, Osney Mead,
Oxford, OX2 0ES, UK

www.solarisbooks.com

ISBN: 978 1 906735 42 0

10 9 8 7 6 5 4 3 2 1

A CIP catalogue record for this book is available from the British Library.

Designed & typeset by Rebellion Publishing

Printed in the UK

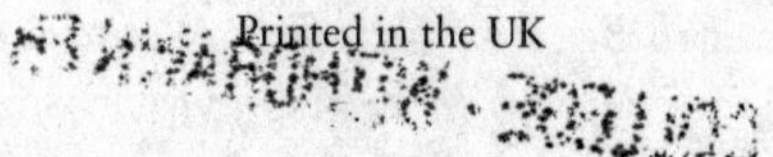

ENGINEMAN

ERIC BROWN

For Rog Peyton,
Birmingham's own Engineman,
with thanks.

Chapter One

It was another hot night out on the tarmac of the old Orly spaceport when Ralph Mirren saw what he thought was a KVI ghost.

He was tired and uncomfortable. The base of his skull throbbed painfully, a sure sign that he was due another flashback. The darkened cab of his grab-flier was like an oven. He couldn't win: with the sidescreens down, the breeze blowing across the 'port carried the alien spores which had drifted in through the interface two days ago from Chenowith. The spores caused respiratory complaints, and word had gone out to all 'port workers at the start of the shift to protect themselves. With the sidescreens sealed, the temperature inside the cab climbed into the high nineties. It was a basic design fault of these old Citroën grab-fliers that the cab was situated between the twin jet engines.

He killed the electro-magnet. The container he was carrying dropped into place beside the dozen others like the penultimate piece of a giant mosaic. He was turning to collect the last container when something flashed in the corner of his eye. He snapped his head around. The electric-blue spectre darted down an alley between the stacked containers. Shaken, Mirren lost control of his vehicle. It lurched for a second like a seaborne vessel rocked by a wave. He gathered himself, righted the flier and brought it to rest on the tarmac. The dying whine of the jets gave way to a sudden silence. If his senses were to be trusted, then what he'd seen was the manifestation of what some Enginemen called a KVI ghost – hard though that was to believe. Mirren had always treated stories of the fleeting banshees, which came screaming from the *nada*-continuum via the portals of the Keilor-Vincicoff interfaces, with a healthy degree of scepticism.

He sat for seconds in the silence of the cab before cracking the hatch and climbing out. He knew he wouldn't find anything. The image he thought he'd seen was no more than a hallucination, the product of too much work and not enough sleep.

He stepped from the flier towards the containers, their corrugated flanks washed by the blue light of the interface across the spaceport. He turned sideways and edged into the gap down which he'd seen the spectre disappear. There was no sign of anything untoward. A hallucination – it could be nothing else.

He turned a corner in the maze of containers, and there it was again. The ghost stood ten metres from him, its human form giving off a dazzling electric-blue glow. Cautiously he stepped towards it and the ghost took flight, disappearing between two containers. Mirren gave chase. When he reached the corner he turned and stared. The ghost had passed down the length of the container and emerged on the tarmac beside the flier. It paused there, as if regarding him. He approached the shape, the sound of his heart loud in his ears. As he stepped from between the containers, the scene before him was transformed. At first he thought it was a trick of his eyes; then he realised that the out-fall of light from the Keilor-Vincicoff Interface, towering over the spaceport, had downshifted from the brilliant cobalt of its deactivated phase to pastel shades of blue and green: through the 'face could be seen the hills and sky of a distant colony world. Instantly, the figure before Mirren was dispossessed of its burning vestments and stood revealed for what it was. Mirren stared at the frail old man garbed in a spacer's silversuit, clutching a bottle before him like a leper with a bell.

"Stay clear and allow me on my way!" He was obviously terrified. There was something at once pathetic about the plea, and yet dignified.

Mirren held out a hand and stepped forward.

"You can't stop me!" the old man called, swinging the bottle in a crazy sweep.

Hard on the realisation that he was dealing with flesh and blood, and not ectoplasm, Mirren assumed that the man was an old drunk who had wandered onto the spaceport by mistake. Then it came to him that, a drunk though the oldster might be, he once had been something more – and that his presence on the 'field was intentional. He recognised the look of bewildered abandonment in the oldster's eyes, heightened by the wild grey hair and straggling beard. His physical enfeeblement spoke of a similar state of mental disorientation. Mirren looked for and found the bulky spar of an occipital console spanning the oldster's shoulders beneath his silversuit like a miniaturised yoke.

"No closer! Leave me be!" He swayed, swinging the bottle in his fist. It slipped from his fingers and shattered at his feet. A dark stain spread across the tarmac and the reek of cognac rose in the hot night air.

"Mirren. An Alpha with the Canterbury Line on the *Martian Epiphany* for five years. Then five on the *Perseus Bound*. Take it easy, I'm on your side."

The old Engineman looked up from the broken bottle. Something in his gaze softened. "An Alpha with the Canterbury Line?" Their eyes met, and more was communicated in the silence than either man could possibly have spoken.

"Macready," the oldster whispered. "Beta. Javelin Line. Twenty years on the *Pride of Idaho*."

Their hands locked in a shake. Mirren felt as if he were crushing the fragile bones of a small bird.

He noticed, tattooed on the crepe-textured skin of Macready's right bicep, the infinity symbol of the Church of the Disciples of the *Nada*-Continuum. Aware of what the old Engineman had planned to do here tonight, Mirren felt both awe and horror at his certainty, his faith.

It was as if Macready had read his thoughts. "You can't stop me," he said softly. "I've thought long and hard about it. I have my reasons. I'm old, and ill. Now, if you'd kindly let me by."

Mirren indicated the alien landscape through the distant interface. The 'face stood as high as a towerblock and twice as long, braced in an arc-lighted girder frame. The juxtaposition of a daylight scene set against the backdrop of the Paris night was like something from a surreal work of art.

"It's activated, Macready. You'd end up on that world – even if you managed to evade security. And one planet is much like any other without the flux."

"If you'd not come after me–"

"You still wouldn't have made it in time."

"When does it close again?"

Mirren shrugged. "One hour, two. Whenever they're through with the deliveries." He stepped past Macready, opened the hatch of his flier and pulled out a half litre of scotch from the dash.

"I've almost finished here. We could sit and watch the transfer...?"

"And when it's finished, I can go on my way?"

"How can I stop you?" Mirren asked. In an hour or two, Macready would be in no fit state to go anywhere.

As he helped the frail old man into the passenger seat, Mirren asked himself what right he had to deny the ex-Engineman his destiny. Macready had faith – which was more than he had – and all he wanted was a return to the One.

Mirren engaged the up-thrusters. He banked away from the containers, sped across the 'field and collected the last unit. It hung from the magnet on the base of his vehicle, projecting fore and aft, fully three times as long as the flier. Mirren returned to the stack, dropped the last container and mach'd away on a parabolic course around the periphery of the 'port.

"Where we going?" Macready asked.

"I know where we'll get a good view."

They approached a crescent of abandoned mansions overlooking the 'port. The buildings were three centuries old, ornate and foursquare. Alien creepers shrouded their facades, bearing blood-red orchid-like blooms and other spectacular flowers.

Macready screwed round in his seat. "You said you were Mirren?" He paused. "Surely not Bob Mirren?"

Mirren stiffened, as if liquid nitrogen had replaced his spinal fluid. "I'm Ralph," he said. "Bobby's my brother."

"I knew Max Thorn," Macready said. "Second man to go down with the Syndrome."

Mirren said nothing. He hoped Macready would drop the subject. The silence stretched in the darkness, and as if Macready had sensed Mirren's distress, he said, "I'm sorry."

Mirren cut the thrust and the flier settled on the flat rooftop of a central mansion. He climbed out and helped Macready down. The old man was weak with an infirmity that could not be wholly the result of his advanced years.

Mirren pulled an old chesterfield from beneath a polythene awning and positioned it at the edge of the roof, where the roots of an extraterrestrial vine gripped the edge like clinging fingers. He assisted Macready to the thick, sprung cushion and sat down beside him.

Macready whistled in appreciation. "Fernandez!" he said, invoking the name of the physicist who'd discovered the *nada*-continuum.

They had a grandstand view of that area of the 'port directly beneath the rearing interface. Down below, giant container-hovercraft and juggernauts approached the hazy membrane of the 'face and were processed through, their shapes giving off sparkling coronas of ball-lightening. Instantly they were light years away, trundling across the tarmac of the distant colony planet.

Mirren fumbled with the cap on the scotch, took a slug and passed the bottle to Macready.

He came up here when there was no other way to vent his rage. He'd drink his scotch and hurl the empty bottle and curse the invention which had ended his affair with the numinous flux.

The interface did its job with disdainful ease and precision, opening portals to worlds separated by light years so that they were connected for periods of up to six hours. Goods could be driven – *driven* – from world to world. Alien planets no longer had mystique; the stars had lost their romance. Space travel was a thing of the past, and so were Enginemen.

Mirren spent a lot of time on the rooftop of the Rivoli mansions. He'd watch the bright points of familiar constellations wheel over the interface; Sagittarius, Virgo, Orion... He'd relived his time among the stars, his travels from one colony world to the next. For ten years all he'd lived for was his stint in the tank every twelve days, when his pineal bloomed and he pushed a 'ship through the realm which underlay the physical universe. The time spent in the tank, the sensation of the flux, had been a thing of wonder, which had left him blitzed for hours after de-tanking and craving *more*. Many of his colleagues held the belief that in flux they were finally conjoined with the One, Nirvana, Afterlife. Mirren held a more materialistic rationale for what he'd experienced. He considered it nothing more than a psychological side-effect of having the logic-matrix of a bigship plugged into his brain. He might have felt at one with the *nada*-continuum through which he pushed the 'ship, but there was no actual concrete proof that the continuum was anything more than the null-space its founder Pedro Fernandez had christened it. Nevertheless, Mirren had lived for the ecstasy of the flux, and even nowadays the wonder of it was a tantalising memory on the edge of his consciousness

– like a moving passage of music which resisted recollection, but at others flooded him with a hint of transcendence, and the sadness of knowing that he would never again experience such joy... Always he would leave the rooftop before dawn in tears, garage the grab-flier at the 'port, pick up his own vehicle and head home to his darkened rooms. Like all Enginemen, everywhere, Mirren abhorred the day.

Mirren had considered, in the early days after the shutdown of the Lines, having his recollections of the flux wiped from his consciousness through the process of mem-erase. He'd even approached a consultant about the treatment, but before he could undergo the process which would have done away with great chunks of his memory, mem-erase was withdrawn as unsafe – tests revealed that the erased memories could resurface years later in bouts of trauma or psychosis – and Mirren was condemned to a life-time of craving.

Macready took a long swallow of scotch and passed the bottle. He laid back his head and exhaled in alcoholic relief. Whisky trickled from his lips, beading in the tangle of his beard.

Mirren indicated the spaceport. "Look."

On the tarmac, before the interface, was a bigship. Both men stared down at it with a kind of silent wonder tinged with despair. It was as if the 'ship had been rolled out before them as a final insult.

It was as big as a towerblock laid on its side – a bull-nosed behemoth moving with agonising slowness towards the screen. The 'ship was like some proud and magnificent animal, blinded or lamed. It had had its flux-tank and logic-matrix ripped out, and all it was now was a feeble husk, a shell ferrying goods through the interface, powered by auxiliary engines and steered by drivers.

The bigship fed its colossal length into the 'face, and there was something horribly symbolic about the 'ship's submitting itself to the very device which had brought about its downfall.

Mirren recalled times, on the many spaceports across the Expansion, when bigships phased rapidly from this reality to the *nada*-continuum and back again, creating a stroboscopic effect like the image on a spinning coin. There had been times when the Lines were so busy that some spaceports had a hundred bigships phasing out simultaneously. To witness this was to be given a foretaste of the flux, as if the flickering 'ships, shuttling between realities, granted mundane reality the tantalising miasma of the *nada*-continuum.

Mirren was brought back to earth by a question from Macready.

"Why did you come after me down there?" There was grievance in the Engineman's tone.

"To tell the truth, I thought you were a ghost."

"A KVI ghost?" Macready spluttered a laugh. "I was a kay from the 'face!"

"Does that make any difference?"

Macready took a slug. "Ghosts are manifestations of the continuum," he said. "They come through the interfaces because the 'faces are the only link between the continuum and this... this reality. They're the souls of the departed and exist only briefly."

Mirren stared at the interface. "To be honest I don't believe–"

"But you thought I was one?"

"Just for a second."

Macready was shaking his head. "But you're an Engineman! Didn't the flux do anything for you?"

"Of course, but..." How could he explain to a believer that he had no belief?

"I pity you, Mirren. I really do. Listen, I've seen ghosts – dozens of them. When I left the Line I worked for a time as a driver on Deliniquin. I piloted 'ships like that one down there. No substitute for the real thing, but at least I was working on a bigship. I could convince myself that entering the interface was the next best thing to experiencing the *nada*-continuum. Some nights on the field we'd see flashes of light streak out from the 'face and approach us, then fade in seconds. Not really human in shape, just bolts of light. Souls..."

Mirren had heard hundreds of stories about Enginemen witnessing the so-called 'ghosts', and although they all claimed to see the same phenomena there was one aspect of the stories that made Mirren sceptical: only Enginemen ever saw the ghosts. It was as if they and only they were granted special audiences with the spectres as recompense for being deprived of the flux. Mirren assumed that the compensatory phenomena was nothing more than a product of the Enginemen's psyches – they wanted to believe, they wanted to see the ghosts, outriders from the continuum that Enginemen were now denied, and they did.

"Here..." Macready was rooting about in an inside pocket of his silvers. He withdrew a glowing card and passed it to Mirren. The card advertised the Church of the Disciples of the *Nada*-Continuum, situated on Rue Bresson, Montparnasse. Mirren had seen pictures of the Church, an old smallship converted into a chapel for believers.

"If you're in doubt, Mirren, go to a service. They'll put you right."

Mirren decided not to argue. He returned the card and smiled at the old Engineman. They drank in silence for a while, watching the activity on the tarmac far below. The bigship had returned through the interface, and now the column of fliers and trucks drove through like a column of ants. They unloaded their cargo on the distant world, then made their way back, traversing the light years in seconds. Later, the arc-lights around the frame of the interface winked out one by one, signalling the imminent closure of the link.

Mirren stared past the interface at the great sprawl of the city. The avenues and boulevards of some districts were illuminated like rigorous constellations, while other areas were plunged into darkness. Paris was the spiritual capital of the universe for the hopeless, disaffected guild of ex-Enginemen. The city had been home to generations of spacers, and when the Enginemen found themselves out of work it seemed the natural thing to do to make the pilgrimage to the shrine of Orly spaceport and the icon of the Keilor-Vincicoff Interface. Some Enginemen came to Paris because it was the city they knew best; others, mainly the more religious, because they believed that by being close to an interface they were also close to the *nada*-continuum.

Mirren counted himself among the former. He had made his home in the city whenever he'd docked on Earth, and rather than start a new life on one of the colony worlds or elsewhere on Earth, he'd decided to return to Paris and try for work at the 'port. He was successful – fliers, indeed workers of all types, were in short supply. But the Paris to which he returned was not the Paris he had left. The city no longer had the monopoly on interstellar trade – the Keilor-Vincicoff Organisation had opened interface 'ports in Kuala Lumpur and Buenos Aires, and investment had moved away from the West and to the richer countries of the South. Also, in the first year that the interface was open, it had admitted a host of breeze-born viruses, spores and seeds. The city had been transformed from the carefree European capital Mirren had known and loved into a sultry alien backwater; plagues and epidemics had ravaged Paris, and as the seeds took hold the city had become a phantasmagorical floral wonderland. The banks of the Seine were overrun by a riot of exotic alien vegetation, so that the river resembled more the jungle-fringed stretches of the Zambesi. Lianas, vines and virulent lichens gained purchase on old buildings and monuments. The girders of the Eiffel Tower were enwrapped by a creeper which sprouted giant sousaphone blooms so that it resembled a radio mast from the nightmare of a crazed surrealist. Plant-life was not the only invader; animals had taken the opportunity to migrate. In the early days, never a week had gone by without Mirren spotting some animal or bird that was not native to Earth. Rodents the size of dogs roved the deserted streets of the Latin Quarter, and exotic, winged creatures, half-bird, half-bat, had the freedom of the skies.

Macready cradled the empty bottle in his lap. He stared into the interface with unseeing eyes.

All activity had ceased on the tarmac below. The fliers and trucks were parked up on the perimeter of the 'port and the bigship had returned to its hangar, a sad animal at the end of its life.

The broad screen of the interface no longer showed the distant alien landscape. Now, deactivated, it coruscated cobalt blue. Rumour among Enginemen, especially those who believed that the *nada*-continuum represented Nirvana, was that in its deactivated state the 'face provided a portal to the infinite, a shortcut to eternity. They could have taken their lives in the privacy of their own homes, of course – and over the years many had – but there was a certain esteem to be had, a status gained in the hierarchy of martyrs, when one single-mindedly and with intent aforethought rendezvoused with the screen and destroyed oneself in a spectacular blaze of glory.

As Mirren watched, a suicide prepared his exit. He came in from the south, slung horizontal beneath the triangular wing of a power glider. Arc-lights dazzled off the propeller and the silver struts. There was about the suicides an element of the innovative that had less to do with the theatrical than the practical: suicides had to find new ways to evade the guards and fry themselves.

The drunken Macready, with his bottle of cognac and desire for oblivion, would have tried to dodge the guards and leap into the 'face in an act as humble as it was ill-planned. Mirren had saved the oldster, if temporarily: if Macready wished to end his life, then sooner or later he would succeed.

Macready had seen the glider. The oldster was leaning forward in the chesterfield, his attention fixed on the small, emerald triangle as it banked over the mansion and dived for the 'port. He wore an expression of fascination, as if he knew he would not make the 'face tonight and was vicariously sharing the pilot's final approach.

The glider arrowed towards the interface and slammed into the screen. Contact was brief and blinding. For a fraction of a second the outline of the glider and its spread-eagled pilot remained etched in silver on the blue screen, then dissolved and vanished. Mirren fancied he could hear the suicide's scream, diminishing, and smell his roasted corpse on the night air. He was at once appalled by the wanton forfeit of life, and awe-struck. He marvelled at the faith of the suicide, his certainty that absorption into the *nada*-continuum was the reward for so spectacular and beauteous an incineration.

Beside him on the chesterfield, Macready attempted to climb to his feet. Mirren restrained him, and the old man was too insensate with drink to resist.

"Let me go, damn you!" He slumped back into the cushions, exhausted.

"You'd never make it down there," Mirren said. "And even if you did, you wouldn't get past the guards–"

"Then I'll die trying!"

Mirren gripped the stringy, tattooed bicep. "Why?" he asked. "Why not just jump off the damned building and have done!"

Macready tipped back his head and cried at the stars. "When I was discharged I... I swore to myself that an interface death was the only way–" He struggled to stand again, but was too weak and fell back, crying. "Life's hell, Mirren. If only you could feel the pain."

"Damn you – and you think I don't miss the flux, too?"

The oldster cackled. "I mean I'm ill, Mirren. I'm dying."

Mirren stared at him.

Macready went on, "It's a terminal condition, Mirren. There's no cure. No cure at all. Only..." His head fell back, as if the fight had drained from him, and his breath came in ragged spasms.

Mirren averted his eyes, aware of the slow thump of his heartbeat.

Down on the tarmac, the guards were clearing up what remained of the kamikaze pilot and his glider – a few charred spars, scraps of clothing, larger chunks of what might have been charcoaled flesh. They disposed of the remains with little ceremony, scooping them up in the shovel of a tractor.

In the quiet aftermath of the spectacular suicide, Mirren found himself saying, "I was married before I became an Engineman. I had a child, a daughter in Australia. I thought I loved them both... Then I signed on the Canterbury Line, experienced the flux. When I came back – you know how it is. Nothing's the same. I lived only for the flux..." He wondered whether to add that his wife had come looking for him recently, but decided that the oldster wouldn't want to hear about his problems.

He glanced at Macready. He tried to remember the last time he'd spoken to someone about his life before the flux.

Macready sat unmoving. His head rested against the back of the chesterfield and his mouth hung open. Mirren reached out and touched the withered cheek. The old man's head fell forward, chin on chest. He felt Macready's frail wrist for a pulse.

He returned his gaze to the interface. He closed his eyes. Even the darkness was tinged with the blue light that glowed through his eyelids. If the Disciple's theology was to be believed, then right now Macready was being absorbed into the vastness which underlay everything, the infinite realm of the *nada*-continuum.

Silently he cursed the flux and its terrible consequences.

He heard the vehicle before he saw it.

When he opened his eyes and turned his head, the police cruiser was settling on the rooftop beside his flier. The cop climbed out, stretching after a long shift. Mirren knew the officer from the nightly patrols he made around the 'port. He'd even joined Mirren on the chesterfield, sharing a drink and appreciating the dawn view.

"Ralph," the cop said, striding over. He saw Macready. "Got company?"

"He's dead." Mirren laid back his head and stared at the stars. He was aware of the cop, kneeling beside him. When he looked, the officer was performing a routine on-the-spot autopsy. He strapped a sleek black device to Macready's forearm, and a dozen sub-dermals pumped a host of nanomedic drones into the dead Engineman's moribund circulatory system.

The cop stood with the device, reading off the cause of death. "Don't worry yourself," he said, misinterpreting Mirren's silence. "You couldn't have done a thing."

Mirren smiled to himself. "He came to the 'port to kill himself." He indicated the interface.

The cop laughed. "He did? That case, it'd save a lot of work if I just dumped him in the 'face."

"He was a Disciple of the *Nada*-Continuum," Mirren said. "In the circumstances I think he would have wanted a formal funeral."

The cop strode away and spoke quietly into his handset. Mirren looked at his watch. There were still a few hours to go before dawn broke over the city.

Fifteen minutes later the ambulance arrived, landing on the rooftop in a wash of revolving light. Mirren moved from the chesterfield – he really wanted to remain where he was, lethargic with apathy and depression, but that might have appeared crass. He watched the paramedics load the body of the old Engineman onto a stretcher and carry it across to the ambulance. It lifted, turned on its axis and banked away towards the centre of Paris, followed by the police cruiser.

Mirren tried to analyse his feelings, find within himself some compassion. He wondered if what he did feel was nothing more than the fear that he too would one day end his life as Macready had, one more unmourned Engineman. As he sat in silence and stared at the constellations overhead, he began to regret that he had denied the oldster his final wish to be taken by the flames of the interface.

Chapter Two

Ella Fernandez surfaced from her dream like a diver coming up for air. She sat bolt upright, gasping with panic. As the dream receded and became abstract she managed to control her breathing. Soon all she could recall was the ill-defined image of her father, walking away from her. She tried to persuade herself that the figure could have been any male, or a representation of every man she'd ever known, but she knew she was selling herself a lie. It was ironic that ever since she'd left him ten years ago, her father had followed her, turning up in her dreams with the regularity of a one-time star guesting on crummy vid-shows.

Ella fumbled in the darkness for the light-pad beside the bed. The room was large and high-ceilinged, the walls decorated with abstract murals. Her other work, her *serious* work – oils, acrylics, a few plasma graphics – leaned against the walls in back-to-front stacks.

The double-doors to the balcony were open to admit the warm breeze, the fragrance of flowers masking the stale smell of the mould which rashed the ceiling. While she'd slept, an alien creeper had found the opening and worked its way in. The magnificent red-and-yellow striped bloom hung above her head, presenting its spread petals and erect stamen like a gift. Ella smiled at it. "Too bad you aren't a golden-flower, buddy," she said. They were a new extra-terrestrial plants whose spores had blown through the interface recently, the golden pollen of which was mildly hallucinogenic. The authorities let the ghettos rot and fall to pieces, but they had been pretty damned quick last week to send out teams to eradicate the alien flowers.

She glanced across the room, looking for the jar of pollen on the upturned crate which doubled as her dressing-table. She could see a bulb of toothpaste and a few buckled tubes of oil paint – but no bottled sunshine. *Eddie, you cheating bastard...* Thing was, she'd have gladly given him the stuff if only he'd asked. He'd been on a downer for the past week and probably needed the pollen to get him through.

She swung herself out of bed and pulled on a wrap. She gently back-handed the flower from her path, ducked beneath the gnarled vine and pushed her way through the tangle of vegetation which had invaded the balcony during the day. Before she'd gone to bed that morning she'd cleared the balcony, cut back the persistent fronds and vines and dumped them in the street below. Now, in just eight hours, they were back again, forceful and vital as ever. She leaned against the balcony rail and stared out over what could have been an exo-botanical garden.

The sun had set and the street was in darkness. As her eyes adapted, she made out the pale pastel colours of the luminous blooms strung out along the facade of the opposite buildings, like a replacement for the neon shop-fronts and the advertisements of a long-gone, prosperous Paris. Directly below, the Rue Chabrol was a dense riot of tropical vegetation, as if a strip of jungle had been laid down between the buildings. The occasional tall shoot arced above the mass, extending great green leaves like spinnakers, nodding in the breeze. At ground level, tunnels and runs had been forced through the undergrowth to connect the few inhabited buildings with the central, caged strip which ran the length of the street to the nearest cleared thoroughfare.

Over the past year, Ella had seen many friends and fellow squatters give in and move out, a combination of the fecund plant-life and the decline in services finally driving them away to the suburbs. At one time, about four years ago when Ella had moved here with Eddie, there had been a dozen other artists living and working in the street – a community of like-minded people doing their own thing in the face of the authorities' displeasure. They'd been good times, and Ella had accomplished some of her best work. Now she was the only artist in the area, and she didn't have too much to do with the freaks and weirdoes she had as neighbours. She liked eccentrics – real, hundred-proof kooks who were original and had something to say – but over the past few months the free accommodation along the street, and the fact that the law rarely patrolled this far into the ghetto, had attracted the kind of people usually only found on the inside of secure psychiatric units.

Increasingly, Paris was becoming rapidly depopulated, the exodus from the city indicative of a much more widespread exodus from Europe itself. Those that could afford to were fleeing the Union and moving to the prosperous haven of Oceania, or off-world entirely to the colonies which the interfaces were opening up in ever-increasing numbers. Only the poor were left – or sorry bastards like Eddie, Enginemen who were unable to tear themselves away from the once-proud centre of the space age – the poor and the very rich who, cushioned against the privations of a ruined Europe, built themselves magnificent strongholds in cultivated Babylons and lived like siege-lords... Ella wondered where she fitted in.

She leaned over the balcony rail and peered south. The interface at Orly, three kilometres away, was in its deactivated phase: a vast membrane of cobalt blue notched between the buildings on either side of the street. Ella shivered. The interface filled her with a strange crawling sensation of dread. She wondered if she should suggest moving away, but she knew what Eddie would have to say about that.

With luck, she told herself, Europe will become so impoverished that the 'face will no longer be viable and Keilor-Vincicoff will relocate it...

She returned inside, wiping the soles of her sap-sticky feet on the filthy carpet. In the tiny, overcrowded kitchen she found her own chipped mug and boiled some water. She never bothered with breakfast, but drank cup after cup of *real* coffee – her one luxury – to sustain her through the nights while she worked. She'd become nocturnal on moving in with Eddie Schwartz. Enginemen were night creatures, and it didn't bother Ella when she slept – she could create just as well at three in the morning or three in the afternoon. She'd soon got used to never seeing the sun. In her down cycles, she told herself that darkness suited the state of her psyche; when she was up, high on the buzz of creating, she knew that she liked the night because it reminded her of the long, balmy twilight phases on the planet of Hennessy's Reach, where she'd spent the happiest years of her life.

She poured herself a black coffee and left the kitchen, holding the mug in both hands and taking tiny sips. She paused outside Eddie's room, deciding to try and wake him. He'd be blitzed on the gold dust he'd stolen, but she could have fun watching his confusion as she asked him nonsense questions. Ella had finished a painting the night before; she was feeling good. She pushed open the door with her toes and saw that his bed was empty.

No doubt he'd be up on the roof, staring at the interface. He'd been spending a lot of time up there, lately.

She stared around the room. Like her, Eddie was not materialistic. He had few possessions. The walls were bare – no pix or graphics to remind him of his time pushing for the Chantilly Line; no ornaments, books or discs. Just a bed, a chair, and a crate containing his clothes.

Ella stepped inside, unable to suppress the feeling that she was trespassing. She could not recall the last time she'd been in his bedroom, nor when he'd last been in hers. Although they'd been together for the last seven years, in real terms they lived very much apart, Ella spending all her time painting and sculpting, and Eddie working nights at the food-irradiation plant in north Paris. Their relationship was very much platonic. She was like an elder sister to him – even though Eddie in his mid-forties was twenty years older than her – advising him, and looking after him during his periods of sickness, both physical and mental.

Even in the early days there had been a certain distance between them. Ella had needed someone she could rebuild her life around – someone who could have looked after and protected her would have been ideal, but the alternative, a man *she* could look after and protect, was better than nothing. Eddie had needed, though he probably hadn't realised it at the time, someone to keep him alive in the dark years after the closure of the shipping Lines. He was a physically big man, solid and greying, not at all imaginative or artistic, and Ella's friends had said that they were ill-matched, that it couldn't possibly work, and given them a year at best. As things turned out, her friends were right on two counts – they were ill-matched and it hadn't worked. But here they were seven years later, still together, mainly due to the fact that Eddie still needed someone, and Ella had found no-one else.

She left the room and closed the door behind her. At the end of the hall she was confronted by her image in the wall-mirror. She set little store by how she looked, and was often surprised when she encountered her reflection. She was short and thin, permanently drawn and tired-looking – even when she was on a high and felt energised. She shaved her head regularly, and this, together with the lines that delta'd from the corners of her eyes, made her look ten years older than she was. And yet today, she told herself, I feel young and confident, full of life. She smiled at herself. She'd just completed a piece she was happy with, which accounted for her high. Tomorrow, when the creative glow diminished and she could regard the sculpture more critically, and see its weaknesses, she'd become depressed, tell herself that she could do better, had to do better – even though she would doubt that she could ever create anything original again... It was all part of the cycle.

Thinking about her work reminded her that she had a painting out at the moment, a triptych canvas she'd sent to her agent a couple of months ago.

She finished her coffee, went to the kitchen for a refill, then approached the vid-screen in the lounge. The room, like the rest of the apartment, was run-down and in need of a good interior decorator, not that Ella gave a damn about things like habitat pride. However, one corner of the room, which faced the screen, was done out with flock wallpaper and a square of carpet she'd found dumped in the street. A mock Schreiber recliner, which she'd made herself on the cheap – faced the screen. The effect was a minor work of art in itself, a mini film-set in the grimy chaos of her living room. Vasquez was a snob, impressed by things like *appearance*.

Ella sat cross-legged in the chair, tapped in Vasquez's code. She decided not to come straight out with, "What do you think of my latest piece, Carmen?"

Five year ago, Vasquez had sold one of Ella's paintings to an off-world art-collector for a good sum. The oil, entitled *Conversion* – a visual attempt to convey the wonder she'd experienced upon her conversion to the Disciples – was one of her favourites. For years she had not bothered about the identity of the purchaser, but a couple of months ago – wondering on which far planet her work might be hanging – she'd written to Vasquez asking her if she could reveal the identity of the buyer.

Now, Ella would remind her agent about the enquiry, and then ask what Vasquez thought about her latest piece.

The calling tone purred. The screen remained blank, then scrolled up the fact that Carmen Vasquez was in a meeting, but if the caller would like to leave a message after the tone...

Ella composed herself, drew her wrap closed at the throat. The tone played out. "Ah, Carmen – Ella Fernandez here–" Damn! That was obvious! Vasquez would be watching the recording of Ella, wouldn't she? "I was just wondering – it isn't really important – but I wondered if you could tell me who bought *Conversion*? Ah... that's all – if you could call back when you have the time, there are one or two things I'd like to ask you. Okay, see you later. Bye." She grinned at the screen, waved her fingers, then felt self-conscious and cut the connection.

She was still laughing at herself when the roar sounded outside. The apartment shuddered as if in an earthquake. When the vibrations came to an end and the flakes of paint stopped snowing from the ceiling, she got up and crossed to the door. She belted her wrap and leaned against the jamb, waiting for Eddie to appear from the escalator across the hall.

His flier had been in the garage of some third-rate mechanic down the road for a month now, until such time as Eddie came up with the credits to pay for the repairs. Now she realised why he'd stolen the gold dust.

After three minutes Eddie had still not shown himself, and Ella began to feel a little silly in this nonchalant-cum-confrontational pose. She pushed herself from the jamb and rode the elevator to the roof.

It was a warm night. The stars were out in a clear sky. Vines and creepers were growing around the girder stanchions of the landing pad, despite Eddie's daily efforts at clearing them. He was sitting on the hood of his battered old Peugeot, his thick-set middle-aged frame and the flier's *art deco* bulk somehow complementary. They were silhouetted against the glow of the interface like a cinema advertisement for Libyan hash.

Ella padded across to him, holding her shoulders. She leaned against the flank of the flier next to Eddie's silversuited legs and feigned an interest in what he was watching. Over at the spaceport, the interface had activated. Through the screen could be seen the busy 'port of some distant colony world.

She felt his hand on the back of her neck, warm and strong. He had a stock of these gentle, affectionate gestures which he used in lieu of conversation. Sometimes he went for days without speaking.

"You took my dust," she said at last.

He made a sound in his throat which might have been an admission of his guilt, squeezed her neck as if that might make things better.

"I wouldn't care. If you'd asked, Eddie... You know that? If you'd asked, "Ella, I need creds to get the flier fixed." I'd've given you the damned dust."

He said, in his soft, slow Californian accent, "I needed the flier. I've got a job lined up at Orly. I'll pay you back next week, okay, Princess?"

She supposed she should have been glad he'd condescended to speak to her, but she was troubled that he'd found work at Orly. She hitched herself up onto the hood and looked at him.

He was watching the interface with that far-away look in his eyes, as if remembering the time when the stars had been his, and recognising the fact that now they were denied him forever. Ella was aware that he'd been slipping into a depression over the past week, and she feared that it might culminate in another protracted bout of drinking, of her having to scour the streets of Paris for him, comatose in some gutter.

"Eddie," she whispered. "Have you been to the Church recently? You know, they have good counsellors there. They'd be able to help you."

Eddie grunted something non-committal.

She sighed. It worried her, the fact that he no longer attended the services or counselling sessions, even when she tried to drag him along. At one point, concerned by his indifference, she had accused him of no longer believing. Eddie had replied, simply and calmly, that he did believe – but that he did not need *faith* as she needed it because he had fluxed, had achieved the numinous union with the *nada*-continuum, and did not need the dogma of the Church to uphold his belief. Unlike Ella, who as a civilian had never experienced the flux, and therefore required blind faith to sustain her belief.

The vast majority of Disciples on Earth were Enginemen and Enginewomen. Ella was one of only a dozen non-spacers in France who'd undergone conversion. She was that rarity, a believer who'd never actually experienced the flux, and thus her faith was questioned and probed all the more rigorously by the devout. She had never opened up and divulged to anyone – not even to Eddie – the circumstances of her conversion during her teens on the colony world of the Reach.

She laid her head on Eddie's shoulder, felt the occipital console beneath the material of his silversuit. Over at the 'port, the screen had deactivated, returned to its cobalt blue phase. She shivered.

Eddie put an arm around her and squeezed. *What you thinking, Princess?* his hug said.

"This place, Eddie... The nearest store is an hour away. The apartment's damp, smelly. The gangs... Eddie – have you seen the street gangs around here?"

Another squeeze. *Don't fear the gangs*.

"Let's just get the hell out of here, Eddie."

This provoked a more definite response. He actually turned his head and looked at her.

"Move out to ...," she went on, "buy a place by the river."

"That'd cost, Princess."

With the fee she'd received from selling a couple of sculptures last year, she had enough for a down-payment on a small unit by the Seine. She didn't tell Eddie this, because in her heart she knew that there was no way he'd agree to leaving Orly. And if he knew she had credits, he'd want them.

"If I sell the picture I have out now..."

"You want to be back in with your artisan friends–"

"I want to leave this place!"

"Or do you want a little house by the river as another statement?"

She pulled away and stared at him. "What?"

"Like your motorbike, your hair–"

"What hair?"

"Exactly, my little shaveskull."

"My bike, my hair; they're me, Eddie. It's not a damned statement, it's who I am."

He turned a gentle smile on her. "It's what your father made you, Princess. A rebel."

Before she could find the words for a half-hearted denial, the chime on the vid-screen sounded, floating up from the open window in the lounge.

"That'll be for you," Eddie said, and turned his gaze back to the interface.

Ella hurried down to the lounge, arrived breathless and pressed the *accept* stud. She sat on the recliner as the screen flared into life. She just had time to arrange the collar of her wrap before Carmen Vasquez appeared, standing beside a marble fireplace and smoking a cigarette in an ivory holder. She wore a long, black strapless gown and, with her tanned oval face and Latin poise, looked as though she'd just stepped off a cat-walk.

"Ella, darling – I received your call." She had the socialite's practised ability of dispensing endearments without really seeming to mean them.

"I hope I didn't interrupt anything," Ella began.

"Of course not. I had intended to call you anyway."

"You had? You can tell me who bought *Conversion*?"

Vasquez drew on her cigarette, her cheeks hollowed. She exhaled and fanned away the offending smoke with a languid wave. "Part of the deal, Ella darling, was that the buyer should enjoy absolute anonymity. I'm afraid it's not my place to divulge client's private details."

Ella felt as though she'd been chastised. "I don't suppose you have any idea which planet the buyer–"

"All I can tell you is that my client was an off-worlder," Vasquez said coolly. "If I were you. I should be thankful for the fee you received."

Implicit in which statement, Ella thought, was the suggestion that Vasquez thought the fee exorbitant.

"Ah... I was wondering about my latest piece," Ella ventured.

"Actually, it's that I was meaning to call you about."

"It was? I didn't mean to rush you. It's just that – well, it *has* been two months..."

Vasquez nodded, tapping a centimetre of ash into an onyx tray on the mantelpiece. She returned her attention to Ella. "As a matter of fact, the piece has been causing me no small amount of difficulty."

Ella's heart sank. "It has?"

"It's a rather angry piece, isn't it?"

Ella was taken aback. "Well, I suppose it is."

Vasquez frowned, examined the length of her cigarette. "It's full of anger and hatred."

Ella was at a loss for words. She feared what was to come. She shrugged. "It's a personal statement, of course. It's how I was feeling at the time."

Vasquez was staring at her. "But didn't you know, darling – hatred is out at the moment."

"Excuse me?"

"Hatred, anger, rage – my customers don't want to adorn their walls with such images. Hatred is out."

"*Out*?" Ella echoed. She tried not to laugh. She could hardly believe what she was hearing. "But art... art's supposed to reflect reality."

"Reality does not exclusively consist of anger and hatred, Ella, darling."

She wanted to shout that *her* reality did.

"Ella..." Vasquez began in a placatory tone.

Ella leaned forward. "Look around you. The world is full of hatred. Look at what's happening in Africa, China. Christ, look at Europe!"

"But there are other images you could employ."

"I don't want to employ other images!" Ella cried. "I'm angry. Look, for Chrissake. Look!" And before she could stop herself, she picked up the screen and staggered with it over to the window ledge. She turned it around, so that the relay cameras presented to her agent the street scene, the crumbling buildings opposite.

She wished she could carry the screen around the ghetto with her, so that Vasquez might witness all the filth, the poverty and the wretchedness.

She swung the screen back to face her. Vasquez wore an expression of fastidious distaste. "Europe is fucked. The people who live here are fucked. And you want me to paint bunches of flowers. I paint from experience, damn you!"

"If you intend to take that tone–"

She swept on, "It's okay for you to dictate what I do, Miss Privilege in your fucking penthouse suite in the richest country in the world." Ella stopped herself, panting, aware that she'd gone too far.

Vasquez was silent, regarding her. "Thank you for making your views so abundantly clear, and so eloquently expressed, Ella. As we seem to have irreconcilable differences of opinion as to what can constitute a work of art, I think it would be best if we parted company. Don't bother sending me any more of your work, Ella. I'll return your latest forthwith."

Ella smiled through her rage. "There's something I'd like to say."

Vasquez raised an imperious eyebrow. "Oh, and you haven't said enough?"

"Too right," Ella smiled. She raised her foot, placed it in the image of Vasquez's face, and pushed the screen off the ledge.

"You bastard!" she yelled after it. She leaned from the window and watched it fall. It sailed through the air, crashed through the undergrowth and hit the street with a dull explosion.

Ella straightened, massaging the small of her back. She stared up at the stars. The adrenalin rush at what she'd done gave way to the sobering realisation of her circumstances. She didn't know whether to be more appalled at Vasquez's view of art, or the fact that she was back at square one, without an agent. She supposed she could always go back to selling her work on the Champs-Elysées.

She wandered into the kitchen, not sure whether to laugh or to cry. Vasquez's expression when Ella thrust her bare foot into her face... It was just as well she hadn't confronted Vasquez in the flesh.

She pulled two beers from the cooler and returned to the roof. Eddie was still sitting on his flier, unmoving, staring intently at the deactivated screen of the interface in the distance. Ella interposed herself between the screen and the Engineman. "Here." She held out a beer. "Brought you this."

He made no move to take the bottle, but reached out and touched Ella's shoulder, signalling that she should move. She stood her ground, defiant. Eddie leaned to his right to get a better view of the screen. He seemed to be in a trance.

She unscrewed the top from her beer, took a long drink. "That was my agent," she said at last, aware that she was talking to herself. She shrugged. "I don't have an agent any more, Eddie." She laughed. "I dropped her."

She looked up at Eddie. No response.

"What am I going to do?" Something in her tone moved him to look at her, but only briefly. He returned his gaze to the screen.

"Fuck you," she whispered. "You're as blind and uncaring as that bitch..." Then: "Eddie! Look at me. I need to talk."

He gestured. "Not now, Princess."

"Not now? But I need to talk *now*."

He was far gone, lost.

"You bastard!" Impulsively, she flung the full beer bottle at him. It missed, sailed way over his head. He didn't even flinch.

"Hey," she said. "You know what? Why don't you fly over there and throw yourself through the screen? Go fry your fucking self and see if I care!"

She hurried away, her anger suddenly usurped by regret, and the hope that Eddie hadn't heard her. She ran to her room, sickened suddenly by the plethora of her failed work stacked against the wall, mocking her. She curled up on her bed and cried out in frustration.

She had no idea how long she'd been asleep when she rolled onto her back and blinked herself awake. The noise that had begun in her dreams continued now, and as she stared up at the ceiling she wondered when her tired mind would stop taunting her.

Then the walls of the room began to shake, and the noise became thunderous. A sudden dread clutched at her. "No," she said to herself, jumping from the bed and running to the balcony.

The ugly bulk of Eddie's flier edged from the landing pad, filling the sky above the street as it moved off in the direction of the spaceport, the roar of its jets diminishing. "No, Eddie!" she screamed. "No!"

She pulled on a jacket and trousers and, still barefoot, ran down the stairs, taking them in threes and fours. Her heart was pounding and she was hardly able to comprehend what Eddie was doing. She told herself that what she feared just could *not* be happening, while the realist in her thought back over the week and recalled all the tell-tale signs of Eddie's increasing disaffection.

She dragged open the cubby door beneath the stairs and hauled out her bike, an old Suzuki turbo she took on long rides into the country when she was feeling low. She pushed it down the hall and through the gaping front door. A tangle of vines and brambles, not cleared for a day or more, barred the way. Using the bike as a battering ram, she charged ahead, thorns catching her clothing on the way through. She came to the caged run down the centre of the street, mounted the bike and kicked it into life. She shot forward, fish-tailing on the slime that slicked the tarmac, then accelerated. The headlamp illuminated the narrow corridor ahead.

She came to the cleared intersection and turned right, down a wide avenue lined by derelict buildings. A street gang on the corner jeered as she passed, hurling insults and beer bottles. The avenue took a bend and straightened up, and Ella opened the throttle. If she could get to the 'port before Eddie, warn the authorities of what he intended... The disadvantage was that, while her bike was faster than his beat-up flier, she was restricted to following the roads, while Eddie could fly directly across Orly to the 'port.

He might want to kill himself now, she told herself – but that's because he's low. He'll snap out of it in a day or two, return to his normal stoic self, look back and realise how close he came...

If only she could get there before him.

She cut down side-streets and alleys, zigzagging between derelict tenements in what she calculated was a short-cut to the massive 'port complex. Her heart surged when, up ahead, she made out the ponderous shape of the Peugeot, flying low, and beyond it the bright blue halation of the screen in the night sky to the south.

"Eddie!" she screamed, the wind chapping her cheeks where her tears had coursed.

Almost as if her subconscious was acknowledging the fact that she'd lost him, the image of Eddie when she'd first met him appeared in her mind's eye. In his thirties, not yet run to fat or greying; kind, gentle, haunted by his loss and yet amazed by his good fortune at being the recipient of all her affection...

She skidded around the bend of the approach road to the 'port, perhaps half a kilometre away. As she straightened up and increased speed, she realised that she had lost the race. Eddie had lifted his flier and accelerated over the perimeter fence. The security guards were firing at the vehicle, bright tracer hosing through the night sky. The flier took a hit and lurched, but continued on towards the screen. Ella screeched the bike to a halt and it skidded out from under her. She rolled, fetched up in a sitting position on the grass verge. She watched the flier limp pathetically towards the brilliant membrane of the interface.

She climbed to her knees, then to her feet, and limped towards the fence. She hooked her fingers through the mesh and hung there, her face pressed up against the diamonds.

"Eddie, stop. Please stop..."

Six metres away, through the fence, a uniformed security guard turned and stared at her.

"Please... please stop him."

The guard was young, in his late teens, and later, when Ella went over and over the sequence of events, one of the inconsequential images that would enter her mind would be that of the guard's young face, his stricken expression as he looked from Ella to the flier, and back to Ella again, unable to do anything to halt the flier, and prevented by regulations from leaving his post and trying to console her.

She watched as Eddie approached the interface. Even at this late stage she maintained the ludicrous hope that the authorities would activate the screen, open the portal to some colony planet, so that Eddie would pass through unharmed. She should have realised, though, that the expense of opening the 'face would far exceed the worth of one crazed Engineman.

The flier hit the interface and vanished in a blinding white explosion. The detonation travelled across the 'port, reaching her a second later, followed by the patter of shrapnelled debris raining down across the tarmac. Ella closed her eyes, and the explosion bloomed again in the darkness.

When she opened her eyes, the guard was running towards the terminal building, and before he could summon medical assistance for her, or whatever he intended, Ella stumbled across to where her bike lay on the grass embankment next to the fence. Dry-sobbing, she hauled it upright, kick-started it and raced off at high speed away from the 'port. As the blue light of the interface sent her shadow sprawling ahead, Ella tried to convince herself that Eddie had not heard her telling him to fly into the screen...

She raced around Paris at breakneck speed, as if tempting fate to take her where it had taken Eddie. The wind in her face, she circled the Eiffel tower, phantasmagorically adorned, tore across the traffic island and through the Arc De Triomph, then accelerated down the Champs-Elysées. Beside the majestic silver dome which covered the tourist quarter of central Paris, she came to a halt. She sat astraddle the stilled engine of her Suzuki, aware of the bike ticking beneath her in the quiet morning air, aware of the pain in her chest, and the fact that she was still alive.

By the time she arrived back at her apartment, dawn was touching the eastern horizon, and she knew what she was going to do.

From beneath the mattress in her bedroom she took the photograph of her father, and the disc he had sent. She dropped the photo on the bed without looking at it, and played the disc.

"I have seen the light, Ella. I need to see–"

The rest was music. Three weeks ago, on receiving and playing the disc, the sound of his voice had caused her so much pain that she had stopped the disc instantly and recorded over the rest of the message.

He had seen the light...? By which, did he mean that he realised and acknowledged all the mistakes of his past?

Surely not...

She dropped the disc on top of the picture, obscuring his face. She changed, found one of Eddie's silversuits. As she pulled it on, the material shrank, nestled around her thin body. She considered the irony of wearing an E-man's silversuit where she was going. She packed a bag and pocketed her savings. She looked around the bedroom, at her work bearing silent testimony to her lack of success. As she stood on the threshold, she was tempted to leave the bedroom door unlocked, let fate take away her past. But something, some deep and abiding belief in her ability, made her turn the key in the lock.

She turned at a sound from the hall window. Sabine was crouching on the sill, watching her. "You leaving, Ella?"

"Going out to the Rim, Sabby," she told the urchin. "Going to look up my father."

The kid glanced around. "Where's Eddie?"

Ella smiled through her tears. "Eddie's gone. He won't be coming back."

"So you want me to look after the place, make sure the bastards don't trash your work?"

Ella dug in her pocket for loose creds. "Sure, Sabby. You do that."

Then she made her way to an Agency and arranged passage to the Reach.

Chapter Three

Dawn was a uniform grey pallor above the eastern horizon as Mirren garaged the grab-flier and walked across the tarmac to the circular bar annexe of the terminal building. It was Thursday morning, the start of his three day break, and he always made a habit of calling into the bar for a couple of beers to celebrate. He was feeling dead on his feet and even more depressed than usual. He could not shake from his mind the death of Macready yesterday, or the suicide of the Engineman who'd flown his flier straight into the interface a couple of hours ago.

He pushed through the swing doors and entered the bar. The room was furnished with cheap moulded tables and chairs, fitted originally to cater for the hordes of vacationing civilians who had visited Earth in the days when the port catered for bigships. Since the installation of the KV interface, however, and the downgrading of the 'port to the status of commercial/industrial, the only patrons of the bar were site workers: security guards, engineers and fliers. The plastic furnishings of the circular room had been sprayed matt black, as if in mourning, and the lighting turned low. The funereal atmosphere of the bar suited its function as the place to come for a quiet drink after a long shift. Here, Mirren could be guaranteed the luxury of privacy without hassle. In many of the bars around the city he would have been recognised as an ex-Engineman – the occipital console was a give away – and regarded with curiosity, pity or even envy. Any one of which he could do without, especially if the party doing the regarding had no qualms about demanding to know if it were true that he – as the representative of Enginemen, everywhere – had looked upon the face of God.

He charged a stein of lager to his tab and carried it through the gloom to a booth beside the wrap-around viewscreen. He sat hunched over his beer and massaged the base of his skull above his occipital console. His head throbbed, forewarning him that another flashback was on the way. Three days ago, as he'd climbed into his flier for the short flight home, he had flashbacked for the first time. He'd suddenly found himself reliving his last flight aboard the *Perseus Bound*. He had flashed twice since then, each time experiencing consecutive episodes from his last flight. He knew where it would end: a decade ago, the 'ship had crashlanded on an uncharted planet, and though he had survived the accident unscathed, he had suffered extensive amnesia. He recalled nothing at all of the journey, and knew of the crash and his subsequent memory loss from what the medics of the Line had told him. He was regaining his recollection of the events, now, in a most singular fashion.

He took a long swallow of lager and sat back, and it was then that he saw her. She was sitting on a high-stool at the bar. Evidently she had just arrived, as he hadn't seen her earlier. He pushed his drink across the table, then slid around the u-shaped couch so that his back was to her.

She was wearing the light blue uniform of the Orly security team, so perhaps her presence here had nothing to do with him, but he found that hard to believe. A month ago she had called, but he'd ignored her message. "Hi, Ralph. I'm in Paris for a few months – security work for various companies in the city. I thought I'd look you up. Perhaps we could go out for a meal? Call me at the Excelsior, any time." And she had smiled and cut the connection.

What had disturbed him so much was the fact that she had changed so little in twenty years. She was still the elfin-faced, spike-haired twenty-one year-old he had walked out on in Sydney with all those years ago. Except she was over forty now, and her breezy confidence and self-assurance told him that she had grown in the interim.

He had not returned her call.

He was about to quickly finish his drink and escape, hopefully without being seen, when he heard footsteps on the tiles, heading his way.

She paused before the booth, arms folded across her chest, leaning forward slightly. "Ralph? It is you?"

He knew that her uncertainty had nothing to do with the low lighting. He had changed a lot in twenty years.

He sat up. "Caroline."

She hugged her shoulders and gave a kind of shrug, a gesture he recognised from years ago which indicated she was nervous. "Carrie, please. Not so formal."

Mirren gestured across the booth, and Caroline slipped along the seat with a quick wan smile at him. She was, he knew, shocked at how the years had treated him.

He had met Caroline Bishop when he was twenty, studying aeronautics at the Jet Propulsion labs in Sydney. She'd worked there one day a week, on release from the college of the Australian Internal Security bureau. Until then he'd thought that love at first sight was nothing more than a concept dreamed up in retrospect by incurable romantics, but when he first saw Caroline in the student canteen he'd experienced an inexplicable surge of desire to possess and protect – which years later he rationalised cynically as the tyranny of biology to gain its own ends.

A year later they had married – a declining institution in the latter half of the century, but Caroline's parents were Catholic, and although Mirren was atheist he'd not objected to the ceremony.

Mirren had joined the Canterbury Line as an Alpha Engineman six months later, and a year after that, with no explanation to Caroline and without being able to explain his motivations even to himself, he had kissed his wife and daughter good-bye and never returned. He'd set up home in Paris, made sure Caroline was financially secure with monthly cheques, and from that day until her call a month ago had never set eyes on her.

He had returned unread the dozens of letters she'd sent him care of the Canterbury Line over the first couple of years.

He tried to find in himself some scintilla of conscience for what he had done, but he felt nothing other than a distant regret that, but for circumstances which in retrospect seemed inevitable, it could all have been so different.

He tried to speak now. His mouth was dry, making words impossible. He took a swallow of lager. "How are you, Carrie?" The cliché was so obvious he thought she might laugh.

Instead she smiled. "I'm fine. You know, working hard..." She was either a very fine actress, hiding her hurt, or the years had worked to heal her wounds. "You?"

He shrugged. "Okay. I have regular work, an apartment." He could look objectively at the situation and see that she would be quite justified in hating him. "What a coincidence this is..."

She shook her head. "I've been looking for you. I'm here on business."

She pulled the front of her jacket open and looked down as she fingered through papers in an inside pocket. Her frown of concentration, her pursed lips, brought back memories. A characteristic of hers had been to exaggerate her facial expressions; she had a theatrical mask for happy and sad and the many grades of sentiment in between, all manner of quirks and tics to express her feelings. He had found it very becoming, years ago.

He wondered if by 'business' she meant legal business, a demand for more payment. "You came all the way to Paris looking for me...?" he began.

She looked up, frowning. "I'm in Paris because I wanted to work in Europe for the experience, and I'm working here because Orly wanted a top security executive."

She pulled something from her pocket and looked at it.

"A guy came to the 'port this morning, looking for you. Recognise?"

She pushed a photograph across the table-top. Mirren picked it up. It was a head and shoulders shot of a man around sixty, with a distinguished mane of silver hair and a tanned face – or rather, half a tanned face. The right side, from his hair-line to his chin, right around to his ear, was covered with a scaled, crimson growth like half a mask.

Mirren was reminded of *The Phantom of the Opera*.

He hook his head. "What did he want?"

"He approached my second-in-command, asking for you. He was referred to me. He had a security clearance from KVO. I thought it best to get a pix and see if you recognised him. He said he'll be back at eight this morning, if you want to meet him."

"Never seen him before in my life. He didn't say what he wanted?"

Caroline bit her bottom lip, shook her head.

Mirren tapped the picture. "What's that?"

With one finger she turned the pix to face her. "I don't know. It's even more striking in the flesh. I guessed he's an off-worlder. He spoke with a very correct accent, like a Brit from a hundred years ago. And he had a couple of tough-looking bodyguards with him."

For the past ten years, Mirren had kept pretty much to himself, hardly going out and shunning personal contact. He wondered if he'd met the off-worlder years ago, on one of the planets he'd taken leave on. But surely he'd recognise someone so disfigured?

"He didn't give his name?"

"He called himself Jaeger. But it wasn't his real name."

Mirren looked up. "How do you know?"

She smiled. "I'm trained in things like that. I know when someone's lying."

Uneasy, he picked up the pix. "Mind if I keep it?"

"Be my guest."

He wondered, for a fleeting second, if the picture was nothing more than an excuse to talk to him, the opening gambit in her scheme to pay him back for what he had done all those years ago. It was a possibility, but then Caroline had never been a person to bear grudges. Of course, she could have changed a lot in twenty years.

He looked across at her. "Can I get you a drink?"

"Mmm, please. That'd be nice. A lager."

Mirren signalled to the bar for two more lagers, wishing that he'd made some excuse, got up and left, returned home to him room and his safe, insulated solitude.

The drinks arrived and Caroline lifted her stein with both hands and peered at him over the rim.

He asked, "Do you mind if I ask you a question?"

"Of course not..."

"What do you want?"

She lowered her glass, frowning. "What do you mean?"

"It's too much of a coincidence that you wanted to work in Europe and just happened to find yourself in Paris, and just happened to take a posting here..."

Caroline pouted, regarding her hands laid flat on the table between them. She looked up. "I came to Paris because I honestly wanted the experience. When I got here... I must admit that I thought about you. When the chance came up to work here – I suppose I could have turned it down, but I wanted to see you, to catch up."

He smiled bitterly. "To see what a mess I've made of things?"

Her gaze hit his like a clash of swords. "No! I didn't come here to score points." Her stare faltered, dropped, rather than take in his bedraggled appearance. "What happened back then, happened. I'm not angry."

He caught his reflection in the tinted viewscreen. He was three day's unshaven and ten year's balding, the little hair he did possess wild and uncombed. His hands were stained with grease, his fingernails rimmed black. Added to which, no doubt, he stank.

He pushed his glass around the table, making a comet's tail of condensation on the plastic surface. "So... what have you been doing with yourself?"

"I started my own security service in Sydney. It went okay, but I didn't like the admin. side of it. I sold at a profit and got back to grass roots. Worked on Mars for ten years, came back here. Australia for a year – then the opportunity came up to work in Europe. So I thought, why not?"

"You never remarried?"

"Ten years ago I met a wonderful man. He worked on the Martian irrigation programme, which was why I left Earth to live there. We married, had nine good years–" She stopped.

"You separated?"

She shook her head, didn't look up. "He was killed in the Olympus sub-orb accident just over a year ago."

"I'm sorry." It was a reflexive response.

"Are you? You never knew him."

"I mean, I'm sorry for you. I can't imagine..."

She took a long drink, something in her haste telling him that she regretted her last statement. She smiled brightly. "Anyway, what about you?"

He waited a good ten seconds, wondering what to tell her. "I pushed for the Line after leaving Australia, and then the Line was closed down. For the past ten years I've worked here." There, simple and brutal; two sentences that comprehensively summed up his last twenty years.

She hesitated. "You never found anyone else?"

Mirren shook his head.

She dropped her gaze. "I realise things weren't perfect between us, Ralph. We had our differences. But we just never talked. Then you walked out, didn't say a word."

"It was a bastard of a thing to do."

"Oh, so you realise that now?"

"I realised it then, objectively."

"But why didn't you say anything? Why didn't we talk?"

"What could I have said? You wouldn't have understood."

"Thank you. Thanks for giving me the chance!"

"Caroline, I just couldn't bring myself to care. That's being perfectly honest."

"But why? What happened to us? At first everything was so good... I don't understand, Ralph. What happened?"

He looked across at her. He could see that beneath her calm, trained exterior, she was shaken.

He let the silence lengthen, then said softly, "When I got back after that first flux... all I wanted was to return to the 'ship, experience the flux. Nothing else mattered." He couldn't bring himself to feel anything for anyone – Caroline, his daughter Susan, or his father. "I never once visited my father after I graduated."

"I know. He never forgave you. He died twelve years ago."

Mirren said, "I heard."

"I went to his funeral. Your absence was noticed."

Mirren regarded his lager. Some part of him wanted to feel guilty, to regret the actions of his past. But he knew that anyone, in his position back then, would have been unable to act any differently.

He lifted his shoulders in a protracted shrug. "I felt nothing, nothing at all for anyone or anything accept the flux."

"That's an excuse!"

"No, that's the reason. You experience the flux, and nothing is ever the same. People don't matter–"

"All Engineman weren't affected like that," Caroline countered.

"No, not all. But many were. I was one of them. I didn't have any choice in the matter. There was nothing I could do about it. It was like a drug."

"Would you have had it any other way?"

He thought about that. He shook his head. "No, not at the time. I was hooked... Later I realised what had happened, but by then it was too late."

"What? Ten years ago, when the Lines closed down?" She wore an expression of exaggerated horror. "But you could have come back, got in touch."

Mirren almost laughed. "You don't understand. By then it was too late. Just because I couldn't flux again, it didn't mean that the desire diminished. I couldn't just cure myself like that!"

"But what about now? Surely..."

"Even now, Carrie. Even now I'd give anything to flux again. What happened ten years ago..." It was an indication of his despair that he could only become emotional about the closure of the Lines.

A silence came between them. He saw the compassion in her eyes, and her pity merely mocked, unwittingly, his inability to respond to it.

Outside, beyond the viewscreen, the interface had activated. The bright cobalt portal flickered and, hesitantly, like the image on a defective vid-screen, the scene of some far planet's spaceport appeared, backed by a dwarf star binary system in a magenta sky and fringed by alien trees. A convoy of trucks and coaches waited to cross to Earth, along with a queue of patient foot-passengers.

Caroline was turning her glass between her palms. She whispered, "What was it like, Ralph? The flux?"

He smiled. "Indescribable. The sense of union, the joy, the incredible feeling of well-being... it was a hundred times greater than the effect of any terrestrial drug. It wiped me out, left me wanting more, looking forward to nothing but the next push. Was it any wonder I couldn't respond to anyone, to feel emotions? Nothing mattered. This reality simply didn't matter."

She looked up at him and smiled. As if to salvage some consolation from the wreckage of his life, she said, "Well, at least you have the next reality to look forward to, Ralph. The afterlife."

Her smile faltered when she saw his reaction. "What...?"

He said, "I don't believe. I can't bring myself to accept that what I – what all Enginemen – experienced in flux was anything more than just a psychological phenomenon existing up here–" he tapped his head "–and nowhere else."

She stared at him. "You don't belong to the Church?"

"Of course not. Unfortunately I've never been able to stomach blind faith. The concept of afterlife that a lot of Enginemen believe in is exactly what they wanted to believe. How can something that so perfectly fits the bill for what follows death have any basis in fact?"

She was shaking her head. "I don't know. I don't believe myself, remember?"

"And all those school fees your parents paid to have you convent educated..."

She smiled at him and shrugged. They lapsed into silence. Mirren felt incredibly weary and his head throbbed. He thought of the darkness of his room, the oblivion of sleep.

Across the tarmac, the first of the foot-passengers passed through the interface, walking from one world to the next, crossing light years, without so much as breaking their stride. He cursed the Organisation that developed the interface technology.

He drained his beer. He hoped Caroline would take it as a signal that their conversation was at an end.

She did. She pushed her glass, still half full, to one side and glanced at the digital watch melded into the fabric of her cuff. "I really should be getting back to work, Ralph. It's been nice seeing you again."

He made an effort and smiled.

She rose, paused, fingertips on the edge of the table. "You haven't asked about Susan," she said.

Susan... He hadn't asked about his daughter because, in all honestly, he had not thought about her in months.

"I'm sorry." He tried to sound enthusiastic. "How is she?"

Caroline smiled, as if to show that she wasn't taken in by his deception. "She's fine, Ralph. She's twenty-one in a couple of weeks. She's working as an engineer for KVO on Mars."

Mirren grunted a laugh. "Traitor."

"She wants to see you some time."

"Well, next time she's in Europe..."

"I'll send her along." She hesitated. "I have some photos of her, if you're interested. Perhaps we could meet for a meal. How about tonight?"

"Afraid I'm busy tonight," he lied.

"Then some time next week?"

"Okay, why not?" He could always make his excuses when she called.

Caroline smiled. "I'll look forward to that. Look after yourself, Ralph."

He gave an affirmative salute and watched her walk from the bar. He ordered another beer, and when it came he sat and watched the bubbles rise to the foaming head. He reflected that for years he'd lived a life of quiet despair and at times had achieved a state of perverse contentment: only when he was reminded of the past was he filled with a sense of impotent dissatisfaction, a reminder of what might have been, and a hatred of what he had become.

"Mr Mirren? Mr Ralph Mirren?"

He looked up. Two heavies, thick-set and swarthy, obviously Jaeger's bodyguards, stood at the end of his booth.

After three beers Mirren felt distant, removed. Being confronted like this by the bodyguards of a disfigured off-worlder was such a novel turn of events, compared to his usual dreary routine, that his curiosity was aroused.

"Yes?"

"Mr Jaeger," said one of the bodyguards, "is in the Graveyard."

Mirren looked up at the speaker. He was dark, Italian-looking, but obviously a colonist from a planet with gravity greater than

Earth's: he was squat, broad, and powerful-looking.

"What does Mr Jaeger want?" he asked.

"That's his business," the other guard answered. "But we have to inform you that he won't be wasting your time."

Curiouser and curiouser... It was certainly his day for meeting people.

"If I were you," the first heavy said, "I'd go and see what he wants. Avenue five, lane three, lot seven."

They nodded fractionally and left the bar.

Mirren sat for another five minutes, drinking his beer and considering the summons. For all their veiled threats, the bodyguards had been too polite to be intimidating. He pulled the pix of Jaeger from the pocket of his flying suit and wondered what the off-worlder might want with him.

He finished his beer and left the bar.

Chapter Four

He walked around the terminal building and across the tarmac towards the quiet eastern perimeter of the spaceport. The sun was rising. The horizon was a blaze of gaudily beribboned strata, tinted rose and umber from the effluvia of the recently erupted Etna. The Graveyard stood in stark silhouette against the sunrise.

In the ten years he'd worked at Orly, Mirren had done his best to avoid the Graveyard, working in the vast lot only when he could find no other flier to take his shift. The last time had been five years ago, when his nostalgia for the hey-day of the Lines had been at its height. Since then, and especially over the last year or two, he'd often gazed across the port to the regimented ranks of the derelict starships receding into the distance, and told himself that for old time's sake he should revisit the last resting place of these mighty behemoths.

He paused and gazed left and right along the phalanx of excoriated and rusting bigships, rising from the tarmac like epitaphs to their own extinction. Dwarfed beneath the rearing hulks, he walked until he came to avenue five. Pushing his own pain at the closure of the Lines to the back of his mind, he experienced a stab of sadness for the 'ships themselves. It was sentimental, he knew, but he nevertheless thought it wrong, unjust, that such magnificent examples of engineering should have been superseded by a form of transportation as effete as the interface portals.

He turned and walked down the avenue, and it was as if he had entered another realm, a nightmare past in which the symbols of his younger days had been perversely maligned by the ongoing process of entropy. One either side, rows of wrecked and dilapidated starships dwindled to vanishing point – bigships and smallships, scout-ships and survey-vessels, colony-liners like compacted cities and planetary ferries, life-boats, tugs, salvage-ships as ugly as deep-sea fish, sun-divers, two-man boats, express cutters and slowboats pushed once by Gamma crews... He slowed his pace, gazing around in wonder. Every type of spatial architecture was represented here: vertical ships as streamlined as needles, horizontal craft like bulky leviathans; squat blocks on bent stanchion-legs like crabs, oval vessels like polished gems. Many gave the impression of being gloriously intact – though Mirren knew that their innards had been ripped out – and many more, tragically, had been strategically dismembered to prevent cannibalisation or salvaging by renegade Enginemen. He passed lots given over to portioned quarters of bigships: tail-sections and lone nose-cones, stranded mid-sections and rearing fins as large as smallships themselves, honeycombed radiation baffles, observation domes, astrodomes, flanks and bulkheads and pitiful cross-sections of 'ships like the carcasses of slaughtered beasts. Perhaps even more devastating than the piecemeal state of the vessels, however, was the attention of the extraterrestrial flora. Some of the smaller 'ships were cocooned, others had their legs and tori enwrapped in clinging skirts of jungle growth. Mirren did not fail to see the irony: for years these vessels had ranged among the stars, vanguards of humankinds' conquest; now the flora of the planets they had conquered was exacting an eloquent revenge.

He found lane three and turned down the narrow aisle. He passed the shell of a rusting smallship, then a bigship missing the domed section of its forward command bridge like the unfortunate victim of some abandoned brain surgery. He came to a halt, there was something painfully familiar about the nose-cone of the bigship which obtruded from its resting place and overhung the lane. The curving panels of its flank were obscured by a beard of purple-leafed vine, but Mirren glimpsed an ornate name-plate through the leaves. He climbed onto the back of a wrecked tug-tractor, reached out and swept aside the vine.

The *Pride of Paramatta*... He repeated the name, savouring the alliteration on his tongue, the flood of memories it provoked. He had never actually pushed the *Paramatta* – it was an early Class II survey vessel decommissioned the very year he graduated – but as a boy he'd often watched it phase into the Sydney spaceport and dreamed of one day becoming an Engineman, never for a second imagining that thirty years later the 'ship would be a thing of the past, and he with it.

He released the vines, allowed them to spring back into place and obscure the name-plate. He jumped down, dusting his hands together, and continued along the lane. He had never before realised quite how beautiful a mausoleum could be.

He came to lot seven. Parked upon it was an old-fashioned perpendicular exploration vessel, an attenuated arrow-head of blue steel. It was tall and proud against the rising sun, intact but for its nose-section fins. Mirren wondered how many planets this 'ship had discovered, how many other suns it had stood proudly beneath.

He looked around the weed-choked tarmac for Jaeger.

"Hello down there!" The cry echoed from high above.

Mirren craned his neck. Halfway up the tapering flank of the bigship, someone stood on a railed observation platform. The grey-suited figure waved. "Mr Mirren! Please, join me."

Mirren crossed the tarmac to the makeshift stairway – a metal chock, an oil barrel – and climbed through the arched hatch. The gloom was pierced by shafts of sunlight slanting in through vacated viewscreens, illuminating dust motes. He climbed a tight spiral staircase, passing levels stripped of fittings and furnishings.

He stepped out onto the observation platform.

Jaeger was leaning against the rail, admiring the view. "Magnificent, is it not, Mr Mirren?"

Mirren glanced from the off-worlder to the vista of superannuated starships spread before him. "Jaeger?"

The off-worlder turned to Mirren and held out his hand. Warily, Mirren shook it. "Jaeger is my little conceit, Mr Mirren. My *nom de plume*. The name is Hunter, Hirst Hunter. I'm delighted to make your acquaintance."

Hunter was a head taller and half as broad again as Mirren. Despite his impressive size, he emanated an aura of casual amiability. He could have passed on Earth for a well-preserved sixty, though living conditions and life expectancy varied so widely on the many planets of the Expansion that he might have been anything from fifty to a hundred standard years old.

The crimson disfigurement covered the left half of his face. On the photograph Mirren had thought it a birthmark, but now he saw that the pustulant mass, raised perhaps a centimetre from the skin, resembled more closely an outgrowth of mould or lichen. His left eye was closed and crusted over, and the side of his mouth was drawn shut and pulled down in a permanent scowl. The remainder of his face was bronzed and smiling, as if bequeathed the humanity so lacking in the ravaged hemisphere.

He was gazing out over the starships, a sad smile on his halved face. He gestured at the graveyard. "I find the sight achingly beautiful. Don't you agree, Mr Mirren?"

"Despite what it represents... yes, I do."

Hunter pointed over the domes, spires and pinnacles of the gathered starships. "Do you see the Boeing cruiser; the 'ship with its navigation bay removed? It was an exploration vessel for the Valkyrie Line, oh... ninety years ago. It surveyed the habitable planets of Kernan's Drift. I was thrilled to come across it today. My homeplanet is Fairweather, the first world it made landfall on in the Drift."

Mirren smiled. Oddly, he felt comfortable in the company of the stranger.

"And now," Hunter said, "they explore new worlds by sending unmanned drones through portals. No romance, no adventure..."

"But cheaper," Mirren said. "More profit for the organisations."

Hunter was sadly shaking his head. "I could weep when I consider the advent of the interfaces, Mr Mirren, and that is no exaggeration."

Mirren glanced at the off-worlder. He was not augmented, but he could have had his console removed.

"Did you push?" he ventured.

Hunter turned to regard Mirren. The crazed, cracked surface of his facial growth was suppurating in the sunlight. "Me? Unfortunately not, Mr Mirren. When I was young I studied to be an Engineman, I wanted nothing more than to push a starship, but I never made the grade. Of course, I could have worked in space, but the thought of working alongside *bona fide* Enginemen would only have served to remind me of my failure."

"You should consider yourself lucky," Mirren said, then stopped himself before he became too self-piteous.

Hunter smiled. "I have something to show you which I think you will find of interest. Please, this way."

Hunter ducked through the hatch and tapped quickly down the spiral stairway. Mirren followed, not for the first time wondering what the off-worlder wanted with him.

They emerged into the fierce sunlight of the new day and walked down the lane side by side. Hunter gestured and they turned right, down an avenue flanked by nothing else but dismembered observation domes and astro-nacelles. Here, the alien plant-life had run riot, shoots and spores finding their way into the accidental glasshouses of the nacelles and domes and blooming in colourful abundance.

Hunter touched Mirren's elbow and indicated to the left. They passed down a wide avenue, then halted before the carcass of a bigship sliced lengthwise, its gaping cross-section cavernous. They climbed a staircase and Hunter led the way along a cat-walk spanning the length of the 'ship above a dense tangle of brambles. They passed through a bulkhead and came into a vast astrodome, humid in the sunlight and home to a hundred varieties of beautiful alien blooms. Their scent filled the air, thick as honey.

They crossed the circular floor to the exit hatch and strode down a corridor, Mirren's curiosity increasing by the second. Hunter pushed open a swing door and stepped through, and Mirren followed. They were in the crew's lounge – a long, comfortably-appointed relaxation area which obtruded through the skin of the 'ship. Hunter strolled up to the vast, concave viewscreen and looked down the length of the bigship. Mirren stopped on the threshold and stared at the great rococo name-plate affixed to the curving flank of the 'ship.

Hunter lifted the mobile half of his mouth. "The *Martian Epiphany*, Mr Mirren. The 'ship you pushed for five years, two of them as team-captain, before your transfer to the *Perseus Bound*, if I am not mistaken."

Mirren crossed the lounge. The air was cloyingly humid, making him feel dizzy. He took in the low, plush loungers, the sunken bunkers in black leather. He was taken back in time fifteen years. Between stints in the tank and hours sleeping in his cabin, he would come down here and stare out at the cobalt-blue magnificence of the *nada*-continuum, shot through with streamers of milky luminescence like streaks in marble which believing Enginemen claimed were the souls of the dead and departed. How many hours had he spent here, gazing out in dazed wonder?

He recalled who he had been back then, what he had been, a team-commander with authority and confidence...

Hunter was smiling at him with an expression that seemed cognisant, in its compassion, of his distress. "Wasn't this the 'ship where you first commanded the Engine-team you were to be with till the end?"

Mirren stared at the off-worlder. "How do you know so much? This 'ship, my team...?"

"I've read Mubarak's memoirs, *E-man Blues*. It's all in there. Have you read it?"

"Started it. Couldn't read much. I found it too painful." He'd worked with Mubarak in the early days on the *Martian Epiphany*. His memoirs had become a bestseller around the time the Lines were folding.

"He painted a glowing portrait of you, Mr Mirren. A fine Engineman – strong, capable, respected by your fellow E-men, a pusher destined to go on and lead your own team, which of course you did. You were also one of the few Enginemen not to be associated with the Disciples. A disbeliever."

Mirren said, more to himself than to Hunter, "Mubarak was a rabid Disciple. We were equally scathing about each other's views, but we didn't let our differences get in the way of our work."

"He has nothing but praise for the team you commanded aboard this 'ship and the *Perseus*."

"They were the best," Mirren stated simply. The thought of his team, the events they had lived through, tortured him.

Hunter strolled the length of the lounge beneath the arc of the viewscreen. Down below was an avenue, and across it more ranked starships. He gazed through, silent, as if contemplating his next question.

"Are you in contact with any of your team, Mr Mirren?"

The question took him by surprise. "One or two... The others..." He shrugged. "I suppose we've drifted apart."

The truth was that he had hardly kept in contact with even the one or two he claimed. Dan Leferve, his second-in-command back then and closest colleague, he had last seen five years ago. Leferve ran an investigation Agency in Bondy, and he was religious – and it seemed to Mirren that they no longer had anything in common. Which was really just an excuse for his inertia and apathy.

He'd last seen Caspar Fekete seven years ago, before the Nigerian became a big noise in the bio-computer industry. For all his agreement with Fekete's atheism, he had found the man arrogant and opinionated. The other two, the Enginewomen Christiana Olafson and Jan Elliott, he hadn't seen since their discharge from the Line. He'd heard that Olafson was living in Hamburg, but he had no idea, or real interest, in what she was doing there. As for Elliott, she had taken the news of the closure of the Line far worse than the others, and though no Engineman or Enginewoman found life easy after the shutdown, he expected that Elliott had found it harder than most.

Mirren turned to Hunter. "Why do you ask?"

"Curiosity, Mr Mirren," Hunter said, as if that adequately answered his question. Before Mirren could press him, the off-worlder went on, "You couldn't tell me, by any chance, how the various members of your team have been affected by the closure of the Lines? I mean, specifically, how they have fared without the flux?"

"How the hell do you think they've been affected? I know for a fact that Elliott, Olafson and Leferve were devastated–"

"And Fekete?"

"Fekete, too – for all his bluster about not needing the flux. I mean, he never resigned before the closures."

"And yourself, Mr Mirren?"

He guessed, then, what Mirren was about: the bodyguards, Hunter's questions, his spurious interest in the Enginemen and the Lines. Mirren had heard that there were people like Hunter at work in the city.

He turned on the off-worlder. "Of course I was affected! You don't for a minute think it's something you can get over in months?"

Hunter gestured placatingly. "I thought perhaps due to your lack of belief you might have rationalised your craving."

Mirren laughed bitterly. "It's a biological thing, Hunter – or rather a neurological craving. Like a drug. And I can't do a thing to prevent it." He stared at Hunter, hating him for playing him along like this. "If anything, it's even worse because I don't believe. I don't live with the certainty that when I die I'll be gathered up safely into the afterlife."

"I'm sorry, Mr Mirren. I didn't mean to upset you."

"Just what do you want, Hunter?"

The off-worlder regarded him, as if contemplating how much to divulge. "If you meet me at the Gastrodome at midnight tonight, then perhaps we could continue this discussion. Do you think you might contact those members of your team living in Paris and bring them along?"

Mirren's mouth was suddenly dry. "Leferve and Fekete, maybe. I don't know about Elliott."

"Bring as many of them as possible, and then we can get down to business."

Mirren felt the words catch in his throat. "What business?"

Hunter waved. "We can discuss that tonight, in more convivial surroundings." He signalled through the viewscreen, and a black Mercedes roadster advanced slowly along the avenue and came to a sedate halt before the lounge.

Hunter turned to Mirren and held out his hand. After a moment's hesitation, Mirren took it. "I have very much enjoyed our conversation, Mr Mirren. I look forward to seeing you tonight."

"I'll contact Leferve and Fekete," Mirren heard himself say above the pounding of his heart.

"Excellent." Hunter made to leave the lounge. "Oh, just one more thing, Mr Mirren. How is your brother keeping these days?"

"Bobby's fine." He was guarded. After all the press coverage his brother's condition had received nine years ago, Mirren was suspicious when it came to strangers asking about him.

"He's coping with his predicament?"

"He's managing."

"Good, Mr Mirren. I'm pleased to hear that. Now, if you will excuse me..."

Hunter ducked through the hatch. A minute later he appeared in the avenue. One of the bodyguards jumped from the roadster and opened a rear door. Holding the front of his jacket together, Hunter slipped inside. The Mercedes accelerated down the avenue of bigships.

Mirren remained in the lounge, considering what little the off-worlder had actually told him. Then he made his way outside and walked down the avenue between two rows of rusting salvage vessels. He got his bearings from the control tower of the terminal building rising behind the bigships, and headed west.

He was aware of a deep, barely containable excitement within him. Five years ago, Mirren had heard rumours that there were shady entrepreneurs at work in Paris who had somehow managed to obtain, against the law and at great risk, the flux-tanks of starships. They had contacted Enginemen and Enginewomen and offered them stints in the tanks at exorbitant prices – prices which, because Enginemen were so desperate for the flux, they would gladly pay. Mirren had made enquiries, toured the city, made contacts with members of the Paris underworld he would rather have had no business with. He'd found that, yes, there were such dealers in France, but that their services were over-subscribed, that Enginemen who were receiving flux-time were paying way over the odds to have more stints than were absolutely necessary. He'd heard other rumours to account for the unavailability of the service: that either the dealers had been caught by the authorities, or had emigrated off-planet with their earnings, and even that a group of Enginemen had killed a dealer and kept the tank for their own use.

At least it had given his life a purpose for a couple of months.

But if Hunter was a flux-pusher then why would he come touting for trade to him, Mirren, a menial flier pilot with an income that hardly kept up the payment on his apartment? And why the interest in the other members of his team? There were hundreds of Enginemen in Paris willing to part with hard-earned creds for the luxury of experiencing the flux again...

But, then, what else could the off-worlder be hinting at? What else could explain his interest in how his team was coping without the flux?

If Hunter was indeed a pusher, then Mirren didn't know whether to despise him as an opportunist – a low-life entrepreneur peddling a quick fix at an exorbitant price to those too weak to resist – or a saviour.

Even the mere thought that he might – just *might* – one day flux again was enough to lift his spirits immeasurably.

He reached his flier in the lot beside the terminal building, climbed in and engaged the vertical thrusters. He banked away from the spaceport, headed north and followed the sinuous curves of the tropical-green Seine as it meandered east through the city. Down below the suburbs rolled by, quiet in the morning sun.

Ten minutes later he eased the two tonne weight of the flier down onto the landing stage of the apartment block, climbed wearily out and took the clanking downchute to his rooms on the top floor. He switched on the hall light, adjusted the dimmer. The first door on the left was ajar; a recording of a Tibetan mantra seeped out. Mirren paused, considering whether to enter. He decided against it, fetched a beer from the kitchen and collapsed on a battered foam-form in the shuttered, darkened lounge. The only light, a comforting orange glow, issued from a long tank on the mantelshelf: within it, the miniaturised sun of Antares rose over a panorama of sand and a silver-domed city. The floor was littered with cushions, discs and old papers. Mirren lodged his feet on the coffee table and drank his beer. He took the pix of Hunter from inside his jacket and stared at the terrible yin-yang of his face, considering what the off-worlder might be selling... He reached for the cord attached to the vidscreen and was lowering it on its angle-poise boom from the ceiling when the base of his skull seemed to explode and a fiery irritation shot up his extended arm. The periphery of his vision shattered, and he could make out only a circular patch of clarity straight ahead, like a bullet hole in glass.

He was about to undergo an attack – his headache all morning had warned him, and he should have been ready for it – but he knew that there was nothing he could have done to prepare himself for the wrenching dislocation.

Hunter's photograph slipped from his fingers. He flashbacked–

AND FOUND HIMSELF once again aboard the *Perseus Bound.*

He was sitting on the slide-bed of the flux-tank, arms stanchioned beside him, head bent forward so that Dan Leferve could adjust his occipital console. He felt a sense of anticipation that he was about to flux, and at the same time a terrible pre-emptive sense of loss that this would be his last push.

Christiana Olafson sprawled in the lounger before the viewscreen which looked out upon the *nada*-continuum, blitzed from her stint in the tank. Jan Elliott, the pale, ginger-haired Irish Enginewoman stood watching his en-tankment, biting her lip worriedly. She'd spent the entire voyage so far in the engine-room, as if unable on her last flight to tear herself away from the centre of operations. Caspar Fekete, outwardly blasé about the whole issue of the closedown, stood beside the tank and called out the sequencing countdown to Dan.

Mirren felt the jacks slip into his skull one by one.

"*Grant him smooth union,*" Elliott was babbling, "*With the majesty of the Sublime, the Infinite.*" Although he allowed the believers in his team to conduct religious rituals before their own en-tankment, he forbade such nonsense before he fluxed.

Despite the distant feeling creeping over him, he lifted a warning finger. "Shut it, Elliott, okay?"

She looked away, her words faltering.

The final jack slipped home.

Fekete slapped him on the back. "Have a good mind-trip, sir!" He pulled a face at Elliott.

Mirren lay on the bed as it entered the tank, glad to be leaving behind the petty banter of his team. Darkness enclosed him. He heard nothing. Within seconds he was no longer aware of his body. His last sense of all, the awareness of himself, his identity, would remain with him, but reduced, modulated, like the feeble consciousness of some primal animal.

He had the sensation of hovering on the edge of some infinite vastness, a pool of immanence which would bathe him in glory. Then, in the second that he fluxed, he was one with the vastness, and his soul, or rather his mind, was flooded with rapture.

What was happening to him had two explanations, one religious and the other secular. If the Disciples were to be believed, then his soul was briefly conjoined with the ultimate reality, the source of all things, which underpinned the everyday, physical world. It was this union, or rather being wrenched from it, that brought about the Enginemen's sense of craving, the desire for reunion... The secular, scientific explanation, which Mirren subscribed to, was that upon neurological union with null-space, or the *nada*-continuum, the only part of the human brain able to function in such a void, the pineal gland, bloomed and activated and produced the power to push the bigship through the medium which underpinned reality. As simple as that – even though scientists were still theorising over the precise cause of the effect. There was no evidence of an afterlife, Mirren maintained, no souls departed or those awaiting birth, just the wondrous mind-trip produced by the excitation of one's pineal gland, and the subsequent craving was the effect of denial.

For a timeless duration, Mirren fluxed.

Then, one by one, his senses returned. The hatch was cracked and the slide-bed withdrawn, and Mirren emerged into the dazzling, though muted, light of the engine-room. He sat up, dazed, knowing that anything from six to twelve hours had elapsed but unable to believe the fact. Dan unjacked him, and as he did so it came to Mirren in a rush that *that* had been the very last time he would ever mind-push a starship.

"Ten light years," he thought, "in almost an instant."

Before the tank, Olafson was holding Elliott, who was clearly agitated. She was sobbing in the arms of the taller woman, shaking her head and trying to say something. Mirren looked at Dan, who shrugged. "She can't bear the thought..." he began.

"Elliott!" Mirren snapped. "If you're in no condition to flux, We'll en-tank Olafson and you can go without, understood? We're all in the same situation, so don't think you're a special case. Pull yourself together. Fekete, set the tank. Leferve, jack her. Elliott..." The tone of his voice held a warning.

Sniffing, Elliott nodded. Olafson assisted her to the tank.

Mirren climbed from the slide-bed and made his way unsteadily towards the viewscreen. He collapsed into a lounger and stared out at the cobalt depths of the *nada*-continuum, and as he did so he heard Dan intoning, *"Grant her smooth union/ With the majesty of the Sublime, the Infinite."*

Mirren closed his eyes, let the residuum of the wonder he'd experienced percolate through his whole being. Enjoy it, he told himself, because it won't happen again.

He sensed someone beside him and opened his eyes. Dan was sitting on the edge of a lounger, staring at his clasped hands.

"What is it, Dan?"

"Weren't you rather hard on her?"

Mirren looked at the Breton, the bearded giant, the *peasant* – as he sometimes called him – who should be ploughing the earth rather than ploughing the continuum.

Mirren sighed. "I know I was, Dan." He shook his head. "She isn't the only one who's going through this."

"But it's affecting her more–"

"Is it? How the hell do you know how it's affecting me? At least fucking Elliott here can shoot herself when she gets back to Earth, achieve union that way."

Dan said, "Knowing Elliott, she might just do that."

Mirren waved. "I'm sorry. You know how it is... I can't take three months without the flux. How will I cope after three years...?"

Dan said, "Or thirty."

Both men looked out at the white light marbling the blue of the continuum, and fell silent–

And the vision that Mirren was reliving became diffuse, distant, and he knew the flashback was drawing to a close. He was back in his apartment, the sudden translocation disconcerting.

He blinked, and watched Hunter's photograph complete its pendulum drift to the carpet. He returned his arm from its outstretched position, feeling within him the vivid recollection of the union.

In reality, the flashback had lasted for a fraction of a second, while subjectively Mirren had experienced the events aboard the 'ship for what seemed like hours. What the hell was happening to him?

He looked up at the screen. Dan Leferve could wait. He'd contact him later. It was all he could do to drag himself to his room, swallow two sleeping tablets with a mouthful of water and fall into bed.

Chapter Five

Ella Fernandez sat in the 'port transit lounge on the colony world of A-Long-Way-From-Home, staring at her fingers and reliving again the explosion that had taken Eddie from her. She shifted position in the uncomfortable bucket seat, her silversuit squeaking against the padded mock-leather. Around her, a hundred travellers waited patiently for the interface to open on their destinations.

"Ms Schwartz." A tanned, blonde woman was crouching before her. She wore a bright two-piece uniform in the blue and yellow national colours of Sweden.

"Oh..." Ella looked up, too tired to realise the mistake the woman had made.

"We'll be processing travellers to Carey's Sanctuary in fifteen minutes."

The courier's gaze lingered on the Schwartz name-tag stitched to the chest of Ella's silversuit. The tags were much sought after among those who held Enginemen and Enginewomen in high esteem.

Christ, Ella thought, yawning and stretching. The courier obviously thought she looked old enough to have been an Enginewoman.

The courier was still smiling, as if expecting words of wisdom from someone she thought had communed with the ultimate. Ella smiled uneasily in return. She recalled Eddie's frustration, sometimes anger, at how he was often regarded. Civilians held E-men in awe, and Eddie had found that this misplaced respect served only to emphasise the fact of his redundancy.

"I think you're very brave," the courier said, "using the 'face. I've met some E-women who can't do it."

Ella shrugged. "I need to travel," she murmured.

The courier appraised her. "You're obviously feeling the strain. Good luck, anyway." She tapped Ella's knee, stood and scanned the lounge for other travellers in her tour group.

Ella pulled her feet onto the seat and sat cross-legged, hanging her head. She was touched by the Swede's sympathy, mistaken though it was. She closed her eyes, and the afterimage of the explosion bloomed in her mind's eye. She was aware of Eddie's body odour in the material of the silversuit.

She had watched Eddie kill himself just ten hours ago, though it seemed like much longer. It felt like a week ago when she had hung on the fence at Orly, watching the slow progress of his flier towards the interface. Even now Eddie's death was an abstract concept. She wondered if the curious absence of feeling was due to the fact that his suicide was too much to comprehend, or that she comprehended it all too well and was unable to grieve over someone she had never really loved, and who had ultimately deserted her. Was what she felt now nothing more than self-pity, the fear of the future without the reassuring and familiar presence of Eddie around to give her life a centre?

She opened her eyes and stared through the sheer crystal viewscreen that fronted the terminal complex. She certainly was, she thought, a long way from home. So far she had made three jumps out towards the Rim – from Earth to Addenbrooke, to Rousseau, and then to the Swedish colony world. Each step she had taken through the interfaces had carried her approximately three thousand light years through space, though, of course, the concept was just too much to grasp. She told herself that the journey so far, nine thousand light years across the spiral arm to the threshold of the Rim, which had taken just six hours with medical examinations and identity checks, would in the old days of the bigships have taken the better part of a standard month. The advent of interface technology, invented and developed on Mars twenty years ago and installed in stages throughout the Expansion over the following ten years, had had the effect of shrinking the human-populated quadrant galaxy to the size of a single planet. In the time it took a traveller to get from London to Sydney by sub-orbital jet – ten hours – the interstellar traveller could pass from Earth, via the junction planets, to the outermost colony on the Rim. Far-flung outposts settled in the Galactic Core, which had been lucky to see a 'ship from Earth once a year, now enjoyed a monthly influx of goods and tourists. Among the hundred densely-populated worlds in the vicinity of Earth, the portals were often opened on a daily basis. The Keilor-Vincicoff Organisation ran the interfaces in the more populated sectors of the Expansion, but in the Core and out on the Rim the operation was conducted by smaller companies.

Ella appreciated the obvious benefits of interface transportation, but at the same time she mourned the passing of the bigship Lines, the tragedy and suffering of the Enginemen, and the simple lack of *romance* of the portals compared to the gut-wrenching, heart-warming sight of the bigships which had dominated the spaceports like magnificent leviathans.

And, of course, portal travel was *painful*.

She looked out across the 'port to the interface a kilometre away, a high blue membrane set against the only slightly paler blue midday sky. Beyond the 'face was the city of New Stockholm, looking impossibly clean and prosperous: a panorama of glass towers, forests and parks. A greater contrast to Paris she could not imagine. The staff working in the terminal building, and the citizens come to see off friends and family, were all well-built, blonde and bronzed, descendants of the Scandinavians who had made the planet their home more than fifty years ago. She compared these people with the travellers who had left Paris with her, harried and beset individuals, either leaving

Earth for good or glad to be getting away from a fragmenting Europe if only for a short time.

She considered the teeming crowds of travellers she had seen over the past few hours. The multitude of citizens in the Expansion, and the multiplicity of events, made her realise the insignificance of her attempt at communicating her thoughts and feelings through the medium of her art. Hell, even in a culture which understood the type of work she did, there were people like Vasquez and her father who shut their minds to what she was saying – and Eddie, too, she had to admit. In the years she had known him, he had made no effort to try to understand what she was doing: that he had appreciated the degree of difficulty involved in producing a piece made the fact that he could not interpret her work all the more frustrating. She gained heart from the knowledge that for every hundred people like Vasquez, Eddie and her father, there was perhaps one who loved and cared for works of art – like the off-worlder who had bought *Conversion*.

Her thoughts were interrupted by the activation of the interface. The blue light flickered and coruscated briefly, hinting at the vaguest outline of the 'port on the other side – then disappeared to be replaced by the rain-slicked tarmac, dull terminal building and overcast sky of Carey's Sanctuary. The slit portals and viewscreens in the frame of the interface glowed warm and yellow against the grey winter scene beyond.

The call went out for travellers to Carey's Sanctuary to assemble at the identity check-point. Perhaps fifty people stood and gathered their possessions. Ella remained seated, watching her fellow travellers move in line towards and through the security check. There were few families making their way to Sanctuary; the majority of travellers seemed to be business-people and soldiers in uniform.

Ella shouldered her bag and tagged onto the end of the queue, her pass and identity card at the ready. The Swedish courier was smiling them through. "I trust you've enjoyed your stay on

A-Long-Way-From-Home, or if you were a transit traveller that you might return one day to enjoy our hospitality. Thank you."

Ella was the last traveller through.

"Excuse me," the courier said. "I thought you might like this. I found it in lost property." The women held out a black synthetic-leather jacket. 'Sanctuary is a Danzig-run world, they might give you a hard time if they knew you were a Disciple." She indicated the infinity symbol tattooed on Ella's arm.

"Thank you." Ella accepted the jacket. "That bad, is it?"

"They're clamping down on the passage of Disciples, E-men and -women to the Rim," the courier said. "At least this'll cover your tattoo."

Ella smiled and shrugged on the jacket. As she was zipping it, she saw the frayed name-tag on the chest of her silvers. She looked up at the Swede, who was watching her still – then ripped off the tag and handed it to the woman.

"Here," she said, "you might as well have this."

She hurried through the identity check.

A hover-coach carried them in a long arc across the tarmac to the interface, where it idled in a convoy of wheeled vehicles and hover-trucks passing though the 'face, ball-lightning sparking off their outlines as they made the transition. The coach edged slowly forward.

Ella watched the passengers seated before her pass though the advancing membrane of the interface. She awaited her turn with the kind of trepidation she had once experienced when awaiting surgery – the awareness that what was about to happen might go wrong, would be painful, but at the same time was necessary. Not many people had actually perished travelling this way, at least not since the early days, but it was the physical sensation of the process that scared Ella, rather than the danger of an accident. She tried to recall the sensation from the last time she'd interfaced, but she found the recollection of pain impossible – which in a way made the anticipation all the harder to bear. All she knew was that it hurt.

The man in the seat before her braced himself at the approach of the hazy membrane that hung between A-Long-Way-From-Home and Sanctuary. Silver lights outlined him briefly, and then he was on the other side. Ella took a deep breath as the interface hit her. The pain was intense, but mercifully fleeting – though in retrospect it seemed to go on forever. Cruel, invisible hands reached into her body and squeezed her vital organs. Nausea swept through her in a hot wave and she gasped.

Then she was on Carey's Sanctuary, and the pain was a thing of the past.

The portal deactivated with a swift rushing sound like a thousand birds taking flight. The sunlight that had poured through the interface was suddenly extinguished, and the blue light of the deactivated 'face washed over the coach as it crossed the spaceport towards the terminal building. A fine rain misted from the overcast sky.

The terminal was low and shabby. The courier who led them from the coach and into the building was garbed in the green uniform and the black beret of the Danzig Organisation. "All travellers onwards to Mephisto and Jet, continue through to lounge two. Passengers bound for Hennessy's Reach, please take a seat and wait here."

The majority of travellers continued through to the second lounge. Five others, besides Ella, seated themselves before the rain-spattered viewscreen: three low-ranking soldiers in uniform, an officer with a peaked cap and over-the-top epaulettes, and a businessman with a briefcase. Ella took a seat well away from them, conscious of being the only woman and casual traveller, and stared out at the bleak scene of the 'port.

Two minutes later the 'face activated, and before she had time to hope that the first world onto which it opened would be the Reach, she recognised the familiar sky-scape of the Rim world. Framed in the exact centre of the portal was the apex of the fiery red giant, like a plasma graphic committed by an incurable romantic. Before the giant primary was an expanse of dark sea, the great Mérida ocean which covered a quarter of the planet's surface. In the foreground was the 'port, a collection of functional terminal buildings and control towers. Ella found herself staring at the low arc of the red giant, at the great loops and geysers of flame erupting from its circumference in majestic slow motion. She recalled her last summer on the Reach, a certain friendship prematurely ended, and experienced a sour-sweet pang of sadness.

A long convoy of armoured vehicles trundled across the rain-swept tarmac and approached the interface. Before she could remind herself of the repression represented by such a show of force, something elemental within her thrilled to the power, uniformity and synchronised precision of the military convoy. The vehicles rumbled through the 'face with a deafening roar of engines. Ella recognised tanks and personnel carriers, nuclear rocket launchers like long tankers and fliers lashed to the flat-beds of low-loaders – but there were other vehicles, bulbous pantechnicons and things that looked like helicopters without rotor-blades, the function of which she could only guess at.

She recalled Hennessy's Reach from the days in her teens. It had been a quiet, backwater world on which nothing ever seemed to happen. She remembered that her father had considered his posting there as a demotion, which might have been a contributory factor to his moods at the time. Now she wondered what had happened, in the ten years she had been away, to account for the military build-up.

She stared through the interface. In the fifteen minutes since the 'face had opened, the sun had set fractionally. Sunrise and sunset lasted for five hours on the Reach, with correspondingly long days and nights – approximately fourteen standard hours each. The sunset phase had been Ella's favourite time of day, warm and balmy. She'd spent long evenings swimming in the sun-warmed lagoons of the Falls with her friend L'Endo-kharriat.

The bitterness provoked by these memories was stopped short when the military courier called, "Everyone for Hennessy's Reach..."

She shouldered her bag and crossed the lounge to the desk, standing in line behind the military officer. When it was his turn to be processed, the official at the desk gave his card a cursory scan and saluted. "Pleasant trip, Major."

He was not so swift in dealing with Ella.

He examined her card, then slipped it into a computer scanner. He read the information revealed on the screen, frequently glancing at Ella. She pulled the lapels of her jacket together, conscious of her silversuit beneath.

"I take it that 'Fernandez' is an assumed surname?" he asked.

"Right."

"And that you're a Disciple."

What good would come from denying it? "Right again."

The official tapped at his keyboard, entering the information. "Your profession?"

Her details were on the identity card. He was trying to intimidate her with his authority.

"I'm an artist," she answered evenly.

"And why are you visiting the Reach, Ms Fernandez?"

"Pleasure. I'm visiting my father."

"His name and address?"

Ella gave him the information.

The official entered the details, then waited. Ella guessed he was cross-referencing the name of her father with a list of the planet's citizens. He read something on the screen, then looked at Ella.

"One minute."

He opened a swing door behind his desk and stepped out. Ella watched him cross to where the uniformed courier was waiting by the exit. They exchanged a hurried, whispered conversation, the courier allowing his gaze to remain fixed on her.

The official returned. "How long do you intend to stay on the Reach, Ms Fernandez?"

Ella shrugged. "Maybe a week or two."

"Where will you be staying?"

"At first in a hotel in Zambique City, then perhaps with my father–"

The official interrupted, "Much of the city is out-of-bounds to off-world travellers, and the country north of the twentieth parallel is off-limits to all non-Reach citizens."

"Why?" Ella asked. "What's happening?"

The official smiled. "Civil unrest in Zambique province," he said. "Oh, and by the way, a curfew is operating on the Reach. Eight till eight, and the patrols have shoot-on-sight orders. If I were you I'd be very careful." He returned Ella's identity card. "I hope you find inspiration for your art on the Reach," he said with barely concealed sarcasm.

Ella plucked her card from his fingers. "Merci, Monsieur. I'm sure I will."

She crossed to where the courier was waiting with the other five travellers. She was aware that she had undergone a more than usually rigorous grilling.

Civil unrest in Zambique province? Somehow she found that hard to believe. And since when had it taken nuclear rocket launchers to quell civil unrest?

The coach ferried them across to the interface. The convoy had long since passed through, and were drawn up in columns on the other side. This time when the coach approached the portal, Ella closed her eyes. The pain hit without warning. Her innards were constricted, and for a fraction of a second it seemed as though her heart might stop. Then she was on Hennessy's Reach and breathing the familiar, heady fragrance of bougainvillea and assorted alien blooms.

The coach carried Ella and the others – among them the military courier from Sanctuary, she noticed – to the terminal, a long, low building with Spanish colonial columns and shuttered windows in the Latin style. She passed through customs, expecting another comprehensive interrogation. This time, however, her identity card was given hardly a second glance. As she strode towards the exit, she was aware of the courier consulting with a knot of security guards. One of them watched her walk from the building. Her presence had been noted.

She halted at the top of the steps, shocked by the scene that greeted her. She recalled the bustle of activity before the 'port on the evening she had left the Reach ten years ago. The forecourt had been packed with the stalls of a night market selling grilled fish and assorted sea-food, fresh fruit – Terran and alien – hot coffee and coca. Music had belted out from the stall-holder's radios, sambas competing with their cries. The scene had been typical of a busy market place on any bustling, agricultural colony planet.

Now the forecourt was deserted. A single, defective street-lamp fluttered light across the empty, pot-holed stretch of concrete. One combustion-engined taxi stood on the rank, its driver sprawled across the front seats, his bare feet protruding from the passenger window. His radio played a tinny rumba, the music lost in the night.

Across the unlighted coast road, the beach extended north for as far as the eye could see. Timber fishing boats, testimony of the planet's backward economy, were drawn up past the high-tide mark. Five kilometres up the coast, Zambique City was a collection of two- and three-storey buildings climbing the hillside around the bay. Even the city looked deserted; in none of the buildings or streets could Ella see a burning light or any other signs of life. The most vital aspect of the scene before her was the sunset, the filament bow of the red giant suffusing the western sky with a gorgeous roseate glow. Before it, the abandoned, human-built coastline lay in abasement.

Ella hurried down the steps and approached the taxi-cab. She decided to check the truth of what the official had said about the city being off-limits.

At the sight of her, the driver withdrew his feet from the window and started the engine. "Hotel, *senorita*?"

She peered in at him. "Can you take me into Zambique?"

The driver made a pained face. "Not possible, *senorita*. City closed. Military patrols. Local hotel, yes?"

Ella recalled the small town three kilometres down the coast where she'd stayed once with her father. She dumped her bag on the back seat and climbed in beside it. "Do you know the Hotel Santa Rosa, Costa Julliana?"

"*Si, senorita*. No problem."

She sat back as the car chuntered from the forecourt and headed down the coast road. The driver braked, then muttered something under his breath as the military convoy pulled from the spaceport and moved north. The procession of identically camouflaged jungle-green vehicles passing before them soon became monotonous. Ten minutes later, as the last armoured truck left the 'port, Ella asked in Spanish, "What is the problem? Why all the military?"

The driver glanced at her in the rear-view mirror, smiling sadly. He mimed locking his mouth and throwing the key through the window. "No questions, no answers, no awakenings at two in the morning." He drew a finger across his Adam's apple and made an accompanying gurgling sound in his throat.

"Christ," Ella murmured to herself. She stared out at the fields of rice and the occasional sumptuous villa.

Hennessy's Reach was one of half a dozen planets on the Rim settled almost seventy years ago by colonists from the countries that made up the Latin Federation. Over a period of twenty years, two million citizens from Spain, Mexico and South America had made the journey by bigship to the Reach, and settled on the world's three largest continents. It had never been a prosperous colony, even in the early days when subsidised by the Federation. Twenty years ago, the Danzig Organisation launched a successful economic take-over of the planet – one of over two hundred which had fallen domino-like to the Organisation around the Rim – and since then the economy of the planet had declined still further. The four million inhabitants of the Reach managed to feed themselves, but only just. Ella guessed that the Hennessians had finally had enough, and instigated a rebellion – hard though that was to imagine of a people she remembered as being peaceable and easy-going. She wondered why she had heard nothing of the trouble on any of the news channels back on Earth.

The taxi followed the coast road around the headland. The small fishing town of Costa Julliana nestled in a horse-shoe cove ahead. A few lights burned in the windows of the stone buildings on the hillside, but the main square which fronted the ocean was empty, as was the jetty extending from the harbour wall. Ella recalled the town's inhabitants promenading along the jetty on hot evenings.

The driver was cutting though the square, heading for the continuation of the coast road and the hotel, when Ella saw the statue. She leaned forward. "Stop here!"

"But your hotel, *senorita*?"

"That's okay. It's not far. I'll walk from here."

She paid him in the local currency she'd bought back on Earth, grabbed her bag and climbed from the taxi. As it started up and u-turned, Ella stood on the cobbles beside a dry fountain and stared across the square.

A hover-truck was parked on the harbour wall, the crane on its flat-bed silhouetted against the sunset. A corps of green-uniformed engineers stood around, regarding the statue. Ella moved forward, then stopped – close enough to see the detail of the towering figure, but not so close that she attracted the attention of the engineers.

She had never seen the statue before – it had certainly been erected since her departure from the Reach. She found the piece terribly moving not just in an aesthetic sense, but also in what it symbolised. The bronze casting, perhaps three metres high, was of a figure standing and staring inland, a staff in its right hand – a male member of the Lho-Dharvo race, the aliens native to the Reach. To human eyes, the statue seemed to be out of proportion, too tall and attenuated for the insectoid width of its starvation-thin limbs, as if stretched to the point of being unable to bear its own slight weight. Its rib-cage was long, each individual, curving bone distinct beneath its copper and bronze piebald skin. Its head was long and thin, too, with large eyes, no nose other than two vertical slits, and a mouth no more than a thin humourless line. To a human observer, the alien at first seemed *too* alien, and then when the eye accepted its similarities, it appeared reassuringly humanoid. Only then, when the observer had been fooled into accepting the alien as familiar, did its differences reassert themselves and mark the statue for what it was – a member of a sentient species not human.

It was, thought Ella, a fitting tribute to an extinct race. Eleven years ago, the first of the Lho had succumbed to a viral epidemic, and four years later all three million aliens on the four continents of the Reach – or Dharvon, as they knew it – were dead. Ella had read of the extinction in a Paris magazine, and she felt now much the same sense of impotent rage and personal loss.

As she watched, an engineer took a cutting tool and sliced through the statue's thin left ankle. A noose suspended from the crane was slipped around the alien's noble head.

A noise on the other side of the square, behind Ella, made her turn. A flier descended and landed on the cobbles. Someone – in the descending twilight it was impossible to tell whether it was a man or a woman – climbed out and stared across at the statue's removal.

Cautiously, Ella approached the engineers. She stood beside a sergeant who seemed to be in charge of the operation.

She gestured at the statue as its left leg was severed with a shriek of tortured metal. Now only its staff secured the statue to its plinth. The hawser around its neck tightened, drawing the alien off-centre.

"Why...?" she asked, shaking her head.

The sergeant glanced at Ella. He was a tall, grey-haired and patriarchal European, as noble in his own way as the statue.

"I wish I knew," he said in a Scandinavian accent. "It's rather beautiful, isn't it? But I have my orders."

They watched together as the staff was severed. Released from its final mooring, the alien hung from the noose and rotated absurdly. Half a dozen soldiers steadied the statue and directed it towards the hover-truck.

Unable to find the words to express the sense of loss that was like a cavity within her, Ella turned and hurried off across the square.

Someone stepped from the shadow of the fountain. For a second, she thought it was the driver of the flier, but then she saw that the figure was short, dumpy: an old woman.

"Ssst! *Senorita*!" the woman hissed. "A hotel, yes?" She pointed along the harbour to a white-washed building overlooking the sea. She smiled, a gold tooth gleaming in the light of the sun.

Ella hesitated. She had wanted to revisit the Santa Rosa, to stir old memories.

The old woman caught her arm, not unkindly. "*Senorita*, it is almost curfew!" she said in Spanish. "They will take great delight in shooting you in the head at the first stroke of eight! Please, this way..."

Ella judged that there was nothing mercenary in the old woman's concern; she seemed genuinely concerned for Ella's safety. She gestured towards the hotel, taking Ella by the hand and dragging her from the square.

As they turned the corner, the woman looked back over her shoulder at the tall figure standing beside the flier. She hissed something under her breath, then hauled Ella up three steps and through the timber door of a small whitewashed building.

Two old men were bent over a board-game in the bar-room. Wooden chairs and tables stood on a polished timber floor, and supporting the ceiling were what looked like genuine oak beams. Ella reminded herself that she was on the Reach now, a relatively young colony world with abundant natural resources.

The use of timber would not be regarded as profligate here, as it would on Earth.

The woman ordered an old man behind the bar to pour Ella a drink, then all but pushed her into a chair beside an open hearth. Ella took off her jacket, and the woman stared with round eyes at the revealed silversuit. Then she saw the infinity symbol on Ella's arm.

"Mama mia! No wonder they follow you!"

"Follow *me*? Who?"

The woman gestured with her thumb. "Who else? The bastard in the flier. Here, drink!"

The woman took a small glass of colourless liquid from the rough-grained timber bar and passed it to Ella. Hesitantly, she took a sip, gagged and coughed. She regained her breath, her eyes watering.

While she was recovering, the old woman was speaking to the man behind the bar in Spanish so rapid that Ella had no hope of following what was being said.

The woman smiled. "Your taxi driver. He called five minutes ago to tell me that you had been followed from the 'port. He thought you needed help. He was a brave man to even call me, *senorita*. One month ago his son was arrested by the military on suspicion of assisting the Disciples. The following day he was found in an alley with his throat cut." The woman shook her head. "But you cannot stay here, little one. It is not safe. Costa Julliana swarms with the military. My husband will arrange for your people to come and take you away–"

"My people?"

The old woman slapped Ella's arm with her meaty hand. "Disciples, who else? Now come this way."

She took Ella through to a back room. Sheep skins were draped over armchairs and old photographs and images of Christ covered the walls. Ella sat in a comfortable chair. She was still clutching her drink. She took a mouthful, the alcohol helping to calm her.

The woman drew up a three-legged stool. "Now – you need not tell me if you so wish – but why did you come to the Reach? Surely you have heard about the troubles?"

Ella shook her head. "We've had no news on Earth–"

The woman closed her eyes. "I hoped at least that help might arrive from somewhere, if what was happening here was known. So you came here in all innocence?"

Ella hesitated, deciding to tell only half the truth. "I came for a holiday. I lived here as a child. I wanted to revisit–"

"I'm truly sorry. You might have been allowed onto the Reach, but let me tell you, little one, that there's no way they would let you leave the planet. We are under military command. Many citizens have fled south, down the coast."

"But what's happening? Why should they be persecuting the Disciples?"

"Something is happening in the mountains – don't ask me what. For weeks, convoys have been heading north. All over the Reach, Ex-Enginemen and -women, their families and friends, are being rounded up, interrogated. Most are never seen again. I am an old woman – it is a mystery to me. But I know on whose side I stand! Ever since the organisation came to the Reach – no good. Have you heard of the Nazis, little one?"

"Of course – fascists who ruled Germany in the middle of the twentieth century and again in the twenty-first."

The old woman was nodding. "Well, these people are every bit as evil."

Ella raised the glass to her lips. This time, the tequila went down as smooth as honey.

The door from the bar swung open, startling her. Three men entered the room. They wore peasant's jackets and their faces were blackened. Ella noticed that the left sleeve of the first Disciple's jacket was empty, flattened and pinned to his side.

"There she is," the old man said, coming in behind them.

The one-armed Disciple regarded Ella, then grabbed her arm

and roughly turned it over to reveal her tattoo. Far from acting as she might have expected a rescue party to behave, these men seemed nervous, suspicious – perhaps with good reason, if half the things the old woman had told her were true.

The Disciple nodded. "Very well. This way." They turned and hurried through the door. The old woman hugged Ella. "You will be well with them, little one. Do not be scared!"

A trap-door behind the bar gave access to a flight of steps, descending into the darkness. Ella was pushed down after the first Disciple, and the two others followed. By the light of an ancient paraffin lamp she made out a stretch of water and a small fishing boat. She was bundled over the gunwale. A hand gripped her chin and her head was pulled back. Something cold and metallic touched her temple.

"One word, one wrong movement... the slightest sign that you work for them, *senorita...*"

Chapter Six

Bobby Mirren was the Time-Lapsed Man, or the Man Who Lived in Two worlds, according to the headlines of some of the trashier journals which ran stories on him a decade ago. In fact, Bobby liked to think of himself as the man who lived in four worlds. He lived nominally in the present, and more substantially a day in the past; he lived a rich life in his memories, and an even richer life anticipating the future. Some part of him was in contact with the numinous reality of the *nada*-continuum, a tenuous and subtle contact like two spheres touching but never interpenetrating, a contact which promised that some day he would merge, become one, and in so doing totally fulfil himself. On the edge of his consciousness when he meditated he was aware of a sweet calling.

Now – though the word was largely meaningless to Bobby – *now* he sat in his armchair in his bed-sitting room. What he could feel, the threadbare arm of the chair beneath his hand, was out of context with what he was experiencing from yesterday. One day ago he had an open book on his lap and was finger-reading the Braille translation of a Buddhist tract. Now he could see the great tome spread across his lap, could see his hand speeding along the dotted lines, but he could not feel the weight of the book on his lap nor the raised pointillism of the Braille beneath his fingertips. His lap was empty and he could feel the material of the armchair beneath his fingers.

He laid back his head and closed his eyes, and he continued to see what his eyes had been directed at yesterday, the book, the carpet before his feet, the far wall... He heard the sound of a flier passing overhead, but knew that the vehicle had passed by a day ago and would be long gone by now.

Bobby Mirren's every sense, with the exception of his sense of touch, was lapsed by almost twenty-four hours. What he saw today he had looked at yesterday; what he heard now first came to his ears a day ago. Similarly with his senses of taste and smell; he would eat a meal today, and, although he would be aware of the texture of the food filling his mouth, it would be tasteless – until the following day when its taste would flood his mouth. He compensated by taking his meals at the same time each day, so that he could taste yesterday's meal while eating today's. In the early days he had experimented – eating steak and then the following day at the same time eating strawberries, so that he would taste the bloody meat while having the sensation of chewing the soft fruit. He had experimented too with the other odd phenomena of his unique condition. He would set off and walk thorough the streets of Paris, feeling his way around the masonry and railings and glass shop-fronts like a blind man – the difference being that, although in his fumbling hesitation he might have appeared blind, he was in fact seeing what he had looked upon the day before: the interior of his room, a vid-documentary, a meal he had eaten... The following day Bobby would remain in the apartment and finger-read a religious tract, while visually and aurally experiencing his trip outside the day before. The dichotomous sense of experiencing two different realities, both just as unreal, had given him, after the initial, nauseous surge of disorientation, a cerebral thrill, an intellectual high, which he tied in with his wide reading in Buddhist philosophy: simply, that this life with an illusion – and he had been vouchsafed, for some reason, the condition that made this obvious. The strange sensory anomaly, which most people would consider a curse,

Bobby from the outset looked upon as a blessing, a sign from beyond this reality that he was special, even chosen.

He was the only time-lapsed man to have survived. There had been five beside himself in the last couple of years before the closure of the bigship Lines. The first two Enginemen, Black and Thorn, had died after just a few days of hospitalisation and observation. The following three had lasted months. All five had drifted irrevocably into comatose states, and then passed from this existence to the next.

But Bobby Mirren had survived.

He recalled his final shift in the flux-tank as if it were yesterday. It would have been his last push anyway, even if he had not succumbed to Black's Syndrome. The Javelin Line had been bought out by an interface organisation, and portals were to replace bigships in the sector of the Expansion served by his Line. He, along with every other Engineman, had been at first incredulous and outraged at the news that the 'ships were being phased out, and then when the fact and its implications sank in, psychologically devastated. Enginemen lived for the flux; it was what made their lives worthwhile, a contact with the infinite that nothing – no amount of worship, prayer or study – could replace. Bobby had gone into the tank for the last time hoping that he would die a flux-death, so as to be spared the years of terrible deprivation. In the event, he almost got his wish.

It was a haul like any other, a three day push from Earth to Reqa-el-Sharif along the spiral arm. He had jacked-in and laid on the slide-bed with the usual reverence that the ritual called for, but with a sense of poignancy also that this time would be the last. He had slipped into a trance as he entered the tank, suddenly aware of the vast, numinous infinity of the *nada*-continuum, and his part in it; a tiny, insignificant speck of life. He wanted nothing more then than to cross the cusp all the way and become one with the sublime.

Then – and he had been sure that some part of him experienced it at the time, sure that it was not a retrospective illusion – he was conscious of a *presence* within his mind, a crawling, probing heat that seemed to be investigating the many layers that made up his being. He felt areas of his brain closing down, becoming stagnant – and he received the distinct impression that he was being stripped down to his essence, his basic animal self, before being accepted more fully than ever before into the continuum. He was dimly aware of a consciousness at work within him, a guiding intelligence behind what was happening, which was benign and had only his well-being at heart.

On the very edge of his awareness he heard the intelligence, calling to him...

Then with a sudden, terrible wrench, he was ejected from the flux-tank. He felt his body being manhandled from the slide-bed, the medics giving him a thorough examination – but all he could see was darkness, and all he could hear was the quiet humming that accompanied the process of en-tankment... He had read about Black's Syndrome, and he knew then that he was its sixth victim.

Bobby had spent almost a year in a private medical institute in New York, his senses lapsing by a few minutes each day, until the time they ceased their drift and halted at almost twenty-four hours. He had been quite prepared for death – he had after all experienced the wondrous realm that followed – but, a month after his senses had stabilised, he was told by the medics that he had survived, could lead an *almost* normal life, and part of him had been disappointed at the news, cheated at the thought of being unable to follow the other sufferers of the Syndrome to a better place.

He had tried to find out what, medically, neurologically, had happened to him – but the medics, although they blustered, had no real idea. They talked of malfunctions in the tank-leads which had affected certain areas of the brain, and gave Bobby lectures on complex neurological dysfunctions which meant nothing at all to him.

The very fact that he had undergone the mysterious transformation and survived convinced him that he had been affected for a reason – this and the fact that ever since his final push he had been blessed with a greater recollection of being united with the infinite. Usually after a push, the fleeting, elusive awareness lasted only hours, but with Bobby it continued, so that even now all he had to do was relax, meditate and concentrate, and he would experience again some measure of the rapture of the union. At these times he could almost hear the calling, a signal from the intelligence that had tried to ease him into the continuum ten years before.

He had come to Paris, moved into his brother's apartment, and after the sickening, sycophantic attention of the media during which he became a nine day wonder, eliciting pity, proposals of marriage – even death threats from a Muslim sect who considered his claims of contact with a higher force as blasphemous – he had settled down to a quiet life of study.

Over the years he had read widely of all the various mystical religions on Earth, and several from beyond, but always came away dissatisfied, aware that none of them addressed what he had experienced while in flux. Even the Disciples, who he had joined when becoming an Engineman, were too obsessed with ritual and dogma. He had stopped looking for answers in human religions, realising that he had experienced the ultimate truth in the *nada*-continuum and occasionally in meditation – and merely read Buddhist and Disciple tracts out of interest, a second best as there was no real codified treatise to explain the continuum; it merely *was*...

Now, Bobby saw what he had looked at yesterday – his vision dictated by the movement of his eyes almost twenty-four hours ago: the book, the carpet. As he watched, he saw his hands close the great book, its cover the size of a trap-door, and hoist it over the side of his armchair to the floor. He sat upright now and experienced his vision tilt dizzyingly as he had leaned over the arm of the chair. He watched his hands return and settle on his knees. He recalled that he had sat like this, in silent contemplation, for fifteen minutes. He thought back a day, and realised that he had been watching and listening to, from the previous day, a vid-disc documentary about the exploration of a newly discovered planet in the Crab nebula. He had stopped his reading when the programme started, to give his full attention to the vid-screen. He could not read normal printed books, newspapers or magazines; unable to see these in real-time, he could not train his eyes to scan the exacting lines of print. He fared much better with the vid-screen, where the visual target was much larger – he'd rest his head against the wing of his chair and stare straight ahead. He tended, though, to watch only hired documentary discs on the 'screen, bored by the combination of brutality and triviality of the networked programmes. He spent a lot of time listening to the radio and his own music pins. He remembered that yesterday at six he had put some music on the player, Tibetan mantras followed by a classical symphony, lay down on the bed in the corner and closed his eyes – while continuing to watch a news programme about the decline of Europe. Now he snapped open the glass cover of his wrist-watch and felt for the hands. It was almost four. In two hours he would get up, put some music on the player, and go and lie down, while listening to the music he had selected yesterday; tomorrow, he would repeat the process, and duly enjoy the music he would select in two hours... Unlike everyone else in the world, Bobby could not spontaneously gratify his desires – to see a film, listen to music, taste a certain meal, or whatever. If he wished to listen to a mantra or a symphony, or taste a favourite food now, this second, it was of course impossible. He would put the music on, or eat the food today, and listen to the music and savour the meal a day later. In the early days he had found this frustrating. He was accustomed to it by now, had become practised at looking forward to whatever experience he had selected for himself the day before.

When four o'clock approached, Bobby was ready.

Yesterday at this time he had climbed to his feet and left the room. Now, as soon as he saw his hands move to the arms of the chair and begin to push himself up, he matched the movement with hands he could not see, and stood smoothly. It had taken months of practise to synchronise today's movements with yesterday's vision – for a long time he'd swayed like a drunk, and often fallen over. Now it came as second nature to him.

He walked across the room to the door, seeing what he had looked at the day before – substantially the very same scene he would have seen now if his vision had been normal. When he opened the door yesterday, his hand had lingered on the worn wooden handle, feeling the grain of the wood in his hand. The day before yesterday he had foregone his habitual routine, he recalled, and had climbed up to the roof. He remembered that yesterday at this point, with his hand caressing the door handle, he had been looking out across Paris towards Orly in the north, and the distant glow of the interface. Now, movement and vision were satisfyingly synchronised. He saw his hand holding the handle, and in real-time he held the handle, pulled back the door just as he had yesterday, watched it move towards him, stepped back and then proceeded from the room.

He followed his vision of yesterday across the gloomy hallway. The day before, he had paused for a minute outside his brother's bedroom, before entering. Today he did not want to enter the room on the off chance that Ralph would be awake and would wish to 'chat' with him – not verbally, on Ralph's part, but with a touch-language he would tap out on Bobby's palm.

Now Bobby deviated from the visual route he had taken yesterday. He turned towards the kitchen and felt his way along the wall until he came to the door. He felt his way around the kitchen until he came to the cooler, and pulled it open. In effect, he was doing all this blind, as he was watching what he had been looking at yesterday. Twenty-four hours ago, he had opened his brother's bedroom door and, unable to hear himself, slurred, "Ralph, it's only me."

Now, in the kitchen, he heard the words. He felt for a beer in the cooler, pulled out the bottle and chugged down the ice cold liquid. He saw the interior of Ralph's bedroom, the bed and the tangled sheets and Ralph, lying in his shorts on his back, staring at him. Sometimes, around this time, Ralph would be getting up for an early evening shift, and they might eat together and 'converse'.

He enjoyed the feel of the beer coursing down his throat. Tomorrow he would taste it.

Yesterday he had stood at the door, unable to see whether Ralph was in bed, or had left for work – watching, still, the skyline of Paris from the day before. Now he held the cold bottle in his hand and tracked his erratic vision of the day before. Ralph was looking at him, Bobby could see peripherally, with no expression on his face.

He had not seen his brother smile in years. Ralph was forever pale and haggard-looking, often unshaven. His gaze carried that habitual, haunted look of the most severely affected Enginemen. Whenever Bobby saw his brother, he had the urge to hug him, tell him that all would be well – but of course by the time Bobby 'saw' Ralph, a day had passed and it was too late, and of course Ralph would have ignored his religiose declarations anyway.

Bobby took another swallow of beer, felt its iciness cut his chest in two.

Ralph, still in bed, sketched a wave. "I'm sorry, Bobby," he said a day ago, the words coming suddenly while Bobby had turned from the room and felt his way out, assuming Ralph had already left for work. "I've had a long shift and I'm not on till ten. I'm trying to sleep, okay?"

At least, thought Bobby, he had said something so that I'd hear his excuse today, rather than feigning sleep.

They had drifted apart over the years, and more was to blame than the difficulty of maintaining a relationship due to Bobby's condition. Years ago they had both pushed 'ships for Lines based in Paris. They had seen each other frequently, toured the bars and jazz clubs together, attended parties and shows. The fact that Bobby had believed back then, and Ralph had not, had done nothing to deter their friendship. They had more in common than not, and they had genuinely enjoyed each other's company. Every time Bobby's 'ship phased-in, the first person he would contact in Paris would be his brother.

It had seemed natural that he should accept Ralph's invitation, almost ten years ago, to come and live in Paris on his discharge from hospital. Since then they had lived their own, separate lives. Bobby tended to absorb himself in his books and meditation, and Ralph...? Ralph read a little, watched a little vid-screen, drank. He seemed constantly depressed, apathetic, living only for a dozen bottles of beer daily and his shift at Orly, which he hated. They had both, at times, attempted to talk openly and seriously to each other, but Bobby's wholehearted acceptance of an afterlife had often run aground on Ralph's uncompromising atheism. They no longer had any common ground.

Bobby thought back to their childhood in Sydney, their father, a severely materialist nuclear scientist working on Australia's first fast breeder reactor programme. Their mother had died when they were too young to recall her, and their father had been over-strict, ruthless in his punishment for minor misdemeanours he considered grave. Ralph, the eldest and least strong-willed of the two boys, had kow-towed to his father, perhaps even subconsciously taken on board his secular world-view. Bobby, on the other hand, had rebelled, stubbornly studied religion, looking for the right one until he became an Engineman and discovered the creed of the Disciples.

Now his vision of yesterday tracked from the hall and moved into the kitchen. He watched the cooler door open and his hand take out a bottle of beer. Seconds later he saw the bottle rise to his mouth, tasted the sweet hopsy wash of it in his mouth even though his mouth today was empty. He soon remedied that, tipped his own bottle and felt it run tastelessly down his throat. Yesterday, he had turned and sat on the chair he was now occupying, and once again his present position and what he could see were synchronised.

Something flashed on the periphery of his vision: Ralph, in the hall, leaving his room and crossing to the bathroom. He saw only a glimpse of his brother, but it was enough to see that he looked thin and ill, far older than his forty-two years. Bobby told himself that suffering was instructive, but knew that this would be no consolation to Ralph.

Bobby had often contemplated taking his own life, but less so nowadays. He had considered suicide not because he disliked his life or was unhappy – life was to be experienced, and all experience was valid – but so as to be finally united with the ultimate. What had stopped him was the knowledge of how his death might effect Ralph. His brother would be unable to believe that he had taken his life to rejoin the wondrous continuum, but assume instead that his existence had been intolerable. Ralph felt guilty enough without being burdened with the thought that he had done nothing to ease what he perceived as the trials of Bobby's existence.

Yesterday at this time Bobby had finished his beer. He did the same now, and followed his vision from the kitchen and across the hall.

He selected three pins from the rack on the wall, inserted them into the player and walked across to his bed.

Bobby Mirren lay down and closed his eyes as he had yesterday. Welcome darkness came as he waited for the music to begin.

Chapter Seven

It was eight in the evening when Mirren awoke. The setting sun showed as a square of rouge filaments around the drawn blinds. He rolled onto his back and stared at the cracked ceiling. The air of the room was oppressive, sultry with the heat of the dying day. He became aware of two things almost at once: he'd slept in his flying suit which was saturated in sweat, and every muscle in his body ached as if with the onset of flu.

Then he recalled Hunter, and what he suspected the off-worlder was offering to him and his team, and his aches and pains became bearable.

He showered and changed into a new flying suit, then fixed himself breakfast: coffee and a mango-like fruit from one of the colonies. As he ate, he heard the recording of a Tibetan mantra seeping from the front room, a bass monotone interspersed with the jangle of bells. He left the kitchen and paused by the bedroom door, staring at the blistered paintwork and listening to the music. He hurried out.

He took the upchute to the landing stage, climbed into his flier and hauled it into the air. The sun had gone down and Paris was illuminated. From the air, the ground-plan of the city resembled a defective pin-ball machine with the lower scores ripped out, leaving only the high scores of the more prosperous quarters in bright halations of light. Dan Leferve had his offices on the Rue Malle, Bondy, a once-fashionable district now falling street by street to the gradual advance of the ghetto.

As he mach'd across the city, he admitted that he was not exactly looking forward to calling on Dan Leferve. Over the past five years he had neglected their friendship, allowed messages to go unanswered, failed to turn up at arranged meetings – not so much out of any active disinclination to see Leferve, but from an inertia and apathy that had its roots in depression. There had been times when he had wanted nothing more than to share too many lagers with his old colleague, but feared the shadow into which his life would be thrown by the energy and bonhomie of the ex-Engineman. Over the years he had become content with his lifestyle of privacy and isolation, and only occasionally wished it otherwise.

He could find no rooftop landing area, which was always a bad sign. He was forced to leave his flier in the street beneath overhanging palms and trust that thieves and vandals were elsewhere tonight. He locked the hatch and crossed the empty street. The social standing of an area in the city these days was indicated by the degree to which alien vegetation had taken hold. Municipal authorities had only limited funds to spend on clearances, and the commercial districts and more exclusive residential areas received preferential treatment. The Rue Malle was going under: soon it would be part of the swathe of jungle which had invaded the districts to the east. The facades of the tall buildings on each side of the street were hung with luminous vines and creepers displaying broad waxy-green leaves, and the sidewalk underfoot was tacky with mould. The building in which Dan had his Agency was the only one occupied; the windows and doors of the others along the street were either boarded up or smashed.

He took the upchute to the top floor, located the appropriate door and knocked. A yellow light burned behind the pebbled pane of glass. A woman's voice called out, and hesitantly Mirren entered. He was in a small waiting room, shabby but comfortable. An Oriental receptionist sat behind a desk. She looked up from a computer screen.

"I'm afraid we closed at eight," she said. "But I can make you an appointment for tomorrow."

"I was hoping to see Dan Leferve. I'm a friend."

She smiled. "You're in luck. I think he might still be in–" She stopped and looked at him. "Are you okay?"

He was aware that he'd broken into a sweat which had less to do with the thought of meeting Dan again than with the illness he'd awoken with. "I'll be fine."

"I'll just check." She spoke into a handset.

"Your name, sir?"

"Mirren. Ralph Mirren."

She repeated it. "Please go right through." She indicated a door.

Dan Leferve was on his feet, open-mouthed with surprise when Mirren stepped into the adjacent room. "Hell, Ralph. You should've told me you were coming. I'd've thrown a party!" He rounded his desk and took Mirren in a bear-hug. Mirren did his best to return it, embarrassed. Dan pulled away and regarded him at arm's length, all beard and black mane.

"It's been too long, Ralph – three, four years?"

"More like five." Mirren shrugged. "I always meant to drop by... You know how it is. Good to see you, anyway. You're looking well."

"Never better, Ralph," Dan said. "Wish I could say the same about you."

"I'll survive."

"Look, let's move into the loft. It's more comfortable. Care for a drink?"

He ushered Mirren from the office, through a second door and up a flight of steps. "Bought this last year, converted it and moved in. What do you think?"

Leferve stood on the threshold and indicated the room. It was long and low, with a large, semi-circular window affording an elevated view across Paris. Two hammocks slung at each end of the loft bracketed polished floorboards covered with Eastern rugs, two alien pot plants and plump foam-forms before the semi-circular window. Plasma-graphics decorated the walls, depicting alien panoramas and sunsets, deep spacescapes of nebulae and planetary systems. The scenes were slowly moving, changing gradually in real-time, so that in one the red super-giant sank infinitesimally towards a mountainous horizon, and in another the planets turned in orbit with the colossal majesty of all stellar objects.

Mirren saw, on a shelf across the room, several pix and holographs of the *Perseus Bound* and his Engine-team.

"Take a seat, Ralph. How about a cognac?"

Mirren sank into a ridiculously comfortable foam-form and admired the view across the city. He indicated the expensive graphics. "Business doing well?"

"I'm not complaining." He passed Mirren a large glass, took the opposite foam-form. "*Salut.* I've expanded over the past few years. Taken a junior partner." He smiled across at Mirren. "Things are okay, considering."

"What kind of work are you getting these days?"

"Much the same as ever, but a bit more of it. Missing persons, stolen property, surveillance. Routine stuff, but it pays. How about you? Still flying?"

"Still flying."

"And hating it?"

"And hating it. But then, I'd hate anything I did..." He was surprised at how easily he slipped into being open with Dan after so short a time in his company. The big man had this effect. They had flown together for almost ten years, after all, and a few years apart could do nothing to diminish the fact.

Mirren took a swallow of cognac. "So... you still a Disciple?"

"Your tone suggests disapproval," Dan smiled. "Don't tell me – you're still a disbeliever, after all the proof?"

Mirren laughed. "What proof?"

"Come on, Ralph. Haven't you read about Degrassi's latest findings? And what about the interface ghosts?"

"Degrassi's an ex-Engineman and a believer, so anything he comes up with 'proving' the existence of the *nada*-continuum is bloody suspect. As for ghosts, I've yet to see one, Dan. And even if I did, what would that prove?"

"You're one of the few Enginemen who hasn't seen one," Dan said. "I saw my first last year. I was in Buenos Aires on business and waiting in the 'port when I saw this silver-blue light flash from the deactivated 'face. No one else saw it but me and another Engineman."

"I don't disbelieve you saw something," Mirren said. "But it proves nothing."

"Isn't it odd that these things should emerge only when the screens are out of phase, resonating on the very same frequency that our occipitals use in the flux? And that only Enginemen see them?"

"Okay, it's odd. But it's certainly not conclusive proof of some ultimate one-state or afterlife."

Dan pursed his lips around a mouthful of cognac. He shook his head. "I've been among believers for so long that I find scepticism difficult to understand. After everything I've experienced, it seems somehow right that the *nada*-continuum is the ultimate."

Mirren smiled indulgently. The alcohol had gone to his head, anaesthetising the ache in his bones, the pain in his body. He was no longer sweating and tense. He felt comfortably heavy, lethargic.

He noticed that the subjects depicted on the plasma graphics had progressed. The M-type sun had set, leaving darkness and a plethora of strange stars in its wake. The view of the solar system had moved on, revealing strange new planets and moons. The pieces were like windows upon the Expansion, showing scenes that Mirren knew he would never behold again.

A dozen snapshots were taped to the nearby wall: Olafson,

Elliott and Fekete in a bar on some distant colony world. Dan and himself, standing before the nose-cone of the *Martian Epiphany*. The other snaps showed various permutations of the five, taken on the many planets they had visited.

"Do you see much of the others?" Mirren asked.

"I haven't seen Olafson or Elliott for years. Olafson's married and working at a flier factory in Hamburg, last I heard. Elliott's somewhere in Paris."

"What about Caspar?"

"Caspar I see about once a month on business. I do a bit of work for him, checking up on potential employees, investigating industrial spies."

"But socially?"

"A couple of times a year. It's strange, but we were never close back then. His rationalism angered me. I couldn't take his smugness. You held the same views as him, but you didn't push them down our throats."

"As the leader of you lot I had to be impartial."

"Caspar never let an opportunity pass to ridicule my belief, argue his reductionist viewpoint."

"How do you get on with him now?"

"Surprisingly well. If anything, our views have become even more radical. Caspar's company is working on Artificial Intelligence. He's involved in trying to record the contents of the human mind. The last time I saw him he did his best to persuade me that the process was a way of achieving virtual immortality at the subject's bodily death. Of course I wasn't having any of it." Dan shrugged. "The odd thing is, he's lost his youthful arrogance. As much as I disagree with him philosophically, I quite enjoy his company."

"Does he ever mention the Line? Does he admit to missing the flux?"

"Not in so many words. But I once argued that he must crave the flux and he said that very occasionally he did feel the need for another fix, but that these periods were infrequent and short-lived."

Mirren grunted. "I obviously wasn't sceptical enough."

He stared through the semi-circular window. To the north, he could see the faint blue glow of the interface at Orly. He recalled the many times in the past when he and Dan had shared drinks in his own rooms and watched the bigships phase-in and out all night long – the silence between them something like the silence that existed now; a remembrance of the wonders of the flux, and the anticipation of it.

Dan stared across at him. "There's not a day goes by when *I* don't recollect, relive, the actual transcendence." Then he corrected himself, "Or should I say, *try* to relive it? What I do recall is a pale substitute. Even the Church is no compensation. There's still a gap somewhere in here." He thumped his chest.

Mirren thought of the disfigured off-worlder, and understood then why he felt so reluctant to tell Dan about him. What if the flux that Hunter promised – if he did indeed promise it – was too expensive for the Enginemen to afford? He'd hate to build up Dan's hopes, just to have them cruelly dashed. Then again, his own hopes were sky high – and there was no way he could possibly afford to pay for a couple of hours in a flux-tank without the financial assistance of the others.

"You recall Zinkovsky, that engineer there were all those rumours about a few years back?"

"Zinkovsky? The flux-pusher? Sure. I followed all the leads like a madman. Came up with nothing."

Mirren stared at the disc of his drink. "I keep hearing stories about other pushers in the city."

"I've heard the same rumours. But I think they're mostly just that. Now and again I get the word from a reliable source that there's a genuine dealer on the make, but I've never come across anything concrete."

Mirren cleared his throat. "I was approached by this guy today – rich-looking off-worlder. He had a couple of bodyguards. He came looking for me at the 'port."

From his slouched position on the foam-form, Dan tipped his head forward and peered at Mirren over his barrel chest. "What did he want?"

Mirren shrugged. "Asked me about my team. If I'd kept in touch. He asked how we'd fared without the flux."

"Does Paris stink!" Dan snorted.

"Exactly. He said enough to make me think he was selling flux-time."

Dan sat up.

"He arranged to meet me tonight. He wants to see us all. I said I'd contact you."

"I don't know whether to believe this."

"I'm not sure we should, just yet. A lot could go wrong. Shit, I don't even know how much he's asking, or if he's legit. Or even if he is selling flux-time. If he is, have you thought about this: we might be able to afford the first flux, but what then? We'll be craving like crazy – and back where we started from." The thought opened an abyss of depression within him.

"At the moment, I'm thinking no further than the first flux." Dan said. "Thing is, I always cursed these bastards as stinking opportunists, living off the dependencies of others. But every time I heard a rumour... I was out there searching with the rest of them."

"I just hope he's on the level."

Dan replenished his glass liberally from the bottle on the floor. "Who's the guy, anyway? He give you his name?"

Mirren withdrew the pix of the off-worlder from his inside jacket pocket, passed it across to Dan. "He called himself Hirst Hunter. Like I said, he had a couple of heavies with him. He drove a Mercedes roadster. Do you know how much those things cost to keep running?"

Dan regarded the pix, frowning. He looked across at Mirren. "But he didn't say for sure that he had a tank?"

"Not in so many words, no. But what else could he want from us? That's probably how he made all his money – fleecing Enginemen like us."

"He didn't tell you anything about himself, where he was from?"

"He mentioned he was from Fairweather, in the Drift."

Dan was nodding. "That'd figure. On some of the worlds in the Drift the settlers are born with viral epidermal infections."

"He said little about himself, other than that he'd trained and failed as an Engineman in his younger days. He told me he regretted the closure of the Lines. He knew a bit about our team – he'd read Mubarak's book."

"Have you contacted the others?"

"Not yet."

"I'll do it." He pulled a handset from his breast pocket, got through to his secretary and asked her to contact Fekete, Elliott and Olafson.

He handed the pix back to Mirren. "Have you any idea how much these guy's charge for just an hour in a tank?"

"I dread to think."

"I heard rumours it's a thousand an hour."

Mirren whistled. A thousand credits was what he was paid for two month's work at Orly.

Dan's handset buzzed. A small voice said, "No reply from Elliott and Olafson, Dan. But I did reach Fekete. He's on line now. I'll put him through."

The wallscreen flared. The three-dimensional screen gave the impression that Caspar Fekete was in the room with them. He was seated in a gold chair – more like a throne – in a plush lounge illuminated by a chandelier. He wore a zebra-striped djellaba, and his face suggested that the rest of him was running to fat: his cheeks on either side of his flattened nose were full, almost cherubic.

He leaned forward, peering. "Dan, is that Ralph you have with you? My word, this is a surprise. Long time no see, Ralph! I trust you are keeping well, sir?"

Mirren suspected that the honorific was sarcastic. He smiled. "Surviving, Cas. I thought you'd be rid of that thing by now."

He indicated Fekete's occipital console, bulky beneath the shoulders of his djellaba.

"Get rid of it! Why, it comes in useful from time to time!"

"You still trying to record what's inside your muddled brain-box?" Dan said.

Fekete laughed. "Right you are, sir. When you possess something worthwhile, hang onto it, is my motto. You know I was always proud of what I had up top, gentlemen. To what do I owe this unprecedented pleasure?"

Dan said, "How would you like to flux again, Cas?"

"I might have known, you old believer! How many times do I have to tell this guy?" He winked at Mirren. "For me the flux means zero."

"Oh, yeah?" Dan said. "You don't ever get the slightest, just the tiniest desire to flux again?"

"If I do," Fekete said, "I go and take a cold shower until the feeling passes. But what's all this about the flux? Have you two come by a tank, perchance?"

"Ralph was approached by a guy this morning, asked him if he missed the flux."

Fekete was nodding. "Sounds like a pusher."

"He was an off-worlder, name of Hirst Hunter. He wanted to meet the team–"

Fekete held up a restraining hand. "Stop there. Did you say Hirst Hunter?"

"That's right. You know him?"

"I know of him, if he's the same gentleman. Is he by any chance handicapped by an extreme facial growth?"

Mirren displayed the pix. "This him?"

Fekete squinted. "I think it is, Ralph. You say he's a flux-pusher?" He sounded doubtful.

"I thought so."

Fekete shook his head. "Sounds highly unlikely. I mean, what would a fellow like Hunter be doing pushing flux like some cheap street hustler?"

"Who is he?" Dan asked.

"He was – and still might be – a trouble-shooter for the Danzig Organisation-"

Mirren interrupted, "The Rim sector interface company?"

"The very same – the Organisation responsible for the military take-over of a hundred or more erstwhile free planets over the past twenty years," Fekete said. "Hirst Hunter was in the news ten, fifteen years ago – accused of organising terrorist strikes against the last of the bigship Lines on the edge of the Expansion. It was never proven, but his name was linked to a number of other dirty tricks campaigns around the Rim."

"So he works for one of the companies who put us out of business?" Dan said.

"Do you recall the attack on a smallship on Emerald ten years ago? Three spacers were killed and the Danzig Organisation was implicated."

"I remember something about it," Mirren said.

"Well, Hunter was reportedly behind that, too."

"But what the hell would a Danzig high-up be doing selling flux-time?" Dan said.

"I think you'll find that he isn't," Fekete said. "You say he wanted to see us?"

"I arranged to meet him at the Gastrodome at midnight."

"If you don't mind, I'd like to come along," Fekete said, "and see what Monsieur Hunter is up to."

"We'll meet you on the corner of Gastrodome boulevard and fifth in... say fifteen minutes?"

Fekete inclined his head. "I'll see you then, gentlemen."

He cut the connection.

Dan indicated the wall-clock. "We'd better get moving."

They took Mirren's flier and mach'd low over the rooftops, passing in and out of lighted districts where the city still functioned. The vast, hemispherical dome which covered the centre of Paris appeared before them, dominating the skyline. The dazzling bauble protected ancient buildings and monuments – many of them moved from their original sites – from the elements and the street-gangs alike.

A *descend* imperative flashed on the windscreen from a traffic control tower, and Mirren followed a channel of laser vectors which stitched the night like tracer. They swooped to street level and idled behind a line of other vehicles, fliers, roadsters and coaches, waiting to be admitted into the central precinct. At the checkpoint, an archway in the wall of the dome, Mirren proffered his identity card to a bored gendarme who barely glanced at it and waved them through. He hovered slowly along the streets – air flight was prohibited within the dome – past ancient buildings and parks. It was a part of Paris he'd had no reason to visit in years, and the grandeur of the architecture, unspoilt by the depredations of alien vegetation, reminded him of the time when Paris was a city of both influence and culture. Hordes of tourists from Oceania and South America strolled along the avenues, admiring the genteel beauty of a bygone age. Later, by contrast, they would slum it in the safer sectors of the ghettos and experience what the city had become.

Mirren steered his flier along the wide boulevards towards their rendezvous with Fekete.

Chapter Eight

Birdsong and the scent of Hennessian honeysuckle...

Ella was in her bedroom at her father's villa, in the luxurious Falls district of Zambique City. Soon her minder would tap on the door and tell her that breakfast was ready, and after breakfast Ella would excuse herself and slip out. With luck, she would not see her father today, would not have to suffer that stern uncompromising scrutiny which seemed critical of her very existence. Since his posting to the Reach he had spent much of his time at his apartment in the city, leaving her minder in charge. Ella found the arrangement to her liking and did not complain. She was fourteen, and the long weeks of her summer holiday stretched ahead like years.

She heard voices, men's voices, outside the room. She opened her eyes, and the illusion of her lucid dream was shattered. Paris, her years as a struggling artist, and Eddie – images came rushing in to fill her mind. She relived Eddie's suicide and her flight to the Reach, the old woman and the Disciples. Her last recollection was of the cold, bitter coffee they had made her drink on the boat last night, quickly followed by her fight against unconsciousness.

She was in a rough stone-walled bedroom. Open shutters overlooked a steep hillside and the distant coastline. Birdsong and honeysuckle brought back poignant memories. She struggled upright, lethargic with the effect of the drug.

Her bag lay on the floor beneath the window. Its contents had been removed and placed neatly on a rough timber table. No sooner had she noticed this invasion of privacy than she realised that her silversuit was open, the zipper pulled down to her crotch. She pulled it quickly to her throat, as if her nakedness were still under scrutiny. A slow, hopeless resentment burned within her.

She stood shakily, found her moccasins beside the bed. She moved to the door and lifted the latch. A little girl with big eyes and a mass of black curls sat on a chair across the corridor. As soon as Ella showed herself, the girl jumped down and ran into the next room. She was barefoot and wore a dirty smock open down the back to reveal the dimples at the base of her spine.

"Mama!" Ella heard her cry. "The *senorita* is awake!"

The girl was clinging to her mother's legs, staring out from behind the folds of her skirt, when Ella entered the room.

The three Disciples sat around a table, their conversation suspended as they regarded Ella.

"I hope you bastards enjoyed yourselves last night," she said.

The elder of the three men – the one-armed man who had checked Ella's tattoo in the hotel last night – gestured with his fork to the dark-haired woman, now holding the girl on her hip. "Conchita searched you. It was a precaution we felt we had to take, under the circumstances."

His tone was apologetic. Ella judged him to be in his sixties, a big European with a grey crew-cut and the far-away, longing, lost look of all ex-Enginemen in his eyes. His left arm was missing from the shoulder, the inside-out sleeve tucked back into his shirt.

Ella waved a hand in a don't-mind-me gesture to excuse her accusation, then walked past the men to the door. The smell of cooking from the kitchen reminded her that she hadn't eaten for more than a day.

She stepped outside. The building was exceptionally crude, brick-built and roofed with terracotta tiles. It stood in the foothills of the mountain range that ran the length of the continent parallel to the coastline. Ella made out the spaceport perhaps twenty kilometres to the north, the deactivated interface at this angle no more than an oblique lozenge, like a sapphire on a ring held at arm's length.

In a cleared, sandy area before the building, an old motorbike stood on a spread tarpaulin. Its engine-casing had been removed, and components laid out in neat rows next to a tool-box. Ella knelt beside the bike, inspecting the damage.

She returned inside.

"Whose bike is it?" Ella asked the one-armed Engineman.

"Mine – or rather it was until this happened." He indicated his shoulder. "Please, take a seat... Do you ride?"

"I've had a bike since I was eighteen." She sat across from him, the two others on her left and right. Conchita placed a bowl of rice in the centre of the table, beside a pot of coffee.

"Max Klien," the grey-haired E-man said, offering his hand. Ella shook it. "This is Emilio Rodriguez–" He gestured to the Disciple on Ella's right, a short, balding man in his fifties – not an ex-Engineman – who smiled briefly while ladling rice onto his plate. "And Dave Jerassi..." The Disciple on Ella's left was in his forties, blonde and well-muscled, whose good looks were marred by the expression in his eyes of incommunicable loss. He nodded, smiling nervously.

"Dave and I pushed nearly twenty years for the Shappiro Line," Max said. "We were at college together in Berlin before that. Emilio is a native of the Reach, and a good Disciple."

Rodriguez laughed. "Converts are often the most devout followers in any religion, Ms Fernandez. I might not have pushed, but in my dreams... You know what I mean?"

Ella smiled. "Enginemen have experienced the ultimate. Because we haven't, we need a greater faith." She thought of Eddie and felt a sudden emptiness within her. "In my dreams, too," she said.

She scooped rice and fried eggs onto her plate, then poured herself a mug of steaming coffee. She was aware of the three men exchanging glances as she bent to her food. She felt as though she was being considered, assessed, that any slip she might make would reveal her as a spy.

They ate in silence for two minutes, then Ella said, "I hope you don't think that I'm anything other than a Disciple, gentlemen?"

Rodriguez and Jerassi shifted uncomfortably, glanced at Klien. Max drew something from the chest pocket of his shirt, passed it across to Ella. It was her identity card. "You seem to be who you claim," he said.

"Thanks." Ella took the card. "I was never in any doubt."

Rodriguez stopped eating. "If you'd been through what we've been through over the past few weeks, Ms Fernandez–"

Max silenced him with a glance. "If you don't mind my asking, Ella, why did you become a Disciple? Isn't every day that a non-spacer civilian converts." He poured himself a coffee, watching her.

She shrugged. How could she tell them the truth without giving away the fact of her privileged past?

"When I was living in Paris seven, eight years ago I met this guy, an Engineman – Eddie Schwartz. He pushed for the Chantilly Line. Ever heard of him?" She glanced around the table. They shook their heads. "He was a lot older than me, but we got on well. I guess we both needed someone. He was a Disciple, of course, and in the early days he attended the services a lot."

Max said, "But only in the early days?"

Ella stared at a forkful of rice, smeared with egg yolk. "Later, he claimed he didn't need the Church. So he stopped going."

"There comes a time when all the ritual is no longer a replacement for what we've lost, just a painful, nagging reminder." Max smiled at her, then asked gently, as if he knew, "What happened to him, Ella?"

She looked up from her food. "A couple of days ago... he just left in his flier and drove straight smack bang into the fucking interface at Orly. There was nothing I could do."

"He's in a better place now, Ella," Max murmured.

"*Yeah*," Ella wanted to say, "*but look where I am*." Instead she shrugged. "Like I was saying, I started going to services with him, and they kind of made sense... Perhaps I needed something to believe in at that time. They had counsellors, welfare workers."

Jerassi looked up. "Paris, you say? The converted smallship, Montparnasse?"

Ella stared at him, to show that she knew what he was doing. "Yeah, the one on the Rue Renoir – all night services, all day counselling sessions. Guy called D'Alamassi runs it. You been there?"

Jerassi smiled. "About twelve years ago, when it was just starting up. D'Alamassi was in charge then, too."

Ella pushed her empty plate away, feeling as though she'd scored a point.

Max rocked his chair back so that it rested against the wall. He regarded Ella. "So, Eddie unites with the ultimate and you decide to come to the Reach. But why here? Hadn't you heard the rumours about the Organisation persecuting E-men and Disciples?"

She shook her head. "There's nothing on the news on Earth. I didn't hear any rumours. When I got to A-Long-Way-From-Home, someone there said the Danzig planets were restricting the movement of E-women, E-men and Disciples, but that's all."

"Why did you want to come here in the first place?" Max asked.

Ella had hoped they might have forgotten that question. "I lived on the Reach for a few years when I was younger. When Eddie died... it just seemed the right thing to do." She stared from one Disciple to the next, defying them to disbelieve her.

Rodriguez was bent low over a second helping of rice, watching Max. Jerassi, the quiet, shy one, stared at his plate without meeting her gaze.

"I take it you were with your parents when you lived here?" Max asked.

"My father. My mother died when I was two. Father worked for a Terran engineering company," she went on, staring at Max, challenging him to call her a liar. "We moved around a lot when I was young. I liked the Reach. I always wanted to come back."

Max stared at her, as if considering his next line of interrogation. "For the past few months," he began, "every E-man and -woman, every Disciple, trying to enter Danzig territory, has either been turned back or arrested. Those suspected of supporting insurrection in the past have been 'arrested and placed in military custody' – a euphemism, I assure you, for executed. For two months, Hennessy's Reach has been, effectively, a closed planet. Only Danzig Officials can come and go as they wish. Then yesterday you suddenly turn up. You sail through all the checks and enter the Reach as if it were a fun park... You must admit that it does look more than a little suspicious."

Ella thought back to Carey's Sanctuary, and the interest the official had taken on finding out the name of her father.

She shrugged. "They put someone on my trail when I left the 'port," she reminded them. "Perhaps they assumed I was meeting fellow Disciples and they wanted to round them up?" She spread her hands in a frustrated gesture. "I don't know. Shit, I have no idea what's going on here. I came for a quiet holiday, and the next thing I know I'm followed, rescued, drugged, then given the fifth degree."

She stared at Max. "Can you tell me what the hell's going on here, Mr Klien?"

Before he could answer, Conchita entered the room and hurriedly swept the used plates and utensils into a bowl on her hip. The little girl padded up to Rodriguez. "Dada–"

"Not now, Maria. Okay?" He patted her bottom and sent her running off into the kitchen.

Max brought his chair forward to rest on all four legs, clasped his hands together and regarded Ella. "Eleven, twelve years ago we – the Enginemen and Disciples of the Reach – formed ourselves into underground cells and began a campaign of armed resistance to the rule of the Danzig Organisation. We hit strategic command structures across the Reach, military depots, ports and airports. We singled out influential members of the Danzig hierarchy to be assassinated, and in a number of cases we were successful. In the past year we have become such a threat that the Organisation have taken retaliatory action."

As Max spoke, Ella glanced at Rodriguez and Jerassi, seeing them no longer as representatives of a harassed and victimised religious minority, but as ruthless guerrilla fighters.

She recalled the convoy she'd seen leave Carey's Sanctuary for the Reach, the tanks and the nuclear rocket launchers.

"But the military build-up I saw...? Against a guerrilla network?"

Max said, "The Organisation's offensive is not directed at us, Ella."

She looked from Max to Rodriguez and Jerassi. They remained impassive, staring at the table-top.

"I don't understand."

"Why do you think suddenly, twelve years ago, we took up arms and declared war on the Danzig Organisation?"

Ella shrugged. "Because they were – still are – a totalitarian regime that keeps the people of the Reach oppressed and economically disabled."

Max smiled. "Oh, we have far more than the mere liberation of the planet in mind."

Ella had to laugh. "But what can be more important that the liberation of the Reach?"

"We took up the fight against the Organisation because of their treatment of the Lho-Dharvo."

She shook her head. "What do you mean?"

"Eleven years ago they designed and released the Lho-specific virus that in three years wiped out the majority of the Lho-Dharvo on the four continents of the Reach."

Ella was aware of a sudden and dizzying rush of blood to her head, and the amplified thud of her heartbeat pounding around her body. In the silence that followed she heard the sound of birdsong from beyond the open door.

"We had contacts within the Organisation, and our own medical experts," Max went on. "We tried to get our findings to the United Colonies forum on Earth, but our delegation was arrested before it reached Earth, and murdered. The Organisation covered their tracks, responding to rumours by inviting UC representatives to the Reach to investigate the plague. But they were very clever. The infection had all the appearances of being the result of a naturally mutating virus, and of course the Organisation was never incriminated. Would you believe that they were actually praised by the investigation team for their work in identifying and isolating the virus?"

"But *why*? Why would they...?"

"The Lho were – are – on our side, actively fighting for the liberation of the Reach. Because of their knowledge of the planet, they were extremely effective in certain offensive situations. The Organisation took exception."

She recalled something Max had said earlier. "You mentioned that the plague wiped out the *majority* of the Lho – does that mean...?"

"A few hundred resisted the plague and are in hiding in the northern mountains."

Ella felt tears stinging her eyes. "But I thought they'd all died, every last one."

"The Organisation circulated that rumour to scotch any further investigations. But the Lho still survive."

Ella made the connection. "In the northern mountains? That's where the convoy was heading yesterday."

"The Lho are hiding in a massive underground temple complex in the heart of the mountain range," Max said. "For some reason the Organisation are desperate to eradicate the last of the Lho, hence the build-up in the past two months. Don't ask me why, or why they feel they need to use nuclear weapons against a few helpless Lho – but something's happening up there which we can't even begin to guess at. We can only do our paltry best down here to help them."

Max looked from Rodriguez to Jerassi, then back to Ella. "What are your immediate plans?"

The question took her by surprise. Would they allow her to go that easily, just walk away after all they'd told her? She shrugged, suspicious. "I don't know."

Which was, she considered, more or less the truth. She wanted to find her father, but what chance had she of accomplishing this if the Organisation was out to arrest every Disciple?

Max said, "We need your help."

Ella almost laughed. "Mine?"

"Do you think you can manage a long cross-country ride with a passenger?"

She stared at him. "Do I have a choice?"

Max glanced at his compatriots. "We'd like to have you along of your own free will."

"What do you want me to do?"

Max looked at his watch. "You and I will be heading out in just under three hours. You'll take me to our destination and wait under cover for me to get back. Emilio and Dave are setting out before then, to meet me later."

"And if I don't agree to your little plan?"

Max smiled at her. "I think you will, Ella. What other options do you have left?"

Ella considered his words. Indeed, what were her options now? Better she helped the Disciples than go her own way in a hostile land. After all, Max and his cell were fighting for a worthy cause. She could always go along with the Disciples, and later attempt to locate her father.

She considered what Max had told her about the Organisation's responsibility for the plague, but she shut her mind to the thought that her father had had anything to do with the genocide of the Lho.

She said, "Very well, then. Okay"

One hour later, Ella and Max were putting the finishing touches to the trail bike when Rodriguez and Jerassi appeared from the house. They were wearing the light blue uniforms of 'port maintenance staff. Conchita followed them, holding her daughter. Ella wiped her hands on a rag, watching as Rodriguez took his daughter from Conchita, swung her through the air and hugged her to him. The little girl giggled, the sound fluctuating through the warm air. Then he kissed his wife in a silence more eloquent than any farewell.

The two Disciples waved across at Ella and Max, then set off along the path that wound down the hillside through the jungle. Conchita picked up her daughter and walked to the top of the track, stood and watched them go.

Ella threw down the rag and joined them.

The woman smiled shyly. "It is more difficult for those who stay behind. The constant worry..."

"Have faith," Ella said. She glanced at the woman's arm, expecting to see an infinity symbol tattoo.

Conchita said, "No, I'm not a Disciple." She looked from Ella's tattoo to her shoulders. "You were never an Enginewoman, and yet you believe?

Ella shrugged. "I have faith," she began, but left it at that. She looked up at Conchita and said, "You must have some belief? Are you Catholic?"

Conchita laughed. "I have no belief – or rather I believe in my husband, in my daughter." She bounced Maria on her hip and kissed the little girl. "The love I have for Emilio and Maria is enough. And you? Besides your faith, do you have special people?"

Ella smiled. "I had. Eddie was an Engineman. He gave himself to the interface. And my father... I haven't seen him for ten years." She shrugged. "We didn't get on..."

To her surprise, Conchita hugged her with her free arm. "You seem so lost, Ella. I hope you find your way."

She smiled at Ella and then carried her daughter into the house.

Ella returned to her room, to change from her silversuit into jeans, a t-shirt and the jacket the courier had given her. She stepped outside, sat in an old armchair on the porch and stared down the hillside towards the coast.

One of the factors that had made Ella decide to leave her father when she was fifteen – indeed, the *main* factor – was the simple fact of his lack of affection. There were many other reasons, a catalogue of specific incidents, acts of thoughtlessness or deliberate instances of cruelty – one in particular involving L'Endo which she could not bring herself to dwell on – but she understood that these acts of unkindness were merely the result of her father being unable to feel towards her the simple love and affection that should unite father and daughter. For instance, Ella could not once recall her father picking her up and hugging her when she was a child. Her upbringing had been left to the care of a series of nannies and minders. Her father had been a stern, saturnine figure who lived a separate life in his own suite of rooms during her early years. From the age of five until twelve, she'd attended a boarding school on the Rim world of Jet, and in that time her father had turned up just twice to take her on holiday, and on each occasion she had spent most of the vacation with her minder. At twelve, on her father's posting to the Reach, he had installed her in a day school in Zambique, within commuting distance of their villa in the Falls. Her father stayed at the villa perhaps one week in six, but by that time years of separation had taken their toll, and they had acted towards each other as strangers.

Ella drew her legs to her chest and hugged her shins. The damned thing was, she could almost bring herself to understand why her father had felt towards her as he had. Her mother had died when Ella was young, leaving him with a child as a reminder of his loss – a child that he had never wanted. His work for the Organisation around the Rim had taken him away from home when she was young, and later in her teens his absence made any rapprochement impossible. She could almost understand her father's disaffection, but she could not bring herself to forgive him.

And then this bolt from the blue. "I have seen the light, Ella. I need to see–" To see you? To finally treat her as he should have all those years ago? It was almost too much to hope for, too cruel a joke for him to play on her. She had built her own life, had almost reconciled herself to the fact that she did not have a father who cared. And then the communiqué, which had made her realise how much she still wanted his love and acceptance.

She watched Max fill the trail bike's tank with petrol. He stowed the canister under the porch and joined her. He leaned against the rail. "Hope you don't mind my saying, but when we came for you last night I thought you were an Enginewoman."

"You're not the first over the past day or two," she said. "I think I must have aged."

"How old are you?"

She squinted up at him. He was a dark silhouette against the sunset. Was she mistaken in thinking she detected a note of genuine interest in his tone?

"Twenty-five – but I know: I look a lot older. Don't tell me."

Max laughed. There was something so warm and gentle, so lost and vulnerable about Enginemen of a certain age that always made Ella's heart go out to them.

"Okay, so I won't say I thought you were thirty."

"Thanks. And how old are you?"

"I fluctuate," he said. "Sometimes I feel a hundred. Other times I feel around sixty-two."

A silence came between them. Finally Ella asked, "What happened...?" indicating his missing arm.

"Last year we attacked a marine base in the south. I got hit in a shoot out." He smiled at her. "I'm lucky to be alive."

"What about today?" She felt a certain tightness in her throat, hindering her words.

"We'll be leaving in about ten minutes. We'll keep off the roads and follow the track we use to get from here to the coast. We're heading for the spaceport–"

"You're not trying to leave the Reach?"

"No – we just have some business at the 'port." He hesitated. "It shouldn't take too long."

Conchita appeared at the door with her daughter when the time came for them to leave. Ella mounted the trail bike, kick-started it and did a practice circuit of the house. Max joined her, and she noticed that he was wearing padding beneath his peasant's jacket, to disguise the bulky occipital console that spanned his shoulders.

He climbed on behind her and held her around the waist. Ella waved to Conchita, then accelerated down the track between the trees. The way was steep, but not as rough as she had feared. The track was a deep gully cut into the red earth, following for the most part an old water course left over from the rainy season. The bike whined and spluttered, bumped and bucked over exposed tree roots and boulders, but only twice were they forced to dismount. The jungle closed in on each side, which, while cutting down the available light, did have the advantage of muffling the sound of the engine. Ella enjoyed the challenge of the ride, the ego-trip of displaying her skill to Max. Not since evading a horde of thugs in the Latin Quarter had she had so much fun.

They hit sea level and the track became a sandy path winding through the dense foliage. The going was easy here and Ella could relax, allow her thoughts to dwell on more than just the ride.

One hour later they climbed a jungle-covered hilltop, stopped and looked down at the extensive, gun-metal grey tarmac of the spaceport.

"There she is," Max said to himself. He was staring at the interface as if it were his personal holy grail.

Ella laughed nervously. "So... what now, Max?"

"Get the bike under cover and wait here for–" he consulted his watch, "– one hour. No more. If I'm not here by then, head off without me. I'll make my own way back. Keep your head down, Ella, okay?"

"Hey, and you take care, too. That's an order."

Max smiled. "I'll be as careful as I have to."

As he started to leave, Ella rushed forward and impulsively embraced him. He returned the gesture, one-armed and awkward. He even seemed reluctant, as if to show her affection now might hurt both of them later. Quickly, he turned and slipped off through the undergrowth. Ella watched him go, then strained her eyes to catch glimpses of him as he slid and scrambled down the hillside. She concealed the bike in the undergrowth, then settled herself in the cradling root system of a giant hardwood tree and peered down at the spaceport.

Was it her imagination, her paranoia, or were there more guards patrolling the 'port than there had been when she arrived yesterday? Sentries stood to attention at regular intervals around the perimeter and patrols made clockwise circuits of the vast strips of tarmac in armoured personnel carriers.

The interface was identical to all the others she had ever seen across the Expansion. Two vertical columns rose like slim towerblocks, portals and viewscreens giving the occasional glimpse of technicians and officials inside, and between them stretched the bright blue membrane of the interface itself. It was not surprising that Disciples considered the portals to be iconic. Even in their industrial, work-a-day aspect they were tremendously powerful symbols, monuments to humankind's incredible achievement of instantaneous star travel.

Ella dug her old digital watch from her breast-pocket. Almost thirty minutes had elapsed since Max had left. She was relieved that she had witnessed no disturbance down at the 'port. She was aware of her heartbeat as she willed the Disciples to return safely, and soon.

The rapid chatter of gunfire almost stopped her heart.

She surged to her feet, desperately scanning the 'port for the source of the firing. Directly below her, half a dozen guards were laying down a barrage of rapid fire across the tarmac, orange tracer creating a complex network in the twilight. At first, Ella could not make out their intended target. Then, when the return fire began, she saw two tiny, blue-uniformed figures – one crouched behind the 'port's courtesy coach and the other, twenty metres away, taking cover behind a small luggage transporter. Rodriguez and Jerassi bobbed up occasionally to return fire, but there was something at once incredibly heroic and hopeless about their stand. Even as they occupied the attention of the perimeter guards, others were closing in across the tarmac behind them. Ella sobbed, trying to shout loudly enough to warn the Disciples. She scoured the 'port for any sign of Max. Had he been arrested already, or killed...?

Then, something jumping and twisting in her gut, she saw the taxi-cab crazily swerving across the tarmac towards the interface, and Max was at the wheel. Their strategy was obvious. Rodriguez and Jerassi were providing the distraction while Max went for the 'face. Even as she watched, adrenalised with fear and despair, she knew with a solid, dull certainty that there was no hope of their surviving. She screamed again as one of the guards fifty metres behind Rodriguez knelt, took aim, and unleashed a withering volley of bullets at the Disciple. Rodriguez didn't fall so much as disintegrate. Jerassi turned and killed his companion's killer. He turned again, took aim – but too late. He was swept away by the continuous fire from two guards sprinting towards him.

Max raced the taxi towards the interface, and only when it was fifty metres from the portal did the guards realise the danger and attack. A line of fire hit the back of the cab, swiping it a full three-sixty degrees and shredding its tyres. The driver's door flew open. Ella shook her head, watching through a veil of tears. Max dived from the taxi, sprinted towards the 'face, dodging the matrices of tracer like a trained combat soldier. Ella was unsure whether he was finally hit by the guard's fire, or if he detonated the explosion himself. The result was the same. Where Max had been, a blinding white starburst exploded. Ella yelled aloud and closed her eyes in pain. When she opened them again, she looked down on a scene of utter devastation. The sunrise laid bloody light across a battlefield. At least two dozen guards lay dead; the taxi was blazing fiercely. Before the interface was a smouldering crater where Max's body-bomb had blown. And the interface itself – Ella stared through her tears, her sobs turning into a kind of crazy laughter... The blue membrane of the interface was no more. The frame was scarred and burnt, the viewscreens shattered, and through it Ella saw the continuation of the tarmac. Never before had she beheld a redundant frame, but however much she tried to tell herself that this had been the aim of her colleagues, she could not accept that their sacrifice had been worthwhile.

She slumped, held her head in her hands and wept.

They'd used her, of course. The bastards had used her to gain their ends – and then deserted her.

Ella sat in the root system of the tree for a long time, considering her options. After perhaps an hour she cuffed the tears from her cheeks, stood and limped with the effects of cramp towards the concealed bike.

She dragged the bike from the undergrowth and, leaving the smouldering ruin of the interface in her wake, headed north towards the Falls.

CHAPTER NINE

HIRST HUNTER STOOD before the arched floor-to-ceiling window and stared out at the darkness stealing over the dying city. For the most part, the advance of night went unopposed: only the occasional district put up a fight in the form of street-lights and neon advertisements. The sight of the moribund city depressed him. It brought to mind the dream he'd been having of late, in which a vast area of light was falling to the gradual encroachment of a black malignancy.

The interface at Orly hung in the air to the south of the city, the blue sky of a colony world contrasting surreally with the Paris night. The portal dominated the skyline, and the pang of guilt it caused him was as sour as heartburn.

He poured himself another brandy and walked across the room to a north-facing window. Here the portal could not be seen, and night held sway totally; the only lights were high in the sky, the industrial orbitals whose profligate illumination mocked the barren land below.

He'd arrived in Paris three days ago and moved his retinue into the top floor of the old Victorian building which had once housed the city morgue. It was situated in a district so derelict and overgrown that the street gangs had been and gone long ago. The building stood squat and solid within its mantle of alien creeper, and the top floor provided the perfect retreat. Hunter had furnished the cavernous chambers of the mortuary with thick carpets, wall-hangings and *chaises-longues* – the polished wood and velvet antiques softening the rather harsh brass and marble fittings of the dissection room and cold storage area.

Hunter stood in his own room, a Spartan chamber furnished with a foam-form on which he slept and a crude bar consisting of half a dozen bottles of Thai brandy. Through the open door he could see the main room with its banks of computers and wall-screens. His bodyguards and advisers sat about smoking or watching vid-screen with a collective air of patient boredom. They had shown surprise at his choice of base, but had known better than to demur. They took it as just another indication of his morbid sense of humour.

Hunter sipped his brandy and considered his meeting with Mirren that morning. It had gone, all things considered, rather well. He had been concerned at first by intelligence reports which stated that Mirren was not a Disciple; he had feared that the Engineman might not crave the flux with the same degree of desperation as some of his believing colleagues. Their meeting had soon dispelled that fear. Mirren might be an atheist, but he desired union just as much as the next Engineman. In Hunter's opinion it was these two factors which were tearing Ralph Mirren apart. He craved the flux, and yet he could not bring himself to believe that it was anything more than an extreme psychological effect. If only he would believe that the wonder of the union had its source in the *nada*-continuum, and not in his own head – and that union awaited everyone in the end – then Mirren might be a more content individual than he was. Hunter wondered whether the only thing that prevented Mirren taking his own life was the perceived oblivion to which he mistakenly believed he would be committing himself. Still, he craved the flux, and that, for the time being, was all that mattered.

Hunter shot the cuff of his silk jacket and glanced at his watch. It was not yet seven. He had another five hours before his meeting with Mirren and the others. He was debating whether to have another brandy when there was a knock on the open door.

Sassoon leaned through, holding the jamb. "We've located a third, sir."

"Excellent! Is it far from here?"

"Clamart, about ten kilometres south-west. Miguelino found it, following up Kelly's information."

Hunter finished his brandy. "Is the car ready?"

"And waiting, sir."

They descended in an ancient, clanking elevator and stepped into the basement of what had once been a spice warehouse. The reek of chilli and petrol fumes filled the air. The Mercedes roadster stood before the elevator gate, doors open and engine running. Hunter slipped into the back seat, Sassoon in the front next to Rossilini.

"Let's hope that this is the one, gentlemen," Hunter said as the car sped from the warehouse. Yesterday they had checked two machines in the northern suburbs, only to find that the first had been cannibalised to repair the second, and that the second was not only unreliable but hardly safe.

He sat back and regarded the passing buildings. They were soon moving through the wide avenues of central Paris, the only road vehicle on his stretch. Overhead, fliers streaked by, tail-lights dwindling, jet engines roaring fit to frighten a less competent driver than Rossilini off the road. They passed the central dome, a giant silver hemisphere surrounded by a fleet of tourist hover-coaches, and then turned south.

Before coming to Paris, Hunter had only ever read about the city, and seen documentaries about it on vid-screen. A great interest in art, which had consumed him for the past five or six years, had contributed to his anticipation of visiting this historic Mecca of so many renowned artists. He had been prepared for a city past it best, living on its reputation – but nothing had quite prepared him for the decrepitude of so much of the place, the apathy of its citizens, and the theme-park tourist attraction it had become.

His wife had been French. In the early days of their marriage he had planned trips to Earth and her native city, but always work out on the Rim had intervened. He had meant to do many things, visit many places, with Marie – and then one day the comfortable certainty of their future together was snatched away, and he faced the galling prospect of empty years alone, with only work to occupy him.

Grief was a strange thing. The old cliché about time healing all wounds was true – over the years the terrible injury of his loss had become almost bearable, but even so, from time to time, memories surfaced and the old wound was reopened.

He wondered whether this was why he resented this changed Paris so much: it was no longer the place of his wife's childhood, the place they had one day planned to visit.

He told himself that once this business was over, and he could relax and enjoy himself, he would become a tourist and visit the galleries and exhibitions under the dome. And, hopefully, by then he would no longer be alone.

He was in danger of becoming maudlin, of dwelling too much on the personal. He returned his thoughts to the business at hand.

"Ah, Mr Rossilini..."

The driver half-turned his head. "Sir?"

"Mirren and the other Enginemen – I take it you've implemented my orders?"

"Of course, sir."

"And everything is running smoothly?"

Rossilini nodded. "Mirren, Leferve, and Elliott are no problem. They live in Paris and rarely venture out of the city. Olafson and Fekete are a bit more difficult. Olafson lives in Hamburg, but I have a private operator trying to trace her, and Fekete has his own security team on the lookout for people showing an interest in him and his affairs. I've put Hassan on him, and he's doing his best."

"And our own operations?" Hunter lived in constant dread that their enemies had discovered what they were doing.

"There's no-one the slightest bit suspicious here on Earth, and the Organisation has no idea where we are."

How many times had Rossilini had to reassure him on that score over the past few days? He must have thought he was losing his nerve...

"Well, I hope you're right, Mr Rossilini. I do hope you are right. I wouldn't want the morgue to find itself in business again."

Rossilini cleared his throat. "Of course not, sir."

They passed from an unlighted, overgrown area – where the alien flora could be seen only in the glare of the headlights, silver-etched and eerie – to a suburb that was just as overgrown but bathed in the illumination of jerry-rigged arc-lights and neons powered by a private generator. The extraterrestrial vegetation obscured the buildings on both sides of the main street, lush and green, like something from the work of Henri Rousseau.

"We're due to meet Miguelino at eight in the Nada Bar," Sassoon said, pointing through the windscreen at a pulsing neon sign.

Rossilini braked the roadster before the bar and Hunter and Sassoon climbed out. Drinkers spilled from the gaudily flower-bedecked premises, many wearing silversuits even though they were too young to recall the hey-day of the space age.

Hunter eased his way through the crowd. The warm night air was heavy with the scent of burning narcotics and loud with computer-generated samba-jazz. Head throbbing, Hunter entered the Nada, a half-lighted, roughly triangular room done up to resemble the bridge of a bigship. As he made his way to the bar, he was aware of the stares directed at his facial disfigurement. On his homeplanet and even on the worlds of the Rim, genetic herpes was such a common trait that it aroused little comment. Only on his arrival in Paris had he been made aware of this facial feature being in any way unique. Indeed, some of his closer aides had questioned the advisability of being seen out on the streets of the city: he was a wanted man, after all, and among the citizens of Paris he was conspicuous, to say the least. In a bid to disguise his identity, he'd employed a cosmetician to extend his disfigurement so that it covered fully half his face, not just the upper left quarter that it had formerly occupied. To be on the safe side he had delegated most of his responsibilities, but had decided to go through with others himself. At this stage of the operation he was, after all, dispensable; any one of his aides could pick up where he left off, if the worst came to the worst, and successfully see through the operation. He wondered if his fatalism had anything to do with his desire to atone for the sins of his past.

Miguelino was sitting on a bar-stool, a tall glass in his hands between his knees. He signalled for two beers when Hunter and Sassoon joined him.

"Mr Miguelino," Hunter greeted the Beta-Engineman, "you've certainly picked the most inhospitable of bars."

"But appropriate," Miguelino said in his usual dolorous baritone, passing them their beers.

"Oh, appropriate, I'll grant you that," Hunter said, glancing at the waiters in the uniforms of the various Lines, and the plasma graphics of the bigships on the wall behind the bar.

Sassoon asked, "Where's your contact?"

The Engineman looked at his watch. "He was due in at eight. The bastard's late." Hunter noted that Miguelino was jumpy, which was not surprising in the circumstances. He was a short, squat Spanish colonial who'd worked with Hunter and Kelly out on the Rim. Indeed, after Kelly – who had remained on the Rim to conduct operations at that end – Miguelino was Hunter's most trusted aide.

He sipped his beer and glanced around the packed bar-room, trying to filter the monotonous thump of the music from his consciousness. He killed time by attempting to spot the colonists among the crowd. One or two of the more freakishly tall revellers were obviously from low gravity worlds – Xyré or Cannon's Landfall in the Core. One particularly squat citizen, almost as broad as she was tall, clearly hailed from a planet of extremely high gravity – Some-day-Soon or Zia-al-Haq. He saw no-one from his homeplanet of Fairweather.

Then he saw the small, dark girl standing against the far wall, talking to a young man. For a second, Hunter's heart skipped – then he realised that he was mistaken. She was so very similar that it pained him to look at her. The girl looked him up and down with a glance of cool contempt. Hunter turned away, embarrassed. Even her superior disdain brought back painful memories.

Miguelino touched his elbow.

He followed the direction of the Engineman's gaze and stared at the man approaching them through the crowd. At first he thought it was a dwarf on stilts. Certainly, his cramped facial features were those of a dwarf, and the fact that he walked with a peculiar lurching gait suggested stilts. Then he emerged from the press and Hunter saw that the man's legs had been amputated at the thighs. From each naked stump a silver rod extended in place of the femur; the artificial legs were articulated at the knees with ball-joints, and terminated in wedge-shaped footpads. The dwarf wore a silversuit, had long grey hair and chewed the end of a cigar.

"Gentlemen," he greeted them nervously. "How can I help you?"

"Cut the shit, Quiberon," Miguelino snapped. "I told you – we know you have a tank."

"You're KVO officials?" Something like panic showed in his eyes.

"Just lead the way, Quiberon," Miguelino said, "and no smart tricks. We have your place surrounded."

Quiberon glanced at the three men. The cigar shuttled from one side of his mouth to the other. He hesitated, weighed up his options, then said, "Follow me."

He led them through a door at the rear of the bar and across an empty street. The music receded in their wake. There were no lights here. Hunter was aware of a disgusting mulch underfoot, the occasional snagging grasp of a ground-vine. They came to a tall iron gate in a stone wall, the bars of which served as a trellis for the climbing plants. Quiberon, bobbing and lurching, unlocked the gate and ushered them through. Hunter clutched a small automatic pistol in his jacket pocket. They were in an ancient, ramshackle cemetery. By the faint light of the stars and the industrial orbitals, he made out lichened gravestones, coy statues of angels with trumpets, kitsch Madonna figures and the occasional blockhouse monstrosity of a family tomb. The alien vegetation had overtaken the place in a riot of vulgar blooms and speckled leaves, a profanity entirely in keeping with the maudlin sentimentality of the ecclesiastical architecture.

Quiberon stilted down a short flight of steps, unlocked and pushed open the timber doors of a subterranean crypt. He touched a wall-switch and flooded the interior with a dull red light. Hunter, Sassoon and Miguelino followed the elevated dwarf inside.

"My customers are eight E-men," Quiberon said. "They wouldn't give me away... How did you find out?"

Ignoring him, Hunter approached the tank installed in the corner of the crypt. Miguelino was beside him, silent, awed.

It was a Larsen Class II, a silver, torpedo-shaped flux-tank that Hunter guessed was no more than twelve years old. By the look of it, the tank had never seen service in a 'ship.

Miguelino was down on his knees, caressing its streamlined length, checking its dials and metres. He might only have been a Beta, Hunter reflected, but all Enginemen, irrespective of their grade, craved the flux.

Quiberon looked from Hunter to Miguelino and back again. "Are you from the KVO?" he asked desperately. "You haven't been snooping around for years. I thought the restrictions were being relaxed, that was the talk on the street. And I do provide a genuine service..." He eyed the Engineman, clearly unable to equate an official KVO investigation with the behaviour of Miguelino.

Hunter asked, "Where did you get it?"

Quiberon hesitated, decided to co-operate. "The Larsen factory. I had contacts when it closed down."

"How good is it? In what state of repair?"

"I've never had a bit of trouble. It's mechanically perfect."

Miguelino looked up at Hunter, a plea in his eyes.

"Set it up for a Beta," Hunter said. "Thirty minutes,"

Quiberon fell to the task like a man reprieved from a death sentence – which perhaps he considered he was. KVO officials would have impounded the tank and arrested its owner: they certainly would not have demanded flux time for an accompanying Engineman.

The dwarf danced around the tank on his flashing silver legs, programming the computer, adjusting its leads. Finally he hauled open the half-metre thick hatch and withdrew the slide-bed. In a daze of anticipation Miguelino unzipped his silversuit, shrugged it from his shoulders and sat on the slide. Quiberon jacked the leads into his occipital console, and as each jack clunked home the Engineman slipped further from this reality. Quiberon and Sassoon laid him out on the bed and pushed him into the tank. The dwarf dogged the hatch and sequenced the monitoring computer.

A faint blue glow showed behind the observation plate in the hatch. Sassoon crouched beside the computer screen embedded in its flank, assessing the tank's performance, reliability and general running condition.

Hunter sat on a low stone shelf reserved for a coffin and waited. Quiberon watched both men nervously, his gaze darting from Hunter to Sassoon and back again. At last he summoned the nerve to say, "You're not KVO officials, are you? You won't turn me in?"

Sassoon was scribbling figures into a note-book.

Hunter decided to keep Quiberon sweating. "You've been hawking the flux for what... ten years? You must have made a small fortune by now, Monsieur Quiberon."

"I provide a service. I keep Enginemen sane."

"How much do you charge for thirty minutes?"

"Five hundred credits, no more."

Hunter pursed his lips. Quite reasonable, if the dwarf was to be believed. He took his wallet from his jacket and counted out five one hundred credit notes. He held them out to Quiberon.

"Here you are. I always pay for what I take."

Quiberon smiled with nervous relief. "No, please. Keep it. This one's on me."

"I said, I pay for what I take." Hunter dropped the credits on the stone slab between them. Quiberon was shaking too much to reach out and take the notes.

"Look," he said, his voice quivering, "if you aren't the KVO, who are you? What do you want?"

Hunter glanced at his watch. Fifteen minutes had elapsed from the time Miguelino had entered the tank. He looked across at Sassoon. "Well, Mr Sassoon?"

His aide looked up, smiled. "I don't believe it. It's very near perfect. Ninety-five percent efficiency, no obvious mechanical deficiencies..."

"So it would appear that this is the one?"

"I'm sure it is, sir."

Hunter returned his attention to Quiberon. "Do you know what the penalty is for hawking flux-time, Monsieur Quiberon?"

The dwarf looked sick. "The bullet," he whispered.

"Tell me, do you believe in an afterlife?"

The dwarf shook his head.

"A word of advice – do so."

Quiberon stammered, "You can't turn me in! You've bought flux time! You can't–"

"My advice was general, Monsieur Quiberon, a recommendation to prepare your mind for the time perhaps years hence when you do eventually cast off this cruel illusion."

Hunter saw Sassoon glance up at him, then look away quickly, half-smiling at his boss's sick sense of humour.

"You must live in constant fear of being found out," Hunter said. "Constant fear of the bullet."

Quiberon swallowed. "I've always been careful. I've taken precautions, never taken risks. How... how did you find out?"

"I have my contacts," Hunter said. Kelly, his man on the Rim, had used Quiberon's services eight or nine years ago, back when the dwarf had had his tank installed in the sewer system below St Denis. It had not been difficult to locate Quiberon. Kelly had provided a detailed facial description, and there were few dwarfs as ugly as Quiberon.

"How would you like me to relieve you of the burden of worrying yourself about being discovered and facing the firing squad?"

"You can't take it–!"

"What do you make in a year, Monsieur Quiberon? Let's see... eight Enginemen every, what, two weeks? At five hundred each that's more than eight thousand credits per anum. That's quite a yearly salary, Monsieur Quiberon. Now listen carefully. I want to make you an offer. I'm taking the tank, whether you like it or not, but as I said earlier, I'm prepared to pay for what I take. I'm offering you twenty thousand credits for the tank. If you refuse, the authorities get to know pretty damned quickly, and you're a dead man. If you accept, you can retire to Sumatra and live like a king." Hunter paused. "What do you say, Monsieur Quiberon?"

Quiberon was shaking his head. "Is this some kind of joke?"

Hunter was in the process of counting out twenty thousand credits in five hundred credit notes. He looked up. "No joke, Monsieur Quiberon. Here is the money. Please check it to ensure I haven't underpaid you." He dropped it onto the stone slab.

Lights sequenced along the flank of the flux-tank. Sassoon opened the hatch and pulled out the slide-bed. Hunter helped him withdraw the jacks from Miguelino's occipital console. While he was doing this he noticed the dwarf quickly snatch the money and rifle through it.

They swung Miguelino into a sitting position on the slide-bed. He was in a daze, the usual look of loss in his eyes extinguished by communion with the ultimate.

"Good work in locating the tank, Mr Miguelino," Hunter said, making a circle with his thumb and forefinger before the Engineman's face. "This is the one."

Miguelino was in no fit state to respond.

Sassoon said, "I'll make the arrangements for shipment immediately."

Hunter was aware of the hard pressure of exultation in his chest. "This means it won't be long now, Mr Sassoon. We're on our way."

Quiberon was still counting the notes when Hunter left the crypt and walked back through the graveyard.

Rossilini had the Mercedes waiting by the gates. Hunter slipped into the back seat and the roadster started up and swept him north through the derelict suburbs. He watched the dark buildings slide by, thinking only of the time when the mission would be over and he could concentrate as much effort on righting the affairs of his personal life.

As they approached the mortuary, Rossilini's communicator buzzed. He spoke in hushed tones, then turned to Hunter. "It's base, sir. Delgardo of the KVO in Kuala Lumpur is wanting to speak to you. He says it's urgent."

"Excellent," Hunter said. "Tell them to put him through to my room. I'll be back in five minutes."

When they reached the warehouse building, Hunter took the elevator to the top floor. He hurried through the main chamber and entered his room, closing the door behind him. He activated the wall-screen and it flooded the previously darkened room with light. The picture resolved, showing a thin, silver-haired man in his seventies seated behind a desk.

Hunter manoeuvred an armchair in front of the wall-screen and sat down. "Jose. Sorry to keep you waiting."

Delgardo smiled. "I've been trying to contact you for hours, Hirst."

"I have a security network filtering and checking on all calls. Secrecy is of the utmost importance."

"Is it possible to ask where you are?"

"I'm sorry. If my opponents were to find out... This is a secure link, Jose, but even so..."

Delgardo gestured. "Not to worry. It's great to hear from you again. It's been a long time."

"Years," Hunter said, aware that they were both beating around the proverbial bush. "Too many years."

Jose Delgardo was something of a paradox: head of one of the Organisations responsible for putting the bigship Lines out of business, he was nevertheless a believer, a Disciple. He had trained to become an Engineman, and even pushed briefly as a Gamma before ill-health had forced his early retirement. Hunter had known and liked him when both men worked for the Hartmann Company on Mars in the early days of interface development. He had been the obvious person to approach about this matter.

Hunter cleared his throat. "I take it you've considered my communiqué?"

Delgardo sat up, equatorial sunlight falling about him through the window-wall of his office. "I must admit, Hirst, that my first reaction to this–" he tapped a sheaf of print-outs before him on the desk "– was that I found it hard to believe."

"And your second reaction?"

The Director of the Keilor-Vincicoff Organisation pursed his lips, considering. "Frankly, my second reaction was still one of disbelief."

"But the consequences, if we ignore it..." Hunter began.

Delgardo made a sound that was part sigh, part laughter. "You don't for a minute expect me to order the closure of all the 'faces, just like that?" He snapped his fingers.

Hunter was ready with a reply. "Not immediately, no. The shutdown could be phased in over a number of years."

"But my investors–" Delgardo began.

Hunter laughed. "You don't sound like a very good Disciple."

Delgardo smiled ruefully. "Five years in this job is enough to corrupt the best."

Hunter leaned forward in his armchair. "We've given this a lot of thought, Jose. Please hear me out. The obvious course of action is for the KVO to reinvest in the shipping Lines. Don't you hold the legal right of tender on many of the main routes? If you began putting capital into ship-building right now, then there's no reason why in two, three years you wouldn't be running a vastly profitable Line."

Delgardo leafed through the report, unconvinced.

Hunter was less nervous now than he had been before speaking to the Director for the first time in years. At least he was giving Hunter a hearing.

"Okay," Delgardo said at last, "just supposing all this is true, supposing I, the heads of the other interface concerns, and the United Colonies agree that we should shut down the network – you don't think for a second that the Danzig Organisation would meekly agree and quietly close down their operations?"

Delgardo turned to a keyboard on his desk and tapped in a command. The entire window-wall behind him darkened, then showed an overview of the galaxy. It focused in on the Rim quarter controlled by the Danzig Organisation.

The Danzig planets flashed orange.

Delgardo said, "They own nearly two hundred planets in this quadrant, and they all have interfaces. Plus they have links to junction planets all around the Expansion. They aren't likely to give it up that easily – especially if we have the jump on them as regards the bigships."

Hunter smiled in complete agreement. This perhaps would be the hardest part of his communication with the Director. "We realise this – and realise also that we might have to neutralise the Danzig Organisation by force–"

"But their militia is second to none! Look what they did to put the rebellion down on Xiang last year."

"If the UC acted as one," Hunter continued, "along with the other interface Organisations, we would overpower them with ease. The only reason they gained such a stranglehold on the Rim is that the UC never squared up to them in the past. They opposed them with petty sanctions which never had any effect." Hunter gestured. "Besides which, to a large extent the conflict would be fought out by guerrilla hit squads. We need only to destroy their interfaces to render them powerless, after all." He paused. "Purely as a humanitarian issue, we can't let them get away with the genocide of the Lho."

Delgardo sat in silence for a long minute. "How can I be certain that your claims are fully justified, Hirst? As I said, I personally find it almost too incredible to believe."

"I don't by any means expect your full and immediate support right this minute," Hunter said. "You have every reason to doubt my story. But I can substantiate it. Just give me time, Jose. Soon, I'll have proof that everything contained in the report is accurate."

Delgardo leafed through the read-out again. He looked up. "How soon?"

Hunter hesitated, took a risk. "In two, maybe three days. I'm coming to Malaysia then. I'm arranging to meet Earth's UC representative at the disused airbase at Ipoh. If you could be present, I promise you won't be wasting your time. Of course I'll be in touch before then to finalise the arrangement."

"Very well, Hirst. I'll do my best to be there – for old time's sake. I've never known the Hunter of old to stick his neck out so far, if it wasn't worth the risk of losing it."

Hunter smiled. "Thank you. You have no idea how grateful I am, Jose."

They chatted for a while longer, before Delgardo excused himself and cut the connection. Hunter sat back in his armchair and released a long breath. Yesterday he had contacted Johan Weiner, the UC representative on Earth, and discussed his report with him. Like Delgardo, Weiner's response had been guarded – but he had not dismissed Hunter's claims out of hand, and had agreed to meet Hunter and his team in Malaysia. It was all Hunter could reasonably ask.

Of course, the meeting at Ipoh would come to nothing if he did not succeed with his plans over the next couple of days.

Which reminded him...

He glanced at his watch. It was almost twelve, and time for his dinner engagement with Mirren and the others.

Chapter Ten

Mirren and Dan Leferve hurried along the crowded avenue towards the golden bauble of the Gastrodome. Hordes of tourists promenaded, enjoying the clement evening. Within the vast dome which covered central Paris the temperature was controlled: not for these rich visitors the sweltering night heat that suffocated the rest of the city. High overhead, tiny lights on the inner curve of the dome simulated the constellations.

Caspar Fekete was waiting for them beside a news-fax kiosk. He was impressive in a magenta djellaba, his bulk emphasised by the console, surely augmented since his discharge from the Line, which spanned his shoulders.

"Ralph, it's wonderful to see you again." He took Mirren's hand in a limp grip, gold bracelets and rings flashing.

He was conscious of Fekete's gaze taking in his unkempt appearance: his balding head, his gaunt, unshaven face. They strolled along the avenue.

Fekete said, "Have you ever been to the Gastrodome, Ralph?"

Mirren gazed at the dome. "I've always thought it a bit up-market."

"You're in for an experience." Fekete smiled to himself.

"I've been," Dan said. "Once. Hated the place."

The restaurant was the decommissioned astrodome of a bigship – or rather the inflated inner mylar membrane – removed and set down on the banks of the Seine. The dome stood on a circular plinth of marble which served as a staircase, and was surrounded by an exotic display of extraterrestrial flora. Unlike in the outlying districts of the city, where xenobiological specimens flourished without restraint, this garden was designed and tended by a team of the finest off-world horticulturists. Similar gardens had been all the rage eighty or ninety years ago, when the first bigships forged their way to the stars and returned with all manner of botanical wonders. Then it had been a status symbol to own land given over to the trees and flowers of Hakoah or Songkhla. With the arrival of the interfaces, however, and the subsequent invasion of the alien spores, such gardens had become *passé*. This one, and everything about the Gastrodome, was an intentional exhibition of nostalgia, a harking back to an era when Paris was the centre of the space industry on Earth – a display, thought Mirren, of kitsch for the *nouveau riche* of Oceania who had never experienced Paris and the space-age in its hey-day.

They mounted the marble steps to one of the triangular entrance hatches. From within drifted the sickly strains of a band playing the hits of twenty years ago. Mirren recognised *Continuum Blues*, but done with an excess of strings to emphasise the sentiment. The *maître d'* met them on the threshold. "Gentlemen... a table for three?"

"We're meeting a Monsieur Hunter at midnight," Mirren said.

"Of course. If you would care to come this way." The *maître d'* was garbed in the dark blue uniform of a bigship Captain – but there was something overdone, almost pantomime, in the width of the scarlet piping, the chunkiness of the epaulettes and the jutting peak of his cap. His dress, like everything else about the place, was more lampoon than honest imitation.

The interior of the dome was a series of ever smaller galleries which rose in tiers from the floor, encircling an inner area where the band played and patrons danced. Each gallery was sectioned off into private dining booths with a view over the surrounding gardens.

As they were led to an elevator plate which whisked them up to the fifth gallery, Mirren turned to Dan. "I see what you mean," he said.

"Wait till you see the prices," Dan said.

"Let's hope Hunter will be picking up the bill."

"To be honest, it won't feel right – dining with someone directly responsible for the closure of the Lines."

They stepped off the elevator and the *maître d'* steered them around the circumference of the walkway.

Hunter was scanning a newssheet when they arrived. He looked up, the disfigured half of his face glowing a fiery crimson in the lighting of the booth. He stood as Mirren made the introductions. "Mr Fekete, Monsieur Leferve, you cannot imagine how pleased I am to make your acquaintance."

They shook hands amicably, Dan and Fekete concealing any hostility they might have felt towards the Danzig Organisation executive. Mirren recalled their first meeting. It was almost as if the big off-worlder had the ability to neutralise suspicion, win people over with his persuasive charisma.

On anyone else, Mirren thought, the growth would be the thing which attracted attention. With Hunter, after the initial surprise, it ceased to be a point of significance beside his attentive demeanour and charm.

"Please, take a seat. May I offer you an aperitif?"

Mirren sat with his back to the soft wall of the dome. He looked around for Hunter's bodyguards but saw no sign of them. He guessed they would not be far away, mingling with the diners. Fekete sat to his right, Dan to his left and Hunter facing him.

"I take it we are not to be joined by Ms Elliott?"

"We couldn't contact her, or Olafson."

Hunter waved in good-natured acceptance.

They ordered. The menu was interstellar and the prices, Mirren thought, astronomical. Hunter exhorted them to try the braised prawns from the waterworld of Shanendoah – the most expensive starter listed. He gave a running commentary on each dish throughout the process of ordering. Mirren calculated that the bill for his meal alone would come to almost double his usual weekly food allowance.

The food arrived and they ate. Hunter sampled his dish. "Delicious! I'll say this for the place, its fare is far more appealing than its appearance, but then how could it not be? I assumed when I booked the table that it might prove an apposite venue. Unfortunately, I reckoned without the city's innate skill in prostituting its former glory."

Mirren had ordered a cut of meat grown in the vats of Amethyst, with a side dish of the planet's finest vegetables. He ate in silence, unable to appreciate the meal. He was aware of a tension around the table, which Hunter strove to defuse with a flow of small talk.

Dan was unable to check his impatience. He laid down his knife and fork. "Forgive my curiosity, Monsieur Hunter, but what did you have in mind when you said that you wished to see us?"

Hunter nodded to himself, suddenly businesslike. "No at all, Monsieur Leferve. We have important matters to discuss."

Fekete said, "I take it that Ralph was mistaken in his assumption that you wish to sell us flux-time?"

Hunter dabbed his lips with a napkin. "Mr Mirren was actually closer to the truth than you might think–"

Dan interrupted. "What the hell is someone like you doing selling flux-time?" Mirren glanced at his friend. Dan was shaking with barely controlled rage.

"Someone like me, Monsieur Leferve–?" Hunter began.

"You work for the Danzig Organisation," Fekete said. "You were responsible for buying out Lines and shutting them down. You were behind the bombing of ships which killed innocent spacers–"

Hunter tossed his napkin into the centre of the table. "I *worked* for Danzig, Mr Fekete. I no longer do so. As for my past actions, I assure you that those deaths were unintentional and deeply regretted. You might find this hard to believe – I know I would if I were in your position – but at the time I believed that what I was doing was for the good of humanity. The methods I employed might have been deemed underhand and unjust, but they were the means that justified a greater end."

"The pre-eminence of the Danzig Organisation in the Rim sector?" Fekete asked, a sneer in his tone.

"The means of easy access to other planets for the average citizen," he said. "Whatever you might argue were the benefits of space travel, it was prohibitively expensive for the average citizen. I genuinely thought that I was working for the good of–"

"You're making me cry," Dan cut in. "You were working to line the pockets of your Organisation, and don't try to deny it."

Hunter smiled. "You are quite welcome to make your own interpretation of my actions," he said. "I have offered my motives."

The conversation lapsed. Down below, the band swung into its own rendition of *Nada Riff*. Thankfully at this range the music was mere background noise.

Mirren cleared his throat, nervous. "You said that I was close to the truth...?"

Hunter sipped his wine. "That's right, Mr Mirren. I am not offering to sell you flux-time. I am giving it to you. Or rather, I intend to pay you to flux again. I have a proposition to make."

Mirren stared at Hunter, his body cold with sweat.

Dan almost whispered, "What proposition?"

From the inside pocket of his grey jacket, Hunter withdrew a silver envelope. He passed it across the table to Mirren. "Please open it and take out the photographs."

Nervously Mirren unsealed the envelope and pulled out three large, glossy pictures. He stared at the first pix, looked up to see Hunter smiling at him. He was aware of Fekete and Dan watching him with a mixture of curiosity and impatience.

He passed two photographs to Dan and Fekete, keeping one for himself. It showed the side view of a short, stubby smallship, its silver paintwork marked with meteor impact slashes and flame excoriations behind the booster exhaust vents.

"An ex-Indian navy cruiser," Mirren said. "Hindustan Class II." He peered at the insignia on the flank and tail-fin. "I'd guess it was built in the Calcutta shipyards about thirty years ago."

Hunter said, "It's actually twenty-five years old, but you are correct in every other detail."

Dan stared at the photograph in his hand. "It's a little beauty. I've actually pushed one – a shuttle flight between Mars and Triton."

Fekete murmured, "It certainly is magnificent."

Mirren was watching Hunter, dry of throat, while the others prattled on. The off-worlder was smiling to himself.

"I am glad you're impressed," he said. "I own the smallship."

Dan was the first to voice an objection. "That's impossible! They were all scrapped, made inoperable. The interface people made sure they bought out every Line and junked every last 'ship. Even those that went to museums had their guts ripped out."

"And the Organisations," Fekete added, "are vigilant in their campaign to ensure that no-one ever gathers the parts and puts them back together."

Hunter shook his head. "They like to give that impression, and they were vigilant in the early days. They owned all the transportation licences and they didn't want their territory invaded. But latterly they've grown lax. Ship parts are expensive, and who would have the funds to put together and fly such a cost-consuming machine?"

"Where did you get it?" Mirren asked.

"I bought the shell of the 'ship itself from the New Delhi Universal Science Museum; the fittings, computers and such from various scrap yards and second-hand dealers in Europe and Asia, mainly London and Seoul. The flux-tank I located here, in Paris. Perhaps the most difficult part of the entire operation was finding engineers and technicians I could trust. But I succeeded." He gestured at the pictures.

Mirren was aware of a hard pressure of excitement in the centre of his chest like an incipient coronary. He could hardy bring himself to ask Hunter the all-important question.

Dan had no such reservations. "What the hell are you planning to do with it, Hunter?"

"I need," the off-worlder said, "a number of Enginemen to push the boat out to the Rim and back."

In that second, Mirren looked upon Hunter as his own personal saviour. He closed his eyes and heard the words again. Whatever capability he might have had to think logically, rationally, had deserted him. All he was able to comprehend was the miracle that Hunter had offered: a smallship to mind-push; an end to all the years of hell he'd endured since the closure; the opportunity to once again acquaint himself with the sublime state of being attained when pushing a 'ship through the *nada*-continuum.

Caspar Fekete brought him crashing back to earth.

The Nigerian sat back in his seat and sipped his coffee, his belly straining at the material of his djellaba. Until now he had been polite in speech and manner. Mirren expected him to graciously thank Mr Hunter, maybe even celebrate the occasion by ordering a magnum of champagne.

"I wonder if you would be so kind as to answer me one question, Mr Hunter?" Fekete asked. "Why should we for one second trust someone responsible for the closure of countless Lines and the deaths of several spacers?"

Mirren stared at the Nigerian.

"Good question, Mr Fekete," Hunter said. "Of course you have every right to be suspicious. I know I would be if our situations were reversed. The fact is that my opinions have changed somewhat since I left the Danzig Organisation."

Fekete laughed. "And you think we should believe you, just like that?"

Before Hunter could respond, Dan said, "How have your opinions changed – or more importantly *why*?"

Hunter caressed his chin where the crimson growth terminated. He considered his reply. "I no longer support the aims of the Danzig Organisation – those aims being the brutal invasion of the free worlds of the Rim, the suppression of political opposition, free speech, free *thought*. The ideals I worked for in the early years are no longer the ideals espoused by the governing forum of the Organisation. I have seen too many atrocities, gentlemen, perpetrated by the Danzig militia, to sit idly by and do nothing."

Fekete clapped his hands. "Words, sir. Mere words! You've succeeded in telling us nothing and making me, for one, even more suspicious."

Dan leaned forward. Mirren sensed that Leferve wanted more than anything to trust in Hunter, but at the same time was wary of being tricked.

"Where do you want us to go," Dan asked, "and why?"

Hunter sipped his wine. He regarded the circle of ruby liquid in his glass for a long time, his face expressionless. "I am afraid that if I told you the details of the mission, then you might be in grave danger if ever the Danzig Organisation found out. I would not wish to place you in that position."

"Ridiculous!" Fekete snorted.

"So it may appear," Hunter said. "But in keeping my own counsel, I have your safety and the success of the mission in mind. I can tell you that upon arriving at your destination, you will rendezvous with the people I wish you to transport back to Earth. I envisage that you will be on the planet no more than a few hours. For this, I will pay you each, in advance, two hundred and fifty thousand units, and the same again upon the successful completion of the mission."

Fekete was shaking his head. "Farcical. No payment can compensate for the fact that we know nothing, neither what we will be doing, nor the reason why, nor the dangers involved."

Hunter hesitated. "You will be in no danger, so long as you remain in ignorance of my intentions."

"I want nothing to do with it," Fekete declared.

Hunter interrupted. "Please, hear me out. Upon completion of the mission, the smallship will become the property of however many of your team agree to take part in the venture. In effect, you will have a smallship to push as the whim takes you. Yes, it will be expensive to maintain, but with what I will pay you..."

Fekete smiled. Droplets of sweat glistened on his high, chestnut forehead. "Very generous. You overlook one small point, however. The owning and running of 'ships is illegal."

"Mr Fekete," Hunter said, "I suspect you have the ingenuity to overcome this slight consideration."

Mirren leaned forward. "Can I ask you where the 'ship is now, Mr Hunter, and when she'll be ready to phase-out?"

Disgusted, Fekete threw down his napkin.

"The 'ship is at a secret location somewhere in Paris," Hunter said. "She will be ready to phase-out when my technicians have finished their final adjustments – perhaps as soon as tomorrow or the day after, if all goes to plan."

"What about a pilot?" Mirren asked.

"I have already hired the best pilot and co-pilot to be had."

"Do *they* know where we'll be going?"

Hunter shook his head. "I cannot take the risk of *anyone* finding out the destination."

"You won't be making the journey?" Dan asked.

"I'm afraid that's impossible. I have work to complete here on Earth to prepare for your homecoming."

The band began playing *E-Man Blues*. Mirren smiled at the song he had known so well back in the old days. "Nada is ecstasy/ I live for the ride/ And life dirtside, man/ Is hard to abide..."

Fekete said, "There's a old expression which precisely sums up this whole situation, Mr Hunter. It is my opinion that we are being sold a pig in a poke."

"Except, Mr Fekete," Hunter responded with icy formality, "that you are paying absolutely nothing at all."

"Nothing but our lives, our freedom if we're caught..."

Hunter gestured reasonably. "But you will not be caught, Mr Fekete. I have planned this venture over a long time and prepared for every contingency. I do not intend to fail at this stage." He paused there, found his glass and took a drink; as if, thought Mirren, to calm himself. He sensed that Hunter had a lot riding on the outcome of this meeting: he had set his sights on getting the best E-team that money could buy.

Hunter looked around the table. "Well, gentlemen, you have heard my side of the story – regrettably brief as it must be. I wonder if I might solicit your agreement to take part... Mr Mirren?"

Hunter's one good eye, piercingly azure, regarded him.

Mirren replied instantly. He was never in any doubt. It might have been illogical, but whatever danger he faced would be worth it for the chance to flux again. "I'm all for it," he said. "Count me in."

Hunter's halved lips rose in what, if matched by the other half, would have been a wide smile of delight. "Thank you, Mr Mirren. Now... Monsieur Leferve?"

Dan hesitated. He regarded the back of his large hands, spread on the table. He looked up. "I'll do it," he said. "But I want to see the 'ship first, check it out."

"By all means. I'll show you over the 'ship myself." Hunter's gaze found Caspar Fekete. "Your decision, sir?"

"I think I have made my position abundantly clear."

"You will not reconsider my offer?"

Fekete sighed. "Mr Hunter, I am not so desperate that I need your money; nor do I need the flux."

"In that case I regret that you will not be joining the team, Mr Fekete, but the choice is yours." Hunter turned to Mirren. "I will be in contact to arrange another meeting very soon. I'll also arrange to have the payments transferred to your accounts. Now, if you will excuse me, I must depart. I have a lot of work to do over the next day or two."

He stood and shook hands with Dan and Mirren. He turned to Fekete. "If you should change your mind..." he began.

"I have made my decision," Fekete said.

The off-worlder nodded. "Then I'll bid you farewell, gentlemen. I look forward to our next meeting." He bowed formally, stepped from the booth and walked around the gallery to the elevator plate.

Fekete was shaking his head. "You two amaze me. What possessed you? The man clearly isn't to be trusted."

"I need the flux, Caspar," Mirren said. "I need the flux more than anything else in the world. It's as simple as that."

"Me too," Dan said. "And I do trust the guy. Don't ask me why. There's just something about him. I believe him when he says he can't tell us for our own good. He's onto something big and he doesn't want to lose it."

"You'll be getting yourselves into serious trouble."

"Do you know something, Cas?" Mirren said. "I couldn't really give a damn. I'd risk anything to flux again."

"Death? Penal servitude?"

Mirren said, "Anything."

Fekete shook his head in a gesture of patronising sympathy. "I give in. Go your own way." He sighed and checked his watch. "I must be going. I'll leave you to your celebrations." He looked from Dan to Mirren. "You two take care, okay? And keep me posted." He left the booth and hurried around the gallery.

Mirren glanced up at Dan and saw his smile reflected as if in a mirror. He leaned back and sank into the soft membrane of the dome. He recalled spending hours in free-fall aboard the *Perseus Bound*, colliding with the trampoline-like inner dermis of the astrodome, as if attempting to merge with the cobalt blue of the enveloping *nada*-continuum outside. He felt euphoria rise in him at the thought.

They took Fekete's advice and celebrated with half a bottle of cognac.

"Here's to Hunter." Dan raised his glass. "To Hunter and the flux – and screw Caspar!"

Mirren smiled. He was considering how his fortune had changed in just one day. Twelve hours ago his life had stretched ahead in a monotonous round of work and sleep; he'd lived so much in the past that the present was an endless time to be endured, the future an abstraction without hope. Now he was on the verge of realising a dream made possible by a disfigured millionaire off-worlder, and it was almost too fantastic to believe.

"Ralph!" Dan cried. "I feel like giving thanks."

Mirren peered at the Frenchman. It seemed like a good idea. He shrugged. "Fine. How? Where?"

"Where else?" Dan laughed. "The Church! The Church of the Disciples!"

Mirren was too drunk, too elated, to voice any philosophical objections. He recalled that the Church was an old smallship – a smallship similar to the one he'd soon be pushing through the *nada*-continuum.

So why the hell not?

Chapter Eleven

THEY LEFT THE restaurant and made their way to the perimeter of the dome. Mirren was too drunk to pilot his flier; it would have detected the alcohol in his system and shut itself down. Otherwise, buoyed up as he was, he might have taken the risk. He considered the irony of dying in a flier accident mere days before he was due to flux again.

They passed through the arched exit and walked into the heat of unprotected Paris. It was four o'clock in the morning and the temperature was still in the eighties. The Church was two kilometres away, in the run-down Montparnasse district, but for once Mirren didn't mind the walk. They passed through the respectable, well-kept streets bordering the centre, but the farther they progressed towards the outskirts, the more neglected and disreputable the streets became. They passed shop-fronts at first barred, then boarded up – though the premises were still in use – then derelict and vandalised, and finally given over to the alien creepers which marked a district as beyond redemption. In one area, as they progressed down an avenue whose buildings on either side were solid banks of vegetation, he and Dan were the only things visibly of Earth in the landscape. They stopped in the middle of the street, a layer of lichen slippery underfoot, and stared at the strip of night sky between the high canyon walls. There, rising slowly beneath the stars of Orion, were the red and white lights of an orbiting industrial satellite.

At one point the undergrowth, which so far had restricted itself to the sidewalks, flowed across the street and became so dense that they stumbled and fell. They proceeded by holding each other like drunks wending their way home over treacherous ice. Mirren clutched Dan's shoulder, feeling the hard ridge of his occipital console.

He pulled his hand away and halted, swaying in the tropical night. "Dan, last... last year I thought of having it removed."

Dan peered at him. "What?"

He touched his shoulder, felt the light alloy spar beneath his flying suit. "My console."

They continued walking, leaving the lichen and the creepers behind as they entered a plasma-lighted district of bars and bistros. Prostitutes stood in groups on the kerb. Garishly lighted shops clearing cheap African electronics belted out the latest popular music; revellers danced. It was as if they had stumbled from a jungle and into a party.

Finally, Dan asked, "Why?"

Mirren laughed. "Because it was... obsolete. The rationalist in me said that it served no purpose. I didn't need it to remind me of the good times. I felt like a walking antique."

"So..." Dan's belch poisoned the air with acid cognac fumes "...why didn't you?"

"Because... because it was part of me. It'd be like getting rid of this." He held a finger before his eyes. "And anyway I couldn't be bothered..." He gestured feebly, aware that he was rambling. He'd lost the point of his little speech.

Dan reminded him. "Fernandez, Ralph! Thank Fernandez you didn't have the op!"

Mirren recalled the sensation he'd experienced on touching Dan's console: the delicious shiver of terror at the thought that he'd decided against the cut.

A young girl fell into step beside them.

Dan smiled and indicated the tattoo on his bicep.

The kid shrugged. "We could always talk."

"About what?" Dan asked.

The girl blinked at something intimidating in Dan's tone, stopped and watched them make their way along the lighted boulevard. They passed jazz clubs and bars named after colony worlds, all-night holo-shows and films from all around the Expansion. The occasional flier roared overhead, drowning out the music.

Mirren clutched Dan's arm. "Dan..."

The big man looked around.

"What do you think Hunter meant when he said we'd be returning to Earth with some people? Why can't they go through a 'face?"

"We'll find out soon enough, Ralph. Have faith. We'll soon be pushing again, that's the main thing. I trust Hunter, whoever the hell he is, whatever he's planning..."

They passed a cafe and the rich, bitter aroma of fresh coffee drifted out on the hot early morning air. They crossed the street and sat at a table on the sidewalk, ordered coffee and croissants and watched an alien bird, as big as an eagle, skim the length of the street.

Mirren stared at the skyline. Far to the north the interface was on an open phase, and the night sky in the vicinity was bright with the light of an alien sun.

Dan said, "It doesn't seem like ten years since we were last doing this. Remember the cafe we used a couple of blocks away?" He frowned, trying to recall its name.

"Rousseau's?" They'd spent many a night on the sidewalk outside the cafe between shifts, watching the bigships at Orly rising into the sky and phasing into the continuum. Life then had seemed a simple fact of fluxing and recuperation, a stable existence which promised a future without threat or change. In retrospect, Mirren could not recall ever looking any further ahead than the next push.

Dan said, "How's Bobby, Ralph?" in a gentle voice which acknowledged Mirren's reluctance to talk about his brother.

Of course Mirren had always been aware, back then, of the infinitesimally rare hazards to which Enginemen were prone. But he had always dismissed them with the thought that they could never happen to him.

It had been so long since he had last spoken about his brother that he was not offended now, but almost relieved. He shrugged. "Much the same as he was five years ago. You saw him. He was introspective then, a little withdrawn." Mirren realised what clichés these were to describe his brother's condition, almost as bad as when, a couple of years ago, he had told someone that Bobby lived in a world of his own.

"But neurologically? There's been no further lapse?"

"No, it stabilised itself around twenty-four hours." He looked up to see Dan watching him. "I should be grateful, really. Bobby was the only Engineman to survive the Syndrome."

"Last time we met you were learning touch-signing."

"I'm fluent now. At least we can communicate."

"Do you take him out?"

Mirren felt guilty now that years ago he'd failed to insist that Bobby accompany him on walks around the local park. In the early days, before Bobby became absorbed in his meditation, he'd been uncommunicative, reluctant to talk. He'd turned down all offers of help, refusing even to let Mirren guide him on simple walks. Occasionally of late Mirren had taken him in his flier on high-speed tours of the city, but Bobby spent so much of his time now meditating and studying that the physical had ceased to have much meaning.

"I take him out about once a month or so – not that he seems bothered one way or the other. I think I do it to salve my conscience."

"Have you ever thought of taking him to the Church?" Dan asked. "He's a believer, isn't he?"

Mirren smiled. "He's not what you'd call an orthodox Disciple, Dan."

For five years before joining the European Javelin Line, Bobby had pushed boats for the Satori Line out of Rangoon. In the countries of the East where the precepts of Buddhism, Zen and Tao had been taken as read for centuries, the discovery of the *nada*-continuum had come as no surprise; it was the Nirvana accepted by their philosophies for so long. Enginemen were looked upon as the enlightened, those who had attained Buddhahood on Earth, and whose destination after this life was Nirvana or the *nada*-continuum. Bobby had taken this belief as his own even before he became an Engineman, and then he had discovered the Disciples. Now, as he liked to remind Mirren, he'd transcended all Earthly creeds and religions.

Dan said, "Have you decided what you're going to tell him about Hunter's offer?"

"No. No, I haven't..." Mirren stared at the grounds of his coffee. The anticipation of the push was soured by the familiar guilt he experienced whenever he considered his brother.

Casually, Dan said, "Bobby could always take Caspar's place and push with us, Ralph." He looked up, his stare a challenge.

"You know I couldn't do that."

"It's what Bobby would want."

"Even so... I couldn't allow him to do it. Would you let your brother kill himself just like that?"

"It's not certain that Bobby would die–" Dan began.

"The medics didn't give him a very good chance of surviving another flux. But you haven't answered my question: if you had a brother in Bobby's condition–"

Dan said, "If the circumstances were the same as Bobby's... then yes, of course I'd let him flux."

Mirren smiled. "You're religious. You've got to look at it from my point of view."

Dan laughed at this. "From *your* point of view! Ralph, you don't know how selfish that sounds. Why don't you look at it from Bobby's point of view?"

Mirren closed his eyes. "I couldn't hold myself responsible if anything happened to him."

"But from Bobby's perspective, and mine, and that of thousands of other Enginemen, you wouldn't be responsible. Can't you accept that?"

As Mirren looked at it, his brother's condition was made worse by the fact that if he were ever to mind-push a 'ship again, the chances were that the effort would kill him. He'd die a flux-death, the death that religious Enginemen considered the ultimate exit, but which he, Mirren, considered just as final and pointless as any other death.

Mirren had always thought that no matter how terrible and restricted his brother's life was, it was an improvement on the oblivion which awaited him upon death.

"Look at it this way," Dan said. "If you asked Bobby whether he wanted to push the 'ship, what do you think he'd say?"

Mirren sighed. "He'd jump at the chance."

"*Exactly!*" Dan hit the table. "Now, could you honestly live with yourself if you denied Bobby the opportunity to flux with us?"

Mirren closed his eyes. The thought of leaving his brother alone in the apartment, while he went off mind-pushing the smallship...

"But how could I live with myself, Dan, if I sent him to his death?"

"It would be what he wanted," Dan said gently. "Please, when you get back, explain the situation and give him the choice. Promise me."

He told himself that Dan was right. There was really no excuse for not telling Bobby; to deny him the right to make the choice would be indefensible.

He found himself nodding.

"Good." Dan looked at his watch. "Come on, it's time we were going. The Church closes for the day in a couple of hours."

"How much further?" Suddenly, the thought of going to the Church no longer appealed.

"Just around the corner."

Mirren clamped the back of his neck, massaging the ache that had been mounting for the past hour.

Dan was watching him. "You okay?"

Mirren wondered whether to tell him about the flashbacks. "Well..."

Dan stared. "Don't tell me you're getting them too?"

Mirren laughed. "The flashbacks? You too? Fernandez, I thought I was going mad."

"We might be," Dan grunted. "I don't understand it. For ten years I've remembered nothing about that last trip, and then suddenly I'm reliving, not just remembering, but reliving the events again."

In the early days after their discharge, when he'd seen more of Dan, they'd both commented on how odd it was that they should all be afflicted with an identical memory loss.

"So what the hell's going on, Dan?" he asked.

"You tell me... I've always wanted to know what happened during and after the crash-landing, and now I suppose I'll find out."

They paid the bill and left the cafe.

A warm breeze sprang up from nowhere, lapping over them. Mirren shivered, overtaken suddenly by the bone-wearying ache he'd awoken to the evening before. He wondered if this bout was no more than a psychosomatic reaction to his dilemma over Bobby.

They continued through the streets in silence.

The Church of the Disciples of the *Nada*-Continuum was an old, converted smallship anchored to an area of wasteground between a burnt-out mosque and a derelict warehouse. It squatted on its belly amid overgrown mounds of bricks, its hydraulic rams long since amputated and its shell a patchwork of rust and old paint. The rear auxiliary engines had been removed and replaced by a set of double doors approached by a rickety flight of wooden steps. The viewscreens along its flanks, and the delta screen above its nose-cone, were concealed by bulky metal units which looked for all the world like refrigerators.

Mirren pointed them out as they crossed the street. "What are they?"

Dan smiled to himself. "You'll see when we get inside."

They were not the only Enginemen attending the Church that morning. Others approached from along the street, stood on the steps awaiting entry. Mirren and Dan joined the queue at the foot of the wooden construction. "It's not usually this busy," Dan said. "There must be a service on."

They passed inside. Mirren was surprised first by the size of the place, and then by the atmosphere of reverence that permeated what was, after all, nothing more than a junked spaceship. The surprising dimensions were easily accounted for: the ceiling which had formerly divided the body of the ship into the engineroom and, on the second level, the crews' lounge, had been removed to create a yawning cavern reminiscent of the nave of a cathedral. In pride of place at the front of the church was a flux-tank – or rather a reasonable facsimile. Above it, the pilot's cabin had been opened up and fronted with rails to form a gallery for the choristers: six cowled Disciples in gowns of light blue chanted in a language Mirren guessed was Latin. The measured, dolorous tone established the ecclesiastical atmosphere, and other religious appurtenances like pews and burning incense left no doubt that this was a place of worship. Above the altar, affixed to the rails of the gallery, was a blue fluorescent infinity symbol. The pews were steadily filling with the devoted who knelt, heads bowed in prayer or contemplation.

Mirren slipped into a pew at the rear, while Dan stood in the aisle and conducted a whispered conversation with a tall, robed figure. As he took his seat he began to wonder what he was doing here, and considered the irony of the fact that in all his years as an Engineman he'd prided himself on never entering any of the similar establishments on the many colony worlds serviced by the Canterbury Line. The Church of the Disciples had been in existence for as long as the starship Lines themselves. Most of the Enginemen he had worked with down the years had been believers, and he had often wondered why he could not believe that what he experienced in the tank was Nirvana. Was it just a cussed streak that would not allow him to follow the majority, even though he secretly knew the truth of their faith; some fatal flaw in his soul which prevented his full absorption into the flux; or the realisation that his fellow Enginemen, like most people, were essentially weak creatures who could not accept the fact of their mortality and needed some bogus abstract belief with which to make their lives bearable?

Mirren thought of Bobby, the certainty of his belief. He felt a deep emptiness like an ache inside him. There were times when he wanted nothing more than to share in the comforting faith that this life was not everything.

Dan joined him, seating himself quietly.

"What's going on?" Mirren whispered. The chanting had increased in volume and tempo and celestial organ music played.

"It's the funeral service of an Engineman," Dan told him. "A believer from Nanterre. Heine's disease."

Heine's...

Heine's was a neurological virus which attacked the victim's nervous system, a highly contagious meningital-analogue that had come through the interface three years ago from the newly-discovered world of El Manaman. There was no cure for the infected, who usually died within a few years of contracting the disease.

The organ music ceased abruptly. The chanting continued, each chorister sustaining a long, mournful note. The lighting in the chamber dimmed, and Mirren was put in mind of the half-light of an engine-room immediately before phase-out. Then the chanting ceased and was replaced by a familiar, low-pitched hum.

Mirren was suddenly flooded with memories and he realised that, for him, this little stage-show would soon be played out for real. He was choked with emotion. Tears welled in his eyes. Through the viewscreens let into the flank of the 'ship, the cobalt blue of an ersatz *nada*-continuum, streaked with marmoreal streamers of white light, gave the illusion that the smallship was actually phasing-out. He understood then the function of the bulky units on the outside of the 'ship that he had noticed earlier. Around him, Enginemen murmured in appreciation.

The robed figure Dan had spoken to earlier climbed into the pulpit beside the flux-tank. The lighting in the Church dimmed; a spot-light picked out the High Priest as he pushed back his cowl to reveal his bald head. The chanting ceased, along with the low-pitched hum, and the congregation fell silent.

"Brothers and Sisters," said the High Priest, his voice resonating in the chamber. "On behalf of the Church of the Disciples of the *Nada*-Continuum and our departed colleague, I thank you for attending. Let us pray..."

Around Mirren, Enginemen and Enginewomen knelt. Mirren followed suit, feeling self-conscious in his ignorance.

"We give thanks to the Continuum/" the Priest intoned, "The Sublime, the Infinite/ Into whose munificence we pass/ At the end of this cruel illusion..."

Spontaneously, the congregation took up the chant. "We give thanks..." Mirren mumbled along, wishing the service would end so that he could escape.

When the congregation had repeated the verse, four dark figures in robes stepped slowly up the aisle, swinging censers and exclaiming in Latin. The scented smoke filled the air, roiling through the beam of the spotlight. The censer-bearers came to the altar and stood on either side of the flux-tank, still chanting. They knelt, heads bowed.

The Priest continued, "We have lived, we are mortal/ For our mortality we give thanks/ Without this illusion we would be without immortality..."

Around Mirren, Enginemen started up, "We have lived..."

The words charged the air, creating an atmosphere that even Mirren, as a none believer, had to admit was powerful, even emotional.

The low-pitched humming of phase-out resumed, a bass note more felt in the solar plexus than heard.

Then, six pall-bearers made their way slowly down the aisle, a streamlined silver coffin on their shoulders. They halted before the flux-tank and placed the coffin reverently upon the slide-bed. Mirren made out the decal of the old Taurus Line painted on the lid of coffin below a blurred pix of the dead Engineman.

"Brothers and Sisters," the High Priest intoned, "we are gathered here today to bless the mortal remains of a fellow Engineman. He has made the great leap to the ultimate we have all experienced, and to which we will all return, and for his release we give thanks. Edward Macready served twenty years pushing the *Pride of Idaho* for the Taurus Line..."

The Priest went on, but Mirren heard nothing for the pounding of his pulse in his ears. He seemed to be aware of the proceedings around him as if from a great distance; he felt suddenly isolated with the burden of his knowledge.

He clutched Dan's arm. "I knew Macready!" he hissed.

Dan glanced at him. "You did? I'm sorry..." And he returned his gaze to the front.

"You don't understand – I was with him when he died!"

Dan leaned over and hissed, "That's impossible! He had Heine's. He'd've been quarantined until he died–"

"For chrissake, I was with him. He broke into the 'port. I stopped him from trying to kill himself. We sat talking for a couple of hours." Mirren recalled the scotch. "We even shared a bottle."

"You sure it was the same guy?"

"How many other Macready's have pushed for the Taurus Line and died recently?" He tried to keep the panic from his voice.

"But Heine's cases are supposed to be kept in isolation."

"Then the bastard escaped. He wanted to throw himself into the interface. He even told me he was ill."

Around them, Enginemen murmured their disapproval.

Dan gripped Mirren's elbow. "How do you feel?"

His stomach turned. "Terrible..." He was shaking again.

Dan ran a hand through his hair. He looked at Mirren. "We're going. We've got to get you to a hospital."

Mirren gave a hollow laugh. "Isn't that a little too late?"

They were already out of their seats and edging along the pew, disturbing disgruntled Enginemen as they went. They hurried to the exit, and behind him Mirren heard the priest intone, "Let us now rejoice that Edward Macready has cast off this cruel illusion..."

Chapter Twelve

Ella leaned expertly into the bend. The snow-capped peaks of the Torreón mountains stood high and distant to her right, and to her left was the ever-present sunset. She came into the straight and accelerated, luxuriating in the feel of the headwind, the illusion of liberty gained through speed and an open road.

She might have been physically free, but mentally she was the prisoner of her thoughts. She could not shake from her head the images of Eddie and Max, Jerassi and Rodriguez. They had given their lives willingly; Eddie through despair, and the others for a cause far greater than their lives, and maybe through despair, too. They were all in a far better place now, but that didn't make the pain of her bereavement any easier to bear. Ella had faith, she believed in the joyous afterlife that awaited everyone, but all she asked was for a little joy in this life, too.

She had been on the road an hour, stopping and pulling into the cover at the side of the road only when she spotted vehicles up ahead. She had no doubt that, after the destruction of the interface, the militia would be all the more vigilant in their search for possible accomplices. So far she had seen only civilian vehicles, farm trucks and the occasional private car, and fortunately not many of either.

Now she slowed as she came to the last bend before her destination, rounded it and brought the bike to a halt.

Ahead, the central plateau lowered itself in ever-widening steps down to the coast. Each semi-circular terrace was bountiful with wild jungle and carefully cultivated tropical gardens, ablaze with bougainvillea and a dozen varieties of alien flowers. Dwellings of different designs occupied the levels, from traditional villas to A-frames, ziggurats in white ceramics to cluster-domes like so many over-blown soap bubbles. But more spectacular than the gardens and mansions was the feature that gave the Falls its name. Perhaps a hundred waterfalls poured cleanly from level to level, perfectly geometrical like arcs of blue glass, each maintaining the water-level of as many dazzling lagoons. The sight always struck Ella as breathtakingly beautiful.

She kick-started the bike and set off, but not in the direction of the residences. Perhaps because she feared the impending meeting with her father, or because his villa held fewer happier memories than where she was heading, she turned right along the track which switch-backed up the steep face of the hillside.

She braked at a bend in the track before she reached the top. In the sudden silence she heard the musical cascade of splashing water. She concealed the bike beside the track, ducked under the branches of a palm tree and found herself suddenly on the very edge of the lagoon.

The sight of the oval sink brimming with bright blue water released a flood of happy memories. The sanguine light of the sunset, filtering through the surrounding foliage, gave the scene a tint of rose which corresponded with her recollections. The unbroken arc of water which tipped from the rockface high above might have been the very same that had surged down ten years ago. There was the flat rock she had used as a diving platform, and there, in the very centre of the lagoon, was the camel's hump.

Between the age of twelve and fifteen she had spent at least one day of every weekend here. During her holidays, summer and winter, she had often defied her father's wishes and camped overnight. What had made the place such an attraction, apart from its obvious beauty, was the fact that it was *secret* – a place she could call her own, a paradise from which her father and her minders were excluded.

Then, in the summer holidays of her fourteenth year, she'd discovered that someone else used her lagoon. What could have been a crushing blow turned out to be a miracle that made her secret extra-special.

She recalled the evening as if it were yesterday.

Her father was having guests for dinner, and he wanted Ella present to serve the food and pour the drinks and talk about how well she was doing at school, but the draw of the lagoon was too much. She had slipped from the house and ran up the zig-zag track to the final bend before the summit.

She had pushed her way through the fringe of shrubs and...

At first she thought the figure standing on the camel's hump of rock in the centre of the lagoon was a naked boy of around her own age. Suffused with rage and indignation, she stepped forward to shout or remonstrate.

Then she stopped. Her rage evaporated, replaced by fear – fear at having her expectations so thoroughly subverted – for the boy was not a boy at all. Ella experienced a sudden, chill dread of the unfamiliar, the unknown.

The boy was not a boy, but an alien; a member of the Lho-Dharvo people. It was tall and spectacularly elongated, and Ella's first reaction was revulsion, even though there was something beautiful about the tone of its copper-bronze skin.

Its stance on the rock was not a human stance. It stood with its arms outstretched slightly behind it, its head tilted back, eyes closed.

A shiver coursed down her spine.

This was the first Lho-Dharvon Ella had ever seen, though she had watched anthropological films about them on vid-screen, and read articles in magazines and on discs. They were a tribal people, nomadic for part of the year, who herded animals similar to goats and lived off the land. They were at the stage of their evolution that corresponded to *Homo sapien's* stone-age, and a xeno-anthropologist working with them over thirty years ago had recorded their religious beliefs in a work known as the Book of the Lho. They lived on all four continents of the Reach, in conditions ranging from polar to desert. Ella had never heard mention of the fact that a tribe was living so close to the Falls.

She watched the alien for the next ten minutes. It maintained its odd pose, unmoving. Wanting to get closer, Ella edged around the lagoon, always ensuring that she was concealed by shrubbery. At last she was as close as she could get to the creature, on an overhang of rock above the water, concealed by scant, sprouting grass. She knelt and stared down.

She could not tell to which sex it belonged. Where its reproductive organ should have been was nothing more than a slight protuberance. It was so thin and long that it seemed that its torso and limbs had been stretched. She stared and stared, and could not decide whether she saw more of its alienness or its humanity: one moment she was taken in by its familiar features and thought it human, and the next it appeared horribly alien in its crude mimicry of the human form. Watching the alien was like looking at an optical illusion that the brain had worked out at one second, and lost the next.

Its eyes were massive, bulging and lidded like those of a toad. Its nose was almost non-existent, two tiny slits, and its mouth was similarly atrophied. Thin lips curved around the hull of its jaw in a thin, stoic, reptilian line.

Ella was wondering whether she had seen enough when the alien opened its eyes – its lids dropping from underneath, she saw – and stared directly at her. In panic she tried to scramble away, but lost her footing and slipped from the overhang. She struck her head as she fell, and in a second of panic she was aware of the warm, cloying water enveloping her as she slipped into oblivion.

She had no idea how long she was unconscious. When she came to her senses she was lying on her side on the flat rock she used as a diving platform. She tried to sit up, and cried out in pain. The back of her head throbbed as if someone was hitting it from the inside with a hammer. She touched her hair, and her fingers came away smeared with blood. She peered at the collar of her blouse and saw that that too was blood-soaked. At the thought of how her father might react, she quickly removed her blouse, crouched at the water's edge and scrubbed it thoroughly.

Only then did she recall the alien. She looked across to the camel's hump on which it had stood, but it was no longer there. Then she looked up at the overhang from which she'd fallen, a good ten metres above her. There was no tide in the pool, of course. There was no way she could have fetched up here without...

Hard on the realisation that the alien had saved her life, she experienced first revulsion that the creature had actually touched her, and then a profound amazement that something so... so *alien* had bothered to save her life – the kind of amazement she might have felt had she been saved by a monkey or a bear.

Then she saw the alien. It was crouching three metres from her, its long shins drawn up before its chest, its elongated head peering at her from above the peaks of its bony knees.

Ella jumped up in fright – at the same time trying to drag on her blouse to cover her nakedness – but the pain in her head forced her down again. Sobbing, she fumbled with the wet, clinging material, finally getting it on and fastening the studs.

All the time she watched the alien, as if it might spring up and attack her at any second.

When it did move, she was ready. The alien unfolded itself to its full height and took a step towards her. She scrambled to her feet, trying to ignore the insistent throbbing in her head. She backed off, sobbing in fear and confusion.

"Don't come near me!" she screamed. "Why did you have to come here anyway?" And she knelt and found a rock and hurled it at the frozen alien. It missed by a long way, sailing over its head, but the creature never flinched. It regarded Ella without expression as she ran off through the bushes to the track.

By the time she reached her father's villa she was sick with exhaustion and shame. The party had broken up – she must have been unconscious for longer than she'd thought. Her minder was swimming in the artificial lagoon behind the house, and her father was in the lounge, staring through the picture window at the sunset. He didn't even look around as Ella hurried to her room. She showered and washed her bloody clothes, hanging them on her balcony rail to dry, then lay on her bed and thought through the events of that evening, the alien and her reaction to it. The contusion at the base of her skull was the size of a racquet-ball, but that had nothing to do with the fact that she slept little that night.

For disobeying her father's orders and not attending the party, she was not allowed out of the villa for a week. In the circumstances she could think of no worse punishment. She wanted nothing more than to find the alien, to make amends for her ungrateful behaviour.

She used the week to good effect; she remained in her room and made a gift for the Lho-Dharvon. On the first day of her freedom, she rushed up to the lagoon. She waited for hours but there was no sign of the alien. The following day she returned, and her heart jumped as she pushed through the bushes and saw, on the rock in the centre of the lagoon, the slim golden Lho, arms outstretched behind it, head in the air. She moved around the water's edge, her resolve to confront the being and apologise diminishing with a renewal of her uneasiness at the creature's very *alienness*.

She crouched on the flat rock and watched for perhaps thirty minutes. At the end of that time, it opened its eyes and gracefully lowered its arms. It did not seem surprised to see her.

Startling her, it dived into the water without the slightest splash, emerged just as cleanly and leapt onto the rock before her. It paused, crouching, and regarded her with massive eyes which nictitated every ten seconds from the bottom up.

She gripped the gift in her hand, but it was as if she were paralysed and could not hold it out for the alien to take. Her mouth was dry; words would not come.

The alien reached out an arm which ended in a long hand with three long, slim fingers and a stubby thumb. Ella marshalled her panic, fought her very real revulsion.

She closed her eyes and swallowed.

She felt gentle fingers probing the bump at the back of her head. When the fingers withdrew, Ella opened her eyes. The alien was staring into her face, its expression unreadable. Perhaps it found the arrangement of her eyelids as strange as she found its?

Then it dabbed the centre of Ella's forehead with its middle finger in a gesture that obviously meant something, turned and walked towards the jungle. Even the spry articulation of its gait was entirely dissimilar to that of a human.

"Wait!" Ella found herself calling.

More, she thought, in surprise at her shout than with any understanding of her command, the alien paused and turned to her. Ella approached, held the painted rock out at arm's length.

The alien accepted it, turned it over and regarded the painting.

"It's you," Ella said. "I did it myself. I thought it appropriate, a rock for the one I threw at you. I know you don't understand, but..." And she shrugged, realising the futility of her words.

The alien looked from Ella to the gift. It was on a long thong, but rather than hang it around its neck, it wound it around its thin wrist, grasping the rock in its hand.

"Before you go," Ella said, and shrugged. "I don't know... Will you be here again tomorrow?"

She took off her watch and stepped a little closer to the alien. She displayed her watch and tried to indicate the passage of thirty-six hours.

"Here, same time, tomorrow?"

But what hope, she told herself, had she of making the alien understand something as abstract as the passage of time divided into human hours?

It regarded her without any sign of comprehension, then disappeared quickly into the jungle.

The following day, when she pushed through the bushes with no real hope, but expectation bubbling within her, the alien was waiting for her on the flat rock.

Now, Ella moved around the lagoon, tears of joy in her eyes. Her memories were so vivid, so alive. There was the camel's hump of rock, and she could see it standing there, could see it diving into the water, emerging with the quick sleek grace of a seal. She stood on the flat of rock on which they had sunbathed, and stared across the water.

Nothing had changed. Everything had changed.

They had met at the lagoon on every weekend for the next four months.

At first they remained within the confines of the lagoon, diving and swimming in the calm blue water. There was little communication between them other than gestures, and they were often so bizarre on the part of the alien – and no doubt hers were to it, too – that she often failed completely to understand its meaning. It spoke occasionally in a soft whispery rush, but the only thing she understood was its name: L'Endo-kharriat, or so she wrote it in her diary, where she kept a detailed account of their meetings. There seemed to be a clicking pause between the consonant and the vowel of the first part of its name, and a shorter pause before the second word. L'Endo-kharriat...

As for its sex... Ella could not be sure. They shared a friendship that was platonic, like that between girlfriends, but for some reason, as time wore on, Ella came increasingly to think of the Lho as a male, perhaps in compensation for the fact that at school no boy had yet shown an interest in her.

At one point every time they met, L'Endo would swim to the camel's hump and perform his strange ritualistic statue-impression, which could last up to thirty minutes. It seemed at these times that he was in a trance, oblivious of Ella and the lagoon around him. One day when he rejoined Ella on the flat rock and lay beside her, golden and spangled with water, she indicated the camel's hump and asked, "Why, L'Endo?"

He stared at her. "*Why?*" he breathed, and said no more. Ella shrugged to herself and reflected that she might never know.

The following week, before commencing his ritual, L'Endo pointed across to the rock. "Why," he said. Then, "Give thanks," he said, but without any indication that he understood the words. "For life."

Ella nodded, intrigued by the fact that there was a member of his tribe who could speak English.

The months passed, and they left the lagoon and explored the upper reaches of the plateau so far left undeveloped by the colonists. It was a magical realm of caves and grottoes, spectacular waterfalls and placid lagoons. L'Endo showed her tunnels which riddled the mountainside, secret passages leading from lagoon to lagoon, strange flowers she had never seen before and even stranger animals.

In return for L'Endo's showing her the wonder of the plateau, on one occasion Ella led him to a nearby dome whose owners were away on vacation. She broke in through a cooling vent and they crawled inside. She had become so accustomed to seeing L'Endo where he belonged, in his home environment where his alienness seemed natural, that seeing him in a human habitat once again made her aware of how very strange – how very *alien*, there was no other word for it – he was.

He seemed uncomfortable in the hi-tech dome, like a stone-age man in a spaceship. Ella showed him all the technological wonders; the synthesiser and vid-screen, the ultra-son shower and the walls of the dome which polarised during the day. L'Endo was quiet and watchful, his eyes half-cupped by their lower lids in an expression Ella thought might denote wonder or suspicion. They left after one hour, returned to the lagoon and sported in the water.

Then, two weeks later, L'Endo failed to turn up at the lagoon. Ella was there at the same time as ever, but there was no sign of the Lho. It was the first time he had failed to show for four months, and Ella was worried. Perhaps their meetings meant less to him than they did to her, and he had quite simply grown bored with the company of the strange human? She had no idea where she might find him, where his tribe was encamped.

Ella waited for three hours, and was about to leave when she saw, through the trees that partially concealed a narrow fissure in the rockface, a familiar alien form. She leapt to her feet, her heart skipping, but the alien was not L'Endo.

It approached Ella with long, nimble strides, an old, bowed Lho whose skin was mottled and faded. It regarded Ella through half-cupped eyes.

"Ella Hunter?" It asked her, and she knew then who L'Endo had spoken to in order to explain his ritual.

"Where's L'Endo?"

"L'Endo-kharriat wishes to see you. This way..."

"Is he okay?" she asked desperately. "Please, what's wrong?"

The old Lho turned and walked away without replying.

Now Ella sat cross-legged on the flat rock beside the lagoon and stared at the sunset. Was it really ten years since she had last been here? She remembered the events of all those years ago as if they had happened yesterday. She recalled minutely what happened next, every last detail of the climb to the summit and what she found there; she relived the horror of it, and also the wonder.

Ella had followed the old alien into the fissure in the rock. As they walked the defile widened, became a gorge with jungle plants clinging to its sides. They climbed a narrow path, the old alien pacing ahead with long, sure-footed strides. The rockface on each side tilted back, opened out to form an ever-widening valley. Well-worn paths striated the sides of the valley like contour lines.

When Ella asked, "Please, is L'Endo okay? Why does he want to see me?" the Lho either failed to understand or chose to ignore her. They passed scampering children, tiny and golden, who hardly reached to Ella's knees. She felt eyes watching her from the entrances of caves on either side of the valley.

More than once she considered turning back. The further they went, the more they entered into alien territory, with animals and plants Ella had never seen before and dozens of aliens who stopped to stare at her. But the thought that L'Endo wished to see her kept her going.

At last the old Lho paused before a dark cave entrance overhung with creepers. He gestured inside. "L'Endo is ill," he said now. "Many of my people have succumbed to the plague." He swept his arm in a scything gesture, his face expressionless.

Ella felt something growing within her; a disbelief that was physical and hard in her chest, threatening to burst with rage and anguish.

Hesitantly she stepped into the cave. A flickering brand lit the nether recesses. In the half-light she made out a figure lying on packed animals skins. Someone crouched beside L'Endo, administering mouthfuls of water from a conch shell. At a word from the old Lho behind Ella, the nurse stood and hurried out. Ella felt a hand on her elbow, gesturing her forward.

She approached her friend and sat down next to him.

L'Endo turned his head and stared at her, and in the hesitant light of the brand Ella saw that the right side of his face had dissolved, the flesh fluid and suppurating, the infrastructure of muscle beneath subsided.

The cry she stifled seemed to resonate in every part of her body, filling her with pain. She quickly dashed tears from her cheeks.

Something clutched her fingers, and when she looked down she saw that it was L'Endo's frail hand. Wound around his wrist was the rock painting she had given him.

"Five of your days he has been ill," the old Lho whispered to her. "L'Endo, and many more of my people. We can do little. We can only rejoice at their passing."

She stared at the old alien through her tears. "What do you mean?" she spluttered.

The alien sighed. "Humans..."

L'Endo moved his head closer to Ella, spoke in a voice even lighter than his usual whispery register.

The old Lho translated. "L'Endo says, 'Do not cry for me, be happy.' This is the moment for which he has lived his life. Truly, Ella, he gives thanks that he is passing. He gives thanks that he has experienced this life and will experience the next."

Ella felt L'Endo's fingers squeeze hers. "The next?"

The old Lho took her free hand. "Only the humans you know as Engineman and Enginewoman believe, like us, in a Beyond. They know that we should rejoice in the gift of life, and not grieve for its passing, for without this life there would be no hope of attaining the Beyond. Look upon L'Endo – do you see a being in mortal agony? He rejoices, Ella. Truly he rejoices!"

She gazed down at her friend. Through the pain, through the obvious affliction of the plague, she recognised in L'Endo something of the inexpressible rapture he had exhibited when standing on the rock in the centre of the lagoon – giving thanks, as he had said, for life.

L'Endo glowed with an energy at odds with his failing life-force. He spoke, and the old Lho translated.

"Can you return in five of your days, Ella, for his passing?"

L'Endo squeezed her fingers.

"His... passing?" she echoed.

"A time of celebration, of joy at his attainment. More than anything, he wishes you to attend. He wishes to share with you his joy as he leaves this life. He wishes to *convince* you..."

"In five days..." she began. "But how can you tell?"

"In five of your days, L'Endo will release his hold upon life and pass from us. He feels it within him, he feels that then the time will be right."

She was in a dark cave with two aliens, she told herself, one of whom, a friend for the past four months, was dying of some horrendous wasting plague, and yet all she could feel was... was *joy*.

She wondered if it was her way of coping with so much grief, but she searched within her and found no such emotion, only the strongest communion with anyone, alien or human, she had ever experienced. Closer to L'Endo than ever before, she shared in his rapture, and felt blessed.

"I'll be honoured to attend his passing," Ella said.

The old Lho translated her words, and L'Endo lay back on the skins with what might have been relief.

Then she took her leave of the dying alien, and the oldster arranged to meet her in five days, and then led her back to the lagoon and said farewell.

For the next few days at home, her life seemed dull and lacklustre. She contrasted the materialism of colony life with what she had experienced with the Lho, and felt cheated. She could never become a Lho, but she could leave the Reach, start a life of her own. She anticipated the time, in three months, when she could legally leave school and the clutches of her father.

In the meantime, she wanted only to re-experience the communion she had shared in the cave with L'Endo.

Then, two days before she was due to attend his passing, her father appeared on the patio above the lagoon where she was swimming. "Ella – my study, this minute."

She shivered, despite the sunlight. He spoke to her rarely, and an official summons to his study could only mean that in some way she had transgressed. She dried herself and dressed quickly, trying to think what she might have done wrong, then hurried inside. The sooner she got this over with...

Her father was seated in a swivel chair behind his desk. To his left stood Conway, her minder. He was dressed all in black today and held, by his side, Ella's metallic-backed diary.

She wanted to scream that they had no right intruding in her private affairs, but she had no intention of giving them the satisfaction of seeing her upset.

Then she realised the subject of the latest entries...

Her father held out a hand, and Conway placed the diary upon it; a set-piece surely rehearsed. He flipped through the pages, came to the last entry and paused, reading it.

Then he closed the diary and laid it very precisely on the desk before him. He looked up at Ella.

She could never guess what her father was thinking. The expression on the only readable part of his face was forever stern, unsmiling.

He tapped her diary with his forefinger.

"This is not permissible, of course," he said. She tried not to smile to herself. He could never address her without resorting to a stilted legalese, as if he were a prosecuting lawyer and she the accused.

"Quite apart from the fact that contact between humans and the Lho is proscribed by colonial edict, there is the very considerable health risk to take into consideration."

She tried to out-stare him, tried not to redden – an impossible combination. She looked away, through the window at the sloping garden leading to the summit of the plateau, and felt herself colour.

She had used phrases like *love* and *feel one with* about the Lho; the admission of which emotions made her feel vulnerable in the face of her father's withering cynicism.

"As you know," he continued, "the Lho have succumbed to a devastating plague. As yet, its full implications are not known."

Ella interrupted. "I've known L'Endo for months and I'm not ill..." She felt a dull certainty about where all this was leading.

"That does not alter the fact that I cannot allow you to attend this... this ceremony."

"But, you don't understand, I must! I promised... If I didn't..." She could only imagine her friend's disappointment if she failed to turn up on the most important day of his life.

She told herself that nothing could keep her from attending L'Endo's passing. Even if her father locked her in the villa, she would find a way out.

"I'm sorry, Ella. But I've taken this matter to higher authorities. You are to transfer schools immediately. From the day after tomorrow you will attend a Danzig boarding gymnasium in the south."

"No!" she screamed. "No, you can't–"

Even then she could not fully comprehend the implications of what he was saying. Nothing could keep her away from the Lho. She would escape now, live with the aliens until L'Endo's passing.

She turned and ran for the door.

She might have known that Conway would be one step ahead of her. As she was hauling open the door, he grabbed her around the waist and carried her kicking and screaming to her room.

The following day, her father left early for Zambique City without so much as a word of farewell. Conway drove her south. Ella went without protest, thinking that if her father had any way of gauging the degree of anger within her, then he would surely feel ashamed.

She vowed she would show the bastard.

For the next three months, before her fifteenth birthday, she paid no attention to her instructors and failed her exams. Her father had once mentioned, at a dinner party held for senior executives in the Organisation, that Ella was a bright pupil who might one day work for the Danzig Colonial Administration.

She'd show him...

The day after her fifteenth birthday, Ella walked from the dormitory of her college and, with savings scraped together over the years, booked her passage through the interface network to Earth.

She attended a third-rate art college in Paris, sold her paintings in the streets. Then she met Eddie, and joined the Church and converted. The day after her conversion, she communicated with her father for the first time in three years. She sent him a photograph. It showed Eddie in his radiation silvers, standing stoically, holding a beer and staring into the camera. Ella was behind him, without clothes, arms around his neck and a leg twisted around his thigh. Her chin was hooked over his shoulder and she was laughing. Displayed prominently on her forearm was the infinity symbol tattoo of the Disciples.

Ella picked up a flat stone and skimmed it across the surface of the lagoon.

She was, she knew, only delaying the inevitable meeting. She checked her watch. It was seven o'clock. The curfew began in one hour. She could make her way down to the villa now, or spend the night here at the lagoon, but she didn't want to do that. The place was full of too many memories, too many reminders of the girl she'd been, a fourteen-year-old full of naivety, hope and ambition. She wondered what that girl might have to say to the woman she was now, who wanted more than anything to make peace with her father.

She left the lagoon. She decided to leave the bike where it was in the bushes and walk down the track. At the first bend, her father's house came into sight – a split-level ranch-style villa, its central section raised above the wings. She wondered if the Organisation had the house under observation. They had no way of connecting her to the sabotage of the interface, but she had evaded their surveillance last night... That set her to wondering *why* they had allowed her onto the Reach. Was it that her father had pulled strings to facilitate her entry?

And that, of course, begged the question of why her father had summoned her. "I've seen the light, Ella. I need to see you-"

She paused at the top of the path that descended though her father's cacti garden. *He'd seen the light...* It came to Ella that he had found out that the Organisation was responsible for the genocide of the Lho-Dharvo. He'd seen the light, seen the evil at the heart of the Organisation, and wanted absolution from the daughter he had so mistreated over the years...

Or perhaps, she told herself, I'm trying to convince myself that he knew nothing of the origins of the plague in the first place.

She descended through the cacti garden, which in her childhood she had considered so symbolic of her father: dry, prickly, and menacing.

Her heart pounding, she walked up the timber steps to the front door. Hesitantly, she pushed the call-bell and waited. The seconds seemed to last forever. How should I greet him, she wondered? Just breeze in shit-tough, or stand here smiling at him like Daddy's little girl returned?

Minutes passed, and she reached up hesitantly and touched the sensor pad. Ten years ago it had been programmed to accept her palm-print... and now the door swung slowly open. She stepped inside, crossed the hall and paused outside her father's study.

The door was open, and she glanced into the room.

The painting... *her* painting. *Conversion.*

As if in a daze, she moved into the room and crossed to the painting.

She experienced once again the sense of transcendence that had overwhelmed her in the cave of the Lho and, again, three years later when she had converted in the Church at Montparnasse. The oil showed a woman in rapture, laid out naked, being transported through an effulgent starscape by shadowy bearers who might have been aliens or cowled Disciples.

On the wall below it was the photograph of Eddie and herself she had sent her father on her conversion.

As if she needed any further proof she saw, across the room on his desk, a leather-bound volume of the Book of The Lho.

Ella stared at the painting again, and wept.

The realisation of the danger she was in came too late.

She heard the flier, the crunch of boots on gravel, and only then did she begin to feel afraid.

A voice, amplified through a loud-speaker: "Ella Hunter – come out with your hands in the air!"

She looked through the window. Armed militia stood between the cacti in the front garden. She slipped from the study, moved to the back of the house. Was it too much to hope that the militia would not have the back garden covered? There was a bolt-hole in the igneous rock beside the lagoon. If she could reach it, lose them, make her way up the track to where her bike was hidden...

She opened the door and slipped out.

A dozen militia-men trained rifles on her. She heard movement in the villa behind her.

"Put your hands in the air," said one of the guards in a slow, bored drawl, "and get the fuck down here now!"

Ella raised her hands and walked calmly down the steps to where the militia waited on the racquet-ball court. The only hope she had was to make them think she would come without a struggle.

Then she made a run for it towards the lagoon.

The first bullet hit her in the thigh, the second in her shoulder. She fell, screaming – hardly able to believe they'd shot her. A phalanx of legs came into view, blurred through tears of pain. She tried to climb to her knees. Something solid slammed into the back of her head. She hit the ground, face first. A small voice told her that the only way to oppose them was with defiance. She knelt, attempted to climb to her feet. Another blow cracked the base of her skull, almost knocking her senseless. She collapsed again and moaned. Someone swung a boot and kicked her in the face. She felt her jaw crack, tasted blood. More kicks from the crazed militia registered like starbursts in her head. She wondered how much more pain she could take before she passed out.

But more than the pain – more than the agony of bullet wounds and broken bones – what hurt most of all was the sound of their laughter.

Chapter Thirteen

The Chagal was an exclusive restaurant on the Left Bank overlooking the river. The scene through the window from Hunter's table – the central dome and the hydrofoils on the Seine – contrasted with the restaurant's old-fashioned interior of polished brass, rosewood and potted palms. The waiters wore white and were discreet, and the brandy was the finest he'd tasted in years.

Hunter felt calm and relaxed for the first time in a long while. When he sent the disc to his daughter a month ago, suggesting she meet him here for dinner today, he wondered later if he had been wise. He might have been too busy while in Paris to keep the engagement, or the Organisation might have been onto him, in which case he would not have dared show himself. In the event, he was neither too busy nor in danger. Circumstances could not have worked out better. Everything was going according to plan, and today he had no other appointments or duties to fulfil. During the night, Sassoon had arranged the transportation and installation of the flux-tank; word was this morning that they had fully integrated the tank with the shipboard logic-matrix and the smallship was almost ready to test-run. As expected, Mirren and Leferve had leapt at the opportunity to push the 'ship; Elliott and Olafson had yet to be approached as back-ups, but it would be no major concern if for whatever reasons they, like Caspar Fekete, declined his offer.

On the wider front, he had heard from the Rim this morning that the resistance was going well. Cells of Enginemen on the Reach had targeted vital Danzig installations, power stations, dams, airports and military bases, and caused maximum damage with a minimum loss of life. Yesterday a suicide squad of Disciples had sabotaged the interface on the Reach, not only putting it out of action temporarily to staunch the military build-up, which was the intention, but wrecking the 'face to the extent that it would be inoperable for up to a month. Hennessy's Reach was effectively cut off, isolated.

Thoughts of the Danzig Organisation led him inevitably to consider his past. When he thought back to the time he had loyally served the Organisation, performing tasks well beyond the call of duty on the planets of the Rim and beyond, he was overcome with such a deep-rooted sense of guilt he wondered if even what he was doing now could atone for his misdeeds. Over the years he had tried to rationalise his guilt – but he found that the rationalisation of one's guilt was as futile a mental exercise as trying to empty one's head and think about nothing... He told himself that at the time he had believed in what the Organisation stood for, and that any action likely to further the cause was to be embraced as right. To this end he had embraced the undercover campaign of divide and rule, infiltrate and subvert, and brought about the closure of the few bigship Lines whose continued operation after the installation of the interfaces had been subsidised by socialist governments around the Rim. Only once had he resorted to actual terrorist tactics, which had resulted in the deaths of three Enginemen. At the time he had considered it a minor price to pay for the pacification of yet another planet.

He wondered if he really did believe, back in the years when he worked ceaselessly for the Danzig cause, in everything the Organisation stood for, or was his main concern himself, his own aggrandisement, his promotion within the Danzig corporate structure with all the attendant wealth, prestige and power that such promotion entailed? He suspected that, at the time, Hirst Hunter the high-flying troubleshooting executive would never have admitted to such failings as egotism: he would have quoted Danzig dogma and pointed to the successful regimes on newly-settled Danzig worlds. Only in retrospect could Hunter see that his younger, ambitious self had been blinded by power into seeing only what he wanted to see.

He was, in short, guilty, as guilty as hell. He would do his best now to atone for his sins, but that would never alter the fact that he had been a shallow, egotistical, power-crazy fool.

And the main casualty had been his daughter, Ella.

He glanced at his watch. It was almost six, the time he had suggested on the disc that they should meet. He ordered another brandy, less to savour its quality than to feel its effect. For ten years he had failed to contact his daughter – and for many years before that he had simply failed her, period – and now that the time was fast approaching when they would meet face to face, Hunter felt more than a little apprehensive.

He wondered how she had changed over the years – hard to imagine she was now a woman of twenty-five. He recalled the photograph she had sent him seven years ago, the one in which she was all over her lover, an Engineman many years her senior. It showed her as tiny as ever, thin and pale, and she had shorn her long black hair. He'd wondered at the time if the photograph was the first step on the road to a reconciliation, or a taunt. He saw it now for what it was – a taunt, an aggressive gesture against everything for which he stood, a statement of Ella's freedom and new-found independence.

Would she be more worldly-wise now, cool and sophisticated and – Fernandez, no! – bourgeois? Somehow, he could not imagine it. She would still be the rebel, the tomboy, the anarchic impressionist shunning success for the type of aggressive art she wanted to produce. Yes, that was more like it. He hoped so... He so much longed to see her that the wait was like an ache within him. He had so much to apologise for, so much for which to make up.

He was wondering whether perhaps the Chagal was the right venue in which to meet his daughter – she would probably turn up barefoot, in radiation silvers – when someone entered the restaurant and crossed to his table, but it was not Ella.

Rossilini cleared his throat. "Excuse me, sir." He was holding a silver envelope.

"Yes, Mr Rossilini?" Hunter gestured to the seat opposite.

"You told me to report when the private operator came up with anything on Christiana Olafson..." Rossilini sat down and laid the envelope on the table before him. Something about his stern expression worried Hunter.

"What is it?"

"We received a report and photographs from the operator an hour ago. Olafson's dead, killed in a flier accident."

Hunter imagined the colour draining from his face, or rather from half of it. He tried to remain calm. "When was this, Mr Rossilini?"

"Two days ago, at seven in the evening, German time."

Rossilini slid the envelope across the table. "I'd give the photographs a miss, sir, if you're thinking of eating."

Hunter withdrew the contents of the envelope and skimmed the operator's report. It detailed Olafson's movements on the day she died, and included the German police report which stated the cause of the accident as engine failure.

Hunter looked up. "Send someone to Hamburg to look into the accident, Mr Rossilini."

"I've already done so, sir."

"Good." Quickly, Hunter leafed through the police photographs taken at the scene of the accident. A microwave pylon had sheared the flier in two. Olafson's remains were scattered across the flat roof of a nearby building. Bosch, Hunter told himself, returning the photographs to the envelope. Definitely Hieronymus Bosch.

"Two days ago I had mentioned to no-one that I was considering employing Christiana Olafson on this mission. I had not at the time even decided myself to approach her. There can be no way this accident is connected with us."

Rossilini said, "I did consider that, sir. But I thought it best to send someone to Hamburg anyway."

"You did right, but I think they'll find that it was what it looks like; an accident." Hunter paused, considerably relieved now after his initial fright. "And anyway, if by any chance our enemies were onto us, they'd surely strike at the very heart of our operations, not at the Enginemen and -women we might employ."

Rossilini picked up the envelope. "I'll leave you to it, sir. I hope you enjoy your meal."

Hunter smiled. "Thank you, Mr Rossilini. I intend to."

He took a mouthful of brandy, the macabre photographs fading from the forefront of his mind as he reassured himself that the accident was not the work of the Organisation.

He looked at his watch. It was six-thirty. Ella was late. He would give her another thirty minutes. He ordered a third brandy and sat back, trying to regain the composure he had felt earlier. The little scare with Olafson, though, and Ella's impunctuality, had served to spoil his optimistic mood.

Did Ella still, after all these years, hate him as she had so obviously hated him as a teenager, and after what he had said on the disc he had sent her? He had made the recording on the free world of Tyler, and it had proved the hardest speech he'd ever had to make. He'd lost count of the number of times he'd had to re-record it. He told her simply of his conversion. He said that he regretted their differences in the past, and expressed the hope that they might build a meaningful relationship in the future, belated though that was. What he really wanted to tell her – the details of this mission which would surely redeem him in her eyes – he could not entrust to disc. He resolved that although he was sworn to absolute secrecy – even his aides did not know everything – he would make an exception and tell Ella what was happening, when they finally met.

He waited until seven, and only then decided that she was not going to turn up. He settled his bill and left, deep in thought. After the air-conditioned chill of the restaurant, the night air outside was sultry and cloying. The Mercedes was waiting at the kerb. Sassoon appeared from where he'd been keeping watch on the restaurant and opened the rear door. Hunter ducked into the car. Rossilini glanced at him in the rear-view mirror. "The morgue, sir?"

"No – take me to Orly. Rue Chabrol."

They set off and motored through the rapidly falling twilight. Hunter leaned forward. "Mr Rossilini..."

"Sir?"

"Am I correct in thinking that you have a daughter?"

The driver glanced at him in the mirror. "Yes, sir."

"How old is she?"

"Nine, sir."

"Have you seen her recently?"

"No, not for two years."

Hunter smiled to himself. "Well, as soon as we've finished with this business, Mr Rossilini, I suggest you take yourself off to... Benedict's world, isn't it? – and make sure you visit your daughter. Understood?"

Rossilini exchanged a glance with Sassoon. They probably thought he was going soft in the head. "Understood, sir."

"Good, Mr Rossilini. Very good." Hunter sat back and watched the passing suburbs fall into dereliction and decay the further they drove from central Paris.

They passed Orly spaceport and turned into the district where Ella lived. They passed down narrow streets between warehouses and storage units owned by the spaceport authorities. Rossilini accelerated over the last kilometre.

The alien vegetation began as a fibrous matting on the pavement, and the further they drove into the district of cheap tenement rows the more prolific the growth became, climbing the facades of the four-storey buildings, crossing the street in great rafts of gnarled and tangled ground-roots. By the time they arrived at the north end of the Rue Chabrol, only the occasional glimpse of building could be seen beneath the all-consuming plant-life: an odd patch of brickwork here, a cleared window there. Rossilini braked and Hunter peered out at the neighbourhood where his daughter had chosen to make her home. Between the overgrown rows of apartment buildings on either side, the street was a trench filled with a riotous jungle. It was hard to imagine how anyone gained access to the shrouded properties. It occurred to Hunter that perhaps Ella had moved out since his contacts had found her address. She might never have received his disc, which would explain why she had not shown up at the restaurant.

He made out the caged run which penetrated the street jungle, a dark tunnel which passed through the slick green leaves and fronds. He opened the door and climbed out, the heat and the heady scent of alien pollen hitting him in a wave. Sassoon was beside him. "Sir?"

"It's okay, Mr Sassoon. Just a little personal pilgrimage."

Sassoon glanced down the run. "Do you think it wise?"

"Stay in the car if you don't feel up to it."

"I didn't mean..." Sassoon began. "I'm coming with you. You don't know what kind of creatures live in there."

Hunter smiled to himself as he gazed up at the overgrown buildings. "Just artists and anarchists, I suspect, Mr Sassoon." He stepped into the wire-mesh corridor and entered the green-tinged twilight. At regular intervals, smaller caged runs branched off at right angles, the wire mesh bearing the numbers of the individual buildings. He strode on before Sassoon, who'd drawn his gun and was following warily.

Hunter stared about him. He could almost believe he'd been miniaturised and set down in the Amazon jungle. On all sides, great blooms and vines had grown through rents in the mesh, impeding their progress.

He came to the number forty-six painted on a board wired to the mesh on his left. He ducked into the narrow corridor.

The collar of mesh finished before the door, and the jungle had poured into the gap as if intent on invading the building. The door was ajar, admitting vines and creepers. Hunter pushed it further open. In the dark hallway he could just make out the shadowy shape of a flight of stairs. He noticed the entrance of a lift, but decided not to trust the mechanical apparatus of such a dilapidated building.

Sassoon entered behind him.

"I'll be able to look after myself now, thank you, Mr Sassoon," Hunter said.

His bodyguard nodded. "I'll stay down here."

Hunter climbed the stairs, broken glass and perished linoleum crunching underfoot. Spectacular drifts of fungus covered the walls, flock-textured. Hunter came to the first landing and climbed the second flight of stairs. By the time he reached the fourth floor he was out of breath and more than a little nervous. Dying sunlight slanted through a window, illuminating damp and unpainted walls. Hunter approached a door daubed with the number twenty-four. The words of greeting he had rehearsed over and over were a jumble in his head. Heart hammering, he knocked. At his first touch the door swung open. He found a light switch on the wall and turned it on. For a second he feared that she had indeed moved out, but then revised his opinion. Had she moved out, she would surely have taken her possessions. The narrow hall was stacked with cardboard boxes full of clothes, in lieu of wardrobes; wooden cartons containing chipped cups and plates, pristine canvasses and plastic back-boards for plasma-graphics. He cleared his throat, called out, "Ella?" He moved down the corridor, squeezing past the boxes. Dust covered every horizontal surface, but he suspected that this was more the artist's aversion to housework than any indication that she'd moved out, for whatever reason, and left her possessions – at least, he hoped so. Of course, there were always other possibilities in a neighbourhood like this...

"Ella!" His call lingered in the sultry air.

He pushed open the first door on the left and entered a lounge. It was furnished with an ancient four-piece suite, none of the pieces matching. No carpet, just bare floorboards. The walls were daubed with a yellow and green psychedelic mural. In the corner of the room was a small area of wall-paper, carpet, and a new-looking recliner, situated before a power point and the antenna of a communications vid-screen, but there was no sign of a set. The pathetic show of respectability brought tears to his good eye. He wondered if the screen had been stolen – certainly it would be the only thing in the room worth taking.

Then he saw the stack of photographs wedged between the cushion and the back-rest of the settee. He sat down, sorted through the thick drift. There were a few pictures of Ella before she left home, at school, on holiday; a slim, pretty olive-skinned girl with long black hair, so painfully like her mother. Most of the photographs were of Ella since arriving on Earth: with a crowd of her bizarre artist friends, at parties and street performances, with the solid, stolid Engineman she lived with. In these pictures, she was a pale, starved-looking shaveskull, and in none of them was she smiling.

At the very bottom of the pile, Hunter found a picture of Marie, his wife...

Its sudden appearance, after so many photos of Ella standing seriously beside her work, caused him to gasp. He stared at the photograph. It showed Marie leaning over a sea-wall on braced arms, her shoulders hunched, her gamin's face mischievous and grinning. So young – Christ, she was so young... He calculated that it had been taken at Zephyr, on the Rim world of New Syria, during one of his too few leave periods. Marie must have been just twenty-two – three years younger than Ella was now – and they had been married just a year. Fernandez, they had been in love. He had known no emotion like it, before or ever since. He'd been consumed at their first meeting, and all through the time of their courtship and marriage, consumed with a love for her that during the next five years had never abated, and consumed with an incommunicable sense of loss, of soul-harrowing grief, when she died giving birth to Ella at the ridiculously young age of twenty-seven.

He quickly slipped Marie's picture into the inside pocket of his jacket, and shuffled to a photograph showing Ella standing on a rock in the centre of a lagoon at Zambique. He wondered who had taken it, for he knew for certain that he had not. It showed her with her arms held outstretched behind her, her head back, but the serious posture was belied by her expression: she was laughing despite her best efforts not to, and her resemblance to her mother was painful.

Fernandez, he had so much to make up for, so much irrational hatred in the early years, so much apathy as she was growing up, so much disaffection that must have seemed to her like casual cruelty, which perhaps it was.

He had been happily, madly, in love with Marie and looking forward to the birth of a son... and then in the space of minutes Marie was dead and he was presented with the cause of it – a disgustingly healthy baby girl – and though he found it hard to imagine now, looking back with shame, he'd been unable to feel anything but resentment towards his daughter.

He had mellowed, or so he thought, in his later years, when his grief for Marie abated and Ella grew into a person in her own right; an attractive, intelligent teenager, even personable when in company, but always mistrustful and reluctant when alone with him. Around the time of her fifteenth birthday, before she'd left the Reach, he began to recognise the mistakes he'd made; though he was totally unable to open up to Ella and apologise or make amends. He had tried to treat her with more understanding, even compassion, hard though that was after so many years of resentment.

Hunter recalled the time when Conway had suspected that Ella was consorting with the alien tribe which had encamped that summer on the plateau. On reluctantly reading her diary, he had discovered her friendship with a certain alien, and knew that he'd have to end the liaison. The Lho were going down with a devastating plague, and at the time he had not known that humans were unaffected. He felt he had to send her away for her own good, and he recalled the scene in his study when he broke the news to her, relived again his inability to express sympathy or regret.

He had so, so much to make up for...

He selected half a dozen photographs of Ella and slipped them into his jacket beside the one of Marie.

He left the lounge and made his way down the hall. He came to the open door of a small bedroom, so bereft of personal possessions he guessed it must belong to the Engineman. The next door was locked. It could only be Ella's bedroom. He knocked. "Ella?" he called, his heart racing. "Ella!"

The timber jamb was rotten. He leaned his shoulder against the door. On the third shove it gave and he entered the room. He found a switch on the wall and turned on the light.

The was no sign of Ella in the bedroom, but there was every sign of her work. Canvasses and plasma-graphic boards in various stages of completion leaned against the walls, stacked so deep in some places that there was hardly room to move around the bed. Hunter flipped through the paintings and graphics, pulling out those that caught his eye. He experienced a strange sensation of pride in his daughter's accomplishments, and at the same time the guilt of a voyeur: looking through Ella's opus was like reading her mind. In canvas after canvas, again and again, he experienced her pain and anger, and he felt the weight of regret and responsibility settle upon him. I made her what she is, he told himself; and by the evidence of her work she is a very unhappy person. Her forte was the depiction of the human form, impressionistically torn and fragmented to suggest the symbolic annihilation of the subject's psyche or soul. In many of the paintings he recognised diffracted aspects of Ella herself.

Then he came across a portrait of himself. He thought – he *hoped* – it might be an early work; certainly it did not possess the technical accomplishment of her later work, and it was certainly influenced. It showed a head, all cadaver – grey with a quarter splotch of crimson, its features twisted and misplaced, the effect almost Mephistophelean. In its brutality and despair it was almost a pastiche of the twentieth-century artist Francis Bacon. Hunter replaced it behind a stack of others, loath to acknowledge the import of the painting, and moved around the room. Pinned to the wall by the head of the bed was a photograph of Ella and the Engineman, Schwartz – according to the name-tag on his silvers – similar to the one she had sent him. In this one, Ella was riding her lover piggy-back, bare legs wrapped around his waist. Her smile contrasted with the total lack of animation on the face of the Engineman. The Disciple's tattoo on Ella's forearm was prominent.

He took the snap from the wall, sat down on the bed and stared at it. He thought back to the time he had received the photograph from Ella, seven years ago. That year had proved a turning point in his life. During that long, hot summer, events had occurred which made him question the morality of the Organisation and his position within it. Danzig militia had put down a rebellion on Esperance, imposed a puppet dictator, and proceeded to rule the planet with brutal efficiency. Thousands of innocent civilians were interrogated and never heard from again. Over the years, Hunter had risen to a position in the Danzig hierarchy from which he could form a historical overview, thanks to records and data hitherto unavailable to him, of the success and failure of the Organisation's political regimes around the Rim. Propaganda had suggested that they were hard but fair, bringing prosperity to the planets they pacified. In fact, Hunter learned that the Organisation's record on the planets they had taken over was abysmal: they ruled with terror; their human rights record was appalling, and the only prosperity they brought was to the ruling elite on the planets they took over – the vast majority of the citizens lived well below the poverty level. Hunter rapidly became discontent and dissatisfied; his position of power and privilege was soured, came to mean nothing. And then, to end it all, he discovered that the plague that had very nearly wiped out the Lho-Dharvon people had been manufactured, in retaliation for the aliens' armed opposition, by the Organisation itself.

In the middle of this plethora of discovery, Ella's photograph had arrived, the declaration of her independence and conversion. Over the months, it had worked slowly on him... More and more he became curious as to why exactly his daughter had converted, and at the same time, perhaps even subconsciously, he was seeking a philosophy to replace his shattered faith in the Danzig Organisation. He had read books, spoken to Enginemen and Disciples, made contacts with heads of the Church. He was duly initiated, after a rigorous vetting by a naturally suspicious jury of Disciples, while still a Danzig executive. For a couple of years he'd remained with the Organisation, and then dropped quickly from sight and worked actively for the resistance.

Soon after that, the Lho had contacted him.

He sat on the bed and stared at the photograph. He ached to talk to her, to explain himself. He placed the picture on the bed beside him, and only then noticed the disc. Beneath it was the small photograph of himself he had sent along with the disc. He picked up the photo; it had been screwed up – worn, white lines criss-crossed his face – but then meticulously straightened and flattened out, as if Ella had had a change of heart following her initial reaction of anger. He picked up the disc, curious as to how his message sounded a month after making the recording. He found the activate slide on its base and thumbed it on.

"I've seen the light, Ella," his voice boomed around the room. "I need to see you–" There was a second of static, and then loud music; Mahler's fifth. Hunter forwarded the disc, played it again – still music. He ran it to the end, but still his words were lost beneath the symphony. She had heard his voice, and quickly obliterated it with the integral recording facility tuned to a classical channel.

Which, he guessed, pretty much summed up her feelings on hearing his voice again after ten years. But what about the photograph? Surely she would not have bothered to straighten it out if her feelings towards him were purely ones of hatred? Perhaps her recording over his message had been an impulsive response. like her screwing up the photo, but one which she could not undo, and which maybe later she regretted?

Or was he being baselessly optimistic?

He was startled by a noise from the hall. Ella, returning? He jumped up and moved to the door, his pulse quickening. At first he thought it was an animal perched on the sill of the open window – an escaped primate – but in the light spilling past his from the bedroom he made out the figure of a small girl, staring at him.

"What do you want?" she cried in rapid French.

Hunter said, "I might ask the same of you." The girl was perhaps ten or twelve, tiny, bird-boned and filthy.

"I'm looking after the apartment for Ella! Who are you?"

He gestured to the paintings in the room. "I'm an art dealer. I buy her work."

She looked at him, suspicious. "Ella feeds me, gives me creds."

"Do you know where she is?"

The girl cocked her head. "Might do."

Hunter pulled out his wallet, counted fifty credit notes. The girl stared, open-mouthed. He held out the notes, just beyond her reach. "Where's Ella?" he asked.

"She left Earth," the girl said. She made a grab for the credits and almost fell from her perch.

Hunter was aware of his increased heartbeat. "Where did she go?" he heard himself asking.

"To the Rim. Don't know which planet. Went to see her father. She told me."

Hunter considered the irony of it, the cruelty. He felt himself rocking on his feet. "When did she go? How long ago?"

The girl shrugged. "Two, three days ago. Gimme the creds!" She made a grab, snatched them this time, and leapt from the sill and down the fire-escape.

Two or three days ago...

Hunter ran from the apartment and down the stairs. Only when he was halfway down the last flight did he remember Sassoon. He slowed his pace, resumed his dignity.

Sassoon was kicking his heels in the hall. "Find what you wanted?"

Hunter brushed past him without replying. He turned to say. "On the top floor you'll find a room full of paintings. Tomorrow I want you to ensure they are safely taken into storage."

Sassoon looked at him oddly. "Very good, sir."

Hunter hurried back to the car, his mind a confusion of ugly thoughts. He felt like one of Ella's diffracted, annihilated subjects. He sat in brooding silence as the Mercedes purred at speed through the darkened Paris streets.

Once back at the morgue he told his team that on no account was he to be disturbed, and retreated to his room. He sat in the darkness and stared through the window at the infrequent points of light.

Ella had left for the Reach two or three days ago. Yesterday the interface had been sabotaged, isolating the planet... His only hope was that they had turned her back as a Disciple, but he knew that this was unlikely. As the daughter of Hirst Hunter, the most wanted man on the Rim, Ella would have been allowed entry and followed, in the hope that she might lead them to him... And when she failed to do so, they would take her in for questioning.

His hands were shaking. "Ella. Oh, Ella..."

There was a knock at the door. He ignored it, to absorbed in his private grief. The knocking became louder. Then the door opened and Sassoon burst in. "Sir?"

Hunter remained sitting in the darkness. "What is it, Mr Sassoon?"

"It's Fekete and Elliott, sir."

Fekete and Elliott? He picked up the remote control and turned on the lights. "What are they doing here, Mr–"

He was silenced by the look on Sassoon's face. "They're not here, sir. Fekete died in a flier accident this afternoon. Elliott was shot dead an hour ago."

Hunter just stared at him. "That's impossible! No-one could possibly know that we planned to use them..."

"But that's three, sir – three out of six, dead."

Hunter shook his head. "I don't understand it, Sassoon. If the Organisation knew of our plans, then surely they'd hit us?"

"I don't understand it either, sir. But the fact remains..."

Hunter looked up. "The others! Round up the others and get them to safety this minute!"

"Yes, sir." Sassoon ran from the room and across to the lift, followed by Rossilini.

Hunter calmly climbed to his feet and closed the door. He crossed to the window and stared out, tears blurring his vision.

The day had started so well. How could it end so tragically?

From his pocket he pulled out the photographs of his daughter and sorted through them, lovingly.

Chapter Fourteen

THEY HURRIED TO the end of the avenue and Dan hailed an air-taxi. He bundled Mirren into the back and climbed in beside him. Mirren felt numb. He heard Dan give their destination as St Genevieve's, then suffered a wave of nausea as the air-taxi lifted and accelerated. He seemed to have weakened appreciably in the last five minutes, since learning about Macready. He wondered how much of it was auto-suggestion; for most of the night he'd felt fine.

Dawn lacerated the horizon. They flew south over familiar suburbs. Dan said nothing. Mirren considered the incredible misfortune of mistaking the drunken Engineman for a KVI ghost. He should have let the bastard fry.

The air-taxi banked over the morning-silvered Seine and approached the ancient, mausoleum-like slab of the hospital caught in a loop of the river. They came down on the rooftop and, when the turbos cut out, the air rang with an explosion of silence as absolute as death itself.

Dan paid the driver, took Mirren by the arm and hurried him to a downchute. They dropped three floors and stepped out into a crowded corridor. The sick and injured sat on benches on either side of the passage; others, too ill to sit, lay on blankets. They had a collective air about them of patient resignation, as if they had been waiting here for years. Mirren heard the occasional whimper and cry. A hundred pairs of eyes watched them as they made their way carefully along the corridor, stepping over the tightly-packed bodies. They arrived at a reception kiosk. Dan said, “I need to see Dr Sita Nahendra.”

The receptionist checked a register. “Do you have an appointment?”

“This is an emergency. I really need to see Dr Nahendra.”

“If you don’t have an appointment...”

Dan leaned over the counter and whispered something to the woman.

The receptionist looked up, saw his desperation and his infinity symbol, then glanced at Mirren.

“If you’d care to wait in that room...” She indicated a peeling door across the corridor, and then bent to a microphone.

They pushed their way through a crowd of patients standing by the kiosk, crossed the corridor and entered a white-walled room: one desk, two chairs, an old diagnostic device hanging from a loose boom on the ceiling. Mirren stood by the door like a spare player awaiting his lines.

Dan said, “Hell, Ralph. Things were going so well. I should have known...”

“What about the others?” Mirren said. “Hunter, Fekete, the Enginemen at the Church? If Heine’s is as contagious as they say...” He found a chair and collapsed into it, the sudden enormity of the situation burdening him like a physical weight. He stared at Dan. “*You...*”

Dan said, “We’ll see what the tests say, then I’ll contact the others.” He looked up at Mirren as if in sudden inspiration. “But there’s no reason why we can’t push the boat, Ralph! Go out in style!” He looked at his watch. “Where the hell is she?”

Mirren shook his head. “I’m sorry, Dan.”

The door opened and an Asian women in her thirties breezed in. She was jasmine scented and her white coat contrasted with her mocha complexion. “Dan! This is a surprise.” Then her expression changed. “What is it?”

“Sita – Ralph Mirren, a good friend of mine. You’ve heard me talk about him. Ralph, Sita...” He took a breath. “Ralph had contact with a Heine's victim... what? Two nights ago? The guy'd slipped quarantine and died with Ralph. We didn't find out until this morning."

Dr Nahendra's calm, oval face turned to Mirren. "I'll have to take a blood and tissue sample from you and I'll be back in... oh, about fifteen, twenty minutes. And cheer up, both of you. The virus is weakened in a carrier close to death." She gave Mirren a smile so bright he didn't want to disappoint her.

"I feel terrible, feverish..."

"Ever heard of psychosomatic symptoms? If you had only superficial contact with the carrier, then you've probably escaped infection–"

"I drank from the same bottle," Mirren said.

She pointedly ignored the admission, her expression set. "Roll up your sleeve, Ralph."

For the next ten minutes she took blood and skin samples from the two men, working quickly and efficiently and without a word. She smiled and hurried from the room with the same breezy confidence as when she had entered.

"Need she be so damned cheerful?" Mirren asked.

Dan forced a smile. "Maybe it's how she keeps her sanity, Ralph. Who'd be a doctor in a place like this?"

Mirren stood and crossed the room to the window. A grey dawn was seeping steadily out of the east, chasing away the patches of darkness in the streets around the hospital and revealing detail: workers leaving their homes, birds both Terran and alien, wind-borne rubbish. Mirren opened the window and felt the breeze in his face, hot and laden with the stench of exhaust emissions and rotting vegetation.

He recalled what Dan had said earlier about still being able to push the 'ship, but the threat of oblivion overwhelmed even the desire to flux again. Why crave ecstasy, when after it there would be no continuation of life against which to measure the experience?

A flier banked over the Seine and settled in front of the hospital, and only then did Mirren notice the ten storey drop to the parking lot below. He looked over his shoulder. Dan was slumped in the chair at the far end of the room, staring at the floor. So why not? He had nothing to lose. Rather instant death than weeks of agony and mental debilitation. He had considered taking his life before, in the years following the closure of the Lines, but always the thought of an eternity of oblivion, and the hope that things might get better – that by some miracle the Lines might be reinstated – had stopped him from going through with the act.

What he faced now was imminent oblivion, or painful weeks or months with the knowledge of his inevitable end...

Then, before he had time to steel himself, the door opened at the far end of the room. Dr Nahendra strode in. Dan was on his feet. Mirren started, and despite himself felt a surge of guilt.

Dan and the doctor seemed not to have noticed his discomfort. They spoke in lowered tones. Dan was nodding. Nahendra looked stern-faced. Mirren felt his stomach tighten.

Dr Nahendra smiled. "Ralph, please – take a seat."

He fumblingly pulled a chair from beneath the table. The doctor sat across from him, consulting a small screen in her hand. Dan remained standing.

Nahendra looked up. "The news is both good and bad, Ralph. The bad first – I'm afraid it is Heine's. The good news is that it's Heine's III, a mutated form of the disease, which means it can be treated."

Mirren experienced a sudden sense of stomach-churning weightlessness, like the sensation of hitting an air-pocket in flight.

"Like they treated Macready?" he wanted to say.

He thought of the oldster he had watched dying.

Nahendra went on, "Heine's is a strange virus, Ralph. In many cases it mutates in the carrier. You contracted Heine's from Macready, but the Heine's you have is not the same as the one which killed him. For one thing, it's not contagious–"

"So Dan and the others–?" Mirren began.

"Dan's fine, Ralph – as is everyone else you've had contact with over the past couple of days. Another 'benefit', if you like, of Heine's III is that it responds to treatment, as I've said." She paused, then continued, "It's still a fatal disease, but with the drugs we have available nowadays it can be controlled."

He felt sick. "How long have I got?"

Nahendra nodded, as if acknowledging his need to be told the truth. "In similar cases of Heine's III, life expectancy is calculated at between four and five years."

Mirren felt their eyes on him. He experienced an ambiguous reaction to the news. He had fully expected Nahendra to tell him that he would be dead in a month, and now he felt as though he had been granted a reprieve, a stay of execution.

Then, as her words sank in, that part of Mirren which considered himself immortal was rocked by the fact that in four years, certainly five, he would be dead. The enormity of the concept was too much to comprehend. Death was what happened to other people, never oneself, however inevitable he knew the fact to be. Intellectually he could grasp the abstract concept that one day he would die – one day in the not too distant future – but on a visceral level it was impossible for him to understand that within five years his viewpoint on existence would be shut down.

He reflected with sudden bitterness that he did not even have the benefit of belief to fall back on.

He felt dazed. He could think only of the obvious questions. "What about pain?" he asked. "How disabled will I be?"

"I can put you on a course of tablets immediately which will control the symptoms and ease the pain. There might be side-effects, but these will be negligible. You'll be active right up to the last couple of weeks. But you never know, by that time, in a few years from now, there might be a comprehensive cure for all forms of Heine's."

Easy words. "There *might* be..." He could only stare blindly at the far wall, too numbed to respond.

"I'll give you these for the time being," Nahendra said. She passed him a bulb of tiny white capsules and a print-out of instructions. "They're analgesics, temperature suppressants. If you can come back say... this time next week, then we can begin the real treatment."

He wanted to ask what the 'real' treatment consisted of, how painful or prolonged it might be, but the coward in him shied from such questions.

Nahendra reached across the table and squeezed his hand. "People with Heine's III are leading full and active lives, Ralph. There's no reason why you shouldn't do the same."

Dan walked Mirren from the surgery and into the upchute. As he left the building in a daze, and crossed the roof to the air-taxi rank, he felt Dan's hand on his shoulder. "Ralph, I can stay with you for a while if you like. If you want to talk..."

Mirren tried to smile. "I'll be fine... I'll call if I need anything."

They boarded the air-taxi. Mirren sat in the back seat and stared through the window as the flier rose and banked away from the hospital. Five minutes later, before Mirren realised where they were, the taxi landed on the rooftop of his apartment. He climbed out, waved abstractedly at Dan and took the downchute to his rooms. He unlocked the front door and switched on the hall light, and then stopped.

Bobby was in the hall, leaving his room. Within two seconds of the light going on, he halted and turned to the door. He cocked his head to one side, his face expressionless. His ultra-sensitive skin had detected the heat of the light.

"Ralph?" he said, slurring the word like a recording played at too slow a speed.

The sight of his brother, his slight body made childlike by the dimensions of the hall, filled him with the urge to reach out and hold Bobby to him, to confess, tell him everything.

Bobby wore his old radiation silvers – not those of the Javelin Line with whom he'd last worked, but of the Satori Line, with its distinctive Bo tree emblem embroidered on the chest. The torso of the suit was regulation silver, the arms and leggings saffron orange.

"Ralph?" he asked again, his face twitching with concern.

His oversized eyes looked straight at Mirren, then moved on around the hallway. The size of his eyes gave his thin, hollowed face a starved, emaciated look, and his unkempt shock of black hair emphasised the pallor of his cheeks.

Bobby turned and moved to the kitchen, walking with the air of calm circumspection characteristic of the blind. Mirren remained by the door, watching his brother.

In the kitchen, Bobby opened the door of the cooler and took out a plastic container of mineral water. Mirren watched as Bobby seated himself carefully and drank, then moved to place the container on the table beside him.

His hand struck the beer bottle that Mirren had left there by mistake yesterday. "Damn!" his brother said. He patted the table-top until he located the upturned bottle, then picked it up and placed it in the wastechute.

Bobby sat very still, taking the occasional mouthful of water. His features remained inert, relatively composed, though etched with basic lines of angst which made his expression, even in repose, seem tortured. Over the years Mirren had come to realise that his brother's physical appearance was no indication of his psychological state. Inwardly, Bobby had come to accept his situation – more, to feel contentment – which one came to understand only in conversation. Outwardly, he forever gave the impression, to strangers and sometimes to Mirren himself, that he was a soul in despair: both the strange nature of his affliction, and his belief, made him dismissive of his appearance and its effect on others.

Bobby replaced the water in the cooler and left the kitchen, his head held upright, staring forward. As he passed beneath the light he stopped, held up his hand to the source of the radiation, and frowned. He reached for the switch and turned it off, clearly troubled by the suspicion that the light had been turned on in his presence. He entered his room and closed the door.

Mirren released a breath and moved to the kitchen. He sat at the seat his brother had vacated and pulled a carton of fruit juice from the cooler. He washed down a couple of the pills Dr Nahendra had given him and considered the events of the night, and then Bobby.

He recalled the day sixteen years ago when he'd learned that his younger brother had graduated from the training college on Mars. He'd felt pride that Bobby would be following in his footsteps, and over the years watched him gain promotion from Gamma to Alpha. There had always been a certain friendly rivalry between them. At home in Australia they had competed evenly at swimming and surfing, skyball and para-gliding: their careers as Enginemen followed a similar course. They had seen each other rarely while Bobby pushed for the Satori Line, then fifteen years ago Bobby transferred to the Paris-based Javelin Line, and when their leaves had coincided they spent a lot of time together – Ralph finding in the company of his Engineman brother a degree of understanding that was lacking in his civilian acquaintances.

Mirren had been working at Orly spaceport nearly ten years ago when he received a call from the Javelin Line. Bobby, on the very last push before the Line closed down, had contracted Black's Syndrome. He was the sixth Engineman to go down with the neurological disorder, and not one of the others had survived. Bobby pulled through, but at the end of the process Mirren wondered if for Bobby's sake he should have died. Later, when Bobby moved in with him, and when Mirren came to some acceptance of his brother's situation, he realised that even the circumscribed life Bobby now led was preferable to no life at all.

Mirren finished the juice, tossed the carton down the chute and sat absorbed in thought. At last he stood and crossed the hall to Bobby's room. He raised his hand to knock – after all these years he still made the same mistake – realised the stupidity of the gesture and opened the door. Bobby was sitting in his large armchair, his eyes closed. Music played, a classical piece Mirren could not place. It was almost nine o'clock. He thought back a day and recalled hearing the Tibetan mantra.

Bobby laid his head against the rest, his expression as contented as Mirren had ever seen it. His right hand tapped a beat – not in time to the concerto that filled the room now, but to the mantra of yesterday.

A low red light burned in one corner, illuminating a sparsely furnished room: a bed, an armchair and vid-screen; shelves full of music discs and many images of Buddha. The walls were draped with tankas and depictions of scenes from the *Bardo Thodol*. It was more like a far eastern shrine or temple than a bedroom in Paris.

Mirren knelt before his brother and tapped his moccasin – their pre-arranged signal – then took Bobby's thin hand.

Bobby smiled. "I thought you would come," he said, his words protracted. He would hear them for the first time in a little under twenty-four hours.

He had moved his head, was staring over Mirren's right shoulder. "Were you in the hall earlier?"

With the forefinger of his right hand, Mirren traced a symbol on his brother's palm: *Yes*–

"Then why didn't you–?"

Mirren felt a constriction in his throat. He adjusted himself so that he was sitting cross-legged on the rug, and so that coincidentally his face was out of Bobby's line of sight. He hesitated, then signed: *Sorry*.

"You should have let me know it was you, Ralph," Bobby admonished.

You know how it is. He was glad, then, that he had to sign to make himself understood: he felt sure that he would have been unable to speak.

Bobby twisted off a wry grin. "Too busy even to make the effort to communicate, Ralph?"

You know that's not true! The exclamation mark was a vicious stab of his forefinger in the middle of the open palm. Mirren moved his head back into his brother's line of sight, so that tomorrow Bobby would be able to see his anguish.

"I'm sorry. I didn't mean that," Bobby said. "Anyway, how's work?"

It's work. I shouldn't complain. He was aware of how clichéd the dialogue was, like that of two strangers – which, he had to admit, they almost were.

He looked down at Bobby's hand in his, his brother's thin fingers, the bitten nails. He was gripping Bobby's hand with unnecessary firmness.

"Ralph...?" Bobby's voice was gentle. "What's wrong?"

Mirren didn't respond, other than to hold his brother's hand all the tighter. He realised that he was crying, tears running down his cheeks.

"There's so much I want to tell you, Bobby." He stopped himself. This was the coward's way of unburdening himself – to confess all now, leave Bobby to hear everything tomorrow.

"Ralph, please... What is it?"

Mirren signed on Bobby's palm, *We haven't spoken in a long time.*

Bobby shook his head. "No, we haven't."

I mean, really spoken – about what matters.

It was a while before Bobby said, "Ralph?"

Mirren stared at his brother's cupped palm, considering his words. *Is your meditation going well?*

Bobby gave a quick grimace. He was always reluctant to discuss his belief with Mirren. "You know..."

No, I don't! He cuffed his eyes dry, trying to find the right phrase to ask Bobby *how* he meditated.

Tell me!

"Well..."

Tell me how *you meditated, Bobby* – the emphasis made by extra pressure. *What do you experience when meditating?*

Bobby stared into space, seeing whatever his eyes had looked at yesterday. How difficult it must be for him, Mirren thought – to have only the sense of touch with which to understand this situation.

"That's difficult, Ralph. I mean, how would you tell a blind man how you see? I'm sorry – I didn't mean to..." He hesitated, shrugged. "I relax, empty my mind, let everything just drift away, forget my*self*. I concentrate on nothing. Then... then I'm in contact with the continuum, Ralph. It's almost as if I'm fluxing again, though with not quite the same rapture–"

But how is that possible?

"I honestly don't know. I think it has something to do with what happened to me, what happened ten years ago in the tank..." He stopped, there.

Go on.

Bobby hesitated, then said, "I haven't spoken about this to anyone... that last time in the tank – it was different. I felt as though what was happening to me – what happened to leave me like this – was somehow intended by someone or something out there, in the continuum. I know that sounds hard to believe, but that's what I felt at the time. I heard a... a calling, almost, a kind of... I don't know – a *telepathic* beckoning." He paused, his face animated as he considered what had happened to him. "Now, when I meditate, I experience the calling again. It's the most wondrous feeling in existence, Ralph."

Mirren shook his head. He signed, *Why didn't you tell me before?*

"Ralph..." Bobby looked pained. "How could I have told you what ecstasy I experienced through my belief?"

You could have told me! Mirren signed. *I wouldn't have ridiculed you!*

Bobby released a sigh. Mirren saw sadness etched in the lines of his face. "The reason I didn't tell you, Ralph, wasn't because I feared your scepticism–"

Then why?

"How could I have told you what rapture awaited, what wonder I was in contact with, when everyday you went through hell craving the flux, unable to believe..." Bobby's expression was blank, staring.

Carefully, Mirren signed, *I wish I could believe, Bobby. More than anything I wish I could believe. I sometimes think that there was something wrong with me.*

"Ralph, Ralph..." His slurred words were freighted with compassion. "Please, listen to me. You might not believe now, but you will when the time comes to unite with the infinite – and that is all that matters. It isn't like the simplistic, barbaric belief system of the Christians and the other cults; belief isn't a prerequisite for salvation. This life is merely a stage through which we pass on to something greater. I know these words will mean nothing to you now, but they're all I can say."

Mirren could not stop his tears. He gripped Bobby's hand.

"Ralph?"

Tentatively, Mirren reached out and hugged his brother. Bobby stiffened, almost reluctant at first, then he too put his arms around his brother's shoulders. It was a release Mirren could never have imagined himself either needing or accepting. He knelt on the carpet, hugged his brother to him and cried onto his shoulder, as if this way he could shed all his fear and anguish, or at least share it. For perhaps five minutes they remained like this, Bobby patting his back, murmuring soothing words.

Mirren pulled away, found Bobby's hand. He signed, *I have Heine's disease, Bobby.*

His brother slowly shook his head. "Ralph... I'm sorry."

Bobby reached out, then, like a blind man, found Mirren's face with his fingers and cupped his cheek in the palm of his hand, soothing him.

It isn't contagious. I can't pass it on.

Bobby merely shook his head.

The medic gave me about four, five years. I... He stopped there, unable to go on. He choked back a sob, glad that Bobby could not hear or see him.

He gathered himself, and with determination signed, *I'm frightened. I realise that even the life I've lived for the past ten years is preferable to no life at all.*

"Ralph..." Tenderly, Bobby swept his hand through the hair on the side of Mirren's head, staring into his face so that tomorrow he could look upon him.

"I wish there was something I could do to make you feel better, Ralph."

Mirren wiped his tears. The very act of telling Bobby of his fear, of communicating his anguish, had had the strange effect of muting it, making it manageable.

Mirren smiled into his brother's unseeing eyes. "Talking to you has helped a lot, Bobby," he said.

They held each other for long minutes.

At last, Mirren signed, *You don't fear death?*

Bobby shook his head. "No, I don't. I believe – no, I *know*, that another life, another existence, awaits us. I wish I could somehow let you experience my certainty..."

Mirren recalled what Dan had made him promise that morning. He signed, *But what if death came tomorrow, next week? Don't you need time to prepare yourself?*

Bobby smiled. "I am prepared, Ralph. I've been prepared for the past ten years."

Then, Mirren almost told Bobby about Hunter's promise of the flux, but he stopped himself. For all his acceptance of his brother's belief, he could not bring himself to allow Bobby to throw away his life. He knew that it would be what Bobby wanted, and he felt guilty denying him his chance to flux – but his own stubborn inability to believe, or rather his own belief that *this* was the only reality – just would not let him tell Bobby about Hunter and the mission.

"Ralph... come and see me more often, okay? It's not always easy for me to find you." He smiled. "We should talk more. We've a lot to catch up on."

Mirren nodded, despite the futility of the gesture. He signed, *We'll do that, Bobby. I'm going to get some sleep now. I'm tired.*

"You sure you're okay? You don't need anything?"

I'm fine. I just need some rest.

He squeezed Bobby's hand, stood and walked wearily to the door. He watched Bobby as he leaned over the armchair and picked up one of his Braille books. For all the limitation of his circumscribed world, Bobby was free as he'd never known anyone to be. As he left the room he felt an odd mixture of delight for his brother, and an inescapable envy of such certainty.

He went to the kitchen and pulled an ice-cold beer from the cooler. He opened the bottle, sat down and absently massaged the back of his neck. He'd been half aware of the pulsing headache for the past few hours.

He was finishing the beer when the vid-screen chimed. Carrying the bottle, he moved to the lounge and turned on the screen. He heard his own recorded voice say, "I'm either out or busy right now. If you'd like to leave a message..."

The screen flared and Mirren saw Caroline, her lips twisted in a characteristically exaggerated frown. On impulse, without really knowing why, he reached out and accepted the call.

Caroline blinked. "Oh, there you are. I was just about to cut off. You know how I hate talking to myself." She smiled out at him. "But you've probably forgotten that by now..."

Mirren sat down. "No, actually, I do remember. You didn't like talking to yourself, or to me when I wasn't listening..."

"And you did a lot of that, Ralph. Especially-" She stopped herself.

Mirren said, "How can I help?"

"I called to see if you were doing anything tonight. I thought... I wondered if you might like to go out for a meal?"

His first impulse was to think of an excuse. He stopped himself. Caroline had, after all, gone to the trouble of calling him. The least he could do was to be civil.

"Sure, why not–"

Carrie stared. "You're sure? You really mean it?"

"I'm sure I'm sure. I'd like a meal. I need to go out."

"Fine. How about the Blue Shift? Around eight?"

"Fine I'll see you there."

Caroline smiled again, cut the connection.

Immediately, Mirren wondered if the only reason he had agreed to seeing her tonight was that he knew he would be fluxing again very soon? There was no danger of emotional involvement because soon there would be the greater attraction of the flux...?

He left the lounge. On the way to his room, he paused and tossed the empty beer bottle towards the waste-chute in the kitchen. It sailed through the air, and in that fraction of a second his vision fractured. He flashbacked–

HE WAS ABOARD the *Perseus Bound* as the 'ship phased prematurely from the *nada*-continuum, hit the turbulent upper atmosphere of Hennessy's Reach and began to break up. The ugly double note of the emergency klaxon screamed through the corridors and lounges – a heart-stopping noise every spacer prayed they would never hear. In the engineroom, Mirren and Leferve hauled Elliott from the flux-tank, strapped her into her pod and secured themselves. Mirren felt the safety harness grip him as his weight shifted with the pitch of the 'ship. He closed his eyes. The bigship rolled onto its side, wracked by a bone-shaking vibration as it tore through the planet's atmosphere. He had never before been aboard a 'ship which, designed for continuum flight, had phased-in early and attempted to ride a gravity well – and as he lay in his pod, every muscle in his body clenched in fear and apprehension, he was aware of the bigship's disintegration. Screams of tortured metal filled the engineroom and muffled explosions communicated themselves through the superstructure as they plummeted towards the planet's surface. Mirren imagined the great auxiliary engines and exterior observation bays coming away and spinning off in the slipstream.

"It's coming apart at the seams!" someone cried. "We don't stand a chance!"

"Be quiet, Elliott," Fekete commanded with impeccable calm. "I actually think the pilot's doing an amazing job. Does anyone know his name?"

"Kaminski," Olafson said through gritted teeth.

"Then Kaminski should be awarded a medal for holding on so long – posthumous, of course."

"Fekete," Mirren yelled. "Just shut it!"

The chaos was accentuated by an electrical fault. The lights dimmed and flickered in synchronicity with a series of explosions which bucked the 'ship throughout its length.

Mirren thought that Leferve, laid out beside him, was humming; no – the continuous, low note was a religious chant. Elliott began gibbering again. Mirren warned her to shut it, or face the consequence of physical violence; which prompted the wry observation from Fekete that he hoped he would be around to watch the fight.

It came to Mirren in an inspired moment of calm reflection that, after all, this was not so bad a way to die: there was a certain irony in the fact that this would have been his and his teams' last flight anyway. He'd often dreaded, since learning that the Canterbury Line was closing down, the prospect of life without the flux. Now his fear was academic.

The *Perseus Bound* hit something – it could only be the ground – and broke up in a series of impacts. He heard multiple explosions, and flaring, actinic bursts of fire seared his exposed flesh. Before he could conceive of being incinerated he was knocked out by a shock wave.

When he came to his senses he was amazed to find himself still in one piece and strapped into his pod.

More amazing still was the absolute calm.

The other pods, arranged around the systems-column like petals, seemed to be intact too. The engine-room had been sheered clean in half, affording a view of the jungle and the main body of the 'ship some distance away. The *Perseus* lay broken-backed in the pit of its own ploughing, ablaze and further torn apart by secondary explosions. The vegetation on either side not destroyed by the crashlanding was alight and burning like an avenue of torches.

Mirren experienced ten seconds of inertia, during which he could do nothing other than marvel that he was still alive. Then he rapidly unfastened himself from the harness. "Dan? Caspar?"

"Well, I must admit this is a surprise," Fekete commented.

Dan was still chanting his mantra.

Elliott and Olafson replied that they were okay.

Mirren pushed himself from the pod and staggered to the jagged edge of what once had been the deck. The engine-room was lodged on a jackstraw arrangement of fallen tree trunks. The heat from the burning wreckage swept over him in a wave. Overhead, unfamiliar constellations burned in an indigo sky.

He returned to the systems-column. From a storage unit he retrieved the distress beacon and emergency supplies and crouched beside the opening. Using the tree trunks as an impromptu stairway, he made his way down to the jungle floor, stood and surveyed the remains of the bigship. At intervals between the larger chunks of wreckage, small parcels of blackened carcasses, some with their extremities still glowing, smoked in the humid night air. The clearing was filled with the stink of cooking flesh. Mirren made a cursory tour of inspection through the red hot wreckage, looking for survivors but knowing that the chances of finding any were remote. He recalled the sight of the hundreds of civilian passengers boarding the 'ship from the terminal on Xyré, and the faces of the dead returned to him.

He entered the details of the crashlanding and the number of survivors into the distress beacon, then launched it into the alien sky. He watched it trail a long, fiery parabolic wake, until it was just another star overhead.

The others had unstrapped themselves and climbed down. Fekete was picking through the debris with what looked like disdain, his natural arrogance shaken and reduced to a fastidious appraisal of the fate which had befallen them. Dan joined Mirren and stared at the wreckage. Olafson sat on a nearby log and massaged her shoulder. Some distance away, Elliott wept and vomited.

"Dan, go get the navigator. Let's find out where the hell we are."

"What do you think happened, boss?" Fekete asked. Mirren always thought he detected a note of insubordination in Fekete's use of the honorific.

"We crashed," he replied.

"What an appropriate way of ending our time as E-men," Fekete went on. "I for one will certainly never forget it."

"Fekete," Mirren warned. "Just shut it, okay? This tour of duty isn't over yet, and until it is you're still under my command – got that?" He stared at the Nigerian until Fekete turned away.

Then, the vision became distant, began to fade–

He was back in the hallway of his apartment. The beer bottle completed its flight towards the wastechute and rattled through the swing lid.

He moved to his room and sat on the edge of the bed, fumbled three sleeping pills into the palm of his hand, and washed them down with a tumblerful of stale water.

He remained sitting for a long while, going over the events of the day. He considered the promise of the flux, and tried to persuade himself that four years was a long time, really.

Chapter Fifteen

Twenty-four hours ago Bobby had turned his armchair to face the window, then sat and stared straight ahead – seeing not the night-time scene of Paris, but the Network Francais nine o'clock documentary about Mars which he had 'watched' on the vid-screen the day before. Now, as nine o'clock approached, he turned his chair and settled himself before the window, and seconds later his time-lapsed vision swung to show him yesterday evening's twilight descend on the city. His physical circumstances and visual vector were synchronised. He stared out across the roof-tops, south towards the bright blue light of the interface at Orly, the scene interrupted momentarily by his fraction-of-a-second blinks of a day ago. He reached out and touched the window sill, felt the ripple-effect of the ill-applied paint beneath his fingertips. It was a strange sensation still, after all these years, to be able to see something, actually touch it, feel its detail with his fingers while his vision corroborated that detail, but be unable to see his hand, his fingers: it was as if his physical reality had been edited out of existence, as if he were already halfway towards absorption into the *nada*-continuum.

He sat back in his seat and stared at the delayed scene his senses were relaying to him, the opposite buildings and the skyline beneath the indigo night. He thought about Ralph, and their conversation that morning. He experienced a pang of intense sadness for his brother. More than anything he wanted to find some way to convince Ralph of the truth, of the fact of continued existence after this one. He recalled a period about five years ago when Ralph had seem particularly down; Bobby had made enquiries through his contacts in the Church – the communications laborious and complex because of his condition – and tried to hire flux-time from a pusher for his brother. His contacts had come up with nothing, and Bobby had consoled himself with the fact that Ralph had pushed bigships for ten years, experienced the rapture of the flux, without succumbing to belief, so who was to say that the experience of the flux now would be any different?

Bobby considered trying again. Even if it didn't bring about the desired belief in his brother, it might make his day to day life worth living, help take his mind off the fact of his illness.

Yesterday at this time, Bobby had closed his eyes, anticipating that his future self would have had quite enough of the scene beyond the window. He had been right. He felt relief at the advent of darkness. In one hour he would go to bed and sleep, as he did every evening at ten-thirty. In the meantime he emptied his mind, abandoned his thoughts, memories, anxieties – allowed his concern for Ralph to slip from his consciousness with the reminder that, in essence, nothing of this realm mattered, that it was just a passing show, that emotions were no more than the excess baggage of the ego. Having done this, he concentrated even harder on washing from his mind the actual thought that nothing mattered. Eventually he bordered on a trance-state, and gradually he attained the peace of mind he had achieved during his last shift in the flux-tank. He felt the joyous unburdened essence of the continuum around him, though without quite the intensity or the rapture he would have had experienced when fluxing. What he felt now was a second best, but a state nevertheless for which he was profoundly grateful.

On the edge of his consciousness he could hear – no, feel, think, somehow *sense*, the calling... the desire of the intelligence, which he had intuited in his last flux, for him to conjoin with the sublime, the infinite continuum.

For an eternal moment, Bobby hovered between this reality and the next.

Quite suddenly he was pitched from his trance. One second he had awareness of the *nada*-continuum, and the next that contact was broken. At first he was disoriented; this had never happened before. Normally he found it difficult to maintain the level of concentration needed to remain in the trance-state, and usually returned to himself slowly to find that an hour or more had elapsed in what seemed like seconds.

This time the transition was abrupt and wrenching.

Something touched his shoulder, and he realised that an earlier touch was what had interrupted his meditation. He felt something on his arm – the touch of a hand, firm but not rough.

Yesterday at this time he had still had his eyes shut. He was still in darkness, for which he was grateful. More hands held him, and he imagined the sensory confusion he would have suffered if his delayed vision had relayed to him an empty room.

The hands were trying to ease him from his chair.

No! he shouted, unable to hear himself. *What do you want?*

Not for ten years had he experienced the touch of another human being other than that of his brother. Now he felt the touch of hands on his shoulders and arms. The sudden intimacy of the unexpected assault filled him with an overwhelming fear.

No!

He struggled; still in darkness, he twisted and writhed. Strong arms clamped his arms and legs, and he felt a disconcerting buoyancy as he was hoisted from his chair and carried through the air.

Bobby screamed in silence.

His yesterday-self had chosen that moment to open his eyes, rise from his chair and walk towards the door. Bobby felt sick with the resulting disorientation. In real-time he was being borne from the room, kicking and struggling, by perhaps four or five men – judging from the restraining holds on his arms and legs – while his vision relayed to him his sedate walk through the hall to the bathroom as he had prepared for bed last night.

He could feel himself being carried along in a hurry, his abductors turning from his room, then moving from the hall into the elevator: with a flailing right hand he struck the plastic interior of the lift cage. The forward motion stopped, but the hold on him was still as strong. He gave up his struggle and felt a belly-lurching sensation as the lift dropped. Visually, he was watching his toothbrush rise to his mouth, and a second later he tasted the sour tang of the mint toothpaste. He had closed his eyes yesterday while doing this, and now he experienced a blessed period of darkness accompanied by the sound of his electric toothbrush and running water.

The lift hit bottom and he was carried out. He could feel the bounce of footsteps, the rush of warm air against his skin as he was taken into the street. He hoped that a passer-by might see what was happening, raise the alarm – or better still that a passing cop patrol might apprehend his abductors. But he knew the chances were slim. Few citizens would be out after dark, and cops rarely patrolled this district.

He was lowered to the ground, stood on his feet. Powerful hands ensured he could not move, then forced him forward. A hand on his head pushed him down and someone lifted first his right leg and then his left. He sat down, feeling the cushioned interior of a vehicle. Evidently he was on the back seat, as he could feel the solid bulk of people on either side of him. He was strapped in. Hands still held his arms.

He was shaking with terror. He tried to concentrate, to rid his mind of the knowledge of what was happening. He told himself that it did not matter, that, even if they intended to kill him, then all he would have to withstand would be the pain – a small price to pay for admittance into the continuum.

He felt an intense yearning for his brother, the desire to hold Ralph and tell him that he was okay, that, whatever happened to him, he should not worry.

The vehicle rose, lurched and tipped its passengers to the right, then sped off through the night. They were taking him somewhere in a flier.

"What are you doing with me?" he asked. He was aware that his words would sound slurred, that even Ralph had difficulty sometimes in making out what he said.

He felt a breath on his cheek – as someone shouted at him? Didn't they even know about his condition?

"Who are you?" he asked.

At that moment, his vision returned. He was leaving the bathroom, crossing the hall, returning to his room. He tried to recall what he had done last night, if he had gone straight to bed, in which case he would soon have the consolation of darkness again.

He watched as his hands undressed himself, carefully folded his silversuit and laid it on the chair next to his bed. He reached out, found the bed-side lamp, and switched it off. Darkness descended, the only illumination the moonlight falling through the window. His vision swung as he climbed into bed, laid back and stared at the ceiling. Yesterday at this time he had been watching and listening to a news bulletin from the night before.

Then he closed his eyes, and now he was encapsulated in total darkness.

"Where are you taking me?"

Someone took his right hand. He felt a finger trace patterns on his palm. So used was he to Ralph's sign-language that it was some time before he understood the form of this communication. He had been expecting something more complex, not the rudimentary sketching of letters on his palm.

He missed the first part of the message. Then, N-O-T-W-O-R-R-Y.

A pause.

W-E-A-R-E-F-R-I-E-N-D-S.

Another pause.

N-O-H-A-R-M-Y-O-U.

His hand was released.

He was aware of the increased beat of his heart. Could he trust these people? Wouldn't even killers reassure him thus, to prevent his struggling?

The flier banked. He tipped in his seat, came up against the solid shoulder of someone to his left. He felt a hand on his upper-arm, almost gentle. He told himself not to worry.

He realised, then, that he *was* worrying – but not for himself. He wanted to reassure Ralph that everything was okay.

The flier landed smoothly. The vibration that had shaken the vehicle now ceased. Bobby felt movement beside him, hands on him again. He was assisted from the flier. He passed into the warm night air. Hands on his arms and shoulders guided him at walking pace along what seemed, by their uneven surface, to be cobble-stones. They paused. His leg was lifted, then the other – onto a step? Again, and again. He got the message, and lifted his feet himself up a long, seemingly never ending, flight of steps.

They entered a building – he could tell by the sudden absence of breeze, the cool quality of the air. He was walked straight forward, and then right, and left, forward again. The hands guiding him were gentle, solicitous.

"Where is Ralph?" he asked. "Please tell me where I am? I want to see him!"

No reply.

They paused briefly, then set off again, this time up an incline. The texture of the surface beneath his feet underwent a change. He had been walking on what felt like stone or concrete, now he felt gridded metal underfoot. Its patterning was incredibly familiar.

Fernandez!

He could not believe it. He was escorted forward, then right. He stood on a metal disc with just one other person. They rose, his stomach lurching with the ascent. Then forward, and right, along a carpeted surface. Right again. He could sense by the atmosphere around him that he was in a small, enclosed space.

The hand released its grip on his upper arm.

Bobby stood in the darkness, heart beating wildly, hardly daring to believe where he was – where he *thought* he was. What could it mean?

He held out both arms, took a step forward. His fingers came up against a wall, its surface familiar. He turned to the left, his fingers tracing the shape of the enclosing walls. He found the oval indentation and knew it for a viewscreen.

To his left, if he were correct, would be a bunk, beside it a hammock sling. He moved to his left, sat down abruptly on the mattress.

Why? Why had they brought him here?

He could not believe it, but it was true.

He was in the cabin of a smallship.

Chapter Sixteen

Mirren arrived early at the Blue Shift restaurant-cum-cabaret club. The place brought back memories. Years ago he'd come here to wind down at journey's end. He had never really thought about why it was so popular with Enginemen and -women, but now he realised that the clientele, far from needing a complete change of ambience on their return home, had required familiar surroundings to ease them back into the routine of Earth. Then, as now, it was fitted out in a series of individual dining-booths simulating the lounges, rest-rooms and observation cells of bigships. The semi-circle of open-ended units, like display modules in some vast habitat emporium, faced a circular dance-floor. Beyond was the raised platform where a band played slow music.

He ordered a second lager and sat back in the comfort of the U-shaped couch. That morning he'd fallen asleep with his head full of the fact that he was dying, and the first thing that had come to him on awakening this evening, swooping down to cloak his thoughts in darkness, was the spectre of his illness. It was ironic that, just as he had been promised the chance to flux again, he should be struck down with Heine's. Still, it could have been worse: he could be dying without the promise of the flux to ease his passing. He recalled what Hunter had told him, that after the mission the smallship would be theirs. The thought of being able to flux for four or five years was a great comfort. He considered Bobby, and his inability to tell him about the mission. Maybe later, he thought, when we have the 'ship; maybe I'll be able to tell him then, grant him his desire to achieve the ultimate union he so believes in.

He glanced at his watch. Caroline was fifteen minutes late. He smiled to himself at the thought that she might have stood him up. He drank his lager and watched the choreographed movements of the dancers on the floor, turning to the music like tesserae in a kaleidoscope.

Five minutes later Caroline edged her way around the dance-floor. She saw him and pulled a face expressing her effort at side-stepping through the close-packed bodies. She was wearing a black bolero jacket, tight black leggings and boots. She'd had her hair cut even shorter since yesterday and bleached gold. Facially, she was very much as he remembered her from twenty years ago. He tried to recall what he'd felt for her back then. He must have loved her – whatever that meant – but all he experienced now at the sight of her was a vague familiarity, a few memories dulled by the years and the flux.

He decided to say nothing to her about his illness. He didn't want her sympathy.

"Ralph. Sorry I'm late." She slipped into the booth across from him. "Been here long?"

"About two lagers. Can I get you a drink?"

"The same. One at a time, though."

She watched him seriously as he press-selected a lager from the table-top menu. Thirty seconds later a waiter deposited it before her. Caroline took a sip. Mirren felt himself withdraw, become an observer of the situation.

"I was surprised that you agreed to meet me, Ralph."

Mirren shrugged. He could hardly tell her that he had been as surprised as her. He'd felt guilty about Bobby at the time, which probably explained it.

"You were so bloody distant yesterday–"

"What did you expect? You turn up after twenty years, breeze in..."

"You acted as if I was about to shoot you for walking out."

He grunted a laugh. "I wouldn't have blamed you." He told himself not to be so self-piteous.

She took another sip of lager, quirked her lips at its bitterness. "By the way, what did that off-worlder want yesterday?"

The question took him by surprise. "Oh... he was an old colleague from the Line. He looked me up for old time's sake."

"With two bodyguards?" She sounded sceptical.

"He's a big name in banking now. He's guarded all the time."

Caroline looked at him. He recalled what she'd said yesterday about being able to detect lies. She obviously decided not to press the issue. "Hey, I'm famished. Shall we eat?"

They press-selected their orders from the panel in the table-top, and seconds later the food issued from a slot in the wall just as meals had aboard the 'ships all those years ago. It even came in compartmentalised trays, producing in Mirren the comfortable feeling of nostalgia and anticipation. Unlike the food at the Gastrodome, this was cheap. To Mirren's surprise it was also good.

As Caroline finished her starter, she said, "By the way, I remembered those photos of Susan I told you about."

Mirren smiled. He'd rather she hadn't. He wondered if she was intentionally trying to make him feel guilty.

She took a stack of a dozen pix from the pocket of her jacket and slid them across to him. He pushed his plate away, went through the snaps one by one.

They showed an anonymous, tall, tanned and blonde Australian girl in her early twenties, smiling in all the shots: in one she was wearing the uniform of the KVO Martian division, in another a ski-suit, Another pix showed her on a beach with someone who was, presumably, her boyfriend.

Mirren recalled the baby he'd left in Sydney.

He tried to feel something, some vestige of the love he must once have felt, or failing that some paternal feelings – but he felt nothing, he admitted; not even guilt.

He returned the pictures to Caroline, who had been watching him closely. "You don't want to keep one?"

He tried to seem enthusiastic as he selected a picture: Susan, skiing on Mars.

"I heard from her last night, Ralph. She's visiting me in just over a month. She asked if I was in contact with you."

Mirren could not help but feel that Susan would be bitterly disappointed when she finally met him. "A month? That's great. We'll go out somewhere together."

Caroline smiled unsurely, pushed her plate to one side. "Ralph, I lied yesterday when I said I didn't come to Paris intending to look you up."

Mirren felt something heavy plummet within him. Please, he wanted to tell her, don't let me hurt you again.

He avoided her gaze.

She went on, "After my husband died... I got to thinking about us. We never gave it a chance – *you* never gave it a chance. I decided to come here and see what you were doing. Look, I don't mean I necessarily want us to get back together, but..." She shook her head.

There was a long silence.

"You're not the man I married, Ralph. You've changed a lot, lost something. That might have been the flux... I believe what you told me yesterday, about the flux. I know you aren't to blame. The very fact that you've had no-one since leaving..."

Mirren picked though his meal. He didn't want her sympathy, her spurious attention on the rebound from her dead irrigation scientist.

"What do you feel about it?"

He looked up. "About what?"

"What do you think?" She sounded exasperated. "Us!"

Carrie, he wanted to tell her, I'm dying and I've been promised the chance to flux again... Instead he just shook his head, folding and refolding his napkin and avoiding her stare.

"I don't mean we should get back together again, okay? But there's no reason why we can't meet occasionally, get to know each other again. No commitment, just friendship?" She reached across the table and took his hand. "I need someone, Ralph, and for chrissake so do you."

He wanted to tell her that he needed no-one. "I see no reason why we can't meet socially," he said awkwardly. He saw the pity in her eyes and it burdened him.

They finished the meal in silence.

When Mirren next looked up, Caroline was staring across the dance-floor towards the bar. Her expression hovered between suspicion and alarm.

"What's wrong?"

"Nothing," she smiled brightly. "Have you finished? I feel like a long walk."

She paid quickly, inserting her card in the table-top slot before he had the chance to argue. "Come on."

Her haste to be away surprised him. "How about another drink?" The alcohol was nicely dulling his senses.

"No, let's get out of here. Follow me."

She stood and side-stepped from the booth. She took his arm in what would seem to observers like an amorous embrace: she almost dragged him around the edge of the dance-floor towards the main exit. Then, without warning, she steered him quickly through a pair of black-painted fire-doors. He was surprised by her strength.

"What–?"

"Run!" They were in a dim corridor. Mirren ran. Caroline, ahead of him, burst through a second pair of fire-doors. They emerged in a darkened alley.

"Where's your flier?"

"Ah... in the central dome. I came by taxi."

"Shit!"

"What is it?"

She pulled him by his arm and ran along the cobbled alleyway. "You were being targeted. A dozen street thugs. They were watching you."

Mirren felt a hot flush of disbelief, then fear. "*Me?*"

"What did that off-worlder character really want, Ralph?"

Behind them, an explosion shattered the quiet night, echoing deafeningly between the narrow alley walls. Mirren looked over his shoulder. A hole gaped in the brick wall of the nightclub. Six thugs leapt through. They knelt amid the tumble of bricks and aimed their weapons. Caroline dragged him to the ground. He heard the air shriek as projectiles sliced overhead, tracer indicating their vector. Caroline pulled a small pistol from her jacket and returned fire. She pulled Mirren upright and hissed, "Run. Turn left at the end!"

She was kneeling, her pistol held in both hands at arm's length, spitting fire. The thugs took cover behind the fallen masonry. Mirren ran, turned the corner and leaned against the wall, panting with a combination of exhaustion and fear. Caroline joined him, tearing round the corner as if all the hounds of hell were on her heels. "Christ, Ralph. You know how to make enemies. These jokers mean business."

The alley terminated in a T-junction with a wider street. Twenty metres to the right was an intersecting main road, full of bright light and pedestrians. To the left, the street descended into shadows and a tangle of alien greenery.

"This way," Caroline said. They sprinted into that section of the street taken over by the alien jungle, Mirren anticipating the lancing pain of bullets between his shoulder blades at any second. Their footfalls no longer rang on the metalled surface; vegetation provided a treacherous carpet underfoot, and overhead the night sky was hidden by a canopy of leaves and vines. A quiet calm closed in around them, reassuring Mirren that the thugs would give themselves away by the sound of their pursuit. At the same time, now that his initial shock at the attack had worn off, it came to him how close he had been to death – and that without Caroline the thugs would have killed him with ease.

If he was being attacked because of his involvement with Hunter... then what about the rest of his team? Dan and Fekete and the others?

Caroline was jogging ahead of him, her breath coming easily. Her whole attitude cried out resolve and Mirren almost wept with gratitude.

She pulled up, placed a hand on his arm for him to hush. She looked back the way they had come, a tunnel forced through the jungle by those who had passed this way before them. Then Mirren saw their footprints in the slime that covered the street, indicating their whereabouts like so many tell-tale arrows. Caroline noticed his panic and smiled. "Do exactly as I say, Ralph. Find the shop-fronts and backtrack fifty paces. Then stop and wait for me?"

"Where you going?"

"I'll be with you in one minute."

He forced his way through the tangle of vines and creepers, barbed brambles catching his hair and flying suit. In the semi-darkness he collided with the wall of the shop-front, and looked back. Caroline was forcing a path through the undergrowth up ahead, creating a decoy trail.

He headed back down the street, squeezing between the brick wall and the vegetation that had adhered to it for years. He counted out approximately fifty paces, then halted and waited for Caroline. He felt vulnerable without her, an easy target. A tangle of foliage closed around him. There was no sound of the thugs; the only noise was the churring of some insect nearby, and the pounding of his heart. The air was humid, rank, and he was soaked in sweat. He told himself that it would be too much to hope for that the thugs had given up their pursuit. He thought of Dan, Fekete, and the others, and he hoped in desperation that the thugs – if they were indeed going after his team – were doing so one by one, and that he was number one on their hit list.

He had to survive in order to warn the others.

Someone grabbed his elbow. His heart lurched and he almost shouted out.

"Ralph!" Caroline hissed. "Follow me!"

She pushed him into the darkened doorway of what had once been a chemist's shop, a cubicle of space that the jungle had not invaded. Caroline forced the door and stepped through. Mirren followed her into the gloom of the interior. The only illumination was a shaft of moonlight falling through a high window overhead. Caroline indicated a door and they crossed to it, their footsteps cracking glass. They passed through a back room and Caroline led the way to a low window. She kicked glass shards from the rotting frame and high-stepped through with pantomime care. Mirren followed her actions like a shadow. The street outside was a replica of the one they'd left. They fought their way through the obstructing vegetation and crossed the street to a facade of shop-fronts opposite, found a gaping door and entered. They hurried through the fusty, rat-infested building and once more came out into a jungle-choked thoroughfare. Again they cut across the street, through the undergrowth, and climbed through the window of a derelict boutique.

There was a gaping hole in the dividing wall. They passed through it into another abandoned shop. A series of doorways gave access along the entire row. Mirren followed Caroline at a jog. It was obvious by the degree of light entering the succeeding rooms from outside that they were leaving the over-run district behind them. They entered a boarded-up mini-market and Caroline crouched against the wall, sitting on her heels. Mirren joined her. "What now?"

"We wait. We might've lost them for a while if they followed my track along the street."

"And if not?"

Caroline just shook her head. She turned to look at him. "They're connected, aren't they? That Hunter guy and all this. What the hell's going on, Ralph?"

He shook his head. "I honestly don't know."

"You aren't telling the truth, Ralph."

Mirren was taken by the sudden need to confide in Caroline; he'd told no-one about what was happening, and he thought that by doing so he might, himself, come to some understanding. He was about to tell Caroline about Hunter's offer when the deafening crump of an explosion devastated the silence.

"Christ, they really mean to finish you off." For the first time, Mirren heard fear in her voice.

She stood and moved to the boarded-up window, prised back a plank and peered through. A lighted shop-front plunged a beam of illumination into their bolt-hole. Caroline crept back to his side. "They've got a guy posted across the street," she reported calmly.

His pulse surged. "They know we're here?"

"I think they've got the whole area staked out." She thought for a second. "Okay, this way." She all but dragged him down an aisle between emptied food racks and old freezer units. They entered a storeroom. Caroline looked around, then crawled through an air-conditioning duct in the far wall. She reached back for Mirren and he scraped himself through head first. She helped him to his feet and he stood, panting. Her expression was grim. "Look," she said.

Mirren could do little else but look. A metre before his eyes was a curving silver surface. It took him seconds to realise that it was the outer membrane of the dome which enclosed the cultural heritage of central Paris, effectively blocking their flight.

Caroline stood with both feet on the curve of the dome, her back braced against the wall. She edged along, foot over foot, came to the end of the building and peered down the street, then returned to Mirren, fast. Her eyes were wide with alarm. "There's about a dozen of the bastards coming down the street." She banged a heel against the silvered surface of the dome. "I could always blast our way through – but they'd soon find the hole and we'd be trapped in there."

Then she saw the inspection hatch five metres to the left. She moved towards it, feet crossing, and Mirren hurriedly followed. The hatch was an oval doorway set into the base of the dome, secured by a finger-print access lock. Without ceremony, Caroline aimed at the lock mechanism and fired once. The pistol spat and the lock disintegrated. She looked left and right to ensure they were unobserved and hauled the hatch open. She crawled through and Mirren ducked in after her, closing the hatch behind him.

The gap between the outer and inner membrane was less than one metre thick, a confined area of supporting girders and air treatment units. Mirren stood awkwardly, his belly and face pressed against the grime-encrusted plastex. It was suffocatingly hot and pitch black; the inner membrane was darkened in its nighttime phase, and the silver outer membrane admitted no light. Further up, where the artificial starfield began, the backwash of the individual halogens provided erratic illumination. The surface of the inner dome was patterned with regular, indented toe-holds allowing the inspectors and engineers to climb between the two great curving planes.

Caroline clutched his arm. "Up there, Ralph," she ordered. "I'll try to shoot a hole through the inner dome. With luck they'll think we went straight through."

Mirren climbed, finding the indents with difficulty. He pushed his way up, his progress impeded by loose hanks of wiring and the pipes of the air-conditioning which kept the precincts within the dome at a pleasant seventy degrees. He paused when he was a couple of lengths above Caroline and peered down. He could just make out her dark shape, spread-eagled between the planes. He heard two sharp shots. Caroline cursed aloud, tried again. Mirren was thankful that the outer membrane was silvered, so they were unobserved. He wondered how long it would be before the thugs noticed the damaged lock of the hatch.

He looked down, saw Caroline moving towards him up the recessed toe-holds. He felt her hand on his leg. "No good, Ralph. The stuff's reinforced."

"Christ!" Mirren yelled. "We're trapped in here!"

"Just keep climbing."

The confined space became suddenly claustrophobic. The heat seemed to increase by twenty degrees. "Where to?"

She thumped his legs. "Just let me do the thinking, will you? Climb!"

As he moved further up the inside of the dome, the gap became narrower, as if the planes of reinforced plastex converged at the apex. Each step became an effort, the toe-holds harder to find, and his fingers ached from supporting his weight when his feet slipped. They entered the region of the starfield. Mirren tried to keep his mind from the terrible thought of being discovered like this by identifying the constellations. He calculated in which quarter of the city they were positioned, and the degree of their elevation, and then recalled the star-charts he'd studied years ago. He recognised Arneb in Lepus. Ahead was Rigel in Orion and beyond it Hatysa, a close-packed nebulosity. He recalled a time, fifteen years ago, when he'd vacationed on Brimscombe, Rigel II... Then he laughed aloud at the absurdity of his present situation. Behind him, Caroline grunted. "What's so funny, Ralph?"

He called, "I always thought I'd die between the stars..."

She hit the sole of his boot with her fist. "Very funny. Now will you hurry up?"

He climbed. His concentration on the stars was shattered when he heard a sound below him – the opening of a hatch. They'd finally found the shattered lock. He screwed himself round, peered down. Caroline was on her belly, reaching out. To her left, a circular hatch hung open, admitting a shaft of light and affording a view of the rooftops twenty metres below.

"Caroline?"

"Not this one, Ralph. Keep climbing."

As he did so, he noticed the outline of a hatch to his left. They were spaced at regular intervals beside the toe-holds, positioned to give access to the cables which connected the ersatz stars. He recalled seeing fliers hovering beneath the dome's inner surface, off-loading replacement parts and tools to mechanics inside. What he'd give for a friendly, passing flier right now...

He peered back at Caroline. She'd opened another hatch, letting it swing on its hinges as she poked her head over the side. She looked up at him. "Damn!"

"Caroline? What the hell...?"

"Your flier's somewhere down there, right?"

A light pressure of elation filled his chest at the thought – quickly chased by despair. "But how the hell do we get down!" he yelled.

"Leave that to me," Caroline said. "Keep climbing, Ralph. Hurry up!"

Something between desperation and an insane belief in the woman behind him spurred him on. He hauled himself past the imitation stars, his flying suit ripped and soaked in sweat. Below, he heard Caroline trying the hatches one by one.

Then he heard an animal cry, as if from far away, and the first tracer illuminated the gloom like orange lightning. He was thankful they that they were high enough to be out of sight of their pursuers, and the curve of the dome made a direct shot impossible. Then more orange tracer lit the darkness. More shouts as more thugs entered the inspection hatch and gave chase. Caroline cried out, "Ralph, stop!"

He'd already done so, in fright and desperation. He clung to the indents, awaiting the *coup de grace* as tracer and bullets filled the space with light and a ceaseless, deafening rattle. He turned his head as Caroline called to him again. She was no longer below him on the track of toe-holds. He caught sight of her to the right, clinging onto the rim of an open hatch and peering through. Her expression, illuminated from below, was joyous.

"Ralph!" she shouted.

He backtracked, edged down indent by indent, until he was beside her. He reached out, gripped the edge of the hatch and hauled himself across to her. The yells of their pursuers echoed in the confines.

Caroline stared into his eyes. "Jump, Ralph!" she cried. "Jump!"

Central Paris waited forty metres below.

"I'll kill myself!" he screamed.

She laughed. "Look, Ralph. Look straight down!"

Mirren hauled himself to the rim and peered over. His heart almost missed a beat. They were directly above the inflated mylar bubble of the Gastrodome.

"Jump! Your flier's down there somewhere. I'll cover you."

He manoeuvred himself so that his legs hung through the hatch.

Caroline turned onto her back and loosed off a fusillade of fire down the incline. "For chrissake, jump!"

She scrambled up beside him and hung her legs through the gap. Mirren looked at her. "What about you?"

She smiled, reached out and pushed him.

He plummeted feet first with a sudden cry of alarm.

He was aware of the cool rush of the air after the glasshouse humidity, and the sudden noise of traffic. He was falling belly first, spread-eagled. The great bauble of the Gastrodome accelerated towards him, its size increasing by the second. He steeled himself for the impact and when it came, taking him by surprise, it was like hitting the slack membrane of a trampoline. The mylar surface gave, accepting him, and he rolled over and over in a constant, moving depression down the side of the dome. He saw brief flashes of amazed expressions on the faces of the diners inside, then longer glimpses of the starfield above.

He fell the last five metres as the curve of the dome became sheer, landing on his knees in the tilled soil of an extraterrestrial flower exhibition.

He looked up. Caroline had jumped and was rolling down the dome. Seconds later she landed awkwardly beside him with a pained curse. She picked herself up, grabbed Mirren and sprinted through a dense plantation of miniature trees. Overhead, the thugs jumped from the inspection hatch one by one, like paratroopers tumbling from a plane. The first thug landed, perhaps thirty metres away, righted himself and looked around. Caroline dragged Mirren after her as they tore through the undergrowth.

They were on the periphery of the alien garden surrounding the Gastrodome. Before them was the iron fencing which separated the garden from a lighted avenue. Across the avenue was a possible way of escape: the darkened entrance of an alley between two tall buildings. Caroline vaulted the fence and Mirren followed, startling a group of passing tourists, and sprinted across the street and into the alley. As he ran after Caroline down the cobbled thoroughfare he realised he was limping. As they came to the end of the alley and paused before continuing into the busy street, he worried that their physical appearance might soon attract attention. Caroline's jacket and leggings and his flying suit were ripped and stained with mud and leaf mould.

"Where to now?" Caroline hissed, looking back along the thoroughfare. "Where's your flier?"

"This way."

They plunged into the crowded sidewalk, attracting stares and comments from passers-by. At the thought that the thugs might have posted lookouts, Mirren broke into a run.

They slowed as they passed the imposing facade of the *Nationale Bibliothèque*. They turned the corner into a deserted street. His flier was where he'd left it. He looked up and down the sidewalk. There was no one in sight. The hatch swung open on identifying his palm-print and Caroline scrambled inside. Mirren slumped into the driving seat, slammed the hatch shut and keyed the command to opaque the windows. The sense of relief filled him with an insane, light-headed elation.

Caroline sat with her head against the rest, eyes closed, breathing deeply.

Mirren gained his breath, adrenalised with a mixture of joy at having survived so far and a retrospective dread at how close they had been to death. The physical strain of the last hour was catching up with him, creating cramps in his legs and a stabbing pain in his solar plexus.

Caroline turned in her seat. Tears streaked her cheeks. She embraced Mirren, and he held her to him, feeling her warmth. They embraced for what seemed an age, silent in the aftermath of the chase.

"Where are you staying?" he whispered at last.

"The Excelsior, St Etienne. Come back with me. I don't know what's going on, but you can't go back to your own apartment–"

"I need to warn Dan and the others."

She stared at him with wide eyes. "Ralph, what's happening? You know, don't you?"

"I suspect," he answered. He hesitated. "Hunter wants us to push a 'ship. Me and my team. I suppose those bastards – or rather the people who hired them – don't want us to succeed."

Caroline was shaking her head. "So that's why..." she began. "I never had any chance against the flux, did I?"

Mirren felt emotion welling in his chest. He wanted to tell her not to blame him, that his motivations were no longer in his control, that he was craving the flux and would stop at nothing to get it. More than that he wanted to tell her not to make him choose between her and the flux.

"Take me to the Excelsior, Ralph."

She sat rigid and stared straight ahead.

Mirren fired the engines, crawled his flier from the kerb and along the street at walking pace, heading for the nearest vehicle exit.

Even at this early hour of the morning, there was still a line of vehicles, roadsters and fliers, waiting to be checked out. To his relief he saw no loiterers around the arched exit – just a bored gendarme perfunctorily glancing at proffered identity cards. When his turn arrived, Mirren showed his card and the official waved him through. He accelerated from the dome and into the skies of Paris, forced back into his seat with the thrust of his ascent.

He banked the flier into the western aerial lane, heading for St Etienne. They made the journey in silence; Mirren could not find the words to explain, to excuse himself. His inability to plead his case increased as the silence lengthened. He sighted the Excelsior hotel and decelerated, coming to rest gently on the landing stage. He thought Caroline intended to climb out without saying a word. She opened the passenger hatch, turned to him and said, "Ralph, go to the police, okay? You needn't tell them about the 'ship, just the attack. They'll give you protection. Failing that, I can give you the name of a private security firm.

"I'll go to the police," he lied.

Caroline smiled sadly. "I meant what I said earlier, about us. Even if it's only friendship..."

Mirren nodded.

"Take care, Ralph."

He watched her climb from the flier and run across the roof to the downchute cupola. He found himself sitting, gripping the wheel, wishing that he'd told her that the last thing he had wanted was to cause her pain. He stirred himself, engaged the vertical thrusters and banked rapidly away from the hotel, the lights of St Etienne falling away beneath him.

He headed north east, a sudden lethargy sweeping over him. At one point he caught himself considering making for his apartment... Then he knew that Caroline was right: he couldn't go back there. The thugs would surely have the block under surveillance on the off-chance that he was fool enough to return.

He brought his flier down in a lighted district a kilometre from Dan's Agency. He parked in the street next to a public vid-screen, climbed out and stepped into the booth. He keyed in Dan's code and waited as the call rang out, sensitive to the fact of every wasted second.

A minute, then two, passed without reply. He tried Dan's mobile, but again there was no answer. He stared at his flier, then along the empty street. He left the booth and made his way towards the Rue Bresson on foot, his pace increasing as he thought of Dan and the events of the night. He would wait in the street until Dan returned from wherever he was, and hope against hope that the thugs had not turned their attentions to the detective.

He turned onto a tree-lined boulevard and crossed the street diagonally, heading for the Rue Bresson two blocks further on. He was leaving a well-lighted district for the run-down area of Bondy. As he stepped onto the sidewalk beneath a line of linden trees, he was suddenly aware of footsteps behind him. He closed his eyes. He knew he'd been a fool. To survive death as he had, only to walk into it quietly on a darkened street...

It began to rain, a fine, tropical drizzle. He increased his pace. He was being paranoid, perhaps – the events of the past few hours lending him to easy fright. He chanced a glance over his shoulder. A rain-coated figure trailed him by a matter of metres.

He began to run. "Mirren!" his pursuer called. He heard footsteps, closing in on him. He turned and lashed out, and the figure launched itself at him and bundled him to the ground. His assailant drew something from his pocket and applied it to Mirren's chest, and he felt an electric jolt lance through his entire body.

He had no idea how long he was out. When he came to his senses he was still on the sidewalk, his mind a confusion of chaotic thoughts. Why had his pursuer not killed him on the spot? Unless he planned to torture him for information he thought he possessed... But why, then, had they tried to kill him earlier?

A roadster drew up, its tyres zipping on the wet road. A rear door swung open and his assailant bundled him inside. The door slammed shut. Mirren made out a dark figure in the rear seat beside him as the vehicle started up and drove off at speed.

CHAPTER SEVENTEEN

THE MERCEDES RACED through the rain-slicked Paris streets.

When Dan released him from the painful bear-hug, Mirren sank back into the padded upholstery and closed his eyes, disbelief and relief sweeping through him. He laughed aloud. "Christ, Dan. If you only knew what I've been through..."

"You? Fernandez, Ralph! What about me?"

"They came after you?"

Dan nodded. "But thanks to these gentlemen..." He indicated the two men in the front of the car. Mirren recognised Hunter's bodyguards. "They got me out minutes before my place was trashed by an air-to-ground missile." Dan hesitated. "You heard about the others?"

Mirren stared at him, shaking his head.

"Jan was shot dead last night. They fixed Caspar's flier sometime yesterday. He didn't stand a chance. They got Christiana the same way a couple of days ago."

Mirren watched the buildings blur by outside.

"How the hell did you get away from the Blue Shift?" Dan asked.

"You heard about it?"

"Heard about it? It was all over Paris in minutes. A vid-cast gave your description. I thought they'd got you."

Something caught in Mirren's throat. "I was with a security guard from Orly. I wouldn't have made it without her."

"Hunter stationed his men around my place in case you got away and decided to look me up. Thank Fernandez you didn't go back to your apartment. The bastards have it pretty well covered."

Mirren started. "What about Bobby?"

"Don't worry. He's safe."

Mirren let out a long breath. "So much for Hunter's assurance that this caper wouldn't be dangerous."

He noticed the bodyguards, in front, exchange a look and then turn their attention back to the road.

They were moving at speed along the Boulevard St Michel towards the Seine. "Where are we going?"

Dan turned to him, the great bush of his hair catching the light from the street-lamps outside. "We're meeting Hunter, Ralph. We're due to phase out in a little under three hours."

Mirren stared through the rain-beaded window at the passing city. After the adrenalin-charged last few hours, this news came as less of a surprise than an inevitability – a just reward for the rigours and hardships undergone. Mirren considered the flux, and the aches and pains of his body seemed to drain away, or rather lose significance beside the fact that soon he would be transcending such petty concerns as he mind-pushed the smallship through the *nada*-continuum.

He took Dan's arm in sudden panic. "Look, don't breathe a word to Hunter about the Heine's, okay? I don't want him to think I can't push."

Dan reassured him. "I won't say a thing, Ralph."

The Mercedes braked suddenly. They were on a cobbled plaza on the Left Bank. The bodyguards climbed out, withdrawing semi-automatic rifles from beneath their jackets. They slammed the front doors, stood beside the roadster and scanned the parking lot before opening the rear doors for Mirren and Dan.

They hurried across the cobbles to a boat-house beside the river. Over the water, Notre-Dame loomed magnificent and gothic against the deep blue light of dawn, its towers and spires dilapidated by years of neglect. The first bodyguard opened a small door in the side of the boathouse and they slipped inside, while the second brought up the rear and locked the door behind them. An ancient bulb snapped on, its sulphurous light revealing rotting wooden rowing-boats and the first bodyguard, hauling open a trap-door in the floor. They descended a flight of steep, narrow stairs until it seemed they were below the level of the river, then hurried for a hundred metres along a concrete corridor dank and dripping with foul-smelling water, their way patchily illuminated by a torch in the possession of the bodyguard behind them. Mirren followed Dan's bulking figure up a flight of steps identical to the first, then through another trap-door. They were in what might have been a wine-cellar or a tomb, its ancient stones scabbed with mould.

They were escorted through arched vaults and up a worn stone staircase, through a heavy timber door into a room that stank of mildewed velvet and damp paper. They passed cardboard cartons full of vestments and old hymn books, then through a door into a chapel.

Mirren slowed his pace and walked like a man in a daze from the side chapel and into the main body of the cathedral – where once the pious had congregated to worship, but which was filled now with technicians and scientists tending to the object of their devotion.

The silver smallship squatted in the vaulted nave, poised on its ram-jets with its nose in the air. It seemed larger than the average smallship – certainly larger than the 'ship the Disciples used as their Church – its bulk emphasised by the confining stonework. Around the 'ship, in recesses and niches between crypts and sarcophagi, technicians in casual dress supervised terminals and monitors. There were perhaps twenty men and women in the cathedral, going about their business oblivious of those who would soon be pushing the smallship. For the first time, Mirren was made aware of the scale and professionalism of the enterprise.

"How the hell did they get that thing in here?" Mirren asked.

"Bit by bit, Ralph. Then they rebuilt it *in situ*. Quite a beauty, isn't it?"

They walked towards the smallship and paused beneath its rearing nose-cone. A nameplate spanned the curve beneath the delta viewscreen: *The Sublime, the Infinite* – the name that believing Enginemen gave to the *nada*-continuum. As they stared up at the 'ship, the first light of dawn poured through a stained-glass window, laying a prismatic effect along its flank.

"What do you think of the hangar?"

"Magnificent," Mirren said. "Does the Pope know?"

Dan laughed. "Hunter bought the place when the Catholic church was having its sale of the century to finance the cathedral on Mars. It suited his purposes right down to the ground: big enough, secluded – once a place of religious observance. I was talking to Hunter earlier. Did you know he was a believer?"

"A Catholic?" Mirren was surprised; like most orthodox religions these days, Catholicism was in decline.

Dan smiled. "No, Ralph. He's a Disciple."

Before Mirren could register his surprise, a bodyguard approached. "Mr Hunter would like to see you. If you'd care to come this way."

They left the smallship and followed the bodyguard through a side chapel and into what once might have been a vestry. The room was furnished and decorated as luxuriously as any penthouse lounge, with thick carpeting, c-shaped settees and tables equipped with drinks. Hunter was not present. The bodyguard showed them to a settee, and for the first time since entering Notre-Dame Mirren realised how bedraggled he was, his flying suit stained with dirt and sweat.

Hunter entered as Dan was pouring a couple of brandies.

"I'll join you in one of those, Monsieur Leferve. I think this occasion deserves celebrating." He raised his glass. "You can't imagine how relieved I am to see you both fit and well."

He stood in the centre of the room, something confident and dominant in his stance – the entrepreneur about to realise an ambition. His disfigurement glowed ruby in the concealed lighting.

For the first time in hours, Mirren had a focus for his antagonism. He felt the brandy burn a path to his stomach. He said deliberately, "So much for your damned assurances, Hunter. I thought you said we'd be in no danger?"

Dan glanced at him, as if in warning.

Oddly, even as he addressed Hunter, Mirren felt treacherous. He was aware that some part of him considered the danger – and maybe even the deaths – worth the reward.

Hunter pursed his lips around a mouthful of brandy and considered his reply. "You might find this hard to believe, Mr Mirren, but I am confident that the killings of your ex-team, and the attacks on your two selves, had nothing at all to do with this project."

Dan glanced up from his drink. "It does seem a bit coincidental, doesn't it?"

"A *bit* coincidental?" Mirren laughed. "More like bloody obvious!"

"Gentlemen, I assure you that these deaths are in no way linked with the project. First, no one but myself, yourselves and Caspar Fekete knew anything about my offer. I told no one, and I presume that you didn't either–"

"We could have been observed at the Gastrodome the other night," Mirren pointed out.

"I made quite certain that no such thing could have occurred. We were not observed or overheard. I had men ensuring that our discussion was conducted in absolute privacy."

"But can you trust all of them?" Dan asked.

"Implicitly," Hunter said in a tone that brooked no argument. "And there is another reason why these deaths and my work are unconnected. Christiana Olafson was killed two days ago, the day before I approached you. No-one but myself knew my motives in contacting you and your team."

Mirren considered. "Olafson died in a flier accident," he said. "But what if it was just that, an accident? Whoever it is that wants us dead would then be spared the trouble of killing her, so they started on Elliott and Caspar."

Hunter was vigorously shaking his head. "I've had my people investigate that so-called accident. It was no accident. Olafson's flier was sabotaged. She was murdered a day before I approached you at Orly."

Mirren laughed without humour. "Then why has each member of my team been attacked, in three cases killed? Who the hell's doing this?"

Hunter gestured. "I wish I knew... I can only assure you that I have my best people working on it. I assure you also that the killings end here. In less than two hours you will no longer be on Earth." He consulted his wrist-watch. "*The Sublime* is about to undergo a test phase-out. Perhaps you would like to observe?"

They left the lounge, made their way through the chapel and into the main body of the cathedral. They halted beside a bank of computers. As they watched, a group of technicians walked up the ramp and entered the smallship. Behind the delta screen above the nose-cone, Mirren made out the figure of the pilot in the command web. The ramp lifted and became a seamless section of the 'ship's flank. A silence settled over the gathered scientists.

Mirren then experienced something deeply poignant and moving as, for the first time in ten years, he witnessed the miracle of phase-out. The smallship, a solid form just seconds before, gradually lost its definition, and faded. The carved knights and saints of the stonework could be seen through its outline; then it pulsed back again, only for it to diminish just as rapidly. For perhaps thirty seconds it shuttled back and forth between this reality and the *nada*-continuum, flickering like the image on a spinning coin. Throughout this process of displacement, the air was alternately sucked in and blown out of the space occupied, and then vacated by the 'ship, creating an eerie whistling sound effect in the cathedral's stonework. Mirren gasped for breath one second, and the next was battered by a raging gale.

Then the *Sublime* vanished with a disconcerting finality which left the eye searching for the 'ship in the middle distance and the senses wondering if it had ever existed. At this moment, *The Sublime, the Infinite* existed apart from the space-time continuum, its actuality translocated to the null-space of the *nada*-continuum. Mirren imagined it hanging becalmed, awaiting the mind-power of an Engineman to push it at ultra-light speed through infinite space.

Mirren looked at Dan and smiled, speechless in the aftermath of such wonder.

Minutes later, the 'ship made its re-entry into space-norm. The process of phase-in was identical to that of phase-out; the *Sublime* showed itself briefly, disappeared, appeared again and then flickered in and out of visibility until establishing its solidity in the nave of the cathedral.

Hunter was smiling to himself. He turned to Mirren and Dan. "Perhaps you would care to board the 'ship, gentlemen? I'll show you around and you can freshen up before phase-out."

The usual complement of Alpha Enginemen aboard a smallship was five, to allow for injuries, illness or just poor performance. The minimum number of Enginemen required for a run like this one, all the way out to the Rim, was three. As they walked towards the 'ship's ramp, Mirren turned to Hunter. "Have you arranged for a third Engineman?"

Dan glanced quickly at Hunter, who cleared his throat self-consciously. They had halted at the foot of the ramp, a tableau stiff with tension. Hunter said, "The third man is your brother."

Mirren shook his head. "I almost told him yesterday," he whispered. "Part of me wanted to. It would have been the right thing to do." He looked at Hunter. "But why Bobby? There's hundreds of other Enginemen in Paris–"

"Ralph," Hunter said, something like compassion in his tone. "This is very hard for me to explain, and even then I doubt you will be satisfied." He paused. "I was instructed by the people I am working for to ensure that Bobby Mirren pushed the *Sublime* from Earth out to the Rim – the choice of Enginemen to accompany him, as back-ups should anything happen to your brother in the tank, was left up to me. It seemed the obvious thing to do to hire you and your old team. I intended to approach you about Bobby before now."

"They want *Bobby* to push the 'ship?"

"I honestly don't know why. They were secretive as to their motives. There are many aspects of this mission that they could not trust me with, for fear of my being captured and interrogated. I am merely the middleman in this operation."

"Who are 'they'"? What do they know about Bobby, his illness?"

Hunter considered, his halved expression pained. "I am supposed to tell no-one about my employers," he said. "I know this might sound melodramatic, but I assure you that the consequences of the wrong people finding out would be catastrophic beyond your wildest imagining. You'll learn the reason for everything – my secrecy, why they need your brother – in due course. All I can beg of you is to trust me."

"But the flux might kill him..."

"I'm afraid that's a risk that must be taken."

Dan said, "Like I told you yesterday, Ralph, Bobby would want to flux."

"Where is he?" Mirren asked.

"In the 'ship." Hunter gestured up the ramp. "He knows nothing about the mission at the moment. We thought perhaps you might be able to tell him..."

Mirren closed his eyes. He considered everything Hunter had divulged, balanced the amount of trust the off-worlder required against the privilege of experiencing the wonder of the flux. He knew in his heart that he had to let Bobby flux, knew that Bobby would want nothing else, yet at the same time he balked at the thought of the oblivion to which he might be consigning his brother.

"Bobby is in one of the rear berths," Hunter said. "I'll take you."

Mirren allowed himself to be ushered up the ramp. They took the elevator pad to the 'ship's second level, then passed down a corridor between the half dozen berths, each comprising a comfortable bunk, a vid-screen, computer terminal and a viewscreen through which to watch the swirling cobalt void of null-space.

Hunter indicated the sliding door to Bobby's berth, then tactfully withdrew. Mirren stopped himself from knocking. He palmed the sensor. The door opened. He stood on the threshold, staring at his brother as he swung himself in the sling. He was wearing his customary Satori Line silvers, his hair as unruly as ever.

His expression appeared troubled.

He inclined his head. "Hello? Is someone there?"

Either a draft or the vibration of the opening door had alerted him. Although he could see no one now, he looked in the direction of his visitor, so he would be able to see that person tomorrow. "I know you're there," he said, panic in his tone.

Mirren stepped into the cabin, shutting the door behind him. He sat on the edge of the bunk, a matter of centimetres from his brother's swinging legs.

He reached out and touched Bobby's moccasin.

Instantly, Bobby proffered his hand. Mirren grasped it.

"Ralph! What's happening?" he said, his words slurred so that Mirren had difficulty making them out. "They drew letters on my hand to tell me that I was safe. Then they put me in here. It's the berth of a smallship, isn't it?"

Mirren signalled assent on the palm of Bobby's hand.

Bobby said, "What's happening, Ralph? Why did they bring me here?"

I don't know where to begin... They want you to push this 'ship, Bobby.

Bobby sat upright, suddenly animated. "Who are *they*?"

I don't know. The mission's fronted by an off-worlder called Hunter. We're going out to the Rim to bring back some people... I'm sorry, I honestly know no more than this. He paused there, considering. *I would have told you yesterday, when we spoke. I wanted to tell you, but at the same time... I don't want to see you kill yourself, Bobby.*

Bobby said, "I object to you using the word 'kill', Ralph. The word's meaningless. I would be giving myself to the flux. Giving myself gladly."

But can't you see – from my point of view you'd be risking your life?

"But from my point of view, Ralph, I wouldn't be. That's what matters, not your... your *guilt*."

Mirren looked up, into his brother's staring eyes. *What do you mean?*

"Ralph, Ralph... Do I really have to tell you? You're guilty that it was me who contracted Black's – not you, who'd pushed more 'ships for many more years than me. You're guilty that you can't find it in yourself to believe. You're even guilty that over the years we've drifted apart."

I'm sorry!

"Don't be. It was as much my doing as yours. You remember that old line about the Middle Way between emptiness and compassion? Well, I was never very hot on the second."

Mirren blinked away the tears. *You're not the only one...*

Bobby squeezed Mirren's hand. "Ralph," he said. "You're wrong to think that if I remained alive we might... I don't know – be as close as we were as kids. That's all in the past. We're as close *now* as we've ever been."

Mirren returned the pressure on his brother's hand.

"Ralph, if you didn't let me flux, if you denied me that, just think of the guilt you'd carry *then.*" He smiled. "So, are you going to let me join your team, or not?"

Mirren signed: *I don't really see how I can refuse.*

"Thanks," Bobby said. "You've made me very happy."

Chapter Eighteen

Ella surfaced from unconsciousness in gradual stages, sense by sense. She recalled the militia at her father's villa and the brutal attack. After that, she had a vague recollection of a hospital, an operating theatre, green-garbed military medics – like images from another life. At the same time she experienced a surge of paradoxical well-being that she did not understand.

She felt a cold, hard surface beneath her. The air was heavy with the rich stench of oil and petrol. She heard the occasional whine of an engine and the laboured *blatt-blatt-blatt* of a helicopter's rotor blades. She opened her eyes. High overhead was a lattice of grey girders supporting a sloping corrugated tin roof. To her right was a wall of expanded-concrete bricks, and to her left the cavernous expanse of an aircraft hanger. A dismantled flier stood at the far end of the chamber, before a tall sliding door.

She was amazed to find that she could sit up without difficulty. What had been the searing agony of bullet wounds and broken bones was now no more than a dull ache. She was wearing a pair of baggy green hospital trousers and her own red t-shirt. She slipped a hand underneath the waist-band, fingered the closed wound on the inside of her thigh. The shoulder of the t-shirt was holed where the bullet had entered and exited. She pulled down the collar and bared her shoulder, peering awkwardly at the stitched flesh, white against her olive tan. She rotated her arm. The joint was tender, but not painful. She touched the line of her jaw. In her memory it was the vicious kick to her jaw that had offended her, an act that seemed more vindictive than the impersonal round of rifle-fire. She opened and closed her mouth experimentally. Her jaw was tender, numb, but again there was no real pain.

She climbed to her feet, and only then noticed the manacle around her ankle. She was chained to a big iron ring bolted to the oil-stained concrete three metres away. Looking down each side of the hangar, she noticed at least two dozen similar shackles. She limped across to a barred window in the concrete-block wall, dragging the chain.

The flat tarmac of a military airbase extended for kilometres. A line of palm trees marked the perimeter. Beyond, low foothills undulated on the horizon. Ella guessed they were the beginnings of the Torreón mountain range, and that she was being held at the Marquez airbase, about a hundred kilometres south of Zambique City.

The base was intermittently busy, transport helicopters taking off and landing every five minutes. Other military vehicles, jeeps and fliers, raced across the tarmac. The only militia she could see were a few hundred metres away, going in and coming out of the control tower and an adjoining building. They wore the same jungle-green uniforms as the bastards who had attacked her at the Falls.

She understood, then, the reason for the odd sensation of euphoria which surged through her still. She recalled her father's message, her painting in his study. Hard though it was to conceive exactly why – because he had found out that the Organisation was responsible for the genocide of the Lho, perhaps? – it did appear that he had converted. "I have seen the light, Ella. I need to see you." He needed to confess, seek forgiveness, share in the joy and certainty of conversion?

Ella rejoiced in the knowledge that he had seen the light, had changed – and regretted only the possibility that she might never share that joy with him.

For the next hour she remained crouched beneath the window, every sound from outside setting her nerves jumping. At one point a platoon of militia quick-marched past, and Ella retched involuntarily. She laid her head back against the wall, regaining the even tempo of her breathing. She wondered if this was a ploy on the part of the Organisation, leaving her alone in a limbo of uncertainty, softening her up for the inevitable interrogation?

She looked down at the leg-iron. It was a measure of her fatalism that she had not considered trying to escape. She bent her leg and gripped the thick iron collar of the manacle. It was loose about her ankle, but her heel stopped it from moving any further. She spat on her fingers, massaged the saliva into her heel, and pushed on the manacle. She gave up when blood trickled from the resulting abrasion.

I believe, she told herself. I believe that life awaits me after this life, so why am I so afraid?

Fear is natural, she reminded herself. A simple survival mechanism. A trick biology plays to perpetuate the flesh.

But what awaits me transcends the flesh...

It was – she laughed through her tears – little help.

Ten minutes later the hangar door opened and three figures stepped through. Two guards escorted a tall man in the dark green uniform of a Danzig officer, the three stripes of a sergeant on his cuff. The guards halted some way off, and the sergeant approached. He halted and stared down at her with ill-disguised contempt.

He was dark-complexioned, hatchet faced – good looking and at the same time brutish. A company man, if ever she'd seen one.

He held out his hand, palm up, and bent his fingers minimally in a horrible, patronising little gesture. "Stand."

Taking her time, Ella pushed herself to her feet. The sergeant was expressionless, staring at her.

"My name, Hunter, is Sergeant Forster," he said. His accent was tight and clipped. "My speciality is the game of interrogation, a game that over the years I have come to play very well. In fact, I never lose." He paused, letting his words sink in.

Ella fought not to let him see her fear.

"But it is a game," he went on, "in which even the loser can win something – or lose everything, depending on how well you understand the rules." Another pause. He was practised in the art of psychological intimidation, of planting pauses and silences to increase the tension.

"The rules are these, Hunter. I ask you a question, and you answer it. If the answer is what I want to hear, then it is correct and you gain a point. A certain number of points, and your life is saved. You will be tried and jailed for between twenty and twenty-five years for belonging to a proscribed terrorist organisation. You might even get out in time to bear children. On the other hand, if the answer is not what I want to hear, you are docked a point. At a certain total of minus points, you will be taken out behind the control tower and shot through the back of the head. As an incentive to answer the questions correctly, there will be certain... shall we say, inducements. Now, are you ready to play?"

Ella just stared at him, knowing that however contemptuous her expression he would have seen it before on the faces of his many victims.

"How do I know," she began, her voice steady and calm, much to her surprise, "that even if I do answer the questions correctly, you won't kill me all the same?"

Forster flashed a white grin. "You don't. You'll just have to take the risk. It is, after all, your only chance."

"Go to hell," she said, her voice almost cracking. "You can take me out now and get it over with."

"Noble sentiments, Hunter. But you haven't heard the questions yet."

Ella shook her head. "Shoot me."

"The first question. With whom did you spend your first night on the Reach? Name your contacts."

"I spent the night alone. I contacted no one."

Forster inclined his head. "Minus one point. Question two. Where is your father, on the Reach, or on Earth?"

"My father?" She stared at Forster, surprised. "What do you want with him?"

"Answer the question, Hunter."

She shook her head. "I don't know. I've no idea. I haven't seen or spoken to my father for ten years–" Why the hell was her father so important to them? Surely the conversion of a Danzig executive would be no great tragedy for the Organisation?

"Minus two points, Hunter. Question three. Who are your father's contacts on Earth?"

"Ella stared at him. "Contacts? On Earth? I've no idea! I don't know what you're talking about!"

"Minus three points, Hunter. I think a little inducement might be called for. Corporal."

One of the guards, immobile until now, stepped forward and reached out to Ella. She never saw the neural incapacitator in his hand, but she felt it.

Her arm burned and her brain exploded. She hit the floor, her neurones misfiring, and convulsed with an induced *grande mal* epileptic seizure. She thought later that it was like being insane for thirty seconds. Her chaotic mind, incapable of coherent thought, peered over the edge of everything known and looked upon oblivion or hell.

Then she was back in the hangar, looking up at her tormentors, her spine arched in pain. She collapsed, sobbing. "You... you–" She wanted more than anything to call them bastards, but the word would not form.

Forster smiled, kneeling beside her. "How do you like the game so far, Hunter? That was just a little encouragement to play by the rules. We have a long, long way to go yet. There are many more questions. Now, let's go back to the beginning. Who were your contacts on the Reach?"

Ella closed her eyes, gritted her teeth. She hissed, "*We give thanks to the Continuum/ The Infinite, the Sublime/ Into whose munificence we pass/ At the end of this cruel illusion–*"

"Again. Where is your father, on The Reach or on Earth?"

"*We have lived, we are mortal/ For our mortality we give thanks/ Without this cruel illusion we would be without immortality–*"

"Again! Who are your father's contacts on Earth?"

"*All essences unite in the Continuum/ Regardless of circumstance/ For all flesh is heir to the vagaries of conditions/ All flesh is capable of evil–*"

"Corporal!"

"No!" Ella screamed.

The Corporal advanced.

A firestorm of pure pain raged through her; it was as if her very soul were ablaze, might burn away to leave nothing of her essence to be saved. Her neurones fired at random, filling her head with a kaleidoscopic nightmare of irrational memories. She was a little girl again, screaming, "Daddy! Daddy! Daddy!" Her father was walking away from her, pacing towards the cobalt screen of the interface. Despite her screams he kept on walking, and exploded in a terminal white starburst. To Ella's shattered mind, it was as if the image was real, and all she craved was oblivion.

The terror passed, the nightmare ebbed and sanity returned. She found herself on the floor of the hangar, staring up at Forster. The thought of what he might do to her, the thought of the beautiful bullet in the back of her head, filled her with peace.

"Kill me..." she demanded.

Forster smiled. "Kill you? But that would be too kind a way out. You don't think for a second that you're going to get off so lightly, do you? Remember – I have been playing this game far longer than you."

He stood and walked away, the guards joining him. Ella tried to sit up, but the effort exhausted her and she lay back down. Her breathing came with difficulty, her chest heaving. Her left forearm was raw from where the incapacitator had burned her, but not as raw as the nerves of her brain. She felt as if her head had been marinated in acid, and when she closed her eyes fireballs exploded. She relived the fleeting, terrible images and brief thought-impressions of entropy and annihilation – the antithesis of everything in which she believed. It was as if her subconscious was mirroring her conscious belief in an afterlife with the exact, terrible opposite – to make her appreciate the wonder and vitality of the realm towards which she was heading.

Her torturers returned.

All she wanted was the promised bullet. Surely she had reached the requisite number of minus points by now? Surely, if they were playing by the rules, she was due her reward. But she should have known. She was dealing with an opponent whose motivation was less fair play than victory at all costs.

Forster knelt, placed his hands on his knees. "Now, Hunter, how would you like to go through that all over again? You can spare yourself the pain, the horror, and at the same time save your life, simply by answering the questions."

She braced herself for the shock of the incapacitator.

"Now, who were you contacts on the Reach?"

How could she inform on the old woman in the bar? Or tell Forster that Max Klien, Rodriguez and Jerassi were her contacts, and in so doing implicate Conchita and her daughter?

She closed her eyes, tortured with the anticipation of the brain-fire and desolation. Through gritted teeth she chanted, "*We become riders of the Infinite/ Shedding our egos–*"

"Two," Forster continued. "Where is you father? On the Reach or on Earth?"

"*Loosing the burden of self/ Becoming One with all things.*" Her body tensed with the expectation of imminent neural annihilation.

'"Three. Who are your father's contacts on Earth?"

"*Bless each one of us as we pass/ From illusion to reality*–"

"Corporal!"

"No! Oh, no – *please Fernandez, no!*"

She screamed. Her brain was burning and would burn forever, the eternal combustion feeding on the oxygen of her pain. All her fears came back to her, all her doubts – her lack of faith, terror that not the afterlife awaited her but oblivion; fear of loneliness, abandonment; images of loved ones walking away from her, ignoring her screamed pleas for protection, affection and love.

Then, as suddenly as it began, the pain sluiced away, leaving only an echoing residue in her head, an ever-present but elusive spectre of all the agony and terror.

Great breaths wracking her body, aware that she'd vomited over herself, she gazed up at Forster. He was standing, staring down at her.

"Kill me!" she gasped.

He gestured to the guards. "Unshackle her. Take her away."

She closed her eyes in relief. Soon it would be over.

The guards unlocked the leg-iron and assisted her across the hangar. She found it hard to walk. The incapacitator had scrambled her co-ordination and she shambled from the building like an old woman. The sunlight was wonderfully soothing on her face. They followed Forster across the tarmac to the control tower.

It struck her in a second of panic that her father might never find out what had happened to her – or that, if he did, he might blame himself for her death. She wanted to tell him that it was not his fault that she had come to the Reach, merely the end result of so many random factors.

She asked herself why the Organisation might be so interested in her father. What did they mean by his contacts on Earth?

They marched her around the back of the control tower. She expected to be put up against the wall and summarily executed. The guards held her between them, looking across the tarmac to a blast-barrier used to test the engines of fliers, twenty metres away. With Forster, they seemed to be watching, waiting for something.

Was this yet another psychological trick, a delay to let her dwell on the fact of her death; as if she might weaken at the eleventh hour, tell him what he wanted to hear?

A truck crossed the tarmac and drew up beside the blast-barrier. Six militia-men jumped from the back of the truck, pulling after them two civilians – one in peasant's garb, the other wearing radiation silvers. They had their hands bound behind their backs, their heads bowed. The guards bundled them across to the blast-barrier.

"Disciples," Forster informed her. "Caught trying to sabotage the Zambique-Guernica mono-link."

She watched, unable to look away or close her eyes. The Disciples were made to kneel, facing the barrier. As they did so, the men raised their heads in a gesture Ella found at once hopeless and dignified. She heard their chant drift through the warm morning air. "We cast off this cruel illusion..."

The guards placed pistols at the base of the Disciple's skulls and fired, the recoil pushing their arms into the air with a flourish like that of a pianist. The Disciples crumpled, legs tucked beneath their bodies in a tragic recapitulation of the foetal posture. The guards took their arms and legs, staggered with the bodies and swung them like sacks of grain into the back of the truck. Then they turned and stared across at Ella.

She looked at Forster, shaking her head. "You can't intimidate me. I'm ready to die. This is one game you've lost–"

Something cunning in his expression made her stop. "Lost?" He smiled. "I don't know the meaning of the word. What you experienced in the hangar was merely the first round of the contest." He signalled to the guards. "Take her inside."

She wanted to scream; she wanted to beg them to kill her. They escorted her through a door and into the control tower, along a corridor. She was taken to a small room furnished with a bed and a chair. A window overlooked the tarmac and the blast-barrier where the execution squad still waited. The door was locked behind her. She sat on the bed, staring down numbly at her shaking hands, watching them through a film of tears.

She wondered what further horrors Forster had in store for her. Would they resort to physical torture? Would she be able to withstand protracted physical pain any better than the attention of the incapacitator?

At a sound from beyond the door, she wiped the tears from her cheeks with the back of her hand. Forster entered the room smartly, leaving the door open. He looked Ella up and down. "Hunter, your clothing is a disgrace. Would you like to change?"

She just stared at him, non-plussed by the banality of his question.

He turned to the door. "Corporal."

The guard stepped forward and handed Forster a folded garment. Forster dropped it on the bed beside Ella. "Why not try it on?" he suggested.

Ella stared at it, her pulse accelerating. She picked it up; it hung from her grasp like a sad, discarded epidermis. She would have recognised Eddie's silversuit anywhere. The name-tag was missing.

Oh, Fernandez... She'd left it at the hillside shack two days ago.

"You do recognise it, don't you?" Forster asked.

"What do you mean?" Ella stammered. "I haven't... I've never seen it before."

"No? Forensic tests revealed that tissue samples found on it belong to you. We found it yesterday, on premises belonging to Conchita Rodriguez."

She looked up at Forster, anguish burning inside her. "What have you done with her?"

Forster smiled, cocked a finger pistol-fashion, indicating through the window. "Rodriguez is in the best of health," he said. "For the time being."

Ella turned, knowing what she would see. Conchita Rodriguez stood before the blast-barrier. Her daughter grasped her legs, face buried in the folds of her skirt. Conchita laid her hands protectively on Maria's head. She seemed to be staring straight at the control tower, through the window, at Ella.

"No..." She shook her head. "No, you wouldn't..."

Forster just looked at her. "No?" he asked.

"But they're innocent. They've done nothing–"

"Rodriguez harboured Disciple terrorists," Forster snapped. "And that's a capital offence."

"But Conchita isn't even a Disciple. She *doesn't believe!* You can't do it–"

"Harbouring terrorists is a capital offence,." He paused, considering. "But... I *might* be able to see my way to commuting the sentence. What do you think?"

Ella looked from Forster to Conchita. There was something noble, almost arrogant, about the way the woman stood, straight-backed, holding her daughter to her skirt, her head high.

"What do you want?" she asked, knowing with a sick inevitability full well what he wanted.

"I want answers – answers to every question I ask. Correct answers, this time. Then Rodriguez and the girl survive. If the answers are not the ones I want, or prove on investigation to be false, then all three of you die." He walked to the window, turned. "What do you say?"

Ella looked past him to the woman. She recalled their conversation. Conchita was not a Disciple – she had no religious beliefs. For her, this life was the only one. Ella could only imagine the woman's terror.

She shook her head wearily. "I'll tell you everything I know, but I know nothing about my father. Please believe me."

Forster was nodding. "We'll begin at the beginning, Shall we? Question number one. Who were your contacts on the Reach?"

Ella hesitated. "Max Klien, Emilio Rodriguez and David Jerassi."

Forster nodded. "The terrorists who sabotaged the interface. Did you accompany them?"

"I left them in the morning, rode to the Falls."

He stared down at her, as if considering her reply. She looked through the window, at Conchita, her heart beating rapidly.

"Very well. Question two. Where is your father, here or on Earth?"

She looked up at him. "I have no idea... I thought he still lived here. I came here to meet him. That's why I went to the Falls–"

"Careful, Hunter. Be very careful. That's a minus point. More than just your survival rests on your answers. You can't play the martyr now."

"It's true. I thought he was still at the Falls."

"When did you last see your father?"

"Ten years ago, a few months before I left for Earth."

"When did you last hear from him, and contact him yourself?"

Ella hesitated. "I contacted him seven years ago. I sent him a photograph. That was the last time. Then he contacted me a month ago. He sent me a disc."

Interest quickened in Forster's jet eyes. "What did he say?"

"Just that he wanted to see me."

"Nothing more – on a thirty minute disc?"

Ella looked up at Forster, tried to hold her tears back. "I wiped the rest of the disc without listening to it. I just heard him say... say that he wanted to see me. Then I wiped it. We never got on... we were never that close."

Forster paced the room, stroking the line of his jaw. "Did he tell you where you were to meet him? Was it here, on the Reach?"

"I don't know. I told you, I wiped the disc."

"Hunter..."

"It's true! I don't know. All he said was... he wanted to see me." She heard then the sound of her father's voice, strong, confident...

Forster considered, tapping his pursed lips. "Did he tell you that he'd converted, joined the Disciples?"

"No – I mean, not in so many words." To hear from Forster's lips that her father had defected, gone over to the other side, made her heart race with joy. "He told me that he'd seen the light. That's all. I thought maybe he'd converted, but I wasn't sure."

More to himself, Forster said, "He's converted, all right." He ceased his pacing and paused before Ella. "Who are your father's contacts on Earth?"

Ella stared, open-mouthed. "I don't know! I haven't seen or spoken to him for ten years!"

"We know he's in contact with Terran Enginemen, Hunter. I want their names!"

"Enginemen? I don't know. I've no idea. Please..."

Forster rushed to the window, hammered on the glass, then signalled. The guards by the blast-barrier motioned for Conchita and Maria to kneel. Ella watched the women lower herself slowly to her knees, her daughter clinging to her.

"Please, no..." Ella wept.

Forster rushed back to her. "Now, answers! Has your father left for Earth?"

"I don't know!"

"Who are his contacts on Earth?"

Ella was shaking her head, her eyes streaming. She swore that if they killed Conchita and the girl, she'd dive at Forster, tear out his eyes...

"I don't know! Please, listen to me..."

"Corporal!" Forster snapped. The guard appeared. "Take her out. Shoot the three of them."

The guard took her arm, almost gently, and brought her to her feet. He escorted her from the room and down the corridor, following Forster.

They passed outside, into the sunlight.

"Please," Ella wept. "Not the girl. Kill me, but not Maria."

Still pacing, Forster turned. "Answers, Hunter!"

"I don't know. I just don't know..." She looked up, then, and saw a line of fliers advancing across the tarmac.

Forster began, "Then the three of you–"

He never finished the sentence.

The explosion knocked them off their feet. Ella hit the tarmac painfully. Dazed, battered by the blast, she rolled over and pushed herself onto her hands and knees. She gazed about her in disbelief. One of the guards was dead, blood trickling from his nose and mouth. The other rolled on the ground, moaning. Forster was groggily picking himself up. Ella screamed and dived across the tarmac to the dead guard. She grabbed the incapacitator from the ground where he'd dropped it, staggered to her feet and ran at Forster. He was drawing his pistol, caught by surprise, when Ella slammed the weapon into his face. He yelled, fell to the ground. She collapsed with him, and brought the incapacitator down again and again on the side of his head. Forster spasmed, his back arching as he convulsed. Sobbing, Ella rolled away from him.

Explosions shattered the air. Across the airbase, the squad of militia beside the blast-barrier lay dead or dying. Ella looked desperately for Conchita and her daughter. She saw them huddling together behind the barrier. As she watched, a flier swooped down and two men bundled the girl and her mother aboard.

Vehicles burned all around the base, and everywhere Danzig militia-men fell. Fliers advanced across the tarmac, hitting anything that moved with shell-fire and grenades.

Ella hugged her legs and curled against the wall of the control tower, watching with terror and disbelief as Forster rolled onto his belly and clawed his way across the tarmac towards her. She looked around desperately for the incapacitator, and saw it – beyond Forster – where she'd dropped it. She tried to move, to summon the energy to pick herself up and run, but she was paralysed by exhaustion and the look on Forster's face as he crawled towards her. Ella screamed.

A battered, turbo-driven flier surged around the corner, came down heavily. At the wheel, a black Engineman casually raised a rifle, one-handed.

He fired, the shot opening a gaping hole in Forster's back. He spasmed, staring at Ella with wide, dead eyes.

"Get in, girl," the Engineman said. "Move it!"

Dazed, she picked herself up and staggered towards the flier. She threw herself over the side and onto the back seat. The flier sped off across the base, swerving erratically to avoid explosions and pockets of Danzig resistance.

A grenade detonated beneath them, bucking the flier. "Hold on tight back there," the Engineman said calmly. "This might be a rough ride."

They accelerated over the perimeter fence, leaving the airbase behind them, and screamed into the jungle. The E-man weaved his way through the trees, trunks flicking by on either side with a sound like rotor-blades.

"You sure don't say much, girl," the Engineman called to her. "You feeling okay?"

Ella wanted to tell him that she'd never felt better.

Instead she passed out.

Chapter Nineteen

Mirren stood with Bobby in the engine-room, an arm around his brother's shoulders. He had showered and changed and felt refreshed, though aware of his bruised and battered body. He was experiencing also a return of the Heine's symptoms: hot sweats, nausea and bone-aching weariness. He had left his medication back at the apartment, though his concern was cancelled out by the thought of the flux. Right now, he told himself, he would gladly die in four years just to be able to mind-push again.

Beyond the triangular viewscreen, the technicians were making final preparations for the phase-out. The irony of the situation was not lost on Mirren. The techs, with their head-mikes and monitors, going about their business in the hallowed chambers of Notre-Dame, were the subjects in a frieze signifying the triumph of science over superstition. He acknowledged another paradox inherent in the situation: that the event towards which the scientists were working would itself be transformed into superstition by credulous believers like his brother and Dan.

Behind them, the engine-room was in the semi-darkness that Enginemen found conducive to their pre-flux preparations. Even a materialist like Mirren had to admit that a darkened room was requisite to proper contemplation of the task at hand. Other Enginemen, believers and Disciples, went in for a long and complex series of rituals, involving prayers, mantras and incense: the engine-rooms on some of the 'ship's he'd pushed were like Eastern shrines and temples. He was pleased to see that this chamber was wholly functional. Alpha-numerics sequenced along the flank of the flux-tank, a tubular silver catafalque on a raised stage against the bulkhead. Beside it was the co-pilot's auxiliary command web, a cat's-cradle slung between a horseshoe console. Black, padded foam-forms and couches gave the engineroom the appearance of an exclusive, hi-tech bar.

Mirren rubbed the back of his neck, hoping to ease the pulsating ache at the base of his skull. He had tried to ignore it for the past thirty minutes, but he knew what it meant.

Dan and Miguelino, the Gamma Engineman who would be the co-pilot on this mission, rode the downchute and stepped into the engineroom. Miguelino moved to his web and strapped himself in. Dan joined them before the viewscreen.

"Ready, Ralph?"

Mirren nodded. Earlier, he'd drawn first push in the tank, Bobby the second and Dan the third.

In the cathedral, the techs monitoring their consoles turned and regarded the smallship. The pilot up in the nose-cone radioed to the co-pilot that phase-out was imminent. As Mirren watched, Hunter stepped forward from a group of scientists, his halved face bright in the wash of light from the 'ship. He raised his arm in a salute of farewell. Mirren and Dan returned the gesture.

"We're phasing," Bobby murmured. "We're phasing, I can feel it!"

As he spoke, the *Sublime* phased out. A low-pitched hum filled the air. Seen from within the 'ship, it was the outside world which seemed to undergo the vanishing process. Reality flickered with ever-increasing frequency: the tableau of Hunter and the technicians in the nave alternated with the cobalt light of the continuum, the effect stroboscopic in the final stages before full integration was achieved. Then the scene inside the cathedral vanished finally and all that could be seen was the deep blue of the *nada*-continuum, shot through with opalescent streaks which flowed like streamers.

Dan withdrew the slide-bed from the flux-tank. The low humming cut out, and the resulting silence was eerie, as if the surrounding continuum soaked up every sound. Mirren experienced a feeling of familiar euphoria as he sat on the padded slide-bed and underwent the process of entankment he had dreamed about for so long. He removed his jacket and touched a command on his occipital-console, opening the dozen sockets of the spar which spanned his shoulders. Dan pulled the first input lead from within the tank, then the next, and jacked them in. They slotted home with solid, satisfying clunks. With the access of each jack he seemed to lose touch with ever more reality until, as the twelfth and final lead connected him to the matrix of the smallship, he was in a trance-like state. He was only half-aware of Dan's strong hands on him as he was laid out on the slide-bed and inserted into the tank. The hatch closed beyond his feet, plunging him into darkness. Outside, Miguelino began the process of easing him into full matrix-integration.

Seconds passed and Mirren became increasingly unaware of his physical self as his senses, one by one, abdicated their responsibility of relaying an outside reality to his disconnected sensorium. He was blind and deaf, his sense of touch diminished. Soon all awareness of his corporeal self fled as his consciousness teetered on the edge of the vastness of the *nada*-continuum. He knew then the infinite wonder of the immanence which underlay the everyday universe. Rapture sluiced through him in a glorious tide of joy.

He fluxed.

The period spent in flux was a timeless duration for Enginemen. Robbed of their senses, they had no awareness of the passage of time. A shift spent pushing a 'ship between the stars might have been over in an instant, or an eternity. Only when they detanked, anything from six to ten hours later, were they able to recollect the instant of the flux and relive the experience of pushing.

Then, Mirren became aware that something was wrong. At first, for a split second, he assumed he was defluxing. But that entailed a gradual return of sensory awareness, a final teetering on the edge of the vastness. Very definitely Mirren had no sensory awareness – no sense of sight or touch, hearing, taste or smell.

He was suddenly aware of an anomalous phenomenon. Deep within his head, on the very periphery of his consciousness, there was a voice, calling to him.

He willed himself to concentrate. The communication became stronger, a definite presence; he was tempted to call it a voice, though it was more a thought.

It was calling his name.

— Ralph, Ralph...

He found he could reply by *thinking* the words: *Who are you?*"

— Ralph, it's me, Caspar.

Mirren was shaken to the core. His mind raced. Caspar Fekete? But that was impossible! He could only assume he was dreaming. The notion that the voice in his head had an external source was too staggering to contemplate.

He thought: *Caspar?*

— Can you... hear me, Ralph? The link is very weak. I can only just make you out...

Then Mirren knew he was not hallucinating – or whatever one did when imagining sounds. The voice in his head was real. His initial shock was overcome by cautious wonder, though at the same time the sceptic in him would not acknowledge the import of this communication. It went against everything in which he believed. And yet that deep, buried part of him, terrified at the thought of his premature death, cried out for Fekete's communiqué to be what he thought it was.

I can hear you – what the hell-? His thoughts became a chaotic scramble of questions.

— I'm dead, Ralph. They got me in my flier eight hours ago-

You're in the continuum, Mirren thought in disbelief. *You've transcended?*

Even as he said this he was so overcome by the marvel of the concept that he hardly thought to ask himself why, on his many shifts in the past, he had not been contacted by the souls, or whatever, of the people he had known in life.

Then Mirren was aware of what might have been a chuckle, like a subtle itch, within his head.

— No, Ralph. I have not transcended – though in a manner of speaking I have. That is, I am not part of the *nada*-continuum or Nirvana or whatever they call it.

Disappointment coursed through Mirren.

Then what?

— Upon my bodily demise, an encoded personality analogue was removed from my occipital console. In simple terms, a recording of my identity, of my thoughts and memories, hopes and desires, a simulacrum of my very self – if, like me, you believe that the mind is the seat of everything that makes us human. Over the years my company developed a means by which to make individuals virtually immortal through cerebral translation into digital analogues. I exist as an information matrix based in my Paris mansion but stretching to the very boundaries of the Expansion. I thought at first that I might feel enclosed, a captive, without the physical freedom endowed by a body, but the reverse is true. I have never been as free in my life...

But where are you now?

— I am transmitting this from my Paris base via a satellite link, accessing the shipboard logic matrix of the *Sublime*. I am also communicating with Dan Leferve in his berth.

Mirren questioned how Fekete could be communicating with two people at the same time.

Again the chuckle. — I am now, in effect, a machine. I can replicate myself *ad infinitum*. I could even, if I so wished, communicate with a million people simultaneously. I am speaking to you via your occipital leads.

A thought occurred to Mirren.

Do you realise that Dan and others of his persuasion will deny that you are any longer human?

Mirren was aware of humour in the reply. — Ralph, I myself doubt whether I am any longer human, as you would define the term. I am, however, a thinking, feeling, morally conscious entity. Call me transhuman, if you wish. I have already had this argument with Dan. We have moved on from that, to the reason for my communicating with you. My time is limited; with each passing second you move farther from the solar system, and my signal weakens–

Why have *you contacted us?* Mirren asked, unable to work out why Fekete, loath to accompany them on this mission himself, should instigate what was surely the most bizarre dialogue in the history of star travel.

There was a pause.

— Upon my death and resurrection in this realm, Fekete began, I learned of Olafson and Elliott's deaths, and investigated. I had unlimited resources open to me, and access to vast amounts of information. I naturally assumed that we, the Enginemen selected by Hunter for this mission, were being targeted and killed because someone did not want the mission to succeed. Coincidental as it may seem, we were targeted for altogether another reason.

So Hunter was right, Mirren thought.

Fekete paused. Mirren thought he had lost the link. Then he continued. -When I discovered the real reason, I attempted to contact Dan and yourself to warn you to abandon the mission. Of course I failed, until my sensors detected the *Sublime*. Now I can but warn you to take care.

The real *reason?* Mirren asked.

— In the days before my death I relived three sudden and involuntary flashbacks of our last voyage and the crashlanding of the *Perseus Bound.* These flashbacks were strange in that with each one I was given an increasing amount of information: I recalled nothing of the journey to begin with, and then with each flashback I recalled more and more... But I suspect I need not go on: you no doubt have undergone the same?

Mirren assented.

— Leferve and Elliott, and Olafson also; which I found out while investigating Olafson's movements before her death. I spoke to her husband, and he mentioned that Christiana too experienced these attacks. He told me that she had contacted her doctor at the firm for which she worked, a subsidiary of the Danzig Organisation. I decided to investigate further. I insinuated probes into the medic's information matrices and discovered a communiqué he despatched to the head of the Organisation.

Fekete paused. The signal was growing appreciably weaker. Mirren was aware that, when Fekete continued, the voice in his head was little more than a whisper.

— What Olafson and the rest of us witnessed in the jungle after the crashlanding was enough to have the Danzig Organisation, when they found out about our flashbacks, order our extermination. For we all witnessed what occurred and we all, if we lived, would eventually recall it.

— I scoured what were now my memory banks. So much – unconscious and subconscious memories, desires, terrors of childhood that made me what I am – is stored in files I rarely access. What happened after the crashlanding had been shunted away into one of these files.

— I found that my recollections of the journey, the crashlanding and the subsequent events had been wiped from my mind by the Danzig Organisation after they picked us up all those years ago; our memories had been edited by the process known as mem-erase. This system was in its prototype stages then, and its faults and flaws were not known. We now know that no memory can ever be truly erased. If they do not resurface as trauma or psychosis, then they return in the form of regular flashbacks. We all suffered these flashbacks of information in increments because that was how, in the days we were quarantined by the psychologists of the Organisation, our memories of what we had witnessed were taken from us, from our first recollections of the journey out, to what we saw later in the jungle. That is the order in which they returned to us. I discovered also that the name of the planet on which we crashlanded had been excised from our memories. We were told that the world was unnamed and unexplored.

There was a pause.

For a timeless duration Mirren considered what Fekete had told him. Then he asked: *Why didn't they just kill us and claim we had died in the accident, if what we saw was so...?*

— From my memory banks I found out that we released a rescue beacon shortly after the crashlanding, and this probably saved our lives. It contained information on survivors, our position and where we were heading. The signal was picked up by a passing bigship of a rival Line, and the Danzig crowd couldn't very well kill us then without it looking suspicious. So they did the next best thing.

Mirren asked the all important question: *What did we see, Caspar?*

When Fekete replied, his words reached Mirren as if from a great distance. He had to concentrate to make them out.

— When we left the crash sight we headed through the jungle to a settlement fifteen kilometres distant. A few hours later we came upon the village and discovered... Here Fekete hesitated, as if either the signal had been broken, or the machine which he had become found the recollection too painful to relate. — We found that Danzig militia-men had massacred over a hundred aliens. In the next settlement, a short distance away, the massacre was still in progress.

Mirren looked into his mind and tried to find a memory of the massacre. He recalled nothing.

— We were discovered when Elliott, unable to bear any more, ran from cover and tried to attack a militia-man. She was knocked unconscious and the militia came after us.

Why? Why were they killing the aliens?

— I don't know, Ralph. There is, of course, no information available on the subject. Officially, the Danzig Organisation reported that the aliens known as the Lho had succumbed to a devastating plague... However, if anyone can tell us why, it is you.

Mirren expressed his surprise. *Me?*

— You of the five of us were the only one to escape when the militia came after us. We were rounded up and taken to a garrison town a hundred kilometres away, where we underwent the mem-erase treatment. You were brought in a day later, beaten and haggard. We heard you being questioned about the aliens. Something about a mountain stronghold of the aliens which the Organisation was intent on discovering.

Before the link was lost completely, Mirren asked, *What was the name of the planet we crashlanded on?*

— The planet was Hennessy's Reach, a Danzig-run world on the Rim. Do you see now why I had to contact you? To warn you...

The signal faltered, crackled.

Warn us about what? Mirren almost cried with his mind.

Fekete responded, the words faint almost beyond comprehension. — I accessed the *Sublime's* programming, Ralph, and discovered your destination. The *Sublime* is headed for Hennessy's Reach.

Mirren asked, *But why?*

— I know as much as you. Perhaps... even less.

The signal was breaking up.

— Take care... Contact me when you return.

And the whispered thoughts in his head were extinguished like the dying flame of a candle.

Without a reference point to determine the parameters of his existence in the tank, Mirren once again experienced the full wonder of the *nada*-continuum. Then, a timeless duration later, he was suddenly teetering on the very edge of the vastness. With part of his mind he apprehended the magnificence of the realm as it faded, became distant.

Dan trolleyed out the slide-bed and Mirren emerged into the blue light of the engine-room. Physically, he might have been withdrawn from the continuum, but mentally he was still suffused with the wonder of the flux: it was as if his circulatory system was filled not with blood but with some effervescent fluid instead – a champagne rush which surged with his heartbeat and filled him with a sublime, light-headed sensation of well-being.

He sat up and Dan unjacked the leads from his occipital console, then assisted him from the slide-bed. He wanted to compare notes with Dan about what Fekete had told him in the tank, discuss the repercussions of what they had learned from the digitalised Nigerian, but he was too blitzed to speak. He knew that this rapturous state of being was what persuaded most Enginemen that they had experienced union with the ultimate, but even now the rationalist in Mirren told him that what he had in fact experienced was no more than a massive over-stimulation of his brain's pleasure cells. Later, the high would ebb away, leaving him to come to terms with mundane reality and craving his next bout of flux.

The *Sublime* was becalmed in the continuum, awaiting motive power. Pacific blue light flooded the engineroom as Bobby climbed carefully onto the slide-bed. Dan inserted the jacks, murmuring some Disciples' mantra, and Bobby's expression became rapturous.

Mirren took his brother's hand. He was filled with an inexpressible sadness, and at the same time he felt the residue of the wonder of the continuum within him, and he knew he had no right to resent his brother's decision to experience that wonder for himself.

CHAPTER TWENTY

BOBBY FELT THE padded surface of the slide-bed beneath him. Dan Leferve adjusted his occipital console preparatory to inserting the jacks. Ralph took his hand. *Good luck, Bobby*, he signed.

"Don't fear for me, Ralph," Bobby said. "I want this. More than anything, I want this."

He was seeing the delayed vision of his room, and recalled that he had been thinking about his brother at this time yesterday, about Ralph's illness. Then, as now, he was ambivalent about the fact that Ralph had Heine's; as far as he was concerned, Ralph was bound for a better place, but that was no consolation to Ralph, and Bobby felt for him. He was aware also of what effect this giving of himself to the continuum, and possible death, would be having on his brother.

While Dan readied his console, Bobby looked at a Buddhist *tanka* on the wall of his room, a cyclic depiction of the cosmos. It was not quite right philosophically, he reflected, but it was perhaps the most appropriate symbol to be taking with him into the flux-tank.

Dan slipped the jacks home one by one, with a care that was almost reverent. Bobby felt their solid, satisfying contact conducted through his skull. For years he had sustained himself with meditation, his tenuous contact with the continuum staving off the craving which affected other Enginemen. Now he was about to achieve total union, and the fact was almost inconceivable.

Gentle hands forced him backwards so that he was lying on the slide-bed. Ralph took his hand, squeezed one last time as the bed drew him into the tank.

He felt the bed beneath him, the padded surface under his fingertips. His vision flittered around the far wall of his room. He could smell the incense burning from the day before. Seconds elapsed. Soon he would be pushing the 'ship through the *nada*-continuum.

He had expected to wait twenty-four hours before experiencing the wonder of the continuum. He would be in the tank, reliving the day before in his room, and only twenty-four hours later would the experience of the union begin, and flood his senses with an ineffable tide of wonder.

He was reconciling himself to the delay when he became aware of some subtle difference... At first he could not specify what had happened, and then realised that he could hear nothing from the day before. He had been listening to the occasional flier passing overhead, and the low, muted hum of distant traffic. Now these had ceased. He could hear nothing. All was silence. Similarly, he could no longer smell the incense.

Then his vision of the room, the *tankas* on the far wall, began to dissolve, fade out, to be replaced by darkness.

He was in the sensory limbo he knew so well from his days pushing bigships for the Javelin Line. Any second now...

It happened. He felt himself drawn from his body, his consciousness teeter on the edge of the continuum in a sudden overwhelming rush of wonder. Then he slipped over the edge, melded with the very fabric of the sublime, the infinite, and the sensation was so much greater than his periods of contact through meditation. He was one with the continuum, he *was* the continuum, and he knew that he had never before in any of his previous pushes achieved this degree of union, never felt quite this joyous flood of wonder, this total affirmation of being. He felt all his human attributes slough from him, along with his ego, his anxiety and emotions. He was aware of himself, but himself as a being transcended, no longer human but something far more, far greater. He knew, then, that he would never be returned to the limited, restricted prison of his body, that he had left it behind when he had transcended – yet at the same time he knew that his body still existed, was still living... He was aware too – some tiny part of him intuited – that he, his body, was no longer in the tank, that he, it, had finished its push. A part of him perceived his former self as a point of light, and around it were other points of light, which he knew to be Ralph, Dan and the co-pilot.

Then the being who had been Bobby Mirren heard the calling. He moved towards it – yet didn't move as he was already part of it – he *became* towards it, was aware then of a teeming multitude of other beings or essences like himself, all the many lifeforms that had ever existed in the physical realm and then passed on, a trillion trillion points of coloured light.

He joined the benign source of the calling, six beings or essences, and they accepted him as one of them.

Chapter Twenty-One

Mirren was drawn from sleep by the sound of voices. He came to his senses slowly, disoriented, unable to tell how long he'd been unconscious. He opened his eyes. He was lying on a foam-form in the engine-room, washed by the blue light of the continuum, where he'd collapsed after his stint in the tank. With sudden panic he recalled Bobby. As he swung from the foam-form, heart racing, he noticed two things almost at once: the view through the screen was of the *nada*-continuum as seen from a becalmed 'ship, and the wall chronometer revealed that he had slept for just two hours.

Dan was in the far corner of the engineroom, speaking with Miguelino in his command-web. The two men were conducting a heated exchange, as if in argument or debate. The co-pilot communicated with the pilot on the flight-deck, at the same time hurriedly striking keys on the console before him.

Mirren staggered across to the flux-tank and peered through the viewplate in the hatch. Bobby was still in there, his head surrounded by a nimbus of blue light. The subject-integration indices on the flank were sequencing in perfect harmony.

"He's still alive!" Mirren yelled.

"We're bringing him out," Dan called. "He's defluxing now."

"But he's only been in there two hours!"

"Check!" Miguelino yelled at something relayed to him from the pilot. "This I don't believe."

Dan hurried from the command web, tapped the keys on the side of the tank. As Mirren watched, the great silver column of the hatch withdrew itself, swung open, and the slide-bed rolled out bearing his brother.

"Confirmed!" Miguelino called. "Just under two hours."

The expression on Bobby's face was beatific; he was so transformed that for a second Mirren hardly recognised him. His eyes were closed with the devotion of a saint in prayer.

Mirren gripped his hand, too overcome to recall the relevant signs with which to express his relief. He hoped the pressure of his grasp would be enough to communicate his feelings.

Dan hauled a diagnostic scanner on its boom from the ceiling, swept it the length of the recumbent figure. The screen in its globular head glowed green with its report. Dan shook his head. "He's fine, Ralph. He's as well as when he entered the tank, but how the hell did he do it?" He batted away the diagnostic device, glanced at Mirren. "His surviving is miracle enough. But his performance..."

Mirren stared, bewildered. "What?"

"He's been in the tank just under two hours," Dan went on, "but he's pushed us all the way to the Rim. We'll be phasing-in in just over fifteen minutes."

"That's impossible..."

Dan spoke to Miguelino, who swung himself around in his web. "Check, Dan. We've traversed twenty thousand light years. We're on the Rim, and no mistake."

Dan said, "He pushed the 'ship to the Rim in just two hours, Ralph. It should have taken over twenty-five..."

Mirren looked down on his brother. It was usual to remain in a trance immediately following defluxing – the wonder they experienced left some Enginemen blitzed for hours – but something about Bobby's total lack of response worried Mirren.

"Dan?"

"After that performance I'm not surprised he's a little out of it." He checked the Engineman's pulse, thumbed his eye-lids. The smile on Bobby's face never wavered. "He seems okay. Let's get him to his berth."

Between them they eased Bobby into a sitting position, then chair-lifted him across the chamber to the up-plate. They rose to the lounge, Bobby limp between them, carried him to his berth and laid him out on the bunk.

"I'll leave you with him," Dan said. "I'll probe the tank, try to work out what happened." He closed the door quietly as he left.

Mirren drew up a seat and sat staring at Bobby.

Almost as if afraid to do so, he took his brother's hand and, after some deliberation signed, *Can you feel this? Can you feel anything Bobby!* – and, though he had meant to end the communication with an appropriate question mark, he mistakenly signed an exclamation instead.

There was no response.

In all his years as an Engineman he had never witnessed this degree of post-flux bodily dysfunction; but then he'd never witnessed the feat of pushing that Bobby had just achieved.

Something flickered on his brother's face – a lessening in the degree of his rapture.

Mirren grabbed his hand again. *Bobby, it's me, Ralph. Can you feel this?*

Mirren watched the wall-chronometer flick away the minutes. He found it ironic that, a few hours ago, he would have been overjoyed if Bobby had survived his stint in the tank. All he wished for now was the return of the brother he could communicate with, even if only through the restricted medium of touch-signing.

Bobby said, "Ralph... Ralph... I know you're there, somewhere..."

Mirren signed, *I'm here. You're okay. You survived.*

Five minutes passed. It was as if Bobby was oblivious to Mirren's signing.

"Ralph... Ralph," he said at last. "This is truly wonderful..."

What is? What's happening?

Mirren cried out loud as Bobby failed to respond.

Five minutes later: "Ralph... When I entered the tank and fluxed, something very strange happened." Bobby fell silent. Mirren told himself that he should be grateful for this sign of animation from his brother, but what he said, and the eerie, removed manner in which he relayed it, sent a chill down his spine. "Something very strange and wonderful, Ralph. I should have gone another twenty-four hours before experiencing the flux, viewing everything that had happened leading up to the time I was tanked, but I didn't... Instead, as soon as I was jacked in, I lost the sights and sounds, tastes and smells of the preceding day and experienced the wonder of the flux immediately. Only... only I experienced it – I'm *still* experiencing it – like never before. I am closer to the immanence, the vastness. It's as if I'm part of that vastness. I am spread across and through the infinite, the sublime nexus of the continuum, sensing every particle of the ultimate reality which underlies the illusion of the mundane, human perceived version of reality. I am in contact with the essence of everyone and every being that ever was..." He lapsed again into silence, and though the sceptic in Mirren tried to explain away his brother's vision as the illusion of a dysfunctioning mind, that part of him aware of his own mortality ached for the wonder that Bobby had described.

He took the limp hand. *Bobby.*

Fifteen minutes passed. Then, suddenly, Bobby resumed. "The truly amazing thing is that, although I know I'm no longer in the tank, I am still experiencing the flux, the continuum. My touch has gone the way of my other senses. I am truly lapsed in time now, Ralph. I think I have achieved that which for years I have been seeking – the ultimate freeing of my ego from my self. I no longer suffer the illusion of worldly reality, the pain of being. I have progressed to a higher state. I have transcended...

"At the same time as I inhabit the continuum," he continued, "I am aware of you, of Dan and the pilots aboard the 'ship. I cannot see you, but you are there – like points of light in the darkness of your reality. I can sense your humanity, Ralph. I am experiencing your essence before you transcend and integrate with the ultimate..."

He said no more then, and the minutes stretched. Mirren felt at once awed and humbled. He became aware that he was not alone. Dan was standing silently at the door.

"Did you hear that?"

Dan nodded wordlessly. They stared at the figure on the bunk.

"I've no idea what happened, Ralph – why he's like that, or how he pushed us all that way. We learned nothing from the tank." Dan's tone was hushed. "I came to tell you that we're about to phase-in."

Mirren released his brother's hand and followed Dan from the berth. They took the down-plate and dropped into the darkened chamber of the engine-room.

Beyond the viewscreen, the blue depths of the *nada*-continuum glowed and pulsed, the white streamers of light stilled now as the *Sublime* came to rest at journey's end. As Mirren watched, the blue field faded. Then, for a fraction of a second, the cobalt backdrop was replaced by their destination. The view strobed – the intervals of its appearance becoming longer, interspersed with brief glimpses of the *nada*-continuum. Finally, the scene outside became solid and constant.

A second later, and without warning, the pain in Mirren's head crescendoed. His vision fractured.

He flashbacked–

HE WAS STANDING in a jungle, beside the wreckage of the *Perseus Bound*. The air was humid, loaded with the sickly-sweet stench of burnt flesh. Jan Elliott sat cross-legged on the ground, weeping. Olafson knelt before her, doing her best to comfort the stricken Enginewoman. Dan jumped from the sheared-off section of the engine-room and made his way across to Mirren, scanning the navigation unit.

"Where are we, Dan?"

"Planet called Hennessy's Reach – a Rim world. Like most of them in this sector it's run by the Danzig Organisation."

The screen on the unit showed a map of the planet's northern continent. A flashing point indicated their position.

"How far to the closest settlement?" Mirren asked.

Dan shook his head. "Nearest human settlement – the city of Zambique, a couple of thousand kays south-west. But there's a native village just fifteen kays north of here."

Mirren peered into the gloom of the jungle. "What about the aliens? Friendly?"

Dan typed in a new set of commands, read the screen. "B3s. Humanoid, sentient. They're an ancient race, apparently friendly. Known as the Lho-Dharvo."

"Is the village likely to have communications with Zambique?"

Dan shrugged. "Doesn't say. I guess there'd be some contact."

"What do we do, Boss?" Fekete asked.

"We either stay here and wait for the salvage team to find us – that might take a few days. Or we make for the village and rest up there..."

He looked out across the wreckage at the bodies, made up his mind. "We're heading for the settlement. Any objections? Fine. Fekete, break out the rations. Let's get the hell out of here."

Mirren led the way as they filed from the crash site and down an avenue of tall, mast-like trees, their progress unimpeded by undergrowth. Mirren estimated that if the terrain remained this hospitable all the way, then it would take four or five hours to reach the village. Dan warned them that the planet had its fair share of man-eating predators and poisonous insects, and Mirren could not shake a feeling of danger as they marched through the twilit jungle. He was trembling. The horrors he'd witnessed back at the crash sight, the fact that he had survived against all odds, were beginning to have an effect: delayed reaction shock. He braced himself against the shakes. He didn't want the others to see him weakening.

They walked for hours, with frequent stops to consult the navigator. Calls and cries accompanied their march, but all from animals and birds in retreat. When the jungle canopy grew threadbare, a thrusting range of mountains could be seen, stark against the starfield. They caught infrequent glimpses of the sun to the west, the upper few degrees of a red giant on the horizon.

Three kilometres from the native settlement, the lie of the land began to change. They followed a worn track, clearly in frequent use, which wound uphill through bushes of broad green leaves and red blooms.

His team was silent. He and Olafson occupied front and rear, ever watchful as they pushed through vines and creepers. Dan was immediately behind him, dependable as ever. Fekete had ceased his wisecracking, and Elliott was quiet after her initial panic.

Ahead, the jungle thinned, and on the sides of the revealed valley was a scattered settlement. One hillside was in shadow, the other bathed in the red light of the setting sun. They emerged from the margin of the jungle and entered the valley, Mirren noticed the air of stillness and silence which hung over the area. The track broadened as it climbed, opened into wide, green slopes. Crude dwellings sprawled up the hillside, timber built A-frames on high pillars.

The settlement was deserted.

They hiked through, stopping to cautiously inspect the interiors of the occasional shack. At the end of the valley the path climbed, and in the crook of a still higher valley could be seen the leaf-woven rooftops of more dwellings. Mirren was about to suggest they continue towards it when Olafson cried out, "Here, Boss!"

She had halted some way back, and was staring into the gap between two timber A-frames. Mirren and the others joined her. Between the stilts of the building was the body of an alien child, lying face down in a patch of mud trodden and churned by domesticated animals. Mirren approached the body and knelt.

Then he looked up and saw the others.

It was a strange sensation: at first he saw just a dozen bodies in the ditch behind the dwellings; then he glanced further along the ditch and saw more, and from that second, wherever he turned his head, right and left and up the hillside, his vision registered dozens, fifty, perhaps a hundred bodies. His first reaction, before he even began to think about who might be responsible, was amazement that he had not noticed the carnage sooner. It was like an optical illusion in which the subject remains obdurately hidden until, by chance, the brain works out the delusion and the eye is flooded with the obvious image.

Mirren stared, overwhelmed by the scale of the slaughter. Many of the Lho were semi- or entirely naked. But for the gold and bronze colouration of their flesh, they might have been so many human beings lying dead beneath the setting sun.

Fekete kept his comments to himself, for once. The others looked on in disbelief, as if unable to come to terms with a second tragedy so soon after the first. Dan passed Mirren and moved up the hillside, stepping between the bodies. From time to time he knelt to examine an alien he thought might still be alive, then stood and moved on.

Mirren gathered himself. "Dan, be careful. We don't know who did this."

"Every last one's been shot in the back of the head," Dan reported.

'They're not an advanced people," Fekete said. "They don't have the technology to produce fire-arms."

Elliott said, "Fernandez, listen!"

Then it came to them, drifting down from the second, higher valley: the distinctive, percussive blast of one projectile shot after another, on and on and on...

Mirren looked at his team, their faces ashen with shock. He made a split-second decision. "Stay here."

He set off at a sprint up the hill towards the second valley. Before cresting the brow, he left the path and approached the second settlement through the undergrowth. He moved with stealth, so as to go undetected by the green-uniformed militia standing sentry at the entrance to the village. A helicopter troop-carrier stood in the clearing between the raised dwellings, and dozens of Organisation men occupied the far crest above the settlement to prevent the herded Lho from escaping up the hillside.

Mirren crouched behind a stand of shrubs and stared out. Beyond the dwellings on the far side of the clearing, six militia-men moved along the rows of kneeling aliens and dispatched them with quick, efficient shots to the back of the head. He heard pitiful cries, moans and screams of terror. As he watched, one alien staggered to his feet and ran, only to be brought down by a bullet between the shoulder blades.

Mirren turned at a sound behind him. Elliott was running up the incline, her eyes wide. "What the hell!" Mirren hissed. "I told you..."

Elliott dodged him and sprinted into the clearing.

Dan and the others appeared over the brow of the incline, exhausted. "We tried to stop her!"

"Elliott!" Mirren cried.

Screaming, Elliott attacked a militia-man bare-handed. The guard recovered, raised his laser rifle and beat Elliott with its butt. The Enginewoman folded, fell at his opponent's feet. The militia-man looked up, in the direction from which Elliott had come, and saw Mirren and the others. Briefly, the killings ceased as the executioners paused and stared down into the clearing.

Mirren turned. "Into the jungle! Run!"

He sprinted down the hillside, veered from the path and went crashing through the undergrowth, falling headlong in his haste to get away. Behind him, he heard the resumption of the sickening, relentless gunfire. He was aware of Dan and Olafson on either side, sprinting through the shoulder-high shrubbery towards the sanctuary of the jungle. Shots whined around them, shredding tree trunks. He lost his footing and skidded down a ravine, sliding on his back through thickets and bushes. He felt nothing but the surge of adrenalin which gave him the strength to pick himself up and sprint into the jungle. He chanced a glance over his shoulder. High up on the hillside, Fekete had halted, arms in the air, and was being manhandled by three militia-men. He saw Olafson fall, screaming and holding her thigh. There was no sign of Dan. Mirren ran on, zigzagging through undergrowth. He heard shouts behind him as the militia co-ordinated their search. The ground sloped. He was climbing the far side of the ravine, losing his footing frequently in the mulch of the jungle floor. The cries became distant, then faded altogether. He had no idea how long he had been running. Probably only minutes, though it seemed longer. The incline went on forever. Doggedly he planted one foot in front of the other, grabbing undergrowth and dragging himself up the hillside. He was sure he had lost his pursuers. He came to an overhanging rock, partially veiled by creepers. He dived into its cover and crouched, aware of the ragged gasping of his breath and the thumping of his heart. He closed his eyes and hugged his legs, striving to control his breathing.

Minutes passed without a sound from outside, and gradually his apprehension turned to relief. Then he thought of his team. He cursed Elliott, then Dan and the others for not stopping her. Then he cursed himself for leaving them in the first place. Christ, if they were dead now it was all his fault. He should have done the sensible thing and ordered an immediate retreat back to the remains of the 'ship. He tried to calm himself and think about his situation. The simple fact was that the militia of the Danzig Organisation were cold-blooded killers. Even if he did somehow escape their clutches now, what chance had he of getting off the Reach and back to Earth?

He felt a hand close around his arm and he almost cried out.

"Engineman," said the voice, "do not be afraid."

In the faint light filtering through the overhanging foliage, Mirren made out a face close to his. It was long and insect-like, with a thin slit of a mouth, a nose no more than two centrally located holes, and massive eyes composed mainly of dark pupil. The alien blinked, its lids operating from below and covering the eye with a disconcerting upward sweep. Mirren had hardly noticed the alienness of the massacred Lho, but faced with this creature he was made aware of how fundamentally dissimilar it was to him. He backed off.

"Engineman," the Lho said in a whispery voice. "We are your friends. We will help you. Please follow."

The alien, bent double, moved off along the overhang from where he'd approached Mirren, peered through the vines and slipped out. The instinct for survival overcame Mirren's qualms. He followed, shaking uncontrollably. The Lho beckoned and ran quickly and quietly up the hillside, dodging fleetly between trees. Mirren gave chase, exhaustion overwhelming him. The alien paused on the crest of the rise. He ducked through the undergrowth. Mirren bent after him and found himself in a tunnel-like track through clinging briars. The natural corridor darkened, excluding the dying sunlight filtering through the jungle canopy far overhead. The alien gripped his wrist and guided him forward. The corridor opened into a circular chamber like the lair of some great beast. A torch gave off a roseate glow and fragrant smoke like incense. Three other Lho occupied the chamber, squatting on their haunches. They looked up and spoke in their own high, fluting tongue as Mirren entered and sank to the ground. His rescuer answered their queries, and as the debate continued they were joined by more aliens – whether survivors of the massacre or outsiders, Mirren could not tell. Each alien approached him, peering, some venturing to touch his silvers in apparent wonder.

"Engineman," they whistled to each other, gesturing at him. "*Engineman!*"

The first Lho called the others to order. He did most of the speaking in the heated debate that followed – either because he was their leader, or had assumed the role through rescuing Mirren.

He was shaking. Fear of the militia gave way to a greater fear. He closed his eyes and tried to calm himself. Despite what his rescuer had assured him, he felt terrified. It occurred to him that he was to be tried as the representative of the race responsible for the slaughter of the villagers.

He opened his eyes, alerted by the sudden silence. Ten alien faces regarded him with unreadable expressions. He realised that in his weariness he no longer recognised the Lho who had rescued him; their faces appeared identical.

One of the aliens moved from the circle, sat cross-legged before Mirren. He assumed it was his rescuer.

"It has been decided, Enginemen..." He read Mirren's name-tag stitched to his radiation silvers. "Mir-ren? I am Rhan."

Mirren inclined his head. He was trembling and didn't trust himself to speak.

"We will do our best to return you to Earth," the alien said, "for ourselves as well as for yourself. You must inform the Terran representative of the United Colonies of what you have seen... He must call an emergency session to debate our situation. The Danzig Organisation must be stopped." Rhan spoke with painstaking care and precision, and the relief Mirren experienced on learning that they would help was followed by confusion.

"But there's a UC representative on this planet," he said, his voice wavering.

Rhan spread his arms wide in what might have been a dismissive gesture. "The UC official on this planet is in the pay of the Danzig Organisation. He reports to Earth that we are succumbing to a natural plague."

"I'll do everything I can to let the UC know the truth," Mirren said. "But why...?" He gestured in the general direction of the carnage.

"One standard year ago," Rhan said, "we approached General Villiers and explained the situation, gave him the benefit of our knowledge. He refused to believe us, so we had no option but to kidnap one of his Majors, take him to the northern mountains and grant him the experience... We hardly expected him to react as he did. We assumed that communion with our Effectuators would have the desired result – that he would report to Villiers the truth of our claims and he would then bring about the closure of the Danzig Organisation interfaces, and those of the other companies around the Expansion... We later heard that Villiers considered the Major to be deranged, or drugged. and that our opposition to the Organisation was merely political, an alliance with the Disciples of the Reach to overthrow their regime. We tried to send representatives to Earth to plead our case, but always we were prevented from doing so, often violently. So, finally, and with reluctance, we joined forces with the Disciples – many of us resorted to armed resistance, forming guerrilla bands and striking at the heart of the Organisation. Their retribution was terrible. Villiers ordered our elimination. Many of my people are falling to the plague they unleashed upon the planet. Those of us who survived are hunted and massacred... You witnessed a small part of that today."

Mirren was aware of the aliens, regarding him intently. He was suddenly very hot. He could not keep a note of disbelief from his voice when he said, "You want the closure of the interfaces?"

Another Lho, seated in the circle to his left, spoke in a fast, twittering tongue. Rhan replied. He looked around his people as if asking their consent. Several made definite gestures.

"Before we attempt to return you to Earth," Rhan said, "we will first take you to the mountain temple. There you will commune with the Effectuators, and learn the truth. You will take this truth to your people."

"The truth?" Mirren asked.

Rhan gestured. "I do not know the human terms to express the concept," he said. "But you will experience it for yourself in two days, when you commune."

Rhan conferred with his people again. Mirren tried to take in what the alien had told him. The heat in the chamber was making him dizzy.

Rhan returned his attention to Mirren. "We wish you to inform your leaders that, in return for the closure of the interfaces, we will endow your Enginemen the ability to push starships at speeds never before imagined. A voyage of five thousand light years will take just minutes. This will compensate humankind for the loss of the interfaces. But we will grant your Enginemen and Enginewomen this ability only if your people agree to close the interfaces."

Mirren stared at the alien. His first impulse was to laugh. "How can you possibly grant..." he began. "It's impossible!"

Rhan said, "We began this process one standard year ago, as a way of persuading you to continue with starflight. Unfortunately, it was less than successful. Our Effectuators contacted certain of your Alpha Enginemen while they were pushing, and... and attempted to absorb them into the Oneness."

As Rhan spoke, Mirren thought of those Enginemen who had suffered the fatal condition known as Black's Syndrome – the time-lapsed men, as they were called – and then dismissed such thoughts as superstitious nonsense. There was, so far as he was concerned, no such thing as the Oneness into which anyone could be absorbed.

"Our Effectuators drew forth these Enginemen in the only way they knew – by one sense at a time, with the aim of leaving the subjects with no conception of the present or self and thus eminently able to appreciate the illusion of this 'reality' and conjoin in the ultimate reality of the continuum. As it happened, the mechanisms of the flux-tanks detected our Effectuators' interference and withdrew the subjects before full absorption was completed, leaving these Enginemen with certain sensory anomalies."

Mirren contrasted the earnest, matter-of-factness of Rhan's delivery with the content of his speech; this simple alien was using terminology and discussing concepts he should, by rights, have known nothing about. The effect, together with the silent regard of the gathered Lho, made Mirren light-headed with the notion that the impossible might not be so impossible after all.

Mirren shook his head. "I can't believe it."

"Please, Mir-ren, believe what I tell you. The Enginemen we contacted were named Black, Thorn, Rodriguez..."

Mirren found himself saying, "You killed these men... You're responsible for their deaths."

"Mir-ren," Rhan said, holding forth a hand. "To begin with, there is no such thing as death. What you call death is merely the end of a certain, physical state of existence. Our experiments with the Alphas were worthy attempts, which did not work. These Enginemen are now part of the One. We have modified the technique of absorption, and we are confident that we can perform it successfully on any willing Enginemen in the future. These subjects will be drawn into the Oneness of the continuum, while still existing in the physical world and thus able to mind-push your starships at, as I have said, undreamed of speeds."

Another alien spoke to Rhan. There was a brief exchange involving every Lho in the gathering. Finally Rhan turned to Mirren. "If you wish, you could be the first Engineman on which a successful absorption is performed."

Mirren stared. How could he begin to inform the alien that he was a sceptic, an unbeliever who considered other

Enginemen's talk of Nirvana or Oneness as nothing more than superstition?

He gathered his thoughts and said truthfully, "I ended my period as an Engineman with this flight. The Canterbury Line is no more." He realised, as he said this, that his old self would be appalled at the prevarication.

Rhan spoke with another Lho.

At length he said, "You have a brother, Robert, who is an Engineman."

Mirren was shaken. "How can you possibly know...?"

"Our Effectuators monitor the flights of every Alpha Engineman. I am informed that your brother is one such. If our Effectuators brought about his absorption, then the chances of success will be high. He will be the first, a new breed of Engineman."

"No!" he said, the rational part of him gaining ascendancy and realising the horror of what they were suggesting. "I can't allow it–"

Rhan gestured. "Perhaps, when you have experienced the communion, Mir-ren, you will be agreeable."

In the silence that followed, one of the aliens rose and slipped from the hide. The others broke into a murmured conversation. It appeared, despite what he might have had to say, that the audience was over. As he watched the insectoid aliens converse in their thin, high tones, Mirren felt at once angered and bewildered – and at the same time curious about the experience of communion which awaited him.

The alien returned and whispered to Rhan.

"We will now proceed," he said to Mirren. "The temple is two days from here, in the high mountains."

Mirren climbed to his feet, his limbs aching. Rhan lay long fingers on his arm and guided him out into the still, quiet twilight of the jungle.

Rhan sent his fellow Lho on ahead, and they flitted swiftly through the trees – quick, lithe figures, their gold and bronze bodies shimmering in the occasional shaft of sunlight slanting through the cover. Rhan, Mirren and a second alien followed at a jog, and once again Mirren experienced the surge of adrenalin familiar from the earlier chase. He thought of Dan and the rest of his team, and the treatment they might have received at the hands of the militia. He was sickened by the thought that the best they could hope for was imprisonment.

There was only one way to take revenge on the Danzig Organisation. He had to escape the planet and get word of the atrocities back to the civilised worlds. He was considering how the Lho intended to get him off Hennessy's Reach when, from up ahead, an alien appeared and called out. Rhan gripped his arm. "We are being tracked," he said, panic evident in his tone.

Mirren heard the whine of turbos overhead. He looked up. Through the high tree-tops he caught a glimpse of a troop-carrier.

Rhan whispered, "This way!"

They darted from the track and through the dense undergrowth. In the distance Mirren heard a sound that filled him with dread. The repeated blast of rifle fire crashed through the humid evening air.

As they ran, Rhan gave instructions to the second Lho, "We stand a better chance if we divide," he said to Mirren. "For the time being, farewell." And he was gone, slipping silently into the shadows.

The second Lho took Mirren's arm and continued with him through the jungle. They increased their pace. The rifle fire grew louder. Human shouts of triumph sounded close behind.

Then, up ahead, he saw a tall militia-man stand squarely in their path. He raised his rifle, fired. Mirren dived, but the alien was not so quick. Mirren hit the ground and rolled, looked up to see the Lho fall beside him, his shoulder shattered.

The militia-man strode towards them, rifle held at a negligent angle in one hand. He wore a bulbous helmet fitted with a com-system – which made him appear more alien than the Lho-Dharvo – and a mirrored visor concealing his expression.

Then, quite casually, he stood over the twitching alien and pumped two bullets into his skull. He turned to Mirren, gestured with his rifle.

Mirren climbed to his feet with his hands in the air. He stared at the silver visor, trying to look into the eyes of the man responsible for such barbarism, but all he saw was his own reflection. The militia-man prodded Mirren in the ribs, instructing him to turn and walk. He allowed himself to be marched through the jungle towards the waiting troop-carrier, choked with impotent rage at the death of the alien and the awful simplicity of his capture.

In the dark confines of the carrier he was shackled hand and foot. He had hoped to find Dan and the others in the hold, but he was the only prisoner. As the turbos roared and the carrier lurched into the air, a militia-man roughly pulled his head back and clamped a pair of goggles to his face, which sucked at the skin around his eyes and rendered him blind. He was aware only of the reek of sweat, the sound of the carrier as it mach'd over the tree-tops, and his increasing fear. Time passed slowly – an hour, maybe more.

He was prodded from a fitful sleep. The turbos were whining down and the carrier no longer lurched; they had landed. Hands grabbed him and bundled him from the hold. He was marched across what might have been the tarmac of an airbase: he could hear the distant roar of jets and the rhythmic *blatt-blatt-blatt* of rotor blades.

The surface underfoot changed. The sound of aircraft died. He sensed an enclosed space – the interior of a building. He was hurried down what might have been a corridor, then shoved in the back. He stumbled forward. A door crashed shut behind him.

He sat down on a hard bunk-bed.

The problem with the blindfold and the total silence within the room was that it turned his thoughts inwards, made him dwell on the atrocities committed by the Danzig militia in the jungle. In turn, he could not help but consider his own fate.

He had no idea how much time had elapsed when he heard the door open and more than one person, judging by the sound of their footsteps, enter the room.

"Take this off!" he said, plucking at the goggles. "At least let me see you."

"Be quiet. Sit down." The voice was stern, uncompromising.

Mirren remained standing. Someone – he felt sure it was not the man who had spoken – backhanded him across the face. He tasted blood in his mouth, staggered in the direction of the bunk and collapsed onto it.

"I am going to ask you a few questions, and I want immediate and truthful answers. If I don't like the answers you give me, I will have you shot." There was something so cold and emotionless in the threat that Mirren didn't for a second doubt the man.

A period of silence, then, "You were found with the Lho in the jungle. What did they want with you?"

Mirren hesitated. Even if he told them the truth, he doubted if it would help the Organisation's cause. But the thought of capitulating, bowing to the coercion of these thugs...

"Go to hell!"

Silence. He trembled with fear.

The blow came, all the more shocking for being unexpected. Pain shot through his jaw.

"We'll try again, Mr Mirren. What did the aliens want with you?"

He heard the percussion of a safety-catch being switched, felt a cold circle of gun-metal against his temple.

He hated himself for giving in, but the instinct for survival overcame his conscience. "They... they wanted to get me to Earth–" He stopped himself.

"Why?"

"To tell the free worlds of the slaughter you're committing here."

Calmly, his interrogator asked, "And what did they tell you of this slaughter?"

Mirren remained silent.

"Did they tell you the reason for our offensive, Mr Mirren?"

He shook his head. "No."

He sensed his tormentors' retreat. A muttered discussion took place at the other side of the cell. Someone returned. Mirren was expecting another blow – not the fine, wet spray that filled his nose with a stinging, antiseptic scent.

He passed out.

When he regained consciousness he felt lethargic, heavy-limbed, and filled with a curious sense of well-being. He also felt amenable. He knew, then, the nature of the spray.

"Glad to have you back with us, Mr Mirren," said the voice from the darkness. "Now, please, tell me who you met in the jungle and what they told you."

He felt as if he had been split into two separate identities. One understood what was happening, and wanted more than anything to resist the drug, to tell his other half not to capitulate – but was prevented from doing so by an overwhelming lethargy. He heard his amenable self talking, telling his interrogator about the crashlanding and the trek through the jungle, his witnessing of the massacre and his audience with the Lho.

"What did they want with you, Mr Mirren?"

"To get back to Earth, to tell the free planets what is happening here. And..."

"And, Mr Mirren?"

"They wanted to take me to their mountain hide, to commune with their Effectuators."

A silence. He could almost sense their anticipation. "Where precisely is their mountain hide?"

This, Mirren felt, was what the Organisation really wanted. He comforted himself that the information he had supplied already would be of little use to them.

He shook his head. "I don't know–"

The interrogator said, "Where, Mirren? Tell me!"

"I said, I don't know. They didn't tell me–"

He sensed their impatience, their anger.

A silence followed, stretched, until it came to him that they must have left the room. Perhaps an hour later, they returned. He guessed he was in for another bout of interrogation. Instead, he felt something being fitted around his head, cold metal bands pressing against his skull, electrodes at his temples.

He knew what was happening to him, and felt relief that they were sparing his life...

He slipped into unconsciousness.

He came to his senses in a hospital bed in a room filled with sunlight. He tried to sit up. An orderly was on hand to restrain him, gently.

"Where am I?"

"On Earth, Mr Mirren."

He fell back, tried to collect his thoughts. His most recent memories were of Paris, the party before his last push for the Canterbury Line.

The orderly was explaining. "Your 'ship crashlanded on an uncharted Rim world, Mr Mirren. You were uninjured, but the trauma of the accident induced comprehensive amnesia..." The orderly went on, but Mirren wasn't listening.

He closed his eyes and tried to remember.

Chapter Twenty-Two

Kelly brought the flier down on a spur of rock overlooking the massed tree-tops of the jungle that extended towards the great ball of the setting sun. Ella stretched, her tired muscles protesting at the effort. The Engineman jumped from the flier and strode across to a rock pool, where he knelt and splashed his face with water.

Ella climbed out. The air was warm, still and silent. Inland, against the twilight, a range of mountains rose grey and imposing, their peaks jagged and faceted like knapped granite.

Kelly made his way back to the flier.

"You're awake at last."

"How long have I been out?"

"Around eight hours," he said. "See the bastards got you with the old incapacitator."

She lifted her arm, peered at it. The skin was red raw and painful, as if boiled. "I'll live." She looked up at Kelly and smiled. "Thanks for saving my life."

"My pleasure, ma'am." He indicated the rock pool. "Water's wonderful if you feel like a swim."

Ella sat on the hood of the flier and held her head in her hands. "I'll pass. Don't think I have the energy."

"Food, then? You must be ravenous."

"Yeah, food'd be great."

She felt as if the trauma of the past two days – her injuries, the torture she had withstood, not to mention the mental torment of not knowing whether she was going to live or die – had finally caught up with her. Every centimetre of her body ached, the pain intense in her jaw, shoulder, and thigh.

Kelly was breaking out rations from the flier. He lifted a cooler on to the hood next to her. "In-flight meals for the Danzig Airways – liberated during a raid last week."

Ella opened a self-heating tray of meat and vegetables. They sat side by side on the flier, eating in silence for a while.

She hadn't introduced herself. "Ella Fernandez," she said through a mouthful of potato. "Pleased to meet you."

"Pleased to meet you, Ella. I'm Kelly. But I know who you are. Why do you think we staged the raid on the Danzig base back there? When we learnt you'd been captured, I thought your father would be grateful if we got you out."

She swallowed quickly. "You know my father?"

"We've worked together with the Disciples and the Lho these past six years. Devising strategy, tactics..." Kelly paused. "Six, seven years ago your father was becoming disillusioned with the Organisation – they'd taken over a couple of worlds further along the Rim and there were rumours of civil unrest and military suppression. He began to look into the Disciples. He read books, made contacts. We were suspicious as hell of him at first. There he was, a Danzig executive, showing interest in Disciples' philosophy, declaring he wanted to join us..."

"But you let him?"

"He supplied information vital to the resistance movement. Over the next few years we worked together, became good friends."

Ella shook her head. "I never think of my father as having friends."

"He has. He's well respected." Kelly paused. "You know, he regretted that you and he weren't closer."

"He told you that?"

"It was always on his mind. He knew he'd made mistakes, but it wasn't easy for him, you know. His work for the Organisation took him away a lot of the time, and you drifted apart."

"You mean he put me in boarding school and forgot about me."

"He was a busy man, Ella."

She laughed. "Yeah – co-ordinating the take-over or destruction of the last of the shipping Lines–"

"That was a long time ago. He's changed. He knows that what he did then was wrong."

Ella whispered, "All I ever wanted was a proper father. He never gave me any affection. It was as if he didn't know how to."

The Engineman shrugged. "Perhaps he didn't," he said. "I think he only came to appreciate you later, once you'd left home. He kept tabs on you, you know? He had people report on how your work was going. He even bought a piece of yours."

"I know. I've seen it." She fell silent, staring at the sunset. At last she said, "Why didn't he tell me about his conversion back then? He could have told me years ago, when it happened." She paused. "If he'd told me six years ago, things would be different now."

The big American leaned back on the hood of the flier, propping himself on one elbow. "It was difficult, Ella."

She looked at him. "Difficult? How come? All it would've taken was a disc, a card even."

"I was with him during those years. We had to be very careful. If the Organisation had had the slightest hint of where we were, more than the liberation of Hennessy's Reach would have been at stake."

Ella stared at him.

Kelly said, "Not long after his conversion, the Lho who'd survived the plague summoned him. He had the right contacts across the Expansion, the right kind of knowledge, and the Disciples had the finances."

Ella shook her head. The thought of the Lho and her father, working in alliance...

"What did they want with him?"

Kelly said, "They wanted him to help them save themselves, the last of the Lho-Dharvo people. They took him into the mountains, where the survivors lived in a temple far underground, and they explained their situation..." He paused, considering. "When he came back, your father was a changed man. If anything, he was more committed, more determined to see the end of the Organisation. He never spoke about what he experienced in the temple, but whatever it was moved him profoundly. There were rumours–"

"Yes?"

Kelly gestured. "I heard it from a Lho that he entered into some kind of communion with their holy people – but the Lho I spoke to wasn't very clear what exactly the communion was all about... Anyway, he returned doubly committed to the cause. We were smuggled off the Reach in a container, through the interface to the free planets of the Tyler-McDermott system. We made them our base and worked to save the Lho and bring about the downfall of the Danzig Organisation."

Ella wondered what her father had undergone in the mountain stronghold of the Lho, if it had been anything like the sense of unity she had experienced all those years ago in the cave with L'Endo.

"Where's my father now?" she asked.

"On Earth," Kelly said. "Specifically, in Paris."

"Paris?"

"He sent you a disc a few weeks ago, arranging to meet you in Paris when he arrived. Obviously you never received it."

"I got it, but I was angry. I wiped most of it when I realised who it was from." She shrugged. "Then things happened. I decided I wanted to see him. So I came here."

"And walked right into the lion's mouth," Kelly said. "Fortunately, we can get you out of here."

She stared at him. "But the interface...

Kelly sat up. "There is another way we can get back to Earth."

Ella peered at him.

"Your father's sending a smallship to the Reach to evacuate the Lho from the temple. With luck, we should be aboard it for the flight back to Earth."

"A *smallship*?"

"Come on, we'd better get moving."

He climbed back into the flier. Ella sat beside him, watching the spur of rock turn away beneath them and disappear. They headed over the jungle towards a jagged, up-thrusting mountain range, skimming low over the tree-tops as the jungle climbed the mountainside and then petered out.

Kelly kept the flier in close to the cliff-face, skirting great planes of rock towering for kilometres above the flier. They wound through a series of pinnacles, each one higher than the last. Ahead, perhaps fifty kilometres distant, was a blunt, rectangular peak Ella recognised as Mt Sebastian.

Ella didn't know which was the most unlikely: seeing her father again after so long, or flying to Earth aboard a smallship. She was twelve when she had last shipped through space, and now smallships seemed an ancient, superannuated form of transport. Compared to the simplicity of the interfaces, the procedure of phasing a smallship into and out of the *nada*-continuum was complex – not to mention dangerous. So much could go wrong between here and Earth. She would rather have returned by interface... not that she was complaining. It was a miracle, after the events of the past few days, that she had survived and would soon meet her father. She closed her eyes and wished that she was already on board the smallship, en route to Earth.

"Hello," Kelly said.

Something in his tone indicated he wasn't speaking to her.

She opened her eyes. He was leaning over the side, looking back towards the jungle. Ella strained her eyes in the same direction, but could see nothing.

Kelly accelerated and swept the flier in a corkscrew ascent of a lofty pinnacle. At the summit he landed and jumped out. Ella followed, alarmed. Kelly was on his stomach at the edge of the rock. Ella joined him and peered down the sheer, dwindling face.

"What is it?"

"There." He pointed straight ahead at the jungle. "See the road leaving the jungle and winding up the mountainside? Directly beneath where the right hand side of the sun touches the land."

She charted down from the sun's circumference, followed the line down through the massed lobes of the tree-tops. She found the road.

An armoured convoy – perhaps the same one she'd seen enter the interface on Carey's Sanctuary – was making its laborious way up the narrow road that followed the contour of the mountainside. There were perhaps a hundred vehicles in the column, ranging from small trucks to colossal rocket launchers. They moved so slowly that from this distance they seemed to be making no progress at all. At the head of the convoy, Ella made out two fliers, scouting the lie of the road in front. These, she suspected, were the immediate danger.

"Obviously they haven't seen us," Kelly said, "or the fliers would have given chase."

"If they haven't seen us, can't we just... just put the mountain between us and head to our destination?"

He glanced at her, then back to the convoy. "There's a missile launcher in the back of the flier, and enough ammunition to take out half the convoy."

"But they'd come after us. We can't take the risk."

"Technically, Ella, we're expendable." He rolled onto his side and looked at her. "For the past month or so the Organisation's been building up its forces in the higher Torreón mountains. They know there's a 'ship due – they had informants in the Disciples, before we eradicated them – but they don't know when or exactly where. When the 'ship phases in, it'll be sending out an electro-magnetic pulse like a homing beacon. It'll be becalmed for up to two hours while it's serviced and made ready for the return flight. The Organisation'll unleash all hell and more. We're pretty deep, and they'd have to flatten the mountain, but they've got a lot of fire-power up here..." He looked down on the convoy. "What I'm trying to say is, if we can knock out a couple of launchers, then we've done the cause a hell of a lot of good. Even if we get zero'd in the process. Your father wouldn't like it if he found out, but I think he'd understand."

Ella regarded the convoy as it climbed at a snail's pace up the mountain road. She glanced at Kelly, aware of his dilemma. He was miles away, staring down at the enemy. He saw her looking and shook his head.

"I'm sorry, Ella. But family reunions come second to the cause. I'm going to surprise the living Fernandez out of the jokers."

He ran back to the flier, opened the hatch in the rear and returned with a case of shells and the launcher on his shoulder. He lay down beside Ella, peering through an eye-piece and tapping co-ordinates into a keyboard on the shaft of the weapon.

He glanced at Ella. "Open the case and take out a dozen missiles."

"Kelly... I want to get back to Earth in one piece."

He turned and peered at her. Instead of shouting, as she'd expected, he took her hand. "Hey, and so do I, girl. You don't think I'm going to let the bastards get us, do you? But I've got to strike while I can. We knock out a few launchers here, we save lives later. Now open the case and slide the missiles into this chamber, okay?" He squeezed her fingers.

She nervously unlatched the case and counted out twelve missiles. The thought of giving themselves away, of falling once more into the clutches of the greatest evil she had ever known, made her sick with fear.

The missiles were tiny, like pepper-pots. She eased them into the launcher.

Kelly saw her expression and laughed. "You wait till you see the damage they do."

She lay down beside him, peering over the edge. The column had advanced. She counted more than a hundred vehicles. Her palms were sweating at the very sight of the convoy.

"Ready, Ella?" He touched the trigger.

With surprisingly little noise, the first missile zipped from the launcher. There was a delay of ten seconds, and then the leading rocket launcher went up in a roiling bloom of flame like an incandescent rose. Delayed, the sound reached them a second later – a hollow crump and a shriek of torn metal like something mortal tortured. Kelly fired five more missiles.

By this time, the militia were on the defensive. Anti-missile projectiles intercepted Kelly's missiles, detonating them one by one in great bursts of flame. A rocket launcher loosed two long, finned missiles. Ella watched in horrified fascination as they speared towards where they lay – shooting overhead with a deafening roar and exploding in a shower of flame and debris against the mountain half a kilometre beyond.

"Kelly!" she screamed. "Let's get out of here!"

Determined, Kelly fired the remaining six missiles. Five were intercepted, blinding Ella. When her sight returned, she saw a rocket launcher on its side down below, flame licking around its blackened carcass.

"That's it, girl. We're gone."

They jumped aboard the flier and Kelly put the pinnacle between themselves and the convoy. They headed towards Mt Sebastian, a towering grey presence in the distance. Ella turned in her seat, stared at the western sky and the flaming hemisphere of the red giant. Against its brightness, any pursuing vehicles would show as tell-tale silhouettes. All she saw was the tiny, dark disc of an inner planet as it traversed the face of the giant primary.

They passed higher into the mountains, flying up valleys and over peaks. Down below the ground was grey, desolate, with no sign of vegetation. In time they put other mountain peaks between themselves and the red giant, so that only its apex showed above the serried range like shark's teeth. Soon, snow appeared on the flanks of the mountains alongside. The air grew chill, then icy.

Ella had been thinking of her father for some time before she asked, "Kelly, when was the last time you saw my father?"

The Engineman glanced at her. "About three weeks ago. Why?"

"Was he okay? I mean, was he keeping well?"

Kelly considered. "He was under quite a bit of strain. A lot depended on him and he was putting in long hours – but I'd say yes, he was keeping pretty well, considering."

She hugged herself against the cold. "Will he be aboard the smallship?"

Kelly shook his head. "He's co-ordinating things from Earth." He smiled at her. "Don't worry. It won't be long now."

Kelly steered the flier under an overhang and into a lateral crevice hewn from the rock, and Ella experienced relief like the unburdening of a great weight. The crevice was shaded from the light of the sun, and illumination was provided by a flickering brand on the wall beside a rectangular opening let into the rock.

Ella climbed from the flier, and then she saw it.

The Lho-Dharvon appeared in the entrance, and the sight of it brought Ella up short. Years had elapsed since her last meeting with a Lho, and in her memory she had anthropomorphised them, allowed her feelings towards the aliens to colour her objectivity. She was surprised anew at how perilously thin the Lho were, how *alien*, almost insect-like.

The Lho approached Kelly, touched him on his forehead with its middle finger, then did the same to Ella.

"Hunter..." it breathed. "Welcome."

"Is the 'ship here?" Kelly asked.

"No 'ship..." the Lho said. "Come."

It ushered them through the entrance in the rock and down a steep, tight flight of stairs. The steps were obviously made for longer Lhoan legs, high and narrow so that Ella jarred her spine as she followed Kelly and the alien. The passage was low – at times the Engineman had to stoop. For the most part it was excavated through solid rock, but occasionally it followed the course of fissures and natural crevices, and here the steps were even narrower and more precipitous. The way was lighted by flaming torches at long intervals, with stretches of half-light in between. They descended for more than an hour. As they plummeted and wound their way deeper into the mountain, the temperature increased. Ella sweated, feeling faint with the humidity and exertion.

At last the stairway terminated and they came out in a wide corridor, clearly an original part of the ancient temple. The corridor too was illuminated by torches, but set at closer intervals to reveal panels carved into the stone depicting stick figures and symmetrical circle-within-circle symbols like mandalas. Ella had no time to give the panels anything but a passing glance. The alien hurried them along and she found herself jogging to keep up. The wonder she felt at being in the temple of the Lho, the sense of experiencing something alien and *other*, was tempered by exhaustion and the thought of the trip back to Earth.

They turned left and climbed down another steep flight of stairs, this one corkscrewing through the rock until it gave onto a vast cathedral-like chamber. The far regions of the circular chamber were in darkness, but nearby was all light and activity. A generator droned, providing power for fluorescent lights and banks of computer terminals and screens. A dozen Enginemen and Enginewomen monitored the screens and pored over read-outs. Perhaps fifty Lho waited – with all the forlorn apprehension of the refugees they were – to one side, crouching or sitting cross-legged on the floor. With them, Ella made out half a dozen aliens on stretchers.

Kelly led Ella across to a rest area – a crude arrangement of old settees and foam-forms set out in a square. Enginemen slept or rested; others drank coffee or chatted among themselves. Kelly embraced a short, wiry Enginewoman in her fifties.

"This is it, Kelly," the woman said. "This is what we've been working towards..."

For the next hour, Ella stretched out and rested on a foam-form, unable to sleep for the noise of the generator, the tense conversation of the assembled Disciples and the sense of anticipation bursting within her.

From among the banks of computers and monitors, someone shouted. The Enginemen in the rest area stood and rushed out. Ella joined them. They stood around the edge of the chamber, staring into the darkness. Seconds later, a fierce gust of displaced air almost knocked Ella off her feet. Grit and dust stung her face as the gale raged around her, blasting her in the face as she watched the squat, silver smallship flicker into existence in the centre of the chamber like the image on a defective vid-screen. At last it established itself solidly in this reality, the sight of the 'ship made all the more poignant by the awed hush of the assembled Disciples.

Ella stared at the smallship through her tears. She was suddenly overcome with a terrible anxiety that had nothing to do with the safety of the imminent flight. The arrival of the 'ship made real the fact that soon she would be returning to Earth, and she experienced a complex mix of emotions – love and hate and everything in between – at the thought of meeting her father again for the first time in ten years.

Chapter Twenty-Three

Mirren stood in the engine-room of the *Sublime* and stared out through the viewscreen. At first he assumed that the 'ship had materialised during the planet's night, as all was darkness outside. Then, as his eyes adjusted, he realised that the 'ship had phased into a vast chamber. Tall, carved figures, attenuated and alien, demarcated the cavern's perimeter. Beneath them, dwarfed, were a group of humans – some in radiation silvers – standing around banks of computers and monitors in the dim light of a dozen jerry-rigged fluorescents. The men and women were clapping, cheering, hugging each other and exchanging handshakes. As they made their way across the floor of the chamber, they were joined by a group of tall, elongated aliens. They moved towards the 'ship with an unhurried circumspection that reminded Mirren of certain insects. They paused in the wash of light from the engine-room and stared up at Mirren and Dan. One of them lifted an arm in an oddly human gesture of greeting, incongruous coming from a figure so alien. Mirren returned the wave and asked Miguelino to open the hatch.

He left the engine-room and dropped to the lounge, where already Enginemen and -women were carrying aboard computers and other technical apparatus. They stopped and greeted him with handshakes, formal in their statement of name, the Line for which they'd pushed, and rank. The Lho walked up the ramp and settled themselves around the lounge, sitting cross-legged on the carpet in patient groups of three or four.

A big Engineman crushed Mirren's fingers with a welcoming handshake. "Kelly, Dunnett Line, Alpha. Are we glad to see you, man. We have forty-five Lho here, as well as six Effectuators and around thirty Disciples."

"Mirren, Canterbury Line, Alpha. We should be set to phase-out in just under two hours, according to my pilot."

"Expect a few fireworks, Mirren. The Organisation know we're down here, and I don't think they'll sit around playing with themselves while we phase-out."

Kelly had his arm around a small woman, less from affection than the need to keep her upright. She looked frail, pale and beaten. Mirren and Kelly helped her across to a foam-form. She collapsed onto it, smiling as if in apology for her exhaustion.

"Hunter," the woman said, "no Line, no rank, but I'm a Disciple and damned glad to be here."

Kelly explained, "Ella was captured by the Organisation, given a rough time."

"Hunter?" Mirren asked. "Are you related–?"

The woman smiled. "He's my father. How is he?"

"He was well when we left. He'll be a lot better for seeing us return."

Ella Hunter smiled and closed her eyes. "Earth, here I come."

Mirren glanced across the lounge. A tall, slight alien stood at the top of the ramp, staring at him. As he watched, it raised its long arm, as if in greeting. Mirren said to Kelly, "You'll find food and drink dispensers by the bulkhead, washrooms along the corridor. Excuse me."

He nodded to Kelly and Hunter and walked across the lounge. With the recollection of the crashlanding and his audience with the Lho so fresh in his memory, it was as if no time at all had elapsed between then and now, as if the past ten years had miraculously ceased to exist.

He halted before the Lho; they all, to his eyes, appeared very much the same, but there was something almost familiar about the alien before him.

"Rhan?" he ventured.

The alien reached out, touched Mirren's brow with its long forefinger. "Rhan was murdered by the militia shortly after speaking with you," said the Lho. "I am Ghaine. I was present when Rhan brought you to our hide. Of the ten Lho gathered there that day, I am the only survivor. I welcome you back to Dharvon, Mir-ren, and thank you."

Mirren reached out and took the alien's hand in his.

Behind Ghaine, twelve Lho carried six aliens on stretchers up the ramp and into the 'ship. They were met by other Lho, who escorted them into the elevator to the astrodome. Mirren watched as the Lho were carried past. They were naked, and seemed to Mirren to be ancient, their limbs thin and their extended rib-cages and pelvic flanges dangerously prominent.

"They are the Effectuators," Ghaine said. "They have been like this for many, many years. They are selected from our finest religious minds. Ideally, there should be twelve at any one time. But as the older Effectuators left us to begin their final journeys into the One, there have been fewer and fewer Lho to take their place.

"Through rigorous mental discipline they have induced upon themselves the process of withdrawal from this universe. They exist on the cusp of this reality and that of the continuum, having relinquished their egos and the burden of self."

"My brother..." Mirren began. He recalled what Bobby had said aboard the *Sublime*, about the *nada*-continuum and his place in it.

"Ten years ago, when the Organisation returned you to Earth, we expected you to relay our messages, both to the UC representative on Earth, and to your brother. We did not know what they had done to your mind. We found out only later, from contacts we had within the Organisation." Ghaine paused, then went on, "The Effectuators contacted your brother and attempted to draw him into the continuum. It was only partly successful. We required him to accompany you on the flight here so that the Effectuators might accomplish the task." He paused, then said, "It was wholly successful. Robert is the first human Effectuator."

Mirren felt his pulse quicken. He recalled what Rhan had said ten years ago, that there was no such thing as death, that all would be explained when he communed.

"Ten years ago I was promised communion," he whispered to Ghaine. "Is communion possible now?"

The Lho regarded him with its large, dark eyes and blinked once, slowly, from the bottom up. "Please, Mir-ren," Ghaine said at last. "Follow me."

They ascended in the elevator to the astrodome.

The Effectuators were laid out to form a six-armed star, heads together in the centre of the dome. Their attendants ministered to their needs, washed down their bodies, massaged them, murmured mantras or prayers.

Ghaine crossed to where four Lho sat beneath the crystal convexity of the dome, cross-legged, their folded shanks jutting. He knelt and spoke to the four, and as he did so they turned their heads and stared across at Mirren.

He remained by the sliding door, something about the unfamiliarity, the sheer strangeness of the scene before him, causing him to have second thoughts about the process of communion. There was something so primitive, almost shamanistic, about the tableau, that he was given to doubt any truth espoused by the aliens – then he recalled Bobby, and what the Effectuators had done for him, and he realised that as crude and primitive as the aliens seemed to be, they were in contact with something that had taken humankind millennia, and the advent of technology, to discover.

For so long Mirren had poured scorn on the tenet of the Disciples, considered it the superstitious belief system of weak-minded people, that to give credence to such belief now, when faced with the prospect of his death in the not too distant future, seemed to him an act of contemptible heresy. Which, he thought, was an admission of weakness in himself. Surely, when faced with the truth, he should be strong enough to admit that he was wrong.

Ghaine stood and rejoined Mirren. The other Lho followed him, gathered around Mirren, staring at him with their odd, up-blinking eyes. One or two reached out, touched his silversuit. Another took his hand and examined his fingers. The fourth alien moved around him, and he felt cold fingers probing the base of his skull above his occipital console.

"Do not be alarmed," Ghaine said, in response to Mirren's reaction. "They are merely assessing your receptivity. Communion is not a process undertaken lightly by anyone involved. It is the most ancient and sacrosanct act known to my people."

Mirren felt the fingers on his skull, but refused to believe that this *assessment* was anything more than meaningless ritual, a superstitious performance that preceded each communion. After a minute the aliens stepped back and spoke to Ghaine in their high, piping voices.

They retreated to their former position across the astrodome, sat in a circle and busied themselves in the shadows with implements that Mirren could not make out.

Ghaine said, "They have decided. You may experience communion. They consider it your reward for saving the Lho, and also the honouring of the promise made by Rhan."

Mirren inclined his head. "Please convey my gratitude," he said. "How...?"

"I will explain the process in due course, Mir-ren. You are only the third human to commune. The first, a Major in the Danzig Organisation, was adversely affected by what he experienced. Hunter, on the other hand, was stronger, and though he found what he looked upon terrifying in the extreme, he overcame his fear, as he had to, and the very fact of your presence here today is testimony to that fact, and the culmination of a long process which began many years ago with his communion–"

"Why is it terrifying?" Mirren asked. "What happens?"

"You will see for yourself," Ghaine said. "This way." The alien led Mirren to the centre of the astrodome where the six Effectuators lay head to head, their emaciated bodies describing the spokes of a wheel. Ghaine spoke to the attendants, who re-arranged the crude wooden stretchers. There was now a space in the arrangement for Mirren.

"Sit down," Ghaine said. "Cross your legs."

Mirren sat as instructed between two recumbent Effectuators. They seemed to be in a trance, perfectly motionless, eyes closed. Their ancient, lustreless skin was like weathered bronze.

Ghaine sat before him, cross-legged too, their knees almost touching. "Soon the process will begin," he informed Mirren. "You will drink *haar*, which I am informed tastes vile to humans. This will prepare you mentally for contact. Please do not be disturbed by the strange effects brought about by the drug. You are in safe hands."

Mirren merely nodded, unable to find the words to express the mixture of curiosity, anticipation, and apprehension he was feeling.

"For fifteen minutes you will be conscious," Ghaine went on. "Then you will lose consciousness, we will lay you out, and you will commune."

Mirren was aware of activity in other parts of the 'ship, the vibration of elevator pads, pneumatic sighs and clunkings from outside as the *Sublime* went through the involved process of pre-flux flight checks. Beyond the hemisphere of the dome, along the length of the 'ship, safety lights flashed.

One of the four Lho who had inspected him earlier now approached, bearing a thick stone bowl. He passed it to Ghaine, who raised it to his forehead and murmured a litany of near-silent words.

Then he passed the bowl to Mirren.

He put his lips to the wide stone rim and tipped the bowl. The thick, white liquid rolled smoothly into his mouth. It tasted, as Ghaine had warned him, vile: at first sweet, and then burnt-bitter in aftertaste – but it was the texture that Mirren found especially unpalatable. It was as thick and cloying as rubber solution, and it slid down his throat in one continuous length that almost made him retch. He closed his eyes and forced down the contents of the bowl.

Ghaine was regarding him, nodding as if in satisfaction. "Good," he said. "Now, relax, empty your mind, wait..."

Mirren tried to do as he was commanded. He was aware that the four Lho, positioned now around the astrodome, were humming deeply within their throats, producing a continuous bass note.

He stared at his upturned palms in his lap. The *haar* seemed to be having an effect already; he felt relaxed, lethargic, heavy of limb. Then he noticed that its effect was not just physical. He found the act of concentration impossible: he could not follow through a logical course of thought. He stared across the dome to the lights on either side of the sliding door, and wondered what they were, what purpose they served – while he was aware that another part of him knew full well the purpose of the lights, but he could not access this information. He was aware of his time-sense becoming warped. He thought that surely the *Sublime* should have phased-out by now, should almost be home, as surely hours and hours had passed while he'd been sitting here, even though Ghaine had told him that he would be conscious for just fifteen minutes...

Then his vision blurred. Shapes and colours ran into each other in a diffuse, impressionistic abstraction. His last sense to go was that of touch; he felt hands on him, the floor beneath his body as he was laid out, and then nothing. He was cradled in a comforting limbo, aware only of his own tiny identity. He had half expected the process of communion to be similar to that of fluxing – but there was no sudden rush of wonder... it came slowly, gradually, and the wonder, when it arrived, was of a degree far greater than anything he had experienced in flux.

At first there was only darkness. Mirren felt six forces drawing him from the physical prison of his body. He was aware of a deep thrumming somewhere within him, like the lingering resonance of a plucked string. Then this vibration slowly intensified until it seemed that his whole being, his every cell and molecule, was oscillating in harmony with some cosmic tempo – and as the vibration reached such a pitch that he thought he must surely explode with the sheer orgasmic pleasure of it, he was flooded with a divine rapture, a sensation of overpowering well-being, and the awareness – surely not visual – of brilliant light. There was no way of comparing what he had experienced in flux with what he was going through now: he was aware of being blessed, of achieving something ultimate. The light in which he bathed was not blue, as it was in the *nada*-continuum experienced through the medium of the flux-tank, but a scintillating riot of every colour imaginable – a billion tiny sparks of glowing, fizzing, darting colour that assaulted his mind and filled him with a sense of being accepted, a feeling of union such as he had never known before.

He made out a voice, or a thought, which seemed to emanate from the vastness of the continuum without, and at the same time to manifest itself within his consciousness.

— Ralph...

He recognised the thought, the cerebral signature.

He responded. He thought: *Bobby*.

— Apprehend the joy, Ralph. The ecstasy. Consider what it must be like for me, who is fully part of the continuum now.

I can't. I can't imagine a joy greater than this.

— You have that to anticipate, Ralph. When you finally leave behind your self, when Ralph Mirren finally succumbs to Heine's, consider the wonder of what awaits...

Something manifested itself 'before' Mirren then, a spark of golden light, comet-like, brighter than those around it.

Bobby? Mirren thought.

— To give your still-human thought processes something on which to focus, Bobby thought at him. — Consider the light as me, your brother, while I show you the wonder of the realm you call the *nada*-continuum; a misnomer, of course. The continuum is not a realm of nothing, but is *full*, bursting with energy and vitality. Come!

Mirren was aware of himself then as a fiery comet very much like that which was now his brother, and he obeyed Bobby and swam, or dived or fell, with him through the vast sea of light and energy.

Bobby maintained a running commentary.

— The continuum is certainly Sublime, but it is not, despite what the Disciples think, Infinite. It is the size of the physical universe, and expanding with it to fill the emptiness beyond. It is still, nevertheless, vast – far larger than you have the time in this communion to experience.

Mirren, or rather the ball of light that was now his point-of-view, followed the comet that was his brother, dashing in and out of the fiery sparks of his tail.

Where are we going? Mirren asked.

— I am taking you beyond what in this realm corresponds to the Rim sector of your galaxy; out beyond the very edge of the 'galaxy' across the interstellar gulf to an area that would be Andromeda in the physical realm.

Even as these concepts formed in Mirren's consciousness, he became aware of a change in the sector through which he was passing. Until now, the substance of the continuum had seemed to be made up wholly of the countless points and sparks of light – as closely-packed as grains of sand. But the further they progressed from this sector, the less frequent the points of light became, until they were passing through a familiar field of harmonious blue that Mirren recognised as the *nada*-

continuum. Only an occasional spark inhabited this area, and these seemed to be in transit, as they were themselves, between one 'galaxy' and the next. As they went, Mirren experienced a diminution of the sense of rapture which hitherto had filled him, and was filled instead by a strange plangent sadness at leaving in his wake so much energy.

The lights, he asked. *What are they?*

— What do you think they are, Ralph?

Mirren thought: *Beings who have passed on? The life-forces of everyone who has ever existed?*

Bobby was a while before answering, as if contemplating his reply. His golden light raced through the cobalt radiance of the continuum. Mirren followed patiently.

— They are not beings, though I suppose they could be described as life-forces. When one transcends, one begins existence in this realm in much the state you are in now, but one soon leaves this stage and joins with all else, melding with the fundamental fabric of the continuum. These lights, these sparks, however, remain. They are no longer individual beings, but carriers of pure information, experience, history, knowledge, memory; in these particles of energy are contained the history of the universe, and everything that has ever existed as a dynamic, living force within it.

So... the light I am following is not really Bobby?

Mirren felt Bobby's amusement. — No, not as such. I am everywhere, united, one with the continuum; however, the light you follow was me, it still could be said to be me, my essence, my history, experience, memories... it is the essence 'I' access when I wish to join with another essence and experience existence as, say, a sundiver in the far galaxy you know as NGC-5194, or experience the life of an amoeba on Mars... This realm makes possible a universal understanding, permits every essence the ability to access every other essence. It takes time, of course; there are trillions of trillions of essences of everything that has ever existed in the long history of the universe, but the comprehensive understanding of everything is the goal of every essence in this realm. After all, what is the purpose of existence, but the transmission and reception of information, in whatever form that information might take?

It seemed mere seconds since they had departed the crowded energy field. Now, as Mirren followed the light that had been his brother and attempted to absorb what he had been told, the blue expanse through which they were travelling once again became populous – with a scattering of essences at first, then more and more, until the blue radiance disappeared and it seemed that the very medium they were passing through consisted of nothing but such essences, vessels, as Bobby had said, of pure information, storehouses of every fact that had ever been.

— These essences tend to remain in the region of the continuum which corresponds to the sector of space where they existed in real-time. Thus, the essences you first encountered were those of our galaxy, humans, aliens, animals, plant-life specific to the Milky Way.

— The essences here, Bobby went on, once lived out their lives in Andromeda. I will now access one, attempt to transmit to you my ability to experience life far away, long ago. Pick a light, Ralph.

Mirren cast about him. *That one – the magenta beacon describing a helix around the slowly rising orange light...*

No sooner had the thought been thought, then the light that was Bobby swooped upon the magenta beacon. Their union produced a small explosion, and then Mirren made out two lights. Bobby's golden comet joined with the pulsing magenta life-force. They spun, embraced in mutual attraction, the helix they described becoming tighter, faster.

— Come closer, Ralph.

Mirren propelled himself closer to the rotating binaries, felt himself attracted – and in a sudden rush he experienced a dizzying overload of information: he knew, in an instant, what it was to be a one thousand tonne gastropod floating in the methane sea of a vast gas giant orbiting a sun going nova. He experienced the creature's emotions, accessed its memories, understood the complex society in which it functioned; for as long as he maintained the contact, he *was* the creature. He could skip through its life, like fast-forwarding a disc, experience its birth, then live through the pain of its death as it was ripped apart by the blast from the exploding sun, and then he was one with the creature's joy as it transcended...

Then Bobby parted company with the pulsing magenta beacon and swirled around Mirren. — Did you feel it, did you experience its pain, and then its rapture as it transcended?

Mirren was hardly able to respond, which was response enough.

— Come, Bobby commanded, and led the way through the sparsely populated region of blue light between the real-time galaxies, towards the massed essences that existed in the continuum's analogue of their home galaxy.

— Do you begin to apprehend the magnificence of this ultimate state, Ralph? Can you understand that the concerns and preoccupations of the humans who still exist as such are petty, trivial, beside the vaulting ambitions of the beings we become?

Of course!

— And yet, Bobby said, something melancholy in his tone, the concerns of the human race are bringing about, albeit unwittingly, the gradual annihilation of this realm. Until now we have existed without threat, free to access and experience the totality of *everything*.

As he followed his brother's golden comet from the barren interstellar gulf towards the teeming pointillism of life-forces, he wondered how humankind might pose any threat to the continuum.

They passed through the sector where the sparks of light were as tightly-packed as atoms, and came to a margin where the blue of the underlying continuum could be seen between the dancing life-forces. As they continued, the last of the lights passed beyond them, so that soon they were travelling through an expanse of blue radiance even emptier than the last one Mirren had experienced.

Are we going to another galaxy? he asked.

— We are still in what corresponds to the Milky Way, Bobby told him. — In fact, this area corresponds to the Rim of our galaxy.

Ahead, or below, or at any rate in the direction Mirren was moving, he perceived a fading of the blue of the continuum. At the same time, as he flew towards and then into the sky blue field, he became aware of an aura of hostility, a sudden iciness which chilled his essence to its very core. Before him, the comet which was Bobby lost its golden glow and its darting vitality.

— Look, Bobby thought at last.

Before them, in the distance, Mirren made out a vast area of what could only be described as anti-energy, black and lifeless. It was growing – even as he hovered, observing, the circumference of the vast amorphous cloud bloated outwards, expanding in great billowing explosions like ink in water, eating up the pale blue of the continuum around it.

— Come, Bobby commanded, and flew ever closer to the cloud.

Mirren balked, hanging back. He recalled what Ghaine had told him about facing terror, and understood that what was before them was the source of that terror.

— Follow me, Bobby exhorted. — Until you have fully experienced what is happening here, you will be unable to appreciate the true wonder and worth of the continuum.

Mirren hurried to his brother's side, so as not to be alone before the relentless approach of the negative force. Side by side they hovered closer to a great rearing, blooming tumour composed of the very absence of everything that made the continuum what it was: light, life, vitality... They hovered like two mayflies before a thunderhead, their very presence taunting the awful immensity of the invader.

On the edge of the continuum, where the black cloud impinged, Mirren perceived what looked like lengths of rope, or roots, leached of colour, lifeless.

— The fabric of the continuum itself, Bobby explained. — The matter which absorbs us upon transcendence, which stores our essences and makes us one. It is dead, killed by this force.

From behind them, Mirren saw a dense flight of united life-forces, like a swarm of hornets or a well-drilled squadron of fighter planes: they swooped, dived at the swelling tumour of cloud and vanished within it, causing the cloud to writhe, to momentarily cease its advance. Then it swelled again, moving ever outwards in its insatiable appetite for more energy.

— They think that by attacking it like this, they might defeat it, but all they succeed in doing is halting its progress for mere seconds, and sacrificing themselves.

A lobe of cloud erupted suddenly, almost swallowing them up. In that second, as they fled to a safe distance, Mirren knew true terror. The very core of his being was shaken as he perceived the heart of the cloud in its essence, looked into it and experienced only a terrible absence.

What is it? he cried at his brother as they retreated. On all sides, the fabric of the continuum squirmed and writhed as the cloud reached and rendered dead all before it.

— This is not the only one, Bobby reported. — Across this sector of the continuum over two thousand of these monstrosities continue to grow, feeding without cessation on the energy of the realm.

But what is it? Mirren screamed.

— It is entropy, Ralph. In time, if it and the others like it are allowed to expand, they will infect the whole continuum. Then, all life as we know it in its higher form will cease to exist. In the physical realm, life will be born, only to face the terrible extinction of absolute death.

— The continuum, Ralph, exists as an eternal mass of light and energy, comprised of vital forces that are the transcended essences of every being that has ever lived and died. The continuum is everlasting, a phenomenon that does not know or suffer the ravages wrought in normal space and time by entropy; the heat death of the universe, the gradual falling apart of the structure of reality.

— Or, rather, the continuum did not suffer entropy...

But what is causing this? Mirren asked.

— The interfaces, Ralph. The continuum did not suffer entropy until the first of the interfaces was opened. You see, knowledge of the *nada*-continuum allowed the scientists working on the interfaces to tap into the vast reserves of energy within the continuum. With this almost limitless supply of power, they annihilated space between the planets and successfully created the portals through which matter could pass instantly from one world to the next. When deactivated, the mechanical systems of the interfaces recharged themselves by leaching energy from the continuum: but the process was not just one way, Ralph. From the two thousand-plus separate interfaces around the Expansion, entropy seeps from the universe which humanity inhabits and spreads throughout the *nada*-continuum.

— You see before you the consequence of the interfaces. This is just one; there are many thousands more, and every further second they exist, they bring annihilation to the continuum. Now do you understand why it is so vital that the interfaces be shut down? You understand why the mission must succeed; to evacuate the Effectuators and their attendants so that the people of the free universe can come to understand the terrible cost of humankind's folly...

As he spoke, a billow of the giant cloud belched towards them, bringing death further into the continuum. Again, a flight of lights made the ultimate sacrifice, bringing about only a temporary cessation of the monster's irrevocable advance.

— They, the life-forces who give themselves, are manifested as the 'ghosts' which sometimes appear around interface portals in the physical universe, and I suppose 'ghosts' is an appropriate definition of these doomed souls. Come, look, all around us the cloud advances.

He was right. Mirren saw that, like an incoming tide, the cloud had edged around them on every side. They sped back the way they had come, the cloud giving chase as if intent on swallowing them. Mirren surged forward after his brother, aware of the dark cloud closing in. As he struggled to save himself, he felt the energy bleed from him, his vitality strangulated by proximity of the decay which abounded and multiplied. He had looked upon energy everlasting in that sector of the continuum so far uncontaminated – here, by contrast, he experienced the ultimate malignancy of death, or rather non-life, and realised that what was all the more frightening was the fact that it was spreading, insatiable, intent on conquering the realm of light, stopping only when the entirety of the continuum was defeated, a lifeless, moribund, burned-out ash of its former self.

His essence was filled with the terror of total oblivion, such as he had never experienced in his human form, an oblivion that, in its hostility to life was the epitome of all that was diabolical.

He screamed...

... And was still screaming when the encompassing darkness faded, and he found himself in the restricted confines of his physical form.

He was sitting up, and Ghaine was kneeling before him, grasping his hands. Mirren ceased his shouting, worked to regain his breath. "It... it was–" Words could not describe the horror of the experience, the residual sense of desolation that lingered in him still.

For the first time, Mirren became aware of a distant rumble, a shudder that shook the *Sublime*.

Ghaine responded to his alarmed expression. "The militia have been attacking us for the past thirty minutes," he said. "They cannot know precisely where we are, just approximately. They are levelling the mountainside. Many of the Temple's upper chambers have been destroyed, but we are deep within the mountain. With luck–"

"How long have I been under?" Mirren asked.

"Almost two hours."

"Then we should be phasing-out!"

"There are difficulties," said the Lho. "Your men are working hard, but they have encountered problems."

An explosion, seemingly directly overhead, rent the air and shook the 'ship. A fall of rock crashed against the astrodome. It cracked with a sound like splitting ice. The *Sublime* yawed, pitching Mirren and Ghaine across the floor. Shards of plastex rained down; a triangular section of dome fell, narrowly missing an Effectuator.

"We've got to get them out of here," Mirren said. "If the 'ship phases-out now we'll all asphyxiate."

"Where to?" Ghaine asked, climbing to his feet and helping Mirren up.

"There's a chamber on the deck below this one. They'll be safe there. We can seal the dome at the air-lock."

Ghaine spoke to the attendants; already they were lifting the stretchers, making their way unsteadily across the dome to the sliding door of the elevator as the barrage continued and the *Sublime* rocked beneath the onslaught.

Mirren opened the elevator, helped load three Effectuators and their attendants. He sent them down to the next level, willing the attendants to hurry and vacate the cage. More explosions crashed overhead. Rock rained down on the dome and the body of the 'ship.

The elevator emptied. He stabbed the command for it to return, and when the door slid open he hauled aboard the three remaining Effectuators. This time he and the rest of the Lho rode down with them, squashed together as the booth rocked back and forth. The door opened on the central chamber and he ensured that the Effectuators were safely housed.

He took the down-chute to the engine-room, holding onto the rail as the *Sublime* pitched like a sea-going ship in a storm.

The engine-room was full of Disciples gathered around the flux-tank and the co-pilot's command web. Mirren staggered across to the tank. "Who's in there?"

Dan Leferve turned, smiled tightly. "Bobby."

"Why the hell aren't we phasing?"

Dan indicated through the viewscreen. Mirren stumbled across to the screen. Beyond, in the chamber, two Enginewomen and an Engineman worked frantically at a bank of computers, occasionally looking up and across at the *Sublime* as if willing it to disappear. The lights illuminating the tableau flickered, for a few seconds going off altogether. Mirren held his breath until the light stuttered back on, picking out the three figures still at their posts. Another explosion shook the chamber. It seemed only a matter of time before the technicians were lost beneath the falling debris.

He heard Miguelino, in his command web, yelling out the phase-out sequence for perhaps the third time in as many minutes, an edge of desperation in his voice.

Mirren was aware of someone by his side – Ella Hunter. The 'ship bucked. He held her to prevent her from falling. Outside, the floor of the chamber began to break up; the surface erupted, throwing up great slabs of rock as unsteady as ice-floes. Still the technicians battled on.

"They don't stand a chance!" Ella cried.

"They're going to a greater thing," Mirren told her.

She looked at him, fear in her eyes. "I hope you're right," she whispered.

"I know I'm right," Mirren said.

The *Sublime* slid sideways as the ground beneath it subsided. The technicians fell into the darkness. Mirren and Ella were dashed against the screen. They fetched up against the padded recess, holding onto each other as if their lives depended on it. A low-pitched hum sounded through the 'ship. Mirren prayed that the blackness outside would vanish for just one second, to indicate that phase-out was under way.

He held Ella to him, and in that second he experienced for the first time the realisation that within her, and consequently within everyone, existed the same vital energy he had first encountered in the continuum. He almost wept with the joy of it. He vowed that if he returned to Earth, he would live his life not as he had lived it to date, but as it was meant to be lived – for however long he had left to him – until the day of his glorious ascension.

When I return to Earth, he told himself... The alternative was too terrible to contemplate.

The humming gained in pitch, but outside the darkness remained.

CHAPTER TWENTY-FOUR

HIRST HUNTER LEANED forward. "Very good, Mr Rossilini."

"Here?"

"This will suit me fine."

The Mercedes rolled to a sedate halt. Hunter climbed out. Rossilini and Sassoon jumped out after him, but perhaps sensing his need for privacy remained beside the roadster, their semi-automatic rifles prominent.

Hunter strolled across the weed-laced tarmac and climbed the grass embankment that marked the boundary of Ipoh airbase. The midday Malaysian heat and the steep incline combined to rob him of breath. By the time he reached the top he was exhausted, an indication of how little exercise he had done over the past few years – years spent closeted in safe-houses, plotting and scheming, unable in the early years even to join the resistance on their missions for fear of capture and interrogation, and later because there was just so much organising to do to ensure the success of the mission.

He turned at the top and stared across the airbase. He had left Paris that morning, taking the sub-orb shuttle to Kuala Lumpur on what he hoped would be the last leg of the long journey that had taken him around the many free worlds of the Rim, and then to Earth. So far, things were running smoothly. The *Sublime* had phased-out from Paris without a hitch, and ten hours into the flight, when contact was eventually lost, no problems had been reported. Feasibly they should have rendezvoused with the Disciples and the Lho in the mountain stronghold without much difficulty, and should make the return trip to Earth likewise. The real danger had always been the possibility that the Organisation might have learnt of his plans *before* the phase-out of the 'ship and prevented it; now that the mission was under way, in fact almost completed, he could stop worrying himself about the possibility of a Danzig intervention. Not that he was being complacent; the airbase was patrolled by Malaysian commandos supplied by the Premier of the state – foot-soldiers and tanks were stationed at strategic points around the perimeter.

Hunter stared out across the flat expense of the airbase. The only prominence on the sky-line, other than the distant hills, was the massive hangar he'd had constructed for the return of the smallship. Next to it was a mylaplex geodesic dome, its triangular facets blacked out.

He glanced at his watch. The dignitaries were due to arrive at one, in a little over fifteen minutes. Besides the KVO Director Jose Delgardo, the UC representative on Earth, Johan Weiner, and the Premier of Malaysia, the heads of three other interface companies would be present. The participation of these three luminaries, cajoled into coming by the good offices of Delgardo, was a bonus Hunter had not expected. It seemed, though he was loath to tempt providence, that the events of the next few hours might prove the beginning of the end of all his hard work. For years he had schemed and sweated for this very day – for years he had lived in fear of the many dangers that might have befallen the mission. Now everything was going according to plan, and he should have been elated.

He told himself that the despair he was feeling was irrational, that he was grieving for the loss of someone he had never really known – or, rather, grieving over the loss of opportunity to get to know Ella in the first place. Early that morning, Hunter had heard from Disciples on A-Long-Way-From-Home that his daughter had indeed gained access to the Reach. The authorities there could only have allowed her entry because they knew that she was his daughter, and either hoped she might lead them to him or could provide vital information as to his whereabouts. They would question her, keep her alive only for as long as she was useful to them – and, as she knew nothing, Hunter guessed that that would not be very long.

She was now, or was soon likely to be, in a better place than this illusion. Her essence would exist in a state of eternal vitality, for which he should rejoice.

Selfishly, he could only mourn the fact that he had never been able to show Ella, in this life, the love she deserved.

He sat down on the embankment and took a small silver book from his jacket pocket. He leafed through Ella's diary, the pages falling open where he had inserted the half dozen photographs of his daughter.

At random, he read entries written in her big, looping handwriting, and it pained him to realise that this would be as close as he would come to knowing the mind of his daughter. It pained him also – though it came as no surprise – that all the entries concerning him were detrimental.

'Last day of holidays, and I haven't seen H once. Good. Back to college tomorrow.'

He turned the page.

'Jay's father is coming with us on the summer trip – that should be good. Mrs T asked me if H could come along to lend a hand, but I said he was off-planet working for the Organisation. I couldn't imagine it! H coming on the trip!'

He let the diary fall open to a later entry, one he had read so many times over the years that he knew it verbatim.

'Yesterday the alien saved my life! I was watching it from the rocks when he saw me and I lost my balance and fell into the water, on the way down hitting my head on some rock. When I came to my senses I was on the flat rock, thinking I should have drowned. Then I saw him looking at me and I knew he had saved me. I was frightened – I mean, he was so *alien*, so different. I ran. H has stopped me from going out for one week for not being at the party. I want to see the alien again, to apologise (does he speak English?) I'm planning to make him something, a present. I sit and think that if it wasn't for the alien I'd be dead, and I try to think what being dead is like.'

Hunter looked up, saw nothing but his daughter as she was then. He turned a couple of pages, read on.

'Today I saw L'Endo on his death-bed, and instead of it being a sad occasion (he was dying of a plague) it was *joyous*. L'Endo was actually celebrating the fact that he was dying. In five days he has his *passing* ceremony, and I am invited. He was so *certain* an afterlife awaited him – I felt his certainty in the air! – that I felt almost at one with my dying friend. I can't begin to explain it. The old Lho said that the only humans who understand what the Lho believe are the Enginemen and Enginewomen. If the Lho are right, then when I die I will experience the afterlife, which is what the Disciples believe.'

One of Ella's last entries read, 'As soon as I can I'm leaving the reach and going to Earth, to Paris to paint and *live* and convert...'

Hunter closed the diary, a sharp knot of pain in his chest.

He considered the beautiful irony of the situation.

Ten years ago, an alien had saved his daughter's life; as a result of this, she had experienced something in the cave where the alien lay on his death-bed that had changed her life, given her the desire to convert and become a Disciple. Three years later she did so, and sent photographic evidence of the fact to Hunter, and he had looked into the religion himself and in due course was converted. Then he was contacted by the Lho and commissioned with the duty to see through the scheme which would not only save the remaining Lho-Dharvon people, but ensure the continuance of what humans knew as the *nada*-continuum.

How wondrous a notion it was that the salvation of the Lho people, and much more besides, had its beginnings in the actions of an alien saving the life of a young girl, so long ago and so far away.

Hunter looked up. Rossilini was standing at the foot of the embankment. He cleared his throat. "Excuse me, sir."

Across the tarmac, a convoy of limousines was heading towards the hangar. The dignitaries had arrived.

He replaced the diary in his jacket pocket and returned to the Mercedes. They drove back to the hangar in silence, Hunter trying to dredge up a scintilla of enthusiasm for what was about to take place.

The last of the dignitaries was being ushered into the hangar by one of Hunter's aides. He followed them inside, check-listing the points he had to make to the VIPs.

The interior of the chamber was divided into two unequal areas. The larger was bare but for banks of computers and sophisticated monitoring equipment; technicians wearing headphones moved about the area where the smallship was due to materialise, making last minute preparations. Like Hunter, these people had worked for years to bring about the success of the mission. If anything, their contribution was greater than his; they had, after all, wrestled with the complex technical problems of launching the first smallship to enter the *nada*-continuum in ten years.

A quarter of the hangar was partitioned and fitted out as a hospitality lounge, with a bar, foam-forms and classical music discreetly playing. The dignitaries stood in conversation with his aides, drinking champagne and casting occasional glances through the gap in the screens to the business end of the hangar.

Hunter squared his shoulders and crossed the carpeted lounge. He greeted Jose Delgardo with genuine warmth, and the KVO director introduced him to the Premier of Malaysia, R.C. Subramanaman, Johan Weiner, and the three heads of the interface organisations, two women and a man whose companies ran operations in the Core.

He raised his champagne. "You have no idea how pleased I am to see you all here today. I thank you for your attendance, and assure you that you will not be disappointed. Today is the culmination of many years of hard and dangerous work on behalf of my team."

"I hope you realise what a sacrifice we're making to spend the entire day here, Mr Hunter?" This was Johan Weiner, the corpulent UC representative.

Hunter smiled, disguising his dislike of the disgruntled Austrian. "I realise and appreciate your efforts, I assure you. As I said, you will not be disappointed."

"When is the 'ship due in?" Jose Delgardo asked.

"It should materialise very soon. We have rooms available for your comfort, and a restaurant."

Several of his guests looked at their watches, Weiner especially making a show of his displeasure. Hunter finished his champagne. "Perhaps, ladies and gentlemen, if you would come this way... I have one or two things to show you which I think you will find of interest."

He escorted them up a flight of steps to a gallery overlooking the main chamber of the hangar. He gave them a run-down on the technical history of the operation, the assembly of the smallship and the recruitment of the technicians and crew. It was, he had to admit to himself, a fascinating story. The dignitaries listened with interest.

As he brought the rehearsed speech to a close, Subramanaman asked, "But how did you become involved with the aliens, Mr Hunter? And what exactly is the nature of this... communion we are due to experience?"

"As to the first part of the question, that is a long story which I'd like to tell you later, perhaps over a meal. As to the nature of the communion... if you would care to follow me."

They passed from the gallery through a door into a narrow corridor connecting the hangar to the adjacent geodesic. Hunter led them onto a circular gallery high up in the dome.

They stared down at the strange monument or sculpture picked out in the spotlights.

One of the Core interface directors whistled. "What on earth is it?"

"Not on *earth*," Hunter smiled. "The original is on the planet of Hennessy's Reach. This is merely a facsimile of the Lho Effectuators' communion chamber." He had commissioned a firm of masons to construct the chamber, less to make the Lho feel at home than to impress the visiting dignitaries.

A great central column rose to the apex of the dome, its length fluted and engraved with arcane alien symbols. At the foot of the column, a dozen stone slabs radiated like spokes. In the illumination of the spotlights, the entire effect was suitably other-worldly.

For the next thirty minutes Hunter gave a short history of the Lho, and then told the dignitaries what little he knew about the Effectuators and the nature of the communion. What he could expound upon in more detail was his own experience in the original chamber almost six years ago, an experience both joyous and terrifying that would live with him forever.

They returned to the lounge in contemplative silence.

"The thing is," Johan Weiner said when their glasses had been refilled, "how can we be certain that our experience of heaven in the communion will be genuine, and not a drug-induced hallucination?"

Hunter was shaking his head. "It isn't heaven," he said. "It cannot be defined as any of the many afterlives described by the organised religions. They all have it wrong–"

"Even the Disciples?" Weiner snapped.

"Many of the Disciples have experienced whereof they speak, so of all the so-called organised religions, they have come the closest to getting it right. Having said that, many of their rituals are merely the trappings of a human-based belief system and have no relevance to what follows this existence. The afterlife experienced in the *nada*-continuum is not a heaven or a hell or a purgatory – it is another realm which exists as a state of positive energy–"

"You still haven't answered my question," Weiner went on doggedly. "How do we know that what you experienced was anything more than a hallucination?"

Hunter paused. He looked around the assembled VIPs. They were waiting for his reply. "I know what I experienced, Herr Weiner. I know that I experienced a state of positive energy, and that that energy was under threat of annihilation. I know that the annihilation I perceived in the continuum was the most soul-destroying and terrifying force I have ever had the displeasure of witnessing... I'm sorry – I can't explain it any better than that, and of course there is nothing I can say to convince you of the truth. Only your own experience of communion will do that."

The dignitaries shifted uncomfortably, exchanging glances.

The Director of one of the Core interface companies said, "Do you realise what you are asking us to do in closing down the entire interface industry, Mr Hunter?" She stared at him accusingly.

He returned her stare. "Perfectly, Ms de Souza," he said. "I am asking you to preserve the realm of existence which follows this one."

Weiner grunted a laugh. "An ecological clean-up of afterlife, you mean?"

"If you wish to put it like that, Herr Weiner, then yes, exactly that."

Weiner muttered into his drink.

De Souza said, "The closure of the interfaces would ruin the economies of so many planets around the Expansion that untold numbers of lives would be at risk."

Hunter restrained himself from saying that human lives mattered little beside the continued existence of the *nada*-continuum. He began, "There are ways of avoiding–"

"I don't think you understand that some planets in my sector rely on the interfaces for their very existence. Dozens of colony planets would be bankrupted by such closures as you envisage–"

"I was about to say that there are ways of avoiding immediate financial catastrophes on the more far-flung worlds. We would not merely cut them off willy-nilly, in fact the closures would be phased out over a number of years, with UC subsidies going to those planets more drastically affected."

Weiner interrupted, "Fine words, Hunter. You don't belong to the UC. You don't have to put your hands on those 'subsidies'."

Hunter continued, not allowing his anger at such petty short-sightedness to show. "If the closures were phased in over years, that would give us time to re-establish and improve the bigship Lines and services they provide."

Another Director of a Core organisation said, "You're talking as if the whole business about the continuum being under threat is cut and dried. I think we should begin such fevered speculation only when your theories have been scientifically tested."

Hunter had been fearing such a pragmatic approach. "A scientific investigation of the malaise affecting the *nada*-continuum might take tens of years, decades we do not have if we are to save the realm. We don't even possess the know-how, much less the technical apparatus, to even begin contemplating such investigations."

"You'd rather we believed the hallucinations brought about by a bunch of alien witch-doctors?" Weiner grunted.

Jose Delgardo said, "Our immediate concern, once we have established the veracity of Hirst's claims, would be less how the free expansion might react, but whether the Danzig Organisation would agree to close down their interfaces."

"They wouldn't!" de Souza said, "Which is why we could not afford to shut down our own portals. Can you imagine the scenario if the Danzig Organisation was the only body with unrestricted access to the interfaces? Preposterous!"

Hunter said, "I wouldn't worry yourselves about the Danzig Organisation. The Disciples have contingency measures to deal with them."

"Meaning?" Weiner asked.

"If need be, we would co-ordinate suicide bombing campaigns to rid the Rim of the interfaces. There are only two hundred interfaces in that sector, and we have more than a hundred thousand willing Disciples capable of taking out more than just the Organisation's portals..."

He allowed his gaze to wonder across the staring faces. Weiner took up his challenge. "You don't mean to say that if we refused to co-operate...?"

Hunter stood his ground. "I mean to say, Herr Weiner, that if the free expansion did not see reason and agree to the closures, then the Disciples would be forced to consider extending their bombing campaign. We have the numbers, the will, and the knowledge that we cannot lose the fight..."

A sudden and profound silence hung over the guests.

"Now," Hunter went on, "if you would care to make your way to the other end of the hangar, I think Dr Chang is ready to show you around the phasing in area."

Muttering, the visitors trudged from the hospitality lounge.

Hunter remained behind, relieved that for the time being the pressure was off. In all his years of preparation, he had underestimated how narrow-minded and pragmatic some people would be when faced with such petty considerations as reduced profits. He tried to look at the situation from their point of view – but that was impossible. He had after all experienced the full and terrible magnitude of the annihilation wrought on the continuum. He tried to convince himself that all, in time, would be well: soon, even the doubters would experience, via the communion chamber, the full horrors of what was happening beyond the illusion of this reality.

And, if all else failed, then the might of the Disciples would succeed.

He left the hangar to get a breath of fresh air and to be alone for a few minutes. He strolled across the tarmac, the weight of his daughter's diary making itself felt in his jacket pocket. The uncertainty of Ella's fate was the most agonising factor in all this: if only he knew, even if she were dead, the truth – then he could begin to grieve, to mourn, and then maybe begin to heal himself. But, knowing nothing, he was in a state of limbo, a void of inertia in which he could do nothing to help himself. There was nothing to grasp and hold onto in this realm of ignorance, nothing on which to gain purchase and orient himself.

He was weeping. Quickly, he pulled a handkerchief from his pocket and wiped his good eye. He took out a photograph and stared at it. Ella was standing beside a canvas, her expression severe. The painting showed what might have been a flayed corpse, spread-eagled against a backdrop of stars. In its agony, the painting seemed to communicate to Hunter his daughter's own anguish. She stared from the photograph, accusingly.

He put the picture away and crossed the tarmac to where Sassoon and Rossilini leaned against the Mercedes. They straightened up as he joined them.

"Did you get those paintings into storage, Mr Sassoon?"

Sassoon nodded. "They're in a warehouse in Passy."

"Very good." He had it in mind to start a gallery in his daughter's name: The Ella Marie Hunter Museum of Modern Art. It had a certain ring. It was the least he could do.

"Sir!" A shout from the hangar. A technician stood at the door. "It's the *Sublime*. We're in contact!"

Hunter returned to the hangar, hurried through the lounge and over to the stacked monitors and busy technicians. There was considerable excitement in the air, an almost palpable sense of relief. The techs called to each other across their machinery. The six dignitaries stood off to one side, an aide talking them through the lead up to the phasing-in manoeuvre.

Hunter made his way to where a technician was standing with a pair of headphones held high. Hunter took the earphones. He preferred to stand, so that he could see where the 'ship would soon materialise.

He pressed the 'phones to his ear. "Reading. Hunter here..."

Static in a deafening burst, then: "Miguelino here. sir..." More static broke up the signal.

"Mr Miguelino, good to hear from you. I take it–"

"... mission was successful. We have the Lho, and around forty Enginemen besides–" Static crackled in Hunter's ear. "... bombed the temple, destroying it. We lost three Disciples and two Lho in the attack–"

"But the Effectuators, Mr Miguelino? Did you get the Effectuators?"

More static. "... safe and sound, sir, all six."

"Excellent work, Mr Miguelino. Congratulations."

"One more thing... Bobby Mirren pushed us to the Rim and back in record time. He's totally lapsed now – a human Effectuator, according to his brother."

So *that* was why the Lho were so insistent that Bobby push the 'ship on the mission. He recalled the Lho's secrecy – their fear that, if the truth was discovered, then all Alpha Enginemen would be in mortal danger.

"ETA just five minutes from now, sir–" A storm of static caused Hunter to pull the 'phones away from his ear. When he returned it, Miguelino was saying, "Kelly, sir. He wants to speak to you."

"Kelly? Splendid. Put him on."

Hunter glanced around, at the dignitaries, at the space in the hangar where the 'ship would materialise. He considered Kelly, the years they had spent planning for this very moment.

"Hirst... you there?"

"Hearing you loud, if not clear, Kelly."

A squall of static obliterated Kelly's first few words. Then, "... have some good news for you, Hirst."

"Miguelino pre-empted you, Kelly. Congratulations on a successful mission."

"Not that, Hirst, for Fernandez' sake!" More static. "... sleeping at the moment, but otherwise okay–"

"I beg your pardon?"

"I said, she's sleeping at the moment. She's taken a beating, but she's otherwise okay."

It was as if a blood vessel had burst in his head. His vision blurred and he felt dizzy. "Kelly?"

"... they tortured her, but she survived. She's looking forward to meeting you, Hirst." He could hear laughter in the American's voice.

"Ella...?" he whispered.

"Who else, Hirst? Of course, Ella – your daughter!" More static. "... so I'll see you then, Hirst. Kelly, out."

Hunter found the tech's seat and his legs gave way beneath him. He experienced an incredible sensation of pressure within his chest, threatening to burst from him in an explosion of joy.

"Sir, is everything okay?"

"Everything's fine. Couldn't be better." He gathered himself, stood and made his way around the computer banks to where a small crowd stood waiting for the *Sublime* to materialise.

"She's looking forward to seeing you..."

Hunter focused on the space before him, trying to imagine the 'ship existing in some realm beneath or beyond this one, the 'ship which was bringing his daughter back to him, after all these years.

"They tortured her... but she survived."

He was oblivious to the activity around him, the scurrying techs and mechanics placing stanchion barriers around the phasing-in area. People slapped him on the back and shook his hand, mouthing congratulations, but all he heard was the countdown. "Ten, nine, eight, seven..."

He had so much to apologise for, so much back-dated affection to bestow on her.

"Six, five, four, three..."

As he waited for the smallship to materialise, he realised that he had never felt so excited before in his life.

"Two, one... zero! Phasing in!"

A wind blasted out from nowhere, storming through the assembled spectators and causing some to turn away or hide their eyes. Hunter stood his ground, gasping and registering the brief flicker of an image, soon gone. The gale changed direction, the air in the hangar sucked into where the 'ship had briefly existed. Again, the silver, streamlined shape appeared, disappeared and then returned. It strobed into existence, the periods of its absence diminishing, so that within fifteen seconds it had fully materialised and sat on the concrete of the hangar as if it had been there all along.

Hunter could see the shapes of figures at the main viewscreen, looking out. He strained his eyes to see Ella, desperate now to gain visual confirmation of the miracle Kelly had announced.

The hatch remained closed for just five minutes, but to Hunter it seemed like an eternity. Mechanics swarmed over the 'ship on ladders, connecting leads and pumps, monitoring exterior gauges. All about him was activity, while all he could do was stand and stare.

Then, quite suddenly, the hatch swung down and hit the concrete with a resounding clang. Enginemen and Lho appeared at the exit, paused and then made their way down the ramp to cheers and applause from the ground-crew. The aliens descended warily, looking about them as if in wonder. Lho stretcher-bearers carrying the Effectuators emerged from the 'ship and were met at the foot of the ramp by armed escorts who ushered them across the hangar to the dome. Disciples spilled out, men and women who had worked with Hunter in the early days. They shook hands with him, spoke hurried words of celebration and triumph, and he returned both handshakes and words, but hardly realised he was doing so, his gaze locked on the exit for the first sign of his daughter.

The first wave of passengers cleared from the ramp, and there was a short delay until the next group appeared. Hunter saw Miguelino and his pilot and three more Enginemen – and then, behind them, the tiny, fragile figure of Ella.

Miguelino and the pilot strode down the ramp, embraced Hunter and spoke greetings he never heard, then passed on.

Ella had stopped at the top of the ramp. Reality seemed to dissolve around her; things vanished from his perception, sound became silence. All he could see was his daughter, all he could hear was his heartbeat.

She stepped down the ramp and limped towards him. Her face was bruised and swollen, her right arm swaddled in a white bandage. She looked so small and frail and vulnerable, ill-treated and in need of what, for years, he had denied her.

She almost fell the last metre into his arms, and she was no weight at all as he caught her and held her to him. He felt her warmth against him and the slightness of her body as she wept against his chest and he repeated her name like an incantation.

Above her head, at the top of the ramp, Ralph Mirren appeared, Dan Leferve beside him. Mirren carried his brother in his arms. He seemed like a man transformed, then, purged of torment and pain. Slowly, they made their way down the ramp and joined Hunter and Ella, and together they crossed the hangar towards the geodesic and the act of communion about to take place.

Chapter Twenty-Five

Mirren sat in a booth at the back of the Blue Shift restaurant bar, nursing a beer and considering the events of the past few weeks.

The bar was quiet, unlike the last time he was here. It was five o'clock, and the serious partying was yet to begin. He enjoyed the quiet, and the solitude. For a week after his return from the Reach, he'd been hounded by news agencies wanting his story. He'd gone to ground, holing up in a luxurious penthouse suite with Dan, Hirst Hunter and Ella. For days they watched the news break with something close to disbelief. Mirren had found it hard to credit that events in which he'd played so important a part had conspired to bring about such radical change.

All across Earth, and across the Expansion, interfaces were being dismantled. In their place, new starship lines were starting up, old vessels, mothballed until now, hauled out of retirement and repaired. It would be a long time before the lines would be at anything like their former strength, but every day he heard of new lines starting up and old ones resuming their trade.

Hirst Hunter had got in ahead of the competition and set up his own business: the Hunter Line, equipped with a fastship, a bigship and several small ships. Effectuator Bobby Mirren was at this minute mind-pushing a fastship out to the Rim worlds, carrying UC officials to oversee the dismantling of various colonial interfaces.

Mirren smiled to himself and ordered another drink.

Over the course of the past week, Dan and Ella had struck up a touching friendship. Despite the age difference – Dan was almost twenty years her senior – they were spending all their free time together, with Hirst Hunter's blessing.

Mirren wondered if it was seeing Dan so happy with someone which had prompted him to make the call that morning.

For days he'd thought long and hard about doing so. He had so much to say to Caroline, so much to apologise for. He wondered how he would begin to atone for his past treatment of her.

He looked up suddenly, aware that he was being watched.

He smiled. "Carrie..."

She stood beside the booth, looking down on him uncertainly. "I got your message, Ralph." She gave a humourless laugh. "I thought it was a joke, at first."

"No joke." He gestured to the padded seat across from him. "I wanted to see you."

She slipped into the seat and ordered a drink from the press-select panel. When the gin and tonic emerged from the slot, she took a quick sip and stared at him.

"I've been watching the news, Ralph. It's... incredible."

"That's the reason I didn't get in touch sooner, Carrie. After you saved me, Hirst Hunter picked me up and we fluxed. Since we got back... Well, things have been rather hectic."

She regarded her drink. "The news reports... They said you'd contracted Heine's." She looked up at him. "Is it true?"

Was it genuine concern he saw in her expression? To his surprise, he thought it was.

He took a chance, reached out and laid a hand on top of hers. She didn't pull away. "A variant of Heine's. It's not as bad as the original strain." He shrugged. "Hunter's paying for me to have the very best treatment there is."

"And?"

"And the medics reckon I have between six to eight years."

At last she said in a small voice, "I suppose it doesn't matter, does it, now that you've found the flux again?"

He squeezed her fingers. "I've been giving it a lot of thought, Carrie. Everything. My life. What happened out there... You."

She looked surprised. "Me?"

"I have a lot to apologise for, Carrie. How I treated you, what I did, walking out like that... Even a few weeks ago, when you got back in touch..." He shook his head. "I was a different person then. I had... certain pressures, years of..." He stopped, then said, "I'm sorry. I'm making excuses. But there's no excuse for what I did. I just want to apologise for everything."

She stared at him, her expression unrelenting. "And now?" she asked.

"Now?"

"What kind of person are you now, Ralph? You're obviously still craving the flux, and what with the opening of the lines–"

He stopped her. "That's what I wanted to tell you, Carrie. I won't be fluxing again." Even as he spoke the words, he was aware of his heartbeat.

She widened her eyes. "You won't? But..."

He shrugged. "What I experienced in the flux, with Bobby, what I saw of the ultimate truth... it's as if that was enough, for now. I know for a fact that it's what I'm destined for... what we're all destined for, ultimately... and that's enough."

"That's quite a change around, Ralph. You were quite the disbeliever."

He shrugged. "I was wrong. I realise that now. Out there, I saw the truth." He took a long swallow of beer. "Anyway, now... now I have things to do on Earth, things I neglected to do for a long, long time."

He looked into her calm, oval face. She swallowed, then said, "And what is that, Ralph?"

He said, "You recall when we met a few weeks ago... you said you wanted us to be friends again."

She squeezed his hand. "You'd like that?"

He felt something constrict his throat. He nodded. "I'd like nothing better, Carrie."

"Oh, Ralph, Ralph..."

He looked up at her, fearing her rebuttal. "What?"

To his surprise, he saw that she was weeping. "Ralph, Susan arrived in Paris last night. She wants to see you. Let's... let's go see her together, okay? Now. She's at the Plaza."

His stomach turned. His daughter... how would he ever find the words to excuse his abandonment?

"Does she hate me, Carrie?"

She smiled. "Of course not. I explained what happened... what demons were driving you. She'll be delighted she has you back."

"For however long, before the Heine's..." he began.

She took both his hands in hers. "Eight years? That's a long time, Ralph. We can make the most of them, okay?"

They stood together and embraced, and some nameless emotion, which he hadn't experienced in years, swelled in his chest.

Carrie said, glancing at her watch, "Come on, let's pick up Susan and go for dinner."

As they made for the exit, Mirren said, "Carrie... I don't think I ever thanked you for saving my life."

She laughed. "Don't mentioned it, Engineman."

Hand in hand, they left the Blue Shift bar and stepped out into the balmy Paris night.

EPILOGUE

DAN LEFERVE SAT on the patio of the bar and gazed out across Orly spaceport. Night had fallen over Paris, but the port was illuminated by dozens of starships phasing-in, phasing-out, or just sitting on the tarmac. It was a sight that never failed to stir something deep within him. He drank his beer and watched a bigship of the Canterbury Line prepare for phase-out: its dorsal lights came on, then flashed like emergency beacons. The streamlined, shark-like 'ship flickered from existence in silence. Within a minute another 'ship appeared in the vacated berth as if by magic, displaced air blowing across the spaceport and lapping over the drinkers on the patio.

Not for the first time that evening, Dan glanced at the towering arrowhead of the fastship *The Sublime Ascension*. Behind its multiple viewscreens he could see the small, dark silhouettes of the crew as the 'ship prepared for phase-out in less than – he glanced at his watch – thirty minutes.

His heart skipped as he watched two white-uniformed officers climb the steps to the patio and approach him. "Alpha Leferve, if you're ready..." The officer's tone was deferential.

"If I can have just five more minutes." Dan glanced across to the door of the bar. "I'm expecting a friend."

The first officer said, "Of course. By all means." They left the patio and Dan exhaled a sigh of relief.

He returned his attention to the activity on the tarmac.

Fifteen years ago the Interface Organisations across the Expansion had, one by one, closed down the portals and ceased operation. Within two years the free Expansion had rid itself of the interfaces. The Rim sector of the galaxy, however, run by the Danzig Organisation, had been another matter entirely.

It had taken a further year of intense guerrilla activity, spearheaded by Hirst Hunter and the Disciples, to destroy every last interface and bring the Organisation to its knees.

Only then was the continued safety of the *nada*-continuum assured.

After the close-downs, the Lines had resumed business and gradually expanded. They were as busy now, if not more so, than even at the time of their hey-day twenty-five years ago. Bigships and smallships, pushed by Alphas, Betas and Gammas, constituted seventy-five percent of the star traffic, and fastships made up the remainder. They were, as their name suggested, super-fast star vessels pushed by Omegas – human Effectuators.

To become a human Effectuator – to hover on the cusp of the *nada*-continuum and push 'ships at fantastic speeds from star to star – was the ultimate goal of all Enginemen and Enginewomen. Not many were chosen, not many were suitable, which made the accolade of becoming an Effectuator all the greater.

Human Effectuators lasted for a maximum of three years in the comatose state required to push fastships through the continuum. Then, inevitably, they slipped finally from the physical realm and merged with the One.

Dan savoured his beer and considered what he was leaving.

Six months after his return to Earth from the Reach, he had sold his Agency and signed up with the newly re-formed Canterbury Line. For the next fourteen years he had pushed bigships from Earth to the Core, for that long he had known again the ecstasy of the flux, and between stints in the tank enjoyed the camaraderie of his team.

Every time he'd returned to Earth, he made a point of looking up Ralph Mirren and Caroline. Ralph had enjoyed his last few years with his ex-wife – ten years, not the forcast eight – and succumbed peacefully to Heine's five year ago.

A year ago, Dan had applied to become an Effectuator – six hours of flux every ten days was just not enough – and after a series of thorough medicals and performance assessments, he was accepted.

He was finishing his beer and contemplating making his way across to *The Sublime Ascension*, when the door of the bar swung open. Dan stood, arms wide, and Ella hurried across the room and hugged him.

She stood back. "Why this late, Dan?"

He shrugged. "I didn't want the goodbyes to drag on."

He smiled down at her. She'd grown a lot since the first time he'd met her, fifteen years ago – not so much in size as in spirit. She had never become the great artist she'd wanted to be, though she still painted. Over the years she had worked with her father to bring aid and succour to the planets liberated from the tyrannical regime of the Danzig Organisation.

"How's Hirst?" Dan asked.

"He's well. I keep telling him that at his age he really ought to think about retiring, but you know my father."

"He's still working for the UC?"

"He never stops. Oh, he send his regards, by the way."

"Say hi when you see him." Dan noticed the officers on the tarmac, signalling to him. "That's the call. You can come as far as the 'ship."

They left the patio and strolled across the tarmac. Last night he'd thrown a farewell party for his friends in Paris. Ella had attended, but he had wanted to say goodbye to her alone.

They stood in the shadow of the fastship. Ella said, "I'll miss you, Dan..."

"I'm going to a better thing," he reminded her.

"Yeah, I know. I'm just being selfish, that's all."

They paused before the ramp that sloped to the brightly illuminated interior of the 'ship. He embraced Ella for the last time.

"Look after yourself, Ella. Work hard."

She stared up at him, tears in her eyes. "Hell, why are farewells always so damned difficult?"

"Hey, this isn't a farewell. We'll meet again, okay?"

Ella laughed. "Don't forget to greet me when I arrive in the continuum," she said. "I'll be a... oh – a red and silver yin-yang comet trailing fire, okay?"

Dan said, "I won't forget."

He walked up and into the 'ship, following the officers. On the threshold he paused and waved down at Ella. She gave a small wave in return as the ramp slowly lifted. Then Dan entered the main chamber of *The Sublime Ascension*, ready at last for the ultimate rendezvous with the glory of the *nada*-continuum.

THE ENGINEMAN STORIES

The Girl Who Died for Art and Lived
The Phoenix Experiment
Big Trouble Upstairs
The Star of Epsilon
The Time-Lapsed Man
The Pineal Zen Equation
The Art of Acceptance
Elegy Perpetuum

The Girl Who Died for Art and Lived

I KNEW LIN Chakra, the famous hologram artist, for two brief days in spring. Our acquaintance changed my life.

I first met her at the party held by my agent to celebrate the exhibition of my crystal, *The Wreck of the John Marston.* The venue was Christianna Santesson's penthouse suite in the safe sector of the city. The event was pure glitter and overkill; big-name critics, artists in other fields, government officials and foreign ambassadors occupied the floor in urbane groups. With *The Wreck* I had, according to those in the know, initiated a new art form. Certainly I had done something that no-one else had been able to do before.

The crystal stood angled on a plinth at the far end of the long room, a fused rectangular slab coruscating like diamond. Earlier, there had been a queue to experience the work of Santesson's latest find. And, when the guests had actually laid hands on the crystal, they were staggered. The critics were pretty impressed, too – and that pleased me. I wanted to communicate my experience of the supernova to as many people as possible, allow them to live the last flight of the *John Marston*. Critical acclaim didn't always guarantee popular success, but I was sure that the originality of my art would catch the imagination of the world.

This was the first social gathering I'd attended since the accident, and I was uneasy without Ana.

* * *

As the party wore on, I eased my way to the bar and drank a succession of acid shorts. With diminishing clarity I watched the guests circulate, and tried to keep a low profile. This wasn't too difficult. The press-release had been brief and to the point. I was described as the sole survivor of an incredible starship burnout, but Santesson's publicity manager had failed to mention the fact that I had no face. Now there was a clique of artists here from the radioactive sector of the city who had taken over the select towerpiles deserted since the meltdown. These people wore fashion-accessory cancers, externalised and exhibited with the same panache as others might parade pet pythons or parakeets. One woman was nigrescent with total melanoma, another had cultivated multiple tumours of the thyroid like muscatel grapes on the vine. I spotted one artist almost as ugly as myself, his face eaten away by some virulent strain of radioactive herpes. They were known in art circles as the Strontium Nihilists, and tonight I was taken as just another freakish member of their band. The observant guest might have wondered, though, at the steel socket console that followed the contour of my dented cranium, or the remains of the occipital computer that had melted and fused with my collarbone.

From my position at the bar I watched Christianna Santesson as she moved from group to group, playing the perfect host. She was a tall blonde woman in her early sixties with the improved body of a twenty-year-old and a calculating business brain. Her agency had a virtual monopoly of the world's greatest artists, and when I joined her stable Santesson had never lost an opportunity to press me for the secret of the fusion process. She told me that she had people who could produce mega-art on my fused consoles, but I wasn't selling.

I was on my fifth acid short when a white light like the nova I'd survived blinded my one good eye. I raised an arm and called out. Silhouetted in the halogen glare I made out the hulking forms of vid-men toting shoulder cameras. Then I became aware of action beside me. Christianna Santesson was being interviewed. The front-man fired superlatives at the camera, stereotyping Santesson as the Nordic Goddess of the art world and myself as The Man With A Nova In His Head. He moved on to me, and I was blitzed with inane questions to which I gave equally brainless replies. Things like how I wanted the world to understand, and how I did it all for my dead colleagues.

Then the painful glare moved away, leaving the bar in darkness. The vid-men dashed the length of the lounge, the spotlight bouncing like a crazy ball. It appeared that the far entrance was now the focus of attention. The party-goers turned *en masse* and gawped like expectant kids awaiting the arrival of Santa.

I thumbed the lachrymose tear-duct of my good eye. "What the hell?" I managed. "I could have done without that."

"Daniel," Santesson said, her Scandinavian intonation loading her words with censure. "I had to have them in to record the arrival of Lin Chakra." And she smiled to herself like a satisfied stage-manager.

Seconds later Lin Chakra entered the spotlight, a diminutive figure surrounded by a posse of grotesques. And I experienced a sudden lurch in the pit of my stomach. Chakra hailed from the same subcontinent as a dead girl called Ana Bhandari, and her resemblance to Ana was unbearable. But then every Indian face sent pangs of grief through me.

Chakra lived in the radioactive sector, though she seemed unaffected by cancer, and compared with the hideousness of her hangers-on she emanated a fragile Asian beauty. She wore black tights, a black jacket, and a tricorne pulled low. Her face between the turned-up collar and the prow of her tricorne was an angry, inverted arrowhead as she scowled out at the assembled guests.

She walked across to my crystal, the cameras tracking her progress. I found it hard to believe that this was being piped live into half the homes on the continent.

She stood on the lower step of the plinth and played her hands over the crystal spread. Visually, it was not impressive, an abstract swirl of colour in the pattern of a vortex; interesting, but nothing more. It was to the touch that the crystals gave out their store of meaning, transforming the object from a colourful display into a work of art. Now, Lin Chakra would be experiencing what I had gone through in the engineroom of the *John Marston*.

She took her time, the guests watching her with silent respect, and soaked up the emotions. She lingered over a certain section of the slab, and came back to it again and again to see if the single crystal node still read as true in light of cross-reference with other emotions. She was being diligent in her appreciation of this newcomer's work.

Then she backed respectfully from the plinth, found Santesson and engaged her in quiet conversation. My agent indicated me with a slight inclination of her head; Lin Chakra's frequent glances my way were like sudden injections of adrenalin.

Then she joined me at the bar. She hoisted herself onto a high-stool and crossed her legs at the knees. "I like your crystal," she said in a small voice.

Seen closer to, her resemblance to Ana was less marked. Ana had been beautiful, whereas Lin Chakra was almost ugly. She had risen from the oblivion of a low-caste Calcutta slum, and her origins showed. Her lineage consisted of Harijan lepers, char-wallahs and meningital beggars. Physically she was a patchwork of inherited genetic defects, with a misshapen jaw and pocked cheeks, the concave chest and stoop of a tubercular forebear. But like her compatriots of the radioactive sector, she carried her deformities with pride, the latest recipient in a long line of derelict, hand-me-down DNA. And yet... and yet she wasn't without a certain undeniable charm, a frail attraction that produced in me a surge of the chivalrous and protective instinct that some people call affection.

When she spoke she looked directly at me, using my misplaced remaining eye as the focus of her attention, and not staring at my shoulder as others were wont to do. My injuries were such that some people found it hard to accept that the slurred, incinerated mass of flesh that sat upon my shoulders had once been a head.

Our conversation came to a close. She slipped a single crystal into my hand and climbed from her stool. She mingled with the crowd, then pushed through the shimmer-stream curtain to the balcony.

In my palm the crystal warmed, communicating. The millions of semi-sentient, empathic organisms gave out their record of Lin Chakra's stored emotion message. The alien stones were sold on Earth as curiosities, novel gee-gaws for entertainment and communication. No-one before had thought of using the crystals as a means of artistic expression. Once invested in a crystal, an emotion or thought lasted only a matter of minutes, and as artists created for posterity the crystals had been overlooked as a potential medium.

Then, quite by accident, I had come across the method by which to change the nature of the crystals so that they could store emotions or thoughts forever. Hence my sudden popularity.

A guest, fancying his chances, parted the curtain and stepped on to the balcony. He returned immediately. "She's gone."

I moved unnoticed from the bar and slipped into the adjacent room. Lin Chakra was waiting for me on the balcony. She had leapt across, and now sat on the rail hugging her shins. I paused by the shimmer-stream curtain. "Hey..."

"I have a fabulous sense of balance," she reassured me.

"I get vertigo just thinking about the drop," I admitted.

"An ex-Engineman shouldn't be afraid of heights," she mocked, jumping down and leaning against the rail.

Behind me, pressure on the communicating door made it rattle.

She glanced at me.

"I locked it," I said. "As you instructed. What do you want?"

"I really meant what I said about your crystal. I like it."

"It's crude," I said. "Honest in what it portrays, but incompetently executed. A kid with six months' practice could do better."

"You'll improve as you master the form," she told me.

I would have smiled, but that was impossible.

"A lot of people would give both arms to know how you fuse those crystals," she said now. "Do you think you can keep it to yourself forever?"

I shrugged. "Maybe I can," I said, and tried not to laugh at my sick secret.

Lin Chakra nodded, considering. "In that case, would you contemplate selling a crystal console already fused, so that other artists might create something?"

"So that's why you're here tonight. You want a crystal?"

"I came," she said, "to see your crystal. But–"

"Forget it," I snapped. "I don't sell them."

"Don't you think that's rather selfish?"

I laughed, though the sound came out as a strangled splutter. "I like that! I'm the one who discovered the process, after all. Aren't I entitled to be just a little selfish?"

She frowned to herself, turned and stared into the night sky, at the stars spread above the lighted towerpiles. A long silence came between us. "Which one?" she asked at last.

I stood beside her and found the Pole star, then charted galactic clockwise until I came to the blue-shift glimmer of star Radnor 66. A couple of degrees to the right was Radnor B, where the accident had happened. The star no longer existed, and the light we saw tonight was a lie in time, the ghost of the sun before it went nova. In fifty years it would flare and die, reminding the people of Earth of the time when a smallship from the Canterbury Line was incinerated, with the loss of all aboard but one.

I pointed out the star.

She gazed up in silence, and as I watched her I was reminded again of her frailty. I wanted suddenly to question the wisdom of her living in the radioactive sector. She seemed so fragile that even something as innocuous as influenza might kill her; but that was ridiculous. No-one died nowadays from flu, or cancer. The freaks in the penthouse were merely exhibitionists; as soon as their pet cancers showed the first signs of turning nasty they would be excised, their owners given a clean bill of health. And anyway, Lin Chakra seemed cancer free.

Her request interrupted my thoughts. "Tell me about the accident," she said.

I stared at her. "Wasn't the crystal enough?"

"I haven't experienced everything," she said shrewdly. "And I want to hear the way you tell it."

"For any particular reason?"

"Oh... let's just say that I want to clarify a point."

So I gave her the full story.

IT HAD BEEN a regular long haul from star Canopus to Sigma Draconis, carrying supplies for the small colony on Sigma D IV. The *John Marston* had a crew of ten; three Enginemen, two pilots, and five service mechanics, the regular complement for a smallship like ours. After the slowburn out of Canopus we phased into the *nada*-continuum with one of my colleagues in the flux-tank. We were due for a three-month furlough at the end of the run, and perhaps that was what gave the voyage its air of light-heartedness. We were in good spirits and had no cause for concern – certainly we could not foresee the disaster ahead. When one of the pilots pointed out that we could save five days, and add them to our furlough, if we jumped the flight-path and cut through a sector of space closed to all traffic, we put it to the vote. Five of us voted for the jump, four were against the proposition, and one mechanic abstained.

The prohibited sector was the size of Sol system, with an unstable star at its centre ready to go off like a time-bomb. The star had been like this for centuries though, and I thought that the chances of it going nova just as we were passing through were negligible... if I thought about it at all. So we changed course and I took the place of the Engineman who had pushed us so far – the only reason I survived the accident. I was jacked-up, laid out and fed into the tank. The last thing I remembered was the sight of the variable sun just outside the viewscreen, burning like a furnace.

I didn't even say goodbye to Ana. But how was I to know?

"When I regained consciousness I found myself in the burns bath of a hospital on Mars. Three months had passed since the supernova."

Lin frowned. "But if you didn't actually experience the nova, how were you able to...?"

"Hear me out. I'm getting to that."

The star had blown just as the *John Marston* was lighting out of the danger zone; any closer and the boat would have been cindered. As it turned out, the ship was destroyed with the death of all aboard – or so it was thought at the time. The salvage vessel sent into the area reported that only fragments of wreckage remained, and that one of these fragments was the engineroom. It was duly hauled in, and the salvage team was amazed – and horrified – to find that I had survived.

If that was the right word to describe the condition I was in. I bore little resemblance to the human being who had entered the tank. Although the flux-tank had saved my life, the flux had kicked back and channelled a blast of nova straight into my head. My occipital computer had overloaded and melted, forcing my skull out of shape and removing flesh and muscle from my face. I suffered ninety-five percent burns and only the null-grav effect of the tank had saved me from sticking to the side like a roasting joint... I was lucky to be alive, the medics told me more than once. But in my opinion I was far from lucky; I would have gladly died to be free of the terrible guilt. The one thing for which I was thankful was the fact that I could not recall the accident or the death of Ana and my friends. But I should have known...

The dreams began a few weeks later.

My occipital computer had recorded the entire accident, and from time to time what was left of the machine, the still-functioning memory cache that interfaced with my cortex, bled nightmare visions into my sleeping mind. I saw the star go nova and the ship disintegrate and the crew, my friends for years, die instantly. Ana's brief cry of comprehension as the supernova blew would echo in my head forever.

WHEN I'D FINISHED, Lin Chakra gripped the rail and stared down at the ground effect vehicles passing back and forth like luminescent trilobites. "Your pain doesn't come through on the crystal," she said at last.

"It isn't supposed to. *The Wreck* is a statement of fact, a documentary if you like, to show the world what happened. I'm working on other crystals to show the agony caused by the tragic decision... Why? Is that what interests you? The agony?"

She glanced at me, and gave her head that typically Indian jog from side to side that might have meant either yes or no. I never realised that the gesture of a stranger could be so painful. "Partly," she said. "And partly I'm interested in death."

I nodded. That was understandable. In a world where death was a rare occurrence, it had become an even more popular subject of artistic enquiry, an even greater source of inspiration.

"The death of my colleagues was almost instantaneous," I told her. "Mercifully they didn't feel a thing."

"Oh, I'm not talking about their deaths," she said. "It's yours that interests me..."

I was glad then that my face could no longer register expression; she would have seen my shock. I was shocked because my decision to die had been a private one, and I had no idea that I'd allowed it to come through on the crystal. Then I recalled the way she had lingered over a particular node on the console.

"You read it?" I asked her.

"Very slightly. I almost missed it at first, like everyone else. I don't think you meant to show it, but it's there, buried beneath all the other emotions but just about discernible."

I remained silent. I had spoken to no-one about my decision, and the fact that Lin Chakra knew made me uneasy.

Then her question came. "Why?"

I had to think for long minutes before I could begin to explain myself. My decision had been a matter of instinct, a feeling that what I planned to do was somehow right. Now, when I came to explain this need, I feared I was cheating a genuine conviction with a devalued currency of words.

"I want to die because I survived," I told her. "I had no right to survive when the others died. I can't get over the guilt."

"I don't understand." She looked at me, her face serious between the V of her collar. "Maybe you want to end your life because you can't stand to go on as you are?"

Again my face failed to show the emotion I felt – anger, this time. "I resent that! That would make my decision to die a petty thing, self-pity masquerading as heroics. And anyway, I needn't remain like this. The best medics could fix me a new face, almost as good as new, remove the computer. I could live a normal life despite the fact that Ana's cry would be in my head even when it was no longer there... I'm sorry I've failed to justify my decision to you, but to be honest I don't feel that I have to."

"There is one way you can do that..."

"I don't see–" I began. Then I did.

She took a small box from her tunic and flipped open the lid. Inside, a fresh crystal sparkled in the starlight. "Take it," she said. "Concentrate on why you feel you have to die."

"I don't see why I should justify my need to you–"

"Or perhaps you're unable to justify it to yourself."

So I snatched the crystal and gripped it in my fist, hearing again Ana's scream as she passed into oblivion. And again I experienced the gnawing guilt, the aching desire to share her fate. The crystal soaked up the fact that I had had the casting vote on whether or not we should take the short-cut. I had voted for it, and by doing so had sent Ana and my colleagues to their deaths.

Ana had voted against the jump.

When it seemed that I'd wrung moisture from the crystal – my hand dripped with perspiration – I passed it back to Lin Chakra. She held the hexagonal diamond on the flat of her palm, staring at it with large brown eyes.

Without a word she slipped the crystal into her tunic.

"The medics give me another six months if I don't agree to a series of operations," I said. "In that time I should be able to finish quite a few crystals. The last one will be an explanation of why I feel I have to die."

We talked of other things until Chakra said she had to go.

"Some Enginemen," she said, "believe that the *nada*-continuum promises an afterlife."

I tried to laugh. "I'm not a Disciple," I told her. "There is no afterlife, as far as I'm concerned."

She nodded and said, "Why not come over to my studio tomorrow evening? The work I'm doing now might interest you."

With reluctance I accepted the invitation, and a little later we left the balcony. She unlocked the door to the party room, and the glare of the spotlight was on her again. I could hear the front-man yammering questions.

Lin pushed through the crowd. Our first meeting was over.

I ARRIVED BACK at my slum dwelling at dawn, and from across the studio an empty crystal console beckoned me. I began work immediately, spurred by my conversation with Lin Chakra. By telling her of my intentions I had reminded myself of the short time I had left in which to complete the crystals. In six months I would be dead; until our meeting, that had been almost an abstract notion. The fact was definite now, substantial. I had work to do, for myself and for my dead colleagues, and I had no time to waste.

The first step in the production of a crystal, even before the choice of subject matter, was the preparation of the thousand or so individual gems. I arranged the console on my workbench and set about the fusion process. I had chanced upon the method to do this almost by accident a few months earlier. Like most people, I had kept crystals and toyed with them occasionally. I found that the stronger the emotion infused into a crystal, the longer it remained. Superficial emotions or simple messages were gone in seconds; but love and hate lingered for long minutes... Now, from time to time, the remains of the computer that linked with my cortex gave me nightmares, blinding images of the nova chasing the ship. And the sheer terror that these nightmares produced in me...

I had been sure that if I could soak a few crystals with this fire-terror, it would last long enough so that people might gain an appreciable insight into what I had gone through.

So the next time I'd awoken with the inferno raging inside my head, I was ready. I'd jacked the leads into my skull-sockets – the same I had used as an Engineman to achieve the state of flux – wound the wires around my arm and attached the fingerclips. I could have simply held the crystals, but I wanted to gain the maximum effect. When the nightmare began I fumbled for the racked crystals beside my mattress and played a firestorm arpeggio across the faceted surface.

The result was not what I had expected; instead of impressing my terror on the crystals, I had unknowingly fused them into one big diamond slab. Not only that, but when I experimented with these transformed crystals later in the day I found that the emotions I discharged – my love for Ana, as ever – remained locked indelibly into the structure of the gems.

I had worked at the technique of bringing about the nightmare at will, and *The Wreck Of The John Marston* was my first effort. Christianna Santesson had snapped it up and signed me on practically seconds after first experiencing it. According to her, I was made.

Now I fused the largest console I'd ever done and began transferring emotions and images. I recreated the atmosphere of the flight before the tragedy, the camaraderie that existed between the crew members. Further on in the crystal I would introduce the accident as a burst of stunning horror. To begin with, I committed to crystal the times I had made weightless love to Ana, relived again the sensation of her sturdy little body entwined with mine in the astro-nacelle. Ana was a Gujarati engineer with a shaven head and bandy legs covered with tropical ulcers the shape of bite marks. We had met when she was assigned to the *John Marston*, and we had been lovers for two years before that last flight.

The sun was going down behind distant towerpiles when I realised that I'd gone as far as I could for this session. I was drained and emotionally exhausted. I had worked all day without thought of food and drink; the task had sustained me. I took an acid short from the cooler, dragged myself across to the foamform mattress and collapsed. I was drifting into sleep – and into certain dreams of Ana – when the call came through.

I crawled to the screen and opened communications. The picture showed a large studio with a figure diminished in the perspective. Lin Chakra stood with her back to the screen and turned when it chimed. "So there you are. You took so long I thought you must be out."

"I very rarely go out," I told her.

"No?" She walked towards the screen and peered through at me, her expression as stern and unsmiling as ever. "Well, how about tonight? Remember what we arranged yesterday? I'd like to show you some work I'm doing."

I considered. I had enjoyed the novelty of her company yesterday, and talking to her had proved an inspiration. "I'd like that," I said. She gave me directions and I told her I'd be over in thirty minutes.

I rode the moving boulevard to the end of the line and took a flyer the rest of the way. The pilot dropped me by the plasma barrier that covered the radioactive sector, and I paid him and stepped through the gelatinous membrane.

The difference between this sector and the rest of the city struck me immediately, and impressed itself on every sense. The air was thick and humid and the quality of light almost magical. The sun was setting through the far side of the dome, transmitting prismatic rainbows across the streets and buildings, many of them in a state of ruin softened by the mutated vegetation that had proliferated here since the meltdown. I walked along the avenue towards the intersection where Lin Chakra lived. The roar of the rest of the city was excluded here, but from within the sector a street band could be heard, their music keeping to the hectic tempo of a Geiger counter. There was an air of peace and timelessness about the deserted streets, and it seemed to me the perfect place for the artist to reside, amid the equal influences of beauty and destruction.

"Dan...!" The cry came from high above. I craned my neck and saw Lin Chakra waving at me from a balcony halfway up a towering obelisk.

I counted the windows and took the upchute to her level.

"In here," she called from one of the many white-walled rooms that comprised the floor she had entirely to herself. I walked through three spacious rooms, each containing holograms like a gallery, before I found her. She was pouring wine by the balcony. She turned as I entered. "I'm glad you could make it," she said.

I murmured something and stood on the balcony and admired the view, to give me something to do while I tried to surmount the pain I felt at meeting her again.

She seemed a different person from the woman of last night, and more like Ana. She wore a short yellow smock, and her thin bare legs were pocked with the tight purple splotches of healed tropical ulcers.

As she invited me to follow her, I realised that she wasn't well. Her hands shook, and her breath came in ragged, painful spasms.

We moved from room to room, the contents of each charting Lin's development from small beginnings through her apprentice work to her more recent and accomplished holograms. She had two main phases behind her: the dozen pieces she produced from the age of fifteen to eighteen, and a triptych called *Love*, which she brought out from the age of eighteen to twenty. These had deservedly earned her world recognition. She had done nothing for more than a year now, and the critics and public alike were eager for the next phase of her work to be released.

She took me into her workroom overlooking the arching membrane of the outer dome. The contents of the room were scattered; hologram frames and benches in disarray, indicating the artist in the throes of production. Three completed holograms stood against the wall, and others in various stages of completion occupied benches or were piled on the floor.

"These three are finished and okay. The others–" She indicated those on the floor with a sweep of her hand. "I think I'll scrap them and release these three later this year."

I stared into the three-dimensional glass sculptures. The imprisoned images were grotesque and disturbing, grim forebodings and prophesies of darkness. I was horrified, without really knowing why. "Dying," I whispered.

Lin Chakra nodded. "Of course. The ultimate mystery. What better subject for the artist who has done everything else?"

I moved to the next hologram. This one was more graphic; inside great baubles and bubbles of glass I made out the shrunken image of Lin herself, her small body contorted in angles of pain and suffering. "You?"

"I contracted leukaemia six months ago," she said. "The medics give me another three."

"And when you've finished you'll go for a cure..." I began.

She averted her gaze, stared at the floor.

"You can't let it kill you, Lin!" I cried. "You're still young. You have all your life ahead of you. All your art–"

"Listen to me, Dan. I have done everything. I've been everywhere and experienced everything and put it all into holograms and there is nothing else for me to do."

"Can't you simply..." I shrugged. "Retire? Quit holograms if you've said all you can?"

She was slowly shaking her head; sadly, it seemed. "Dan... You don't understand. You're no artist, really. Not a true artist. If you were you'd understand that artists live for what they can put into holograms, or on paper or canvas, whatever. When that comes to an end, their lives are finished. How can I go on when I have nothing more to say?" She stared at me. "Death is the final statement. I want to give the world my death."

"Does Santesson know about this?" I asked.

"I told her, of course. She's an artist, Dan. She understands."

I moved around the studio in a daze. At last I said, "But these holograms aren't your death, Lin. These are your dying."

Her eyes brimmed with tears, and she nodded. "Don't you think I realise that? Why do you think I've scrapped all these?" She flung out her arm at the half-completed holograms scattered about the room. "They're imperfect, Dan. Impressions of dying, that's all. These three are the closest in dying that I've come to death."

I thought of Ana, who had died when she had most wanted to live. Lin's slow suicide was an affront to her memory, and it was this knowledge that burned in me with anger. "You can't do it, Lin."

"You don't understand!"

I'd had my fill of pain and could take no more. I left her standing by the entrance and without a word took the downchute. The music had stopped and I walked quickly through the empty streets towards the safe sector of the city.

For the next couple of days I remained in my studio, drank acid shorts and stared morosely at the crystal I had started but could not finish. My old need to create art from the tragedy of the *John Marston* was overcome by apathy; it was as if what Lin Chakra was doing had reminded me that nothing, not even art, could ease the agony of my being without Ana.

Lin called repeatedly, perhaps in a bid to explain herself, to make me understand. But I always cut the connection the second her face appeared on the screen.

I considered killing myself before my time was due.

A few days after my meeting with Lin I stood before a crystal I'd completed months before. It failed as a work of art, but as a statement of my pain and my love for Ana it was wholly successful. I ran my hand over the crystals, reliving again the experience of being with her; reliving the horror of her absence.

Next to the crystal I had placed a laser-razor...

Christianna Santesson saved my life.

The screen chimed and I ran to it, intending to scream at Lin Chakra that I resented her intrusion. I punched the set into life.

Santesson smiled out at me. "Daniel... How are you?"

"What do you want?" I snapped, venting anger on her.

"Business, Daniel." She chose to ignore my rudeness. "Your crystal is showing very well. I'm delighted with the response of the public. I was wondering... How would you feel about producing a sequel to exhibit beside it?"

Her commercialism sickened me.

I told her that that was out of the question, that in fact I'd stopped working.

She frowned. "That's unfortunate, Daniel," she said; then, with an air of calculation, "I don't suppose you've considered telling me how you produce your crystals, Daniel? After all, you did promise that you would, one day."

I nodded. "One day, yes."

"Then perhaps I could persuade you to sell me one single fused console, instead?" There was a look of animal-like entreaty in her eyes.

I laughed as an idea occurred to me. "Very well, I will. But I want a million credits for it."

To my surprise she smiled. "That sounds reasonable, Daniel. You have yourself a deal. One million credits. I'll pay it into your account as soon as the crystal is delivered."

In a daze I said, "I'll do it right away."

She smiled goodbye and cut the connection.

Later, I wired myself up and arranged a crystal console, induced a nova-nightmare and channelled the firepower into the alien stones. As always it took immense concentration and energy to sustain the power required to fuse an entire console without leaching my emotions into it, and I was exhausted by the time I finished. I sealed the slab in a lead-lined wrap and hired a flyer to take it to Santesson. Then I returned to my studio and sprawled across the foamform. All thoughts of pre-emptive suicide had fled. With the million credits I would offer Lin Chakra the stars, buy her passage aboard a starship to give her that which she had yet to experience. I slept.

I dreamed of Ana. We were making love in the astro-nacelle, our bodies joined at the pelvis and spinning as the stars streaked around the dome. Ana moaned in Hindi as orgasm took her, eyes turned up to show only an ellipse of pearly white. Our occipital computers were tuned to each others' frequency, and our heads resonated with ever-increasing ecstasy. Around our spinning bodies cast-off sweat hung weightless like miniature suns, each droplet catching the light of the genuine suns outside. Then, with a surreal rearrangement of fact common to dreams, the nova blew while I was still with Ana, and burned in my arms, though I remained strangely uninjured. Her flesh shrivelled and her bones exploded, and through our computer link she screamed her hate at me.

The horror pushed me to a shallower level of sleep, though I didn't awake. I tossed and turned fitfully, and then began to dream a second time. Again I was in the astro-nacelle, and again I was making love – but this time not to Ana. I held Lin Chakra to me, distantly aware of this anomalous transposition, and she stared in wonder at the starlight wrapped like streamers around the dome.

It was dark when I awoke. I had slept for almost twenty-four hours. Through the slanting glass roof of the studio, star Radnor B winked at me. I got up feebly and staggered across to the vid-screen. I called Lin Chakra, but she was either out or not answering; the screen remained blank. I paced around for an hour, going through the contents of my dreams. Then I tried to reach her again, and again there was no response. I decided to go to her place with my offer of the stars, dressed and left the studio.

I walked through the deserted streets of the radioactive sector and rode the upchute to her suite. I called her name as I passed through the large white rooms, but there was no reply. The words I had rehearsed were a jumble in my head as the time approached for me to use them. I think I realised that she would refuse my offer, point out quite simply that she could have bought the experience of starflight herself, if she had thought it might afford her new insights. In the event I had no need to make the offer. I entered her room.

I found Lin on the floor.

Her naked body lay in a pool of her own blood. Choking, I dropped to my knees beside her. She had taken a laser and lacerated her left wrist almost to the point of amputation. She appeared far more beautiful in death than ever she had in life, and I knew that this was because of the expression on her face. I realised then that during all the time I had known her I had never seen her smile.

I cried something incomprehensible, lifted her body into my arms and began to rock, repeating the name, "Ana..." over and over.

A FEW WEEKS later I met Christianna Santesson at a party.

I had completed a dozen crystals since the first, and they were showing quite well. My last crystal had been an admission of the guilt I felt at consigning my colleagues to death, an expiation that stood in place of my own death. I hoped that soon I would be able to leave the psychologically crippling subject of the *John Marston* and move on to other things. Perhaps in fifty years I would be able to watch the nova of star Radnor B without the pain of guilt.

I had hired the services of a top medic and he had removed the computer and rebuilt my face. I was still no beauty, but at least people could look at me now without flinching. The scars still showed, physical counterparts of the mental scars that would take much longer to heal.

Christianna Santesson did not recognise me.

As I stood beside her in a group of artists and critics, I could not decide if she was evil or supremely good. My attitude towards her was ambivalent; I passed through phases of wanting to kill her and wanting to thank her for saving my life a second time.

Someone mentioned Lin Chakra.

"Her death was such a tragic loss," Santesson said. "But she will live on in her work. Her final trilogy, *Dying*, will be out this summer. I had arranged for her to make a definitive statement on the subject, but the piece was stolen soon after her death. As I was saying..."

I left the party early and returned to my studio.

The crystal lay in the centre of the room, sparkling in the starlight and still covered in blood. Lin had even titled it before she killed herself: *The Death of Lin Chakra*. I knelt before the console and passed a hand across the faceted surface. Agony and pain saturated each crystal, and they communicated the awful realisation that everything she had ever known was drawing to a close with the inevitable approach of death. Lin had achieved her final artistic goal; she had successfully transferred to crystal her ultimate experience. Soon, as she would have wished, I would give her masterpiece to the world, so that everyone might learn from Lin Chakra's bloody death how fortunate they were to be alive.

The Phoenix Experiment

One month after the death of his daughter, Jonathon Fuller decided to leave the city. The life and energy of the place was too stark a contrast to the isolation he had imposed upon himself, too harsh a reminder of his daughter's passing. He needed the tranquillity of the countryside, where his desire to be alone would not be seen as perverse, in order to come to terms with his guilt and eventually, perhaps, to persuade himself to return. He shelved all his projects and told his agent that he was going away for a long holiday.

Early that summer he drove from the city and toured the southern coastline in search of a suitable retreat, somewhere isolated and idyllic, untouched by the technologies of contemporary life. Within a week he discovered a lonely village overlooking the channel, and made enquiries at a local property office. He was told that there were no houses for rent in the village itself, but there were chalets available in the Canterbury Rehabilitation Community, half a mile away.

He'd heard about the Community, but, far from being deterred by the nature of the place, it occurred to him that there he might be allowed the privacy he desired.

When he arrived at the enclosed estate later that afternoon he was met by a big, bulky man in an invalid carriage, who called himself the Captain and showed Fuller to one of a dozen identical A-frames that occupied a greensward beside the ocean. The view of the seascape, and the chalet's relative isolation, cheered him. He thought back to his depressive state in the city and told himself that this was exactly what he had been seeking.

That first night, as darkness fell and the stars appeared, he took a bottle of scotch onto the balcony, drank and stared up at the constellations. The Captain had told him that he would be made welcome by the rest of the patients – at this stage of their rehabilitation, he had said, they rarely had contact with outsiders. Fuller had been unable to bring himself to tell the Captain that he would not be requiring company for some time.

In one of the other A-frames on the gently sloping greensward, a party was in progress: the patients, he thought, doing their best to forget the present. Dark shapes passed across the lighted squares of windows like figures in an Indonesian shadow play, and laughter drifted across to him on the warm night air.

He decided to set up a camp bed on the balcony, in the hope that his dreams of late had been in part a product of the claustrophobia he had experienced in the city. But the open air, the mild sea breeze, could do nothing to alleviate the guilt, and in the early hours he awoke in a sweat and watched his daughter's smiling face vanish into the night.

FULLER TOOK TO going on long walks early in the mornings, so as to avoid the patients who were active mainly in the afternoons. He would spend the rest of the day reading, or drinking, or watching television. It was as if he was purposefully filling his head with trivia, and allotting only the two hours he spent walking for the serious consideration of his circumstances.

At the funeral, and its aftermath, he had been unable to show the slightest sign of grief. Many of his acquaintances assumed that he was still in shock, but his father had seen through his silent facade and called Fuller cold and emotionless, accused him of feeling nothing for his dead daughter.

Only later did he begin to experience the guilt – not so much at being unable to grieve at her death, rather at his inability to show her more affection during the short time that she had been alive. He had kept his distance, remained aloof, believing that by doing so he could insulate himself from the hurt that inevitably followed emotional involvement. He believed that with involvement came the fear of another's mortality, and from that the reminder of one's own – and more than anything else Fuller feared his own death. Over the years, he had succeeded in distancing himself from everyone with whom he had contact, his daughter included. He was rewarded by the inability to suffer anguish at his bereavement. Only now was he coming to realise that his apathy had affected the quality of his daughter's short life.

ONE MORNING, AFTER a long walk, Fuller encountered a patient on the beach beneath the cliffs. Later, he came to think of the brief meeting as prophetic.

He saw the woman as he came around the headland, paused and considered retracing his steps so as to avoid meeting her. She was staring out to sea, with her back to him, and he decided to walk quickly past her towards the steps cut into the cliff-face.

She stood in the wet sand, her hands slotted into the back pockets of her denim cut-offs, a short white tee-shirt emphasising her tan. She was a crew-cut blonde with the figure of a small boy, and it occurred to Fuller, with mounting shock that, if she were so physically perfect, then her debilitation had to be cerebral.

Then he became aware of the subcutaneous network, the threads of gold that embroidered the surface of her arms and legs, the small of her back and belly between cotton shirt and the frayed waistline of her denims.

She turned and caught him staring. Her face was young and open. Fuller tried to hurry past, but her question stopped him.

"Are you one of them?" Her voice was transistorised, straight from the larynx, while her full lips smiled and her green eyes stared at him.

"I arrived here yesterday, from London." He stopped. "But aren't you–?" He gestured to the greensward.

"I'm a patient, but not of the Canterbury Line. We do not mix."

He saw that although she had followed him with her head, her stance in the wet sand had not altered. She stood with a torque to her spine that was at once awkward and becoming, her hands still pocketed behind her.

He gestured to the steps in the cliff-face, suggesting she might care to accompany him. "Why don't you mix?" he asked.

She walked with movements of such brittle care that she might at one time have broken every bone in her body, yet she was far from clumsy. She moved with the fluid grace, the deliberation of an actress in a Noh play.

She said simply in reply, "I scare them." And smiled at him.

At the top of the cliff he made an excuse and returned to his chalet. There, he turned and watched her as she moved off with laborious languor. Her perfection, despite whatever injuries she had sustained, filled him with wonder – and he suspected that it was her perfection that scared the other patients.

TWO NIGHTS LATER he came close.

It was a contradiction that although for thirty years he had absented himself from emotional involvement, so that he might hold himself at some remove from the inevitability of death, now he was contemplating taking his life. A fear of death had made him what he was – and it was as if threatening himself with oblivion he was in fact presenting himself with an ultimatum: either change, and learn to live and give as others do, or kill yourself now in the full knowledge of the futility of your existence... So naturally he had flung aside the pistol with which he had intended to shoot himself through the heart.

Then, in lieu of fulfilling the directive of his ultimatum, he found the bottle of scotch and drank himself senseless.

OFTEN, DURING THE next few weeks, the patients invited him to join their gatherings, and Fuller could not bring himself to refuse. He attended picnics on the greensward, barbecues on the beach, late night parties at which the invalids would sit outside in groups and point to the stars where they had served.

His main concern in capitulating and joining their company, that he might have to explain himself and his presence here, proved unfounded. They had heard of Jonathon Fuller, the historical-scripter, and knew of the loss of his daughter. He found himself accepted without having to explain his past, and part of him – the part that had refused to end his life the other night – knew full well that he was cheating himself.

He soon spent almost every night at their gatherings, and it was ironic that they regarded him – the only fit and whole person among them – with the pity that they themselves deserved; they had come to accept their own injuries, but they found it hard to come to terms with Fuller's loss. They had passed so close to death that the mere thought of it terrified them.

They were daunting company, these survivors of starship burnouts, novae, alien pestilence, war and a hundred other far disasters. They spoke of their experiences with a gentle wisdom at odds with the enormity of their physical deformities. He had thought that, beside them, perhaps his own problems would come to appear slight, but such was not the case. Through their experiences they had come to know themselves with a thoroughness that emphasised his own uncertainty and lack of self-knowledge. All he had that they did not was a fully-functioning body.

He could not talk of himself without appearing superficial, so although he drank and laughed and partied with them, he remained aloof. To save himself he knew that he must accept the intimacies of others, and in turn give of himself, but he was not prepared to open himself to the pain and humiliation that that would entail.

One warm evening, at a party which had spilled from a chalet and across the greensward, Fuller sat on the grass with a bottle in his grip while he listened to the Captain recount the meltdown of his starship.

They were alone, and Fuller had ceased to be revolted by the Captain's extensive injuries. They were rebuilding him piece by piece; he would disappear for days on end, and reappear, at last, a little more human.

Fuller sat well beyond the crimson glow that encapsulated the Captain and his overdose of radiation. A Geiger counter on the spacer's belt churred like a cricket.

He came to the end of his story, and they regarded the star where it had happened. A silence came down between them, like the end of an act, and on the periphery of his vision Fuller was aware of a familiar movement. He turned to acknowledge her presence.

She crouched on the grass twenty metres away, hugging her bare shins and staring at them. Her epidermal network glowed in the gathering darkness like spun gold. She had the aspect of an angel.

In a bid to overcome his unease at her constant regard, he turned to the spacer. "Who's the woman?" he asked.

The carriage swung so that the gobbet of flesh and gristle that was the extent of the Captain's physical being now faced the perfect woman. "She's the Phoenix Line experiment," he said.

Her tragic isolation touched something deep within Fuller. "Why doesn't she join us?"

It was a while before the Captain replied. "She's not one of us," he said, and his carriage rose and hovered off towards the chalet.

Fuller walked over to the woman. He passed across her line of sight, and it was seconds before she compensated and moved her head to regard him.

He crouched beside her. "What happened to you?" he asked gently.

She just smiled, shook her head. Her distant eyes relived the trauma of her accident.

"Why don't you join them?"

Her lips remained fixed in a smile and she shrugged artlessly.

Fuller shook his head to indicate that she mystified him. He wanted to find a question that she might answer, as if to establish her psychological reality within his frame of reference.

She rose and smiled uncertainly at him. The sound of her static-choked voice was sudden. "I really must be going," she said, and still smiling she moved off like a narcoleptic ballerina.

Over the next few weeks he saw less and less of the other patients. He made excuses when they called with invitations: he was working, he was thinking. Of course, he was doing none of these things. The patients frightened him with their personal certainty, their understanding. He felt inferior in their company.

In contrast, the woman seemed weak and lost, and Fuller resolved to spend more time with her.

He continued his long walks around the estate, hurrying until he came to the beach and there pausing to admire the view, perhaps hoping he might happen upon the woman again. He was confused, but no longer suicidal. He had even considered returning to the city, but something, some intimation that he was not yet ready, restrained him.

One morning as he walked along the beach he saw the woman approach him from the opposite direction, moving through the warm air as if wading along at the bottom of the sea.

She paused before him. The process of coming to a halt involved a gradual shut-down of her bodily movements: she settled into stasis like some machine.

As ever she was smiling, distant. "Jonathon, you remind me of my father..."

They walked side by side along the seashore, and although she was present physically, she was absent; it was more than just her silence – she seemed removed as if inhabiting a private universe of her own, a universe that earned the constant praise of her smile. Fuller wanted nothing more than to establish some means of contact with her, to take her in his arms and communicate. It was as if she were imprisoned within her perfect form, and only a show of affection on his part might provoke from her some reciprocal response.

At last she broke the silence. "Why are you here?"

He told her about the death of his daughter, and despite some inner urging said no more. Later, when they concluded their walk outside his chalet, and she said, "Perhaps we might meet again?" – a no-doubt sincere request made formal by the means of its delivery – he was torn between wanting to accede to her request, and wanting to shut her from his life forever.

SUMMER PROGRESSED AND Fuller spent more time with the woman, and the other patients shunned them. No longer came the invitations to picnics and parties, and whenever he met a patient while out walking he was pointedly ignored. The dissociation did not bother him unduly; he supposed, in a way, that he had begun the rift when he sought the woman's company in preference to theirs.

They met every day and walked, lunched, sat on the balcony of his A-frame and drank, then dined and watched the sun set. They never discussed their tenuous relationship, or how it might continue; they simply met and passed the time of day together. She was always distant, present in body but rarely in mind, and when she spoke it was with an objectivity shorn of all emotion. He often had the urge to ask her how she felt, if she had plans and ambitions for the future, joyous memories and old loves. It was as if the accident through which she'd passed had traumatised her, made her loath to become the feeling human being she used to be.

Fuller never demanded from her a statement of commitment, or anything that might require from her an expenditure of the emotion she was unable to declare. Perhaps she saw in him someone who would accept her as she was, and perhaps he saw in her the same.

They spoke of their respective lives in terms of fact, sanitised of feeling. It was the first time he had declared his past to anyone, even though his words were objective and far from comprehensive.

One evening as they watched the sun sink into the ocean, he asked, "Why are you here?"

"I was a xeno-biologist on Thallia, in the Persephone Cluster," she began.

She *was* a xeno-biologist – but she was also something more. She was born on Thallia and lived there until the time of her accident twenty years later. She was fifteen when she joined her father in the study of the alien natives, and they became the only humans the aliens would trust. She lived among them, learned their ways, was accepted by the arboreal, ape-like creatures as *goyu*, "One of us." When the Phoenix Line moved in on the planet, they used the father and daughter team as liaison officers between Head of Command and the native elders. The Line wanted to mine the planet's only island, and as the planet was protected territory they needed the Thallian's permission. The only humans with whom the aliens would consent to discuss the matter were the xeno-biologist and his daughter.

She told him this over the period of an hour, with no stress or inflexion, with no passion that might suggest she was on the side of the natives.

They watched the light die on the horizon.

She continued, "My father and I were in a shuttle accident, coming from the planet's surface to an orbiting starship for debriefing. My father did not survive; I did. They brought me to Earth and began to rebuild me. In one week I return to Thallia, to negotiate with the natives. I am a valuable commodity to the Phoenix Line."

He glanced across at her, but her face was expressionless, with no hint of grief or regret, or anger that she had become no more than a chattel of the Line.

He tried to imagine the shuttle accident, the extent of her resulting injuries. She had said that she had been rebuilt, and he wondered how much of her had survived the crash. The only indication of physical damage was the golden net that held her body together, the only hint of mental impairment her eternal distance.

Two days before she was due to leave for the Persephone Cluster, he led her to the bedroom of his chalet and undressed her as she stood perfectly still with a distant smile on her lips. Then he carried her to the bed and they made love – or rather he, overcome with lust, made love to her, and she moved her limbs with a semblance of passion but without conviction. It was as if the absent part of her disdained physicality, allowed her body only a token role in the experience.

Later he caressed her occipital computer, fitted flush to the back of her neck, and smoothed his hands over her body network, a filigree matrix slightly firmer than the flesh it underlay. She had said not a word during the whole encounter. She stared uncomprehendingly at his tears.

"Jonathon?"

He kissed her and said she was the only person he had ever loved.

"Did you not love your wife?"

"I was never married."

"Then the mother of your daughter?"

He had adopted his daughter when she was two years old, in an attempt to bring something into his life that he might love.

He told her all this now.

She was unable to make an adequate response, as Fuller had suspected. He wondered if this was the reason he had opened up to her; he had experienced the catharsis of confession without an adverse reaction, without the questions that would have accused him – which, he realised, was no catharsis at all. Through replying to criticism, attempting however futilely to defend himself, he might have come to understand more about the person who was Jonathon Fuller: he would have undergone the process of sharing personal pain and anguish which was all part of the exchange of human love but which he, in his cowardice, had never experienced.

She reached out and touched his cheek in a gesture so empty of affection that it was almost brutal.

"I think we are very much alike, Jonathon."

He told her that they were very much different. He thought that, despite the injuries that had left her unable to exhibit the regular run of emotions, she could perhaps feel them – whereas he had the ability to do neither.

"But you said earlier that you loved me," her vocal-assist pronounced through smiling lips.

She lay still beside him as darkness gathered, then closed her eyes and slept.

"Words," he murmured to himself.

In the morning she was gone.

At dawn he left the chalet and attempted to find her; he needed her acceptance, and rationalised that anything other than her refusal to tolerate his presence he could count as that acceptance. She was the only person to whom he had ever admitted the truth, and he could not bear the thought of her rejection.

She was not in her chalet, or anywhere else in the grounds. He spent the rest of the day performing an extended version of his morning walk, but the woman was nowhere to be found.

That evening, as darkness gathered and the patients began another of their interminable soirees, Fuller crossed the greensward to the fireside group and sought the Captain. He knelt beside the carriage and regarded the nub of flesh that, despite its appearance, was nevertheless human.

"Have you seen her?" he asked.

The party noise around him stopped abruptly. Their dialogue became the centre of attention. "Is she missing?" the Captain asked.

"She left this morning. I haven't seen her since."

The Captain seemed to vent a weary sigh. "Fuller... Fuller. Stop this idiocy, man! Don't you see that nothing can come of it?"

"I need her," he said, and the silence around him deepened.

"Oh, Christ... Fuller, please listen to me. Don't you realise – she's dead."

It was as if the Captain had physically assaulted him; for a second he was breathless, incredulous. "She can't be! She was with me just last night–"

"I'm sorry, Fuller. I'm very sorry. We thought you knew. She died six months ago in the shuttle accident. The woman you know is nothing more than programming."

He could feel the weight of their silent pity as he turned and ran.

THE FOLLOWING MORNING he found her on the beach.

She stood in the wet sand, staring out across the ocean. Her shorts and tee-shirt were soaked, clasping her body. Fuller sank into a siting position on a nearby rock.

"The Captain told me about the accident," he said.

She turned to him from the waist and stared. Her face, as ever, was empty of expression.

"Biologically," she said, "she is dead. She died in the accident and all that survived was her body. She was brain-dead, so they manufactured a digital analogue of her mind and re-vitalised the remains of her body. Over a period, here on Earth, they rebuilt her... *me*."

Fuller stood and held the woman. "But you're still *her* – you have all her memories, her knowledge."

She avoided his eyes. "I am a continuation of her."

He sensed her doubt, her reservation.

He shook her. "But you're still human!"

Her eyes found his, accusing. "I tried to drown myself today... I failed, of course. I am programmed to save myself. I am a valuable asset to the Phoenix Line."

He looked into the vacancy of her expression, which he had thought of until now as merely distant. He recalled his own aborted suicide attempt, and he had the first stirrings of an awful premonition.

"Why...?" he released her and took one step back. "Why did you try to kill yourself?"

"I have her memories. She knew love before she died. Yesterday, with you, she would have been able to *feel*. I knew then for the first time that I could no longer pretend to be her. I am no longer human, and the part of me that was her cannot bear the thought."

A silver ambulance, with *Phoenix Line* emblazoned along its flank, drew up on the cliff-top. Two uniformed men climbed from the cab and came down the steps, and the woman allowed herself to be walked away without so much as a backward glance.

He followed, burdened with grief for the woman. He crossed the greensward towards his chalet and, as the vehicle started up, he recalled her words of yesterday, when she had said that they were very much alike. Fuller realised that, of course, they were. He also realised their difference: the woman was condemned to existence with the full and terrible knowledge of her inhumanity, denied release by her programming and unable to regain that which she once had been.

Fuller thought of the city, of the life and the energy there. He turned and watched the silver vehicle drive from the estate, carrying away the woman who was no longer human.

Big Trouble Upstairs

I'M ON THE Barrier Reef pleasure 'plex, looking for a year-wife. Someone small and dark this time – Oriental maybe. The jacuzzi lagoon is foaming around me and my lover, a cute Kampuchean fluxer, when my handset goes *ber-leep*. I wade into the shallows, the kid big-eyed on my hip, and take the call.

"Sorry to come between you and your fun, Isabella." Massingberd stares up from the back of my hand, playing the chaperone. "But you're on."

The spacer senses the goodbye and lays a soft cheek against my breast. I enter her head, tone down the love I've been promoting thus far, damp her synaptic fires.

"Give it me, Mass," I sigh.

"You're gonna love this one," he begins, and gives me a big wink.

There's a laser-slayer loose on the Carnival Sat, wasting innocents like mad-crazy. The bastard zero'd the security team first, along with the mechanical defences – and he has a dozen workers imprisoned on the satellite, to pick off at his leisure.

"It's your kind of job, Is. You're going in there alone."

"Say, thanks..."

"A shuttle's on its way," he says, and signs off.

Soo-Lee clutches me. "Isabella..."

"There'll be other times," I say. But not with me... Why do I do it – *why*? It was love at first sight. I felt that yearning, gut pang the second I set eyes on Soo-Lee a week back. She was picking scabs from her new hand-jack on the beach outside my villa. Of course, she wouldn't have given me a second glance, but I have *ability*.

Ten years ago I tested psi-positive and had the cut – but the operation went wrong. It was *too* successful. Instead of coming out plain telepathic, I emerged *mega*-telepathic. Which meant that, as well as being able to read minds, I had the power to control a subject's thoughts, make them do just whatever the hell I wanted. Pretty neat, okay.

I was the first of a new line.

We're a dozen now, closely supervised.

And I have this thing about kids. Whenever I see one I like I get in there and tamper, fix, and soon they're all gooey-eyed, eager.

This past week on the 'plex we made a striking couple: an anorexic, slit-eyed Enginegirl and a six-six eighteen-year-old Rwandan Watusi with scarified cheeks and dreads. That's me.

The love I promote is doomed, of course. I can't sustain that degree of adoration in a subject for long. The past few years I've instilled ersatz-love for the period of a six-month or one-year marriage contract – then withdrawn. It's kinder that way, to both parties. A year is long enough to live a lie, even when you're in love.

I dump Soo-Lee on the golden sand and sluice apathy around her frontal lobe, and by the time I step into my villa she's beginning to wonder what she ever saw in me. Soon Isabella Manchester will be nothing more than a pleasant event in the memory of her youth, and then not even that.

Massingberd knows. He was the only person I could bring myself to tell. He once asked me why I didn't turn my ability on myself. "Why don't you cure yourself, Is? Fix your head so you don't lust after these kids..."

It's no longer illegal, but oldsters like Mass have throwback morality.

"'Cos if it wasn't kids it'd be women or men. I'd be no better off, just the same. I need love, okay? I guess I'm insecure. I can't change what I am because of *why* I am–" And stopped there.

I didn't even know Massingberd well enough to tell him why I am.

"I need love and it's so easy for me to get it," I'd often say. "But how can that be love?"

Skip six hours and I'm aboard the shutt on autopilot, heading away from the plane of the ecliptic towards the Carnival Sat. And mine's the only vessel going thisaway: all the other traffic is streaming Earthwards, sunlit specks corkscrewing down the gravity-well like gene-data on a DNA helix.

From this far out the satellite is an oblate spheroid, a yuletide bauble set against the Pleiades. The lower hemisphere is in darkness – the maintenance section that keeps the whole show ticking. Above, the working end of the Sat is a fuzzy golden blur. Closer proximity provides resolution: I see avenues and arcades, rides and sideshows. One big fun city down there.

Massingberd's saying: "... carved up two hundred Japanese and American tourists before the emergency shuttles could get the rest out. There's around a dozen workers still in there, plus the killer."

"You sure he didn't sneak out on a shuttle?"

"I had a 'head screening every ship that left, Is." He looks up at me solicitously. "Hey, you be careful, okay?"

The sentimental old bastard. "I'll be fine, Mass."

"I'm putting you through to the Director who's still in there–"

But he's cut off by a screenful of static. I shake my hand impatiently and the screen clears. Now another mugshot regards me – the big cartoon head, all ribbons and grin, of Minnie Mouse.

"I'm fouled up with an entertainment channel, Mass!" I yell. I'm approaching the Satellite fast and I need the Director's talk-down. I can't hit destination cold. I'd be easy meat for the laser-slayer.

"Massingberd!" I cry again.

"Manchester?" Minnie Mouse asks.

"Huh?" I goggle.

"Are you reading, Manchester?" Minnie's fatuous grin belies the impatient tone.

"Reading," I say. "Who the hell...?"

"Director Maria Da Cruz," Minnie says, a girl's voice muffled by latex.

"Why the fancy dress, Director?"

"You'll find out when you get here. Frankly, your surprise cannot equal mine. I was expecting a combat squad, at least. We have a maniac rampant up here, and they send me a..." She subvocalizes the rest, not for my ears, but I make out what might be, "... a witch-doctor."

I smile. "What's the score, Minnie?"

"I'll meet you at rim-lock twelve. The killer's somewhere on the far side of the complex. Could be anywhere within an area of twenty square kilometres. My workers are in the central plaza, in the dorms. They fled there when the shooting began." As Minnie prattles I have the weird sensation of watching a kids' video crossed with the soundtrack of a cop show. "They're pinned down and can't get out."

"Have they tried?"

"You're joking, of course. The fire came from the far rim, and the dorms open onto the central concourse. It'd be an automatic death sentence for the first person who shows their face. You've got to get these people out."

"My job is to get the killer," I tell her. "Then they're safe."

"In that case I hope you're well armed," Minnie says condescendingly.

I have the last laugh. "As a matter of fact I don't believe in the things."

The Minnie head deprives me the satisfaction of seeing her face drop. She grins idiotically until I cut the link.

The shutt makes one hi-altitude orbit of the satellite and glides towards the docking rig in the underbelly, blindside of the killer. We contact with the delicacy of balloons kissing.

Seconds later I float out, cycle myself through the airlock and peer cautiously into the long, curving corridor. I scan for the killer's manic brainvibes, but the coast is clear. I move inside.

Minnie stands arms akimbo, awaiting me.

Maria Da Cruz is tense and afraid, of course, but beneath this I access her identity. She's an intelligent, lonely kid, twenty-one in a week, and in any other circumstances I'd like to get to know her better.

As it is–

"So here you are at last!" She kicks something towards me, a black rubber puddle sprouting ears.

"What the hell?"

"Get into it. Don't argue." She looks me up and down, appraising. "You're tall, but you'll fit at a stretch."

I pick it up. A Mickey suit. I step into the booties and pull up the clinging rubber leggings over those of my onepiece. "Now, if you don't mind telling me what all this is about?" I could take time off scanning for the killer and read her, but I'm jumpy at the thought of being fried alive.

"This allows us greater freedom," Da Cruz says. "The killer isn't potting cartoon characters – they're all robots. I was in the storeroom when the killing began. I saw what was going on and dug these out. They're the last we have in stock, from the days before actors were superseded by 'bots."

I stretch the torso over each shoulder and let go with a snap. Then I pull on the zippered head; my own bulges between the ears like a big egg. Mickey's never been so tall.

"You weren't kidding, were you?"

"Eh?" I'm having difficulty with the zipper.

"You aren't armed."

"Told you so."

"Then how the hell do you hope to kill the killer?"

I give her a big smile before fastening the zipper. "An old African custom," I say. "I'll *think* him dead." Which isn't that far off the mark, minus the ethnic bit.

"Okay, just one more thing," she says. "You gotta walk like the real Mickey. Like this."

I stare at her through the gauze where Mickey's tonsils should be. She's strutting up and down the corridor, waving her arms, twitching her ass. If only Massingberd could see us now.

"Your turn, Manchester."

So I strut my stuff before her, elbows working invisible bellows. "Point your boots! Swing your tail! This has to be perfect, Manchester. If this bastard so much as suspects..."

She doesn't have to finish that line.

"Fine. You got it. Now where you want to go first?"

The thought of parading myself out there like a sitting duck – or rather mouse – gives me the heebies.

I quit wriggling and squat on my heels. The suit is tight and uncomfortable, squashing me short. "First, before I start risking my life – 'cos I don't want to be found dead in this fucking thing – first I want to know more about the killer. Like how he managed to waste an entire security team *and* blow the defence system?"

I keep a probe out for the killer. I have a range of just over a kilometre, though it's getting weak by then. We're quite alone at present.

"The security unit? The killer sprayed them with Procyon animalcules. They reduced the unit to slush one hour before the fireworks began."

"*Yech!* And the mechanical defences? The 'bots?"

"Deactivated beforehand. That should have set off an alarm in computer control, but that'd been fixed too."

"Whoever the killer is, he sure knows his stuff. Could it be someone who works here?"

She shrugs. "Why not? We employ nearly twenty thousand permanent staff."

"Most of them evacuated with the trippers? So that leaves only the dozen workers holed up in the dorms."

"Plus the killer."

I think about it. "Has there been any shooting since the dozen staff made it to safety?"

"No..." Da Cruz is getting my drift.

"So perhaps, just *perhaps*, the killer is a worker. He or she hides with the others after the firing's through – providing an alibi."

"You think that likely?"

"At the moment anything's possible," I say.

Da Cruz pushes herself from the wall with a practised rubber bounce. "Any more questions?"

"Yeah... how come a girl as young as you gets to be the Director of an outfit as big as this?"

That stops her in her tracks.

"How do you know how old I am?"

"I'm well informed," I tell her. "Well?"

She shrugs. "I work hard."

"You must be very talented."

She's suddenly uncomfortable, under the Minnie suit. I read that she was a solitary kid, bullied at school, whose only way of showing *them* was to succeed. But there's still something lacking, I read. Success isn't all.

I have the almost irresistible urge to go in there and help her out, ever so gently. But I restrain myself. This is neither the time nor the place – and there's work to be done. Besides, I'm getting to the stage where I need *real* love, love that isn't forced.

"Lead the way," I say.

"Where to?"

"The workers' dorm, or thereabouts. I can do my stuff at long range."

She regards me. "Okay. You ready?"

We cake-walk into the open, beneath the arching crystal dome, along with a hundred other cartoon characters. They're operating with an attention to duty that could be mistaken for macabre celebration of the surrounding carnage.

The fear I feel at our vulnerability is soon replaced by horror. Gobbets of human flesh occupy parks and gardens, tree-lined boulevards and exhibitions and fun-rides. Families lie in messily quartered sections, each chunk still grotesquely parcelled in the appropriate portion of clothing. Lower halves of once human beings sit in the seats of whirlers and spinners, still whirling and spinning in mechanical ignorance of their dead cargo.

And – this somehow makes the slaughter all the more tragic – robotic Mickeys and Minnies, Donalds and Plutos move from body to lasered body, patting dismembered heads, shaking lifeless hands, posing for pictures never to be taken beside the lacerated remains of Junior and Sis.

Da Cruz continues galumphing along. She's seen it all before. I slow and stare aghast until I hear a, "Psst!" and see a tiny gesture from Minnie up ahead. I quicken up and join her, strutting like a fool.

We leave the boulevard, cross a facsimile Wonderland and come to the croquet lawn. The Queen of Hearts strides around and calls imperiously, "Off with their heads!" And by some ghastly coincidence the Alice 'bot stands, hands on hips, her head removed by a freak sweep of this killer's laser.

Da Cruz ducks behind a hillock and points. "There," she says, indicating the entrance of a large rabbit burrow.

I close my eyes and concentrate on the workers' dorm beneath this make-believe world.

"What are you doing?" Da Cruz asks in a whisper.

"Just casting dem ol' black spells," I jape.

I make out eleven minds down there. I go through them one by one, discarding each in turn as innocent. All I read is fear and apprehension and, in a couple of cases, even hysteria. I'm looking for the bright brainvibes of a maniac. This bunch is clean.

"You a telepath?" Da Cruz asks in a small voice as I open my eyes and clear my head with a shake.

"Something like that," I tell her. "I thought you said there were a dozen workers? I scan only eleven."

"Over there." She points a white-gloved hand beyond the burrow to a hulking structure moored in a white, simulacrum river, part of another facsimile. I recognize it. The steamboat from Huck Finn. "He didn't make it to the dorm," she says.

I concentrate, get nothing. There's a blank where the person should be. The boat's within range, and there's nothing wrong with my ability as I can still sense the eleven down the rabbit hole.

"There's no-one there," I say. "You sure–?"

Then I glimpse movement.

Between balustrades I see a guy sitting on the steps of the upper deck. He's garbed in ancient costume: cloak, frilled shirt, tight breeches and big-buckled shoes. He's there, okay.

Fact remains – I scan nothing.

"I don't get this one bit," I murmur. "You see a guy over there? Or am I hallucinating ghosties?"

"Sure. That's him. He's an Andy, an A-grader. He plays the part of Dr Frankenstein in our latest spectacular."

"Thanks for telling me," I say. "You think I can scan cyber-junkboxes just like living minds?"

She gets the message and stays mute.

So our Dr Frankenstein's an Android? A tank-nurtured artificial human, playing the lead in the Gothic classic. I reckon Mary would just love that.

As for me, I'm suspicious. I have this aversion to Andys. Okay, so this guy's a citizen-grade Android from a reputable clinic, a fellow sentient with all the civil rights of you and me. But he still doesn't scan. I can't read Androids.

Prejudice, I know. And me of all people...

Nevertheless, I avoid them at parties.

"What do you know about this guy?" I ask. And I read her to ensure she's telling me all she knows.

"Well, he's an exceptionally talented actor. He applied for the role of the Doctor in the Frankenstein show. He auditioned well and got the part."

"You think he might be the killer?"

"Him?" She's surprised. "No... I don't think so. When we met he seemed very–"

"Okay, okay. I don't want a character reference. They say the Boston Strangler was a charmer."

"But what makes you think–?"

I shrug. "A hunch, that's all. The eleven workers are clean, and here we have an unscannable Andy."

"The laser fire did come from the other direction."

"Has it occurred to you that he might have got where he is now after he quit firing?" I say in a tone that suggests she shut up.

But why would an Andy go berserk like this, I ask myself.

I'm about to suggest we get the hell out in case the Andy is our man, when he sees us. He stands and stares across the river at the two cartoon mice no longer in role.

I take Da Cruz by the hand and put the Duchess's cottage between us and the Android. "The best way to prove your Andy innocent is if I grill him," I say, pulling off my left glove.

Most Androids are equipped with handsets, and Dr Frankenstein is no exception. I get through to him and stare at his face on the back of my hand: it's heavily made-up, with age-lines and dark smudges beneath his eyes to suggest overwork.

"Worry not, good Doctor. Your circuits have not fused." I unzip the Mickey head and tip it back. "Isabella Manchester. Tactical Telescan Unit. I'm here to save you people like a regular superhero."

The Android inclines his head, not taken with my humour. "I wondered when help might arrive." His tone is measured, cultivated. I almost understand why citizen-graders are so sought after at all the big social events.

"A few questions, if you please."

He inclines his noble head again.

So I ask him where he was when the firing began, what he saw of the slaughter, where does he suspect the killer is now? I try every trick in the book to make him incriminate himself, but he's not that dumb. He answers the questions with a slight Germanic accent, and I get the impression he's mocking me, as if he knows what I'm doing and wants me to know that he knows. He's pointedly civil in his acceptance of suspicion.

I thank him, assure him that I'll get the killer and quick, and cut the link. "Well?" Da Cruz asks.

"What do you expect?" I say, frustrated. "That he admits he's the bad guy?"

"What did he say?"

"He was rehearsing when the killing began and made it as far as the showboat. He saw nothing of the massacre after that. He kept his tin-pot head down."

"You still think he did it?"

"I never said I did... But anything's possible."

"And now?" she asks. She's far from impressed by my uncertainty.

"Where did you say the last fire came from? Across the complex? Okay, so I'll make my way around the perimeter until I come within range. If I were you I'd remain here. I don't want your death on my conscience."

"I feel it my duty to accompany you," she says.

I nod. "Very well, then. Okay." I grab her hand and look for a route out of the Andy's possible line of fire.

She restrains me. "Remember the walk!"

So we be-bop into the open again, heading towards the multiple amphitheatres that scallop the perimeter of the complex. Our only comfort is the knowledge that we're indistinguishable from hundreds of other strutting cartoon characters.

At least, I *thought* we were.

The killer knows better.

The first bolt amputates Minnie's tail at the rump with a quick hiss and a coil of oily smoke. The second bolt misses me by a whisker and roasts a passing Donald Duck at short order.

Da Cruz drags me into the cover of a stage set and we crouch behind a chunk of lichened stone. I trace the bolts back to their source: across the complex beneath the far arch of the dome. I concentrate, but the distance defeats me.

"So the Android *can't* be the killer," Da Cruz claims.

I laugh. "No? You sure about that? Think again, girl. In our disguises we were safe among all the other characters – then we're seen by the Andy. He's the only person who knows we're in this get-up."

"But the fire came from the opposite direction," she complains, reasonably.

"So the Andy has an accomplice, yes?"

That silences her.

Belatedly I realize that we're on the set of *Frankenstein*. The scientist's lab is caught in flickers of electric blue, revealing eerie contraptions, improbable machines. The monster is on the slab, awaiting reanimation.

"And I don't know why we're wearing these stupid things," I say, unzipping the head and flinging it back. Out there, the killer is busy frying every Mickey and Minnie in sight.

Da Cruz says: "But why should he want to...?"

"Slipped cog?" I suggest facetiously. I kick my suit away and it shivers against the wall like an animated jelly. "Take yours off," I tell her. "You're a marked mouse if you don't ditch that suit."

I waste no time and get through to Massingberd.

"Is! You okay?"

"I'm fine, Mass. Look, I need some info. You ready?"

I look at Da Cruz. She gives me the Andy's tag and classification, and I relay this to Mass with the rider, "Not that he's filed under that. Check wide. You know where to find me." I cut the link.

"You not out of that thing yet?" I stare at her. "Hey, you got something to hide?" Which, considering I have access to her head, is cruel.

I peep over masonry. I can't see the Andy or his boat from here, but his accomplice is still junking robot rodents. Bolts hail continuously from the far side of the complex.

"Come on!" I say.

She's out of the suit and staring defiantly at me.

The right side of her face is disfigured by a long scar more suited to Frankenstein's monster. Even in the flickering light I can see that it was once far worse, before plastic surgery. And it's still ugly. She's a nice kid, too – a small, dark Peruvian with skin like Aztec gold.

The scar's much deeper, of course. The surface damage is superficial; it's the scar inside her head that causes all the pain.

I give her my hand. "There must be a service hatch somewhere," I say. "We can approach the killer from below without being seen."

She leads me to a concealed swing door and we hit the underside. Less attention has been paid to illumination and glitz down here. Glo-tubes rationed to every ten metres stitch the gloom. The thunder of machinery is deafening. We jog along a vast, curving gallery, mirror image of the corridor top-side where I met Da Cruz.

And I'm scanning all the time for the killer.

My hand bleeps and we stop to take the call.

"You're right, Is," Massingberd rapps. "The 'droid isn't on our files – under that tag. I came up with a likely candidate, though. A B-grade Andy manufactured in the Carnival clinic twenty-five years ago. It was employed for the first ten years as an extra in kids' films. It applied for up-grading several times but got nowhere. It was transferred to Disneyworld Shanghai, where it worked for another decade. Then – get this, Is – five years ago this 'droid was reported rogue. It dropped out and disappeared. We have a few reports on file as to its alleged activities during the next five years. Apparently it joined the outlawed Supremacy League, that crackpot band of 'droids who demand the rule over humanity. It was involved in the bombings of '65, but was never apprehended. We have a number of reports that it underwent a programme of training as a cyber-surgeon so that the League could expand its up-grading of all the 'droids who joined them. We lost trace of it earlier this year, Is – around the time that your 'droid joined the Carnival outfit. It's quite feasible that it gave itself new retina-, finger- and voice-prints, doctored certificates and became the actor who played Dr Frankenstein. The 'droid returned home, Is–"

"To do a little counter publicity for the largest manufacturers of B-grade Androids," I finish.

"You got it."

"I'll keep you posted, Mass."

We set off again.

Da Cruz is murmuring to herself. "And he seemed so genuine at the audition..."

I ignore her and concentrate on the sudden flare of sentience that's just appeared a kilometre up-front. I've never before scanned anything like it. As we draw closer I realise that I'm not dealing with a normal human being. The thing up there overwhelms me with fear and pain and regret and guilt.

I go for the killer's identity, but I'm either too far away or the signal is weakening. I get the impression, then, that the killer is losing his strength, dying...

We're almost underneath the place where the maniac made his stand. To our right is a viewscreen, showing space and the quiet Earth. On our left we pass a pair of green swing doors, marked with heiroglyphs: the representation of a man and what might be an icicle.

It doesn't hit me for another five paces.

There's something in the head of the killer above us that has no right to be there... something that's keeping him alive.

I retrace my steps and regard the swing doors.

"Isabella?" Da Cruz says.

"Christ," I murmur. "Jesus Christ..."

I push through the doors at a run.

"Isabella!" Da Cruz rushes in after me.

We're in an operating theatre, and the only way it differs from the one in Dr Frankenstein's castle is in the modern fittings; the overhead halogens and the angle-poise operating table. They've both seen the same deed accomplished, one in fiction and one in fact.

I move towards a green, vertical tank as if in a trance.

"Isabella?" Da Cruz is staring at me. "Didn't you know? We brought him up here years ago, equipped this place for when the time is right to bring him back to–"

I open the tank and it's empty.

"Where is he?" she screams at me as I run from the theatre and through the nearest hatch to the upper hemisphere.

I've never really credited Androids with any of the more complex human emotions, like love or hate...

Or even irony.

By playing his role of Dr Frankenstein to the full, this Andy has proved me wrong.

Back in the twentieth century, the king of the greatest entertainment industry on Earth was corpsicled. Put on ice and stacked away until such time as his cancer could be fixed. And now...

Now Walt stands on the balcony of a fairytale castle. Ten metres separate him from where I crouch on the gallery that circles the complex. He rests his weight on a laser-rifle, crutchlike, and sways. His shaven head bulges at the left temple with a dark mass like some morbid extra-cranial tumour: it's a cyber-auxiliary, wired in there by the Android. It's this that is powering him, that motivated him to commit the slaying of the innocents. He's so feeble now, so near death a second time, that it has little control over his body or his mind. For the first time since his resurrection, he is himself.

He sees me and smiles sadly.

His skin, blanched with more than a hundred years of death, is puckered and loose, maggotlike. He is barely conscious, yet a flicker of tragic awareness moves within him. The chemical that is keeping him alive is almost spent.

"Is this a nightmare?" he asks in a voice so frail it barely reaches me.

"A dream," I say.

"Where am I?" I read his lips. "In Hell?"

I almost reply: "In your Heaven, Walt," but stop myself.

I follow his gaze to the deck, as he surveys the carnage of his own doing.

"Watch out!" Da Cruz appears beside me and drags me to the ground. Walt is making one last feeble attempt to lift and aim the laser; it wavers in our direction. I can read in his eyes that he has no desire to kill us, but the choice is not his. The Frankenstein Android controls the cyber-auxiliary.

I close my eyes.

In the nightmare of Walt's failing brain I open the floodgates of anger. I motivate him into action, give him the will to revenge himself.

And while I'm doing this I realise something. How can I ever again use my ability to induce love after using it to promote so much hate?

Da Cruz clutches my arm. "What--?"

I concentrate. "Just call it black magic, Maria." And as I speak, Walt swings his laser-rifle, the desire for revenge overcoming the Android's final command.

He cries out and fires.

The showboat disintegrates in a million shards of synthi-timber, and Dr Frankenstein explodes like a grenade in a brilliant white starburst.

Walt lets the laser fall and slips quietly into his second death, smiling with induced euphoria all the way.

* * *

THREE HOURS LATER and we're surfing down the helix of the gravity-well. Back on the Sat, Walt is being returned to ice, the slaughter mopped up. Maria is taking time off, dirtside.

I break the silence. "Were you orphaned, Maria?" Gently.

She looks at me, suspicious. "How do you know?"

I reach out and touch her head. "Big trouble upstairs," I say. Then: "We're very much alike, you and me."

She gives me the story that I know already, but it helps for her to talk about it. Her mother died when she was ten, and she was taken from her father following the attack that left her scarred.

"And you?" she asks. "Were you orphaned?"

"Something like that–" And stop.

My parents' tribe was hungry and poor. I was their third and youngest daughter, and I checked out psi-positive. A hundred thousand credits bought a lot of cattle, back then.

So the Telescan Unit wasn't exactly slave labour...

But try telling that to a lonely nine year-old.

"Perhaps you'd like to tell me about it?" Maria asks, with affection.

Get that–

Genuine Affection.

I smile. "I think perhaps I might," I say.

Star of Epsilon

Paris was in again and summer found me on the left bank, playing to crowds in the Blue Shift slouchbar. I blitzed 'em with cosmic visions. I sub-circuited direct, employed slo-mo, ra-ta-tat shots, even visual cut-ups, in homage. Goddard and Burroughs were back in, too. Had to do with nostalgia, the harking back to supposedly better times. Hell... Didn't I know that? Wasn't I cashing in on the fact that we all love to live a lie? Wasn't I giving the crowds what they wanted because they'd never get it otherwise?

I met her after a night performance.

The Blue Shift was *the* scene that month.

It wasn't just the drugs they pumped but the live acts, I liked to think. I alternated nights with a cute fifteen year-old sado-masochist on sensitised feedback. It wasn't my kick, but off-nights I'd sneak downstairs and jack-in. And jack-out again, fast. Three minutes was all I could take of this kid – my opposition. The management had it sussed. They played us counterpoint: one night this weird little girl giving out intimations of death and id-grislies like no kid should, and the next old Abe Santana with his visions of Nirvana-thru-flux, the glories of the space-lanes.

The girl intrigued me. The neon-glitz out front billed her as Jo, and that was enough to pull the freaks. Her act was simple.

On stage a sudden spotlight found a small cross-legged figure in a Pierrot suit, white-powdered face a paragon of melancholy complete with stylised tear. She'd come on easy at first, slipping fear sub-lim at the slouched crowd. Her head was shaven, but a tangle of leads snaking from her cortical-implant gave her the aspect of a par-shorn Medusa. The leads went down inside her suit and into the stage, coming out by the cushions. Freaks jacked-in and got fear first, subtle unease. Then the kid shifted her position, sitting now with outstretched legs together, arms stanchioned behind her, palms down. The nursery pose contradicted the horror coming down the leads, the hindbrain terror of mortality. She tapped into us and found our fear of death and gave it back, redoubled – turning us to stone.

First time I jacked-in I wondered how she did this, what magic she worked to show us that which we tried to deny, even to ourselves. So the next night I stayed with it a while longer, and I found out. Little Jo was dying. She was fifteen and she'd never see sixteen and the gut-kick I experienced when I realised this was *zero* compared with her angst. That's when I jacked-out, sickened, got loaded and tried to forget.

Over the next few weeks I was lured back again and again. I knew what I wanted: not the orgasm of terror the rest of the crowd got high on, but the futile reassurance that Jo was not really dying, that her performance was just a death-analogue recorded from some terminal patient, encoded on Jo's computer and used cynically to thrill.

But the more I experienced her act, the more I knew I was dreaming. Jo was dying, okay. She gave out death, and when the audience were convinced that *they* were dying she reversed the feed and drank it back, and you could almost hear the gasp of her soul as its need was quenched. The kid's in love with death, I told myself, as if hoping this might ease my heartache: perhaps, if she were, then I could pity her a little less.

Then I realised the truth. The only reason she reversed the feed was to take from the crowd the knowledge that they too would some day die, to reassure herself that she was not alone in the dying process we all call living.

After that I avoided the club on my nights off. I couldn't go near the place, and those freaks in there – I thought many a time over a drink in some darkened, nondescript bar – they stayed jacked-in for hours! And that brought me back to what I was running from, the fear of death and the terrible realisation that Jo was plugged into that *weltschmerz* for the rest of her life.

AND MY ACT?

How many of the crowd who freaked out on Jo's act came to mine? Their diametric content would suggest none, but I hoped some people needed antidote.

I'd start simple. I'd give them the experience of an Engineman emerging from the flux; the elusive ghost of rapture that haunted his mind; the drone of auxiliary burners; the knowledge that we were lighting into the Nilakantha Stardrift on a mission of rescue. Then I'd hold this sensory input under and come in with the voice-over: "Fifty years ago I mind-pushed bigships for the Canterbury Line..."

I'd take them at hyper-c through the *nada*-continuum, coming out places they'd only dreamed about or seen in travel brochures. Black holes were a favourite, and I took them on a tour of a giant nicknamed Kolkata, courting disaster on the hazardous event horizon, the bigship a surfer on the math of Einstein-Fernandez physics. Then I'd sling the 'ship at a blistering tangent off across uncharted space, on the trail of new and more wondrous adventure... The main theme was always wonder – the hint of Nirvana that every Engineman experiences in the flux.

My customers left satisfied, uplifted.

THEN ONE NIGHT after her performance Jo was stretchered off comatose, and I didn't know whether to feel relief that at last she had died, or sadness at the passing of someone I had hardly known. Later the manager told me that Jo was fine, she'd recover. Would I fill in for her this week? And I said yes, relieved that I might have the opportunity to get to know her, after all, and hating myself because of that.

WE'RE QUARK-HARVESTING a long, long way from Earth. I step from the flux-tank, as we are coasting now. I look through the viewscreen, behold the sweeping sickle sponsons reaping fiery quarks. The 'aft scene is even more spectacular, a panoramic miracle. The converted energy is fired from the bigship in blinding c-velocity bolts, streaking away on a multi-billion light year bend that describes the inner curve of the universe. And I'm moved almost to tears, along with my audience, though for different reasons.

For a long time after the performance I sat yogi-fashion. The crowd cheered and applauded, then moved back to the bar or out into the night. And I was ashamed, like a preacher who has convinced his congregation but does not himself believe.

Technicians dismantled the rig, unplugged me and wound in the leads. A few tourists tried to get to me, to say how much they'd enjoyed the performance. They were stopped by the heavies, who knew how low I felt after my act.

The club never closed, but trade hit a low around four in the morning. I was still there then, in the darkness of the stage, thinking back and regretting the events of all those years ago, the pretence of the present. A few junkies slouched at the bar, getting their fix jugularwise.

As I sat, a kid crawled from a cushioned bunker between the bar and the stage. She headed my way on all fours, galumphing over cushions and the wraparound membranes in the floor. I assumed she was a fan who wanted to rap about how it was to flux on the bigships.

She climbed aboard the stage and sat before me cross-legged, like a mirror-image of myself. She had long black hair, too luxuriant for a kid her age, too sensual.

"I loved your performance," she said in a husky voice which, like her hair, belonged to a thirty year-old.

She had a triangular, coffee-brown face and large green eyes. She should have been a nice-looking kid, but there was some disunity in the planes of her cheeks which made her almost ugly.

"Hey," I said, weary. "Go home, kid. Get some sleep."

A flash of emerald anger. "I said I liked your show."

"And I said–"

"Abe," she smiled, serious. "I know you want to flux again."

I LOOKED AT her, guarded. She had it wrong, but only just.

So I said, "How...?"

She grinned at me. "I experienced your show good, Abe. Your need was in there. Those fools might not have read it, but I did."

Then I saw the teflon protuberance at the base of her skull. I lifted a tress of hair, fingered sockets worn smooth through use.

"Who are you?" I whispered.

"I'm just another German-Turk from Dusseldorf," she shrugged, "with a taste for sick theatrics."

I smiled and shook my head.

"You still don't recognise? How about if I wore a Pierrot suit and a big tear," she said, "just here."

"Jo?"

"Jodie Schimelmann."

I felt a tremor inside. This was the kid who'd rocked me with haunting visions of death. She was fifteen years-old and she'd stared oblivion in the face and she was still here.

I'd be ninety in a month and I felt a burning sense of shame at the injustice.

"I need your help," she said.

I shook my head. "How can I possibly help you?"

So she told me why she was dying.

* * *

UNTIL SIX MONTHS ago Jodie worked in the Orly spaceport. She was a flux-monkey, an engineer whose job it was to crawl inside the exhaust ventricles of bigships and carry out repairs on the auxiliary burners. It was hard work, but she didn't complain; she lived well and saved enough creds to send home to her mother in Germany.

Then one check-up she was found to have contracted some complicated virus that had lodged in the flux-vent of a bigship she'd worked on. She was given a year to live, paid off and discharged. Jodie was rotting inside with some alien malignancy that had attacked her marrow, lymph glands, lungs and trachea... It was a miracle she was still alive and active, but she loaded herself with analgesics every day and went on fighting.

The disease explained her voice, of course, and the fact that she wore a wig. Ironic that that which was killing her also gave her the appearance of someone much older, while in her head she had matured as well.

I said, "Isn't there a cure?"

"Yeah, sure there is. But a cure costs creds, Abe. And not even my pay-off was enough."

I recalled her words. "How can I help you?"

"I need creds. I want the cure. I also want to be beautiful–"

I laughed.

Then she realised how funny that was and she laughed too.

"See that beautiful woman at the bar?" she asked. "The one zonked on jugular-juice and out of it."

"So?"

"So she's dead ugly – honest."

"I thought you just said she was beautiful?"

Jo smiled, "You ever seen her here before?"

"She doesn't come in here when I'm on. I'd recognise her."

"Yeah? Ever noticed an old woman, maybe a hundred and ten? All bags and wrinkles? It's the same woman. She has the latest sub-dermal capillary electro-cosmetics. What you see there is a clever light show, a laser display to deceive the eye into beholding beauty. I want one."

"But you aren't ugly, Jo."

"I'm not beautiful."

"So you want me to get you the creds to buy this device?" I said. I thought I saw her logic. She was almost as terrified by her physical deterioration as she was by the thought of death, and she wanted to die looking good.

But I was wrong.

She said, "That *and* a cure. I want to live, and I want looks. Think I'm greedy?"

I shrugged. "Why live a lie?" I asked her, hypocritical.

"I want both, and you can help me get them."

So I asked, "How?"

"I've got a ship I want you to flux," she said simply.

Why live a lie? I had asked.

Sure I live a lie...

"Tell me about it," I said.

So Jo TOOK me to the Louvre.

I protested that art wasn't my kick, but she insisted. When I tried to find out what she had planned, she clammed up. She stomped along the boulevard, pulling me after her. We made an odd couple, even among countless odd couples. She wore callipers to assist her wasted leg muscles, unadorned leg-irons without automation.

We did the Louvre.

We saw the Mona Lisa and a hundred other art treasures of Earth. Then we strolled around the hall of alien artifacts and came at last to the Chamber of Light, a circular room containing the Star of Epsilon VII. Jo just stared, open-mouthed.

The diamond burned as bright as any primary, filling the chamber with golden light. It stood on a pedestal, protected by a hexagon of high-powered lasers.

"Do you know its story?" Jo whispered. "They call it the 'Healing Stone'."

THIRTY YEARS AGO... An expedition to the Lyra in Beta cluster... A bigship made touchdown on a new world, an Earth-norm planet never before explored. The spacers mapped and charted and came up with another world fit for colonisation, and lifted off. And after three days in space the crew came down with a potentially lethal viral infection, and they re-routed and headed to the nearest Terran base with adequate medical facilities to deal with the hundred-plus dying spacers... And the ship hit trouble, crashlanded on Epsilon VII, uncharted and hostile, light years from anywhere and months away from help... So the crew set to work concocting a cure from the resources at hand on the planet... And on the day that a spacer found a giant diamond, the Star of Epsilon, the drugs administered to the dying crew began to take effect... And they pulled through with no casualties... And the spacers, a superstitious lot at the best of times, put it down to the luck of the largest diamond ever discovered.

The Healing Stone.

"Do you believe that?" I asked Jo.

She smiled. "Do you?"

We drank champagne on a patio overlooking the Seine, and Jodie told me of her dream.

"How long have you had it planned?" I asked.

"Oh... well before they paid me off. I knew I was dying, that I had to have the creds."

"Then why the cabaret?"

"I need the feedback, the knowledge that sooner or later all those fuckers are going with me. Of course, if it works..." She smiled at me. "Abe... do you believe in happy endings?"

I just smiled at her, unable to reply.

She finished her champagne. "C'mon. It's time we were getting there..." And as she rose clumsily from the table I noticed that she was shaking with fear and anticipation and pain.

I wanted to tell her, then – I wanted nothing more than to tell her the truth.

I WAS DESPERATE two months back, before the Paris run.

I contacted my agent. "I need more material! My repertoire's getting stale, all the same old stuff. The competition has everything I've got, and more–"

"I thought you had that black hole original, the Kolkata show?"

I sighed. "I have. It's original now, but how long will that last? How long before someone finds an Engineman willing to sell another event horizon fly-by?"

"So what do you suggest?"

I told him. He said he'd be in touch, and rang off. I spent a tense hour in my room above the club, dreaming of far stars. Then the vid chimed and I dived at it.

"I've found him," he said. "The rest is up to you."

The Engineman emeritus received me in his penthouse suite. A big wall-window overlooked night-time Paris and valuable starscapes adorned the walls.

He wore charisma that scintillated like silver lamé. He was a tall, grizzled African in his early eighties, muscular still despite his age, his years in flux.

"Your agent called. What he proposed I find quite novel. I've never heard of it before."

"It's common," I told him. "The process has been around for years. Space is especially popular now – people need what they've never had."

He poured stiff drinks and we sat on foamforms before the view.

"You pushed a bigship for the Cincinnati Line," I said.

He smiled in recollection. "The bigship *Hanumati* on ten year runs to the farthest reaches of the Out-there."

"They say the flux is ecstasy," I said.

He chuckled. "Ecstasy? More like Heaven, man..." And he described the sensation as best he could.

Then he stopped and looked at me. "Your agent said you wanted to *buy* the *Hanumati* run?"

"I'd like to make an analogue for my show. I'd be able to pay you fifty thousand creds–"

"I don't want your creds!" he snapped. "What do you think creds mean to me?"

"But I couldn't possibly–"

"I'll give you the run," he said. "Or you don't get it at all..."

I had brought along a holdall full of jacks and leads and monitoring equipment.

He jacked the leads into his occipital computer and bled images and sensations of the *Hanumati* run into the monitor. I edited it, strung together the highlights, then interfaced and downloaded the synthesis into my occipital. As always, the analogue didn't include the experience of fluxing – that was impossible, something only Enginemen could get *in situ* – but the rest of the analogue was pure high-powered wonder. The data detonated my synapses in a series of explosions until my cerebellum nova'd.

I couldn't recall leaving. I staggered through the nighttime streets in a daze. When I made it to my room I collapsed in my cot, blasted. I was on a high for twenty-four hours, then came down slow on waves of self-pity and regret.

ORLY SPACEPORT...

It took me back. As a kid I'd watched wide-eyed, fingers hooked through the diamond mesh, as the Bigships trundled home from interstellar runs. And I'd dreamed...

It was a long time to wait for a dream to come true. But, as this dream was likely to be a nightmare, perhaps that was just as well.

Jo had the fence pre-cut, and we crawled through quick, the snipped wire clawing at our clothing. Once inside Jo clank-stomped, stiff-legged, towards a parked mini-roller, and I limped after her. We climbed aboard, Jo took the controls and we jolted off across the lighted tarmac. We passed through the inner fence under the bored gaze of a security guard, who waved us through when Jo flashed her old authorisation pass. We trundled towards a hangar and Jo brought us to a halt outside.

She was about to climb down when I caught her arm. "Jo – I don't think–"

She glared at me. "You can't back out now, Abe! You promised–"

So I swallowed my protest and climbed down after her.

She ran clumsily to the vast, sliding doors, plugged a lead into her implant and jacked into the lock's computer socket. She closed her eyes, summoning codes, and the door clicked and rolled open a metre. We slipped inside.

"*The Pride of Baghdad*," Jo told me, playing a flashlight over the squat bulk of an old Smallship. "Ex-Iraqi space fleet. They sold it to Europe for scrap, but there's one more run in the old tub yet."

We climbed a welded ladder and Jo used her lead again on the hatch. It sprang open and the interior of the *Baghdad* lit up, exuding the aroma of stale sweat and flux.

We dropped into the engineroom.

"You know how to pilot this crate?" I asked, delaying the inevitable.

"I worked on the *Baghdad* last job," she told me. "I shunted her across the 'port once or twice. I know how to pilot her. I got *everything* measured down to the last centimetre." She looked at me. "What you waiting for, Abe?" She had discarded her wig along the way and, bald, she looked thinner and more vulnerable than ever.

I paused by the sen-dep tank that I had experienced only in the memories of other men. I lifted the hatch and stared at the slide-bed, the complication of leads.

"Abe...?"

In a whisper: "I'm not an Engineman, Jo."

She stared at me. "*What?*"

"I've never fluxed before, Jo. I can't do it."

Her expression was more than just horrified. She seemed to die before me, to age. She slumped, a hand going to the tank for support.

Her voice trembled with the imminence of tears. "But... but I jacked into your performance, Abe. I could feel your *need* to flux."

"The performance was just that, Jo. A performance. I used analogues, cerebral recollections from real Enginemen and spacers. My need to flux was just a futile yearning to do what I'd never done, but had always wanted to do."

Jo just shook her head. "Abe...?"

"I was turned down by the Rousseau Line when I was twenty-one," I said. "So I took up cabaret. It was the only way I could experience starflight, convince people that I'd once been a spacer... Sometimes I even managed to convince myself that I'd been up there."

"Can't you do it just this once, Abe?" She was in tears. "Just for me?"

I stared at the tank. "That's one thing I never experienced," I said, more to myself than to Jo. "Even in analogue. The actual experience of flux can't be reproduced. Enginemen say it's almost religious, a foretaste of Nirvana. I've tried to simulate it in my shows, but I don't really know what it's like."

"Why can't you do it, Abe!" Jo yelled at me. "What do you fear?"

"I might not survive, Jo," I lied. "It might kill me." But what I feared was far, far worse than this.

"Abe – *it might save me!*"

So then, shaking with fear, I slipped into the slide-bed and jacked-in, like I'd done a thousand times before in analogue. Sobbing with tears of relief now, Jo leaned all her weight against the 'bed and pushed it home. She slammed the hatch shut and total darkness encapsulated me, then silence. The ship's computer slipped anaesthetic into my skull and soon all physical feeling departed. I sensed a quick, blurred vibration as Jo, up in the pilot's berth, fired the burners.

Then I fluxed.

WHAT I FEARED, of course, was that the promise of Nirvana-thru-flux would turn out to be no more than a myth – a romantic fabrication to enhance the mystique of the Enginemen. For so long I had lived with the hope that Nirvana was real, the ultimate state at which each one of us eventually arrived. I was an old man with not long left, and to have experienced *nothing* in the flux would have destroyed me.

I sensed a strange timelessness to begin with, and I was still aware of myself as a single human entity. And then... something happened. I was no longer myself, no longer human, but part of something larger and infinite. I had a vast understanding of everything – I *was* everything – and the petty human concerns that had filled my life to date were revealed for what they were. I had often wondered at the faraway attitudes of the many Enginemen I had met, and now I understood the reason for their aloof otherness: how could anyone be the same, or like any other human being, after experiencing *this*? With one part of my mind I knew that *The Pride of Baghdad* no longer existed in the real and physical universe. We were surging through the *nada*-continuum now, on a mission to save the life of Jodie Schimelmann.

After what seemed like an eternity, though in fact was a matter of minutes only, the sensation of physicality returned to me. I felt hands on me and I was pulled upright and dragged forward, and all I could think of was the ecstasy of the union in the flux. I could see nothing, hear nothing, and I was aware only of my bodily progress from the ship and out on to what seemed to be sand. I felt the warmth of sunlight on my skin and collapsed.

I came to my senses again and again, and always Jo was kneeling beside me, smiling, trying to impress upon me the success of the venture.

Then I came fully to my senses and elbowed myself into a sitting position. I looked around. I was on a beach, an endless golden crescent with the blue sea metres away. *The Pride of Baghdad* was buried in a dune behind me, and only the hatch was visible like the entrance to some mysterious underground kingdom.

I called out and seconds later Jo emerged from the ship and closed the hatch behind her. "Abe! You're okay?"

"Never felt better," I said, touched by her concern. "Where are we?"

"Brazil, Abe. Ten kays south of Rio."

She passed me a vid-board, tuned to world news. The headlines ran: 'Louvre raided... The Star of Epsilon missing... Chamber of Light destroyed in mysterious raid...'

She held out the diamond, scintillating in her callused palms. "You did it, Abe. You saved my life."

I wanted to tell her that there was nothing to fear from death – that, after life, something more wondrous and magical awaited us. But how could I tell her that? Jo was a young girl with all her life ahead of her, and I was an old man at the end of mine.

"Okay," I said, "let's get you into a hospital."

"And you?"

Me? First, I'd get the occipital computer wiped clean of all the dreams of space that belonged to other men. I had my own experience of flux now, and I no longer needed analogues.

"I'll tell you as we walk," I said.

Jo pulled me to my feet and we left *The Pride of Baghdad* and set off along the road to Rio.

The Time-Lapsed Man

Thorn was not immediately aware of the silence.

As he lay in the tank and watched the crystal cover lift above him, he was still trying to regain some measure of the unification he had attained during his time in flux. For long hours – though it had seemed a timeless period to Thorn – he had mind-pushed his boat between the stars: for long hours he had been one with the vastness of the *nada*-continuum.

As always when emerging from flux, Thorn sensed the elusive residuum of the union somewhere within him. As always, he tried to regain it and failed; it diminished like a haunting echo in his mind. Only in three months, on his next shift, would he be able to renew his courtship with the infinite. Until then his conscious life would comprise a series of unfulfilled events; a succession of set-pieces featuring an actor whose thoughts were forever elsewhere. Occasionally he would be allowed intimations of rapture in his dreams, only to have them snatched away upon awakening.

Some Enginemen he knew, in fact the majority of those from the East, subscribed to the belief that in flux they were granted a foretaste of Nirvana. Thorn's Western pragmatism denied him this explanation. He favoured a more psychological rationale – though in the immediate period following flux he found it difficult to define exactly a materialistic basis for the ecstasy he had experienced.

He eased himself up and crossed the chamber. It was then that he noticed the absence of sound. He should have been able to hear the dull drone of the auxiliary burners; likewise his footsteps, and his laboured breathing after so long without exercise. He rapped on the bulkhead. He stepped into the shower and turned on the water-jet. He made a sound of pleasure as the hot water needled his tired skin. Yet he heard nothing. The silence was more absolute than any he had experienced before.

He told himself that it was no doubt some side-effect of the flux. After more than fifty shifts, a lifetime among the stars, this was his first rehabilitation problem, and he was not unduly worried. He would go for a medical if his hearing did not return.

He stepped under the blo-drier, donned his uniform and left the chamber. Through the lounge viewscreen he could see the lights of the spaceport. He felt a jarring shudder as the stasis-grid grabbed the ship and brought it down. He missed the familiar diminuendo of the afterburn, the squeal of a hundred tyres on tarmac. The terminal ziggurat hove into sight. The ship eased to a halt. Above the viewscreen a strip-light pulsed red, sanctioning disembarkation. It should have been accompanied by a voice welcoming ship personnel back to Earth, but Thorn heard nothing.

As always he was the first to leave the ship. He passed through check-out, offering his card to a succession of bored 'port officials. Normally he might have waited for the others and gone for a drink; he preferred to spend his free time with other Enginemen, and pilots and mechanics, as if the company of his colleagues might bring him closer to that which he most missed. This time, though, he left the 'port and caught a flier to the city. He would seek the medical aid he needed in his own time, not at the behest of solicitous colleagues.

He told the driver his destination; unable to hear his own voice, he moved his lips again. The driver nodded, accelerated. The flier banked between towerpiles, lights flickering by in a mesmerising rush.

They came down in the forecourt of his stack. He climbed out and took the upchute to his penthouse suite. This was the first time he had arrived home sober in years. Alcohol helped to ease the pain of loss; sober, he was horribly aware of his material possessions, mocking his mortality and his dependence upon them. His suite might have been described as luxurious, but the blatant utility of the furnishings filled him with nausea.

He poured himself a scotch and paused by the piano. He fingered the opening notes of Beethoven's *Pathetique*, then sat down in his recliner by the wall-window and stared out. In the comforting darkness of the room, with the lights of the city arrayed below him, he could make-believe he was back aboard his ship, coming in for landing.

Of course, if his hearing never returned...

He realised he was sweating at the thought of never being able to flux again. He wondered if he would be able to bluff his way through the next shift.

HE WAS ON his second drink, twenty minutes later, when a sound startled him. He smiled to himself, raised his glass in a toast to his reflection in the window. He spoke... but he could not hear his words.

He heard another sound and he frowned, confused. He called out... in silence. Yet he could hear *something*.

He heard footsteps, and breathing, and then a resounding *clang*. Then he heard the high-pressure hiss of hot water and an exclamation of pleasure. His own exclamation... He heard the roar of the blo-drier, then the rasp of material against his skin; the quick whirr of the sliding door and the diminishing note of the afterburners, cutting out.

Thorn forced himself to say something; to comment and somehow bring an end to this madness. But his voice made no sound. He threw his glass against the wall and it shattered in silence.

Then he was listening to footsteps again; his own footsteps. They passed down the connecting tube from the ship to the terminal building; he heard tired acknowledgements from the 'port officials, then the hubbub of the crowded foyer.

He sat rigid with fright, listening to that which by rights he should have heard one hour ago.

He heard the driver's question, then his own voice; he stated his destination in a drunken slur, then repeated himself. He heard the whine of turbos, and later the hatch opening, then more footsteps, the grind of the upchute...

There was a silence then. He thought back one hour and realised he had paused for a time on the threshold, looking into the room he called home and feeling sickened. He could just make out the sound of his own breathing, the distant hum of the city.

Then the gentle notes of Beethoven's *Pathetique*.

The rattle of glass on glass.

He remained in the recliner, unable to move, listening to the sound of his time-lapsed breathing, his drinking when he wasn't drinking.

Later he heard his delayed exclamation, the explosion of his glass against the wall.

He pushed himself from the recliner and staggered over to the vidscreen. He hesitated, his hand poised above the keyboard. He intended to contact the company medic, but, almost against his will, he found himself tapping out the code he had used so often in the past.

She was a long time answering. He looked at his watch. It was still early, not yet seven. He was about to give up when the screen flared into life. Then he was looking at Caroline Da Silva, older by five years but just as attractive as he remembered. She stared at him in disbelief, pulling a gown to her throat.

Then her lips moved in obvious anger, but Thorn heard nothing – or, rather, he heard the sound of himself chugging scotch one hour ago.

He feared she might cut the connection. He leaned forward and mouthed what he hoped were the words: *I need you, Carrie. I'm ill. I can't hear. That is–*

He broke off, unsure how to continue.

Her expression of hostility altered; she still looked guarded, but there was an air of concern about her now as well. Her lips moved, then she remembered herself and used the deaf facility. She typed: Is your hearing delayed, Max?

He nodded.

She typed: Be at my surgery in one hour.

They stared at each other for a long moment, as if to see who might prove the stronger and switch off first.

Thorn shouted: *What the hell's wrong with me, Carrie? Is it something serious?*

She replied, forgetting to type. Her lips moved, answering his question with silent words.

In panic Thorn yelled: *What the hell do you mean–?*

But Caroline had cut the connection.

Thorn returned to his recliner. He reflected that there was a certain justice in the way she had cut him off. Five years ago, their final communication had been by vidscreen. Then it had been Thorn who had severed the connection, effectively cutting her out of his life, inferring without exactly saying so that she was no match for what he had found in flux.

Caroline's question about the time-lapse suggested that she knew something about his condition. He wondered – presuming his illness was a side-effect of the flux – if she was aware of the irony of his appeal for help.

One hour later Thorn boarded a flier. Drunk and unable to hear his own words, he had taken the precaution of writing the address of the hospital on a card. He passed this to the driver, and as the flier took off Thorn sank back in his seat.

He closed his eyes.

Aurally, he existed in the past now, experiencing the sounds of his life that were already one hour old. He heard himself leave the recliner, cross the room and type the code on the keyboard. After a while he heard the crackle of the screen and Caroline's, "Doctor Da Silva..." followed by an indrawn breath of surprise.

"I need you, Carrie. I'm ill. I can't hear. That is–" Thorn felt ashamed at how pathetic he had sounded.

Then he heard Caroline's spoken reply, more to herself, before she bethought herself to use the keyboard and ask him if his hearing was delayed. "Black's Syndrome," she had murmured.

Now, in the flier, Thorn's stomach lurched. He had no idea what Black's Syndrome was, but the sound of it scared him.

Then he heard his one-hour-past-self say, "What the hell's wrong with me, Carrie? Is it something serious?" The words came out slurred, but Caroline had understood.

She had answered: "I'm afraid it is serious, Max. Get yourself here in one hour, okay?"

And she had cut the connection.

Caroline Da Silva's surgery was part of a large hospital complex overlooking the bay. Thorn left the flier in the landing lot and made his way unsteadily to the west wing. The sound of the city, as heard from his apartment, played in his ears.

He moved carefully down interminable corridors. Had he been less apprehensive about what might be wrong with him, and about meeting Caroline again after so long, he might have enjoyed the strange sensation of seeing one thing and hearing another. It was like watching a film with the wrong sound-track.

He found the door marked 'Dr Da Silva', knocked and stepped inside. Caroline was the first person he saw in the room. For a second he wondered how the flux had managed to lure him away from her, but only for a second. She was very attractive, with the calm elliptical face of a ballerina, the same graceful poise. She was caring and intelligent, too – but the very fact of her physicality bespoke to Thorn of the manifest impermanence of all things physical. The flux promised, and delivered, periods of blissful disembodiment.

Only then did Thorn notice the other occupants of the room. He recognised the two men behind the desk. One was his medic at the Line, and the other his commanding officer. Their very presence here suggested that all was not well. The way they regarded him, with direct stares devoid of emotion, confirmed this.

A combination of drink, shock and fear eased Thorn into unconsciousness.

HE AWOKE IN bed in a white room. To his right a glass door gave onto a balcony, and all he could see beyond was the bright blue sky. On the opposite wall was a rectangular screen, opaque to him but transparent to observers in the next room.

Electrodes covered his head and chest.

He could hear the drone of the flier's turbos as it carried him towards the hospital. He sat up and called out what he hoped was: *Caroline!...Carrie!*

He sank back, frustrated. He watched an hour tick by on the wall-clock, listening to the flier descend and his own footsteps as the Thorn-of-one-hour-ago approached the hospital. He wondered if he was being watched through the one-way window. He felt caged.

He looked through the glass door and stared into the sky. In the distance he could see a bigship climb on a steep gradient. He heard himself open the surgery door, and Caroline's voice. "Ah... Max."

Then – unexpectedly, though he should have been aware of its coming – silence. This was the period during which he was unconscious. He glanced back at the sky, but the bigship had phased out and was no longer visible.

Thorn tried not to think about his future.

* * *

CAROLINE ARRIVED THIRTY minutes later. She carried a sketch pad and a stylus. She sat on a plastic chair beside the bed, the pad on her lap. She tried to cover her concern with smiles, but Thorn was aware of tears recently shed, the evidence of smudged make-up. He had seen it many times before.

How long will I be in here? he asked.

Caroline chewed her lower lip, avoiding his eyes. She began to speak, then stopped herself. Instead, she wrote on the sketch pad and held up the finished product:

A week or two, Max. We want to run a few tests.

Thorn smiled to himself. *What exactly is this Black's Syndrome?* he asked, with what he hoped was the right degree of malicious sarcasm.

He was pleased with Caroline's shocked expression.

How do you know it's Black's? she scribbled.

You mentioned it over the vidscreen, Thorn told her. *I didn't hear it until I was coming here... What is it, Carrie?*

She paused, then began writing. Thorn read the words upside down: Black – an Engineman on the Taurus Line out of Varanasi. After fifty shifts he developed acute sensory time-lapse. It's a one-in-a-thousand malady, Max. We don't know exactly what causes it, but we suspect it's a malfunction in the tank leads that retards interneuron activity.

She paused, then held up the message.

Thorn nodded. *I've read it. So...?*

She turned to a blank page, stylus poised.

How long did he last? Thorn asked, bitterly. *When did the poor bastard die?*

Quickly she wrote: He's still alive, Max.

Thorn was surprised, relieved. If the present condition was the extent of Black's Syndrome, then what was to prevent him fluxing again?

He wondered at Caroline's tears. If his disease was only this minor, then why all the emotion?

Then he thought he understood.

When can I leave, Carrie? When can I get back to the flux?

He was watching the pad, waiting for a reply. When he looked up he saw that she was crying, openly this time.

He laughed. *You thought you had me, didn't you? Discharged from the Line, your own little invalid to look after and pamper. You can't stand the thought that I'll recover and flux again, can you?*

Despite her tears she was scribbling, covering page after page with rapid, oversized scrawl.

When she came to the end she stabbed a vicious period, ripped the pages out and flung them at him. She ran from the room, skittling a chair on the way. Thorn watched her, a sudden sense of guilt excavating a hollow in his chest.

His gaze dropped to the crumpled pages. He picked them up and read:

Acute *sensory* time-lapse. Not just hearing. Everything. In a few days your taste and smell will go the same way. Then your vision. You'll be left only with the sensation of touch in the 'present'. Everything else will be lapsed...

It went like this for a few more pages, the handwriting becoming more and more erratic. Most of it reiterated the few known facts and Caroline's observations of Black's decline. On the last page she had simply written: I loved you, Max.

Thorn smoothed the pages across his lap. He called for Caroline again and again, but if she heard she ignored him. He wanted to apologise, ask what might happen to him. He tried to envisage the sensation of having all his senses time-lapsed save for that of touch, but the task was beyond his powers of perception.

He lay back and closed his eyes. Later he was startled by the sound of his voice, his cruel questions. He heard Caroline's breathless sobs, the squeak of the stylus, a murmured, "I loved you..." to accompany the written assurance. He heard her run crying from the room, the chair tumble, the door slam shut.

Then all he could hear was the sound of his breathing, the muffled, routine noises of the hospital. For the first time in hours the sounds he heard were synchronised with what he could see.

He slept.

ON THE MORNING of his third day in hospital, Thorn's senses of taste and smell went the way of his hearing. This further time-lapse dashed any hope he might have had that Caroline's diagnosis had been mistaken.

He had not seen Caroline since her hurried departure on the first day. He had been examined and tested by medical staff who went about their business in silence, as if they were aware of his outburst at Caroline and were censoring him for it. On the third morning in hospital, a nurse brought him his breakfast.

He began eating, and soon realised that he could neither taste nor smell the bacon and eggs, or the coffee, black and no doubt strong.

He finished his meal. He watched the nurse return and remove the tray, sank back and waited.

Two hours later he heard the sound of the trolley being rolled in, the rattle of knife and fork. Seconds later the taste of bacon, then egg yolk, filled his mouth. He inhaled the aroma of the coffee, tasted it on his tongue. He closed his eyes and savoured the sensation. It was the only pleasurable effect of this strange malaise so far.

Then he sat up as something struck him. *Two hours!...* The delay between eating the food and tasting it had been two hours! Likewise the sound of the nurse's arrival.

If his hearing, taste and smell became delayed at the rate of two hours every three days – then what would it be like in a week, say, or a month or a year?

And what of his eyesight? How would he cope with seeing something that had occurred hours, days, even weeks ago? He resolved to find out what had happened to Black, how he was coping. He sat up and called for Caroline.

SHE DID NOT show herself for another three days.

Thorn was attended by an efficient platoon of medics. They seemed to rush through their duties around him with a casual indifference as if he had ceased to exist, or as if they assumed that his senses had retarded to such an extent that he existed alone in a bubble of isolation. On more than one occasion he had asked whether he could be cured, how much worse it might become, what had happened to Black? But they used the fact that he could not immediately hear them as an excuse to ignore him, avoiding not only his words but his eyes.

On the morning of his sixth day in hospital, he awoke to silence and ate his tasteless breakfast. The sound of his waking, of the hospital coming to life around him, the taste of his breakfast – all these things would come to him later. He wondered if he could time it so that he tasted his breakfast at the same time as he ate his lunch?

He waited, and it was four hours later when he tasted toast and marmalade, heard the sounds of his breathing as he awoke.

Later, a nurse removed the electrodes from his head and chest. She opened the door to the balcony and held up a card which read:

Would you like to go out for some air?

Thorn waited until the nurse had left, shrugged into a dressing gown and stepped onto the balcony. He sat down on a chair in the sunlight and stared across the bay, then up into the sky. There was no sign of starship activity today.

He realised that, despite the seriousness of his condition, he still hoped to flux again. Surely the state of his senses would have no detrimental effect on his ability to mind-push? He had already decided that when his condition deteriorated to such an extent that he could no longer function without help, which must surely happen when his sight became effected, he would volunteer for a long-shift. He could push a boat to one of the Rim Worlds, spend a week of ecstasy in flux. It would probably kill him, but the prospect of such rapture and a painless end was preferable to the life he could expect here on Earth.

Caroline appeared on the edge of his vision. She placed a chair next to his and sat down beside him, the sketch pad on her lap. She seemed fresh and composed, the episode of the other day forgotten.

He said, *I've been wanting to apologise for what I said, Carrie. I had hoped you'd visit me before now.* And he cursed himself for making even his apology sound like an accusation.

Caroline wrote: I've been with Black.

Thorn was suddenly aware of his own heartbeat. *How is he?*

She wrote: Only his sense of touch is now in the 'present'. All his other senses are time-lapsed by nearly a day.

How's he coping?

She paused, then wrote: Not very well. He was never very stable. He's showing signs of psychosis. But you're much stronger, Max–

He interrupted: *What happens when his sense of touch retards?*

Caroline shrugged. Thorn read: It hasn't happened yet. It's difficult to say. In a way, if it does occur, it will be easier for him as all his senses will be synchronised in the 'past'. But he'll be unable to mix with people, socialise. How could he? Their presence would be delayed subjectively by hours, days. There would be no way for him to relate...

He could still flux, Thorn said.

Caroline looked away. Tears appeared in her eyes. Then she scribbled something on the pad:

Is the flux all you think about?

It's my life, Carrie. The only reason I exist.

She shook her head, frustrated by this clumsy means of communication. She wrote out two pages of neat script and passed them to him.

I could understand your infatuation with the flux if you thought the experience had religious significance; that you were in touch with an afterlife. But you don't even believe that! To you it's just a drug, a mental fix. You're a flux-junky, Max. When you left me you were running away from something you couldn't handle emotionally because you'd never had to in the past. For most of your life, Max, the flux has provided you with a substitute for human emotion, both the giving of it and the taking. And look where it's got you!

Thorn sat without speaking. Some part of him – some distant buried, human part – was stunned by the truth of her insight.

You just feel sorry for yourself because you didn't get me, he said weakly, trying to defend himself.

Caroline just stared at him. She shook her head. With deliberation she wrote one line. She stood up and tore off the top sheet, handed it to him and left the balcony.

I'm not sorry for myself, Max. I'm sorry for you.

THORN PUSHED THE meeting with Caroline to the back of his mind. In the days that followed he dwelled on the hope that he might one day be able to flux again. If his sense of touch did retard, then, as Caroline had suggested, all his senses would he synchronised and his condition made considerably easier. He might not be able to socialise, but that would be no great loss. His only desire was to rejoin the Line.

On his ninth morning in hospital, Thorn opened his eyes and saw nothing but darkness. He called for the lights to be switched on, but instead someone spoon-fed him breakfast. He was unable to tell if it was Caroline who fed him; he could neither see, hear, or even smell the person. He asked who it was, but the only response – the only one possible in the circumstances – was a gentle hand on his arm. After his first breakfast in absolute darkness he lay back and waited.

His sensory delay had expanded to six hours now, and it was that long before the darkness lifted and he was able to see the sunlight slanting into the room. He had the disconcerting experience of lying flat on his back while his gaze of six hours ago lifted as the Thorn-of-this-morning sat up and prepared for breakfast. In his vision the nurse positioned his tray and fed him bacon and eggs. Thorn felt that he could reach out and touch the woman. He tried, and of course his hand encountered nothing.

He had no control over the direction of his gaze; his unseeing eyes of that morning had wandered, and he found himself trying to bring his errant vision back to the nurse, when all he saw was the far wall. His vision was interrupted by frequent, fraction-of-a-second blanks, when he had blinked, and longer stretches of total blackness when he had closed his eyes. The only benefit of this visual delay was that now his sight and hearing, taste and smell were synchronised. He saw the nurse lift a forkful of egg to his mouth, heard the sound of his chewing and tasted the food. The only thing missing was the egg itself; his mouth was empty.

"There we are," the nurse said, proffering him a last corner of toast. He wanted to tell her to stop treating him like a child, but that was the big disadvantage of his present condition: what he experienced now had happened six hours ago. The nurse would be elsewhere, the bacon and egg digested, the sounds and aromas dissolved into the ether.

Over the next few days he remained awake into the early hours, watching the happenings of the previous day. At four in the morning, then six, darkness would descend, and Thorn would settle down to sleep. Around noon he would wake, spend several hours in darkness, then watch the sun rise eight hours late. If the delay between occurrence and perception continued to increase by two hours every three days, as it was doing, then Thorn foresaw a time when he would be spending more time in darkness than in light.

He would be able to cope. There had been many a long period in the past, between shifts, when he had locked himself in his darkened apartment, with drink and fleeting memories of flux.

* * *

After almost two weeks in hospital Thorn began to weaken. He passed through periods of physical nausea and mental confusion. He hallucinated once that he was fluxing again, this time without the usual euphoria of the union.

The day following this hallucination he awoke early and felt the warmth of sunlight on his skin. Eight hours later he was aware of the sun coming up over the sea. He would have liked to watch it, but his eyes of eight hours ago were fixed on the foot of his bed. The frequency of his 'waking' blinks gave the scene the aspect of an ancient, flickering movie. At least it wasn't silent: he could hear the hospital waking around him, the distant crescendo of a starship's burners.

Later, after someone had spoon-fed him a tasteless lunch, he felt a soft hand on his arm. He moved his head, as if by doing so he might see who it was. But all he saw was the same old far wall of eight hours ago; all he heard was his own breathing. He recalled the touch of the other nurse, but that had been light, platonic, reassuring him like a child that everything was alright. There was nothing platonic about this touch. As he lay there, helpless, whoever it was pulled back the sheets and divested him of hospital garb. He shouted out in silence, tried to fend her off – 'her' because his flailing arm caught the softness of a breast. But he could not see the woman and he was unable to prevent the ludicrous rape. He felt a warm, soft weight straddle him, her breasts loose against his chest, and the sensation was what he imagined it might be like to be taken by a succubus.

Caroline? he said. He moved his arms in the clumsy description of an embrace, touched her familiar warm and slender body. He was aroused now despite himself. She found him and he moaned without a sound, ran his fingers through her black invisible hair. He recognised Caroline's brand of love-making from the past, went along with it as though they had never parted, and when climax came it was as he remembered it from many years ago, a brief ecstasy soon gone – like a second in flux but not as satisfying. Even the unusual circumstances of the union, the fact that he could not see Caroline, that the source of his pleasure was as it were disembodied, could only intimate a greater rapture and not fulfil in itself.

The invisible weight of her lay against him now, heavy and sated after orgasm, which Thorn had experienced through the silent contractions of her body. She kissed him, and he felt salt tears fall on his face.

Caroline... Why...?

Her lips moved against his cheek, her breath hot as she formed words. It was like being kissed by a ghost, bestowed silent prophecy.

In the calm aftermath of the act, Thorn began to feel revulsion. The bizarre nature of their love-making sickened him. He felt a return of the old guilt which he thought he had long since banished. It was as if the union was a symbol of their relationship to date; for years Thorn had played at loving someone whose essence was invisible to him, while Caroline for her part had wasted her life chasing someone who was emotionally forever elsewhere.

He cried out now and pushed her from the bed. He felt her fall and almost heard her cry of pain. *Get out, Caroline! Go away!* He faced where he thought she might be, but could not be sure. *I don't want you, for Godsake! All I want–*

She attacked him then. She came at him with painful blows and slaps, and no doubt cries and accusations. Thorn was aware only of the physical violence, the punches that struck from nowhere without warning. And he was aware, too, that he deserved the assault.

He lay on the bed, battered and exhausted. Caroline had ceased her attack. He had no way of knowing whether she was still in the room, but he sensed her continued presence. *I don't know why you came here*, he said. *I don't know what you want from me...*

He half-expected another hail of blows, and flinched in anticipation. But none came.

When he thought he was alone he dragged the bedsheets around him protectively, lay back and recalled Caroline's tears on his cheeks.

There could only be one explanation for her visit.

THORN FELT HIMSELF weaken further during the hours that followed.

He waited with mounting apprehension, his body covered in chill sweat. Visually it was four o'clock in the afternoon, but the real time was around midnight. It seemed a lot longer than the delayed eight hours before Caroline entered his line of sight.

She moved out of it quickly as she came to the side of his bed. She reached out and touched his arm, and Thorn expected to feel her now, but of course her touch had startled him eight hours ago. Then, Thorn had turned his head abruptly, and now he saw Caroline full on. She wore only a white gown and nothing beneath, and she was crying.

He watched as she undressed him, and the sight of her doing this now brought a hot flush of shame and resentment to his cheeks. The sensation of her touch had passed, but as he saw her slip from her gown and climb onto him he experienced a resurgence of the desire that had overwhelmed him eight hours earlier.

The Thorn-of-now lay still in his bed. He was making love to Caroline, but, with his memories of the physical act already eight-hours old, he felt like a voyeur in the head of his former self. He could see her, frenzied blurs of flesh and hair and tongue; he could smell her, the perfume she used and the sweat of sex that overcame it; and he could hear her small moans of pleasure, her repeated cry of his name as she approached climax.

He heard his slurred question: "Caroline... Why...?"

They had finished their loving-making and she lay in his arms. "Because I loved you, Max," she had said. "Because I *still* love you."

He knew what happened next. Again he experienced that overwhelming sense of revulsion, brought about by guilt. He watched helplessly as he pushed her from the bed. "Get out, Caroline!" he heard himself cry. "Get away!" He saw her expression of pain, the acceptance of rejection in her eyes, and had it been possible he would have stopped himself saying what he said next. "I don't want you, for Godsake! All I want–"

She came at him and hit him again and again.

The Thorn-of-now flinched, as if the blows he could see coming might indeed inflict pain upon him; he raised his arms as if to protect himself.

Caroline backed off and yelled at him.

He heard himself say: "I don't know why you came here...I don't know what you want from me..."

Caroline was crying. "I came because I loved you, Max. I came to say goodbye."

She lowered her gaze and murmured, more to herself than to Thorn: "Black died two days ago."

Eight hours later Thorn lay quite still.

He deteriorated rapidly over then next few days.

The knowledge of Black's death robbed him of any will he might have had to fight. In his final hours he experienced a gradual diminution of his senses. His hearing left him first – then his taste and sense of smell, though he hardly noticed their absence. Later his vision dimmed and went out, and he was aware of himself only as a small, blind intelligence afloat in an infinite ocean.

Soon even the awareness of his physical self diminished, and then the last sense of all, the cerebral intuition of his own identity, left him too. A familiar euphoria flooded him, and the man who had been Thorn knew, before he died, that he was being absorbed into the vastness of the cosmos he had known until then as the *nada*-continuum.

The Pineal-Zen Equation

I'm dropping acid shorts in the Supernova slouchbar when the call comes through. Gassner stares from the back of my hand, veins corrugating his mugshot. Gassner's white – fat and etiolated like a monster maggot – but my Bangladeshi metacarpus tans him mulatto. He's a xenophobic bastard and the fact that he comes over half-caste on the handset never fails to make me smile.

I like irony almost as much as I dislike Gassner.

He's muttering now, some stuff about young junkies.

"You wrecked?" he queries, peering.

"I'm fine," I lie.

He wants me in ten. He has customers coming. Distraught parents who have evidence their daughter was butchered. "This is big-time, girl. Some high-up in the Wringsby-Saunders outfit. Don't screw it." I feel like telling him to auto-fellate on a cannibal personatape, but I resist the urge. Maybe later, when I have the funds to fly. He still owns me, still has his fat face stamped on the back of my hand, good as any brand.

But it's only a matter of time now.

I've been out for hours. What I did earlier needed a good hit to help me forget. My head's dead and so are my legs. I stagger through a battlescene of prostrate bodies and make it to the chute.

Outside it's night, and the crowds are beginning to hit the streets. I brazen my way across a packed sidewalk, earning taunts on three counts. I'm a telepath and a junkie – the two go together – and I have no crowd-sense. I admit everything with an insolent yeah-yeah to whoever's complaining and climb aboard the moving boulevard. A breeze, fresh onetime but polluted now with city stench, does its best to revive me. I ride the slide a block and alight at 3rd. Feeling better already, I dodge touts and beggars and home in on the Union towerpile.

"Bangladesh!" The legless oldster grins in my direction, dumped like garbage by the entrance. How does he do it? He gouged his eyes out yearsback and still he knows when I'm coming. Could be he's on to the scent of my hair oil, or even my crotch. His tag's Old Pete, and he's my regular. I slip him creds and he makes sure I'm stocked with 'gum when I see Gassner. "Any nearer?" he asks now.

I try a probe. All I get is jumblefuzz. He's shielded. We have a game, me and him. He reckons he was someone famous, onetime, and I have to guess who. His face is certainly familiar, disregarding the absent nose and evacuated eye-sockets. He went Buddhist, yearsback. Quit the race and mutilated himself to indicate his repudiation of this illusion. I often wonder what it was that drove him to such extreme action. Maybe he was seeking enlightenment, or perhaps he'd found it. Once again I concede ignorance, pass him ten and chew 'gum in the upchute.

I'm feeling great when I hit the 33rd. Gassner has his office shelved this level, though 'office' is a grand title for his place of work. It's little more than a cubby filled with Batan II terminals and link-ups and however much of his blubber isn't spilling through the hatch. I enter bright, my metabolism pumping ersatz adrenalin. It doesn't do to let him see me any other way. He'd gloat if he knew how low I was at being his slave.

A metal desk-top, the bonnet of a pre-fusion automobile, pins his fat up against the floor-to-ceiling window. He's scanning case notes and his grunt acknowledges the fact that I got in with about three seconds to spare. The only light in the place is the silver glow from the computer screen. I clamber over this and sit cross-legged in the hammock where Gassner slings his meat between shifts. Every ten seconds the chiaroscuro gloom is relieved from outside by the electric blue sweep of a misaligned photon display, strobing sub-lim flashes of 'Patel's Masala Dosa' into our forebrains.

I slip my ferronniere from its case and loop it around my head. And instantly all the minds in the building, previously mere distant flickering candles, torch painfully. I strain out the extraneous mindmush, editing the occasional burst of brainhowl from psychopathic individuals, and work at keeping my head together.

Gassner, of course, is shielded. It wouldn't be good policy for someone who employed a telepath to go about with his head open. I'm shut out, *persona non grata* in his meatball. Times are when I'd love to read my master. Then again, times are when I'm glad I'm barred entry. I read too many screwballs in the course of a day without Gassner opening up.

Seconds later Mr and Mrs distraught roll in.

The guy is Kennedy, and he's playing it cool. I'll be lying if I call him distraught; on the Richterscale of personal upheaval he'd hardly register. He's chewing *djamba* to calm himself and he carries his bonetoned body with a certain hauteur. Or call it arrogance. Under one arm he has the silver envelope containing the evidence, and under the other his wife. She's Scandinavian, beautiful in better circumstances, but grief plays havoc with good looks and right now Mrs Kennedy is ugly. I get the impression that Mr Kennedy is embarrassed by the degree of his wife's distress.

They sit down while Gassner murmurs pleasantries, then jerks a thumb up at me. "Bangladesh," he says. "My assistant."

My name's Sita, but ever since the invasion I got the national tag. Here in the West they reckon it's kinda cute. I'm just glad I wasn't born in Bulgaria.

My presence, perched aloft, surprises Mrs Kennedy. She flickers a timid smile, then sees the connected-minds symbol on my cheek. She recoils mentally; she has no wish to have her grief made any more public than she can allow. I think reassurance at her, telling her that I have no intention of prying – at least, not *too* much. There's no way I'm probing deep into the angst-ridden maelstrom of her psyche. Grief and regret and self-pity boil down there, and I have my own quota of these emotions to contend with at the best of times.

As for Mr Kennedy... He's shielded, so I don't waste sweat trying to probe. And anyway I already know enough about him, everything I want to know, and even things his little Oslo-born third wife doesn't know.

He nods at me, his gaze coolly observant.

I give him my best wink.

And my presence here is token, now. Gassner questions them and they answer, and I probe Mrs Kennedy to ensure veracity, not that I really need to. I had the facts of the case even before she crossed the threshold.

Becky Kennedy was snatched inside an uptown gymnasium at ten this morning, her bodyguard taken out with a neural-incapacitator. Their assailant came and went so fast that the bodyguard saw nothing. Around noon the Kennedys, waiting anxiously in their suburban ranch, received a silver envelope.

Kennedy glances at Gassner, who nods. He lays the envelope on he desk and amid fresh whimperings from his wife slides out a glossy photograph. I lean forward. It isn't pretty. The still shows a young girl, spread-eagled in a leotard, with a massive bullet wound in her pubescent chest. Here dead eyes stare at the camera, frozen with terror.

"No note or message of any kind?" Gassner wheezes.

Kennedy replaces the photograph in the envelope. "Nothing. Just this," he says, and adds, without the slightest hint of appeal in his tone, "Can you get my daughter back, Mr Gassner?"

My boss fingers the folds of fat at his neck. "I'm almost certain we can, Mr Kennedy."

"Within the three-day limit? She's due on the Vienna sub-orbital next month. We'd like her to make it."

And Mrs Kennedy breaks down again. She knows that the majority of missing kids are never found, except after the three-day limit. Despite Gassner's reassurances, she can't believe she'll ever see her little Becky again.

Gassner is saying, "The fact that your daughter's abductor sent you this photograph indicates to me that what we have here is no ordinary abduction." By which he means that Becky might not end up as the meat in a necrophilic orgy.

"My guess is that you'll receive a ransom demand for your daughter pretty soon. My Agency will handle the negotiations. On top of whatever ransom demand is made, my fee for the case is two million creds."

Kennedy waves. "Just get my daughter back, Mr Gassner. And you'll get your fee."

"Excellent. I'm glad to see that someone appreciates how dangerous our line of work can be. We are dealing with criminal psychopaths, Mr Kennedy. No price can fully compensate for the dangers involved."

But two million creds will do nicely, thanks... Two millions that Gassner needs desperately. Trade is bad nowadays, and Gassner is struggling to keep his fat head above the choppy water-level of Big-City business.

He arranges to keep in touch and the Kennedys quit. I jump down and squat by the hatch, watching them go. "You got everything?" Gassner wheezes.

I nod. "Everything I need."

Gassner catches my eye as I'm about to leave. "Hey – and if you find the body before they get the ransom demand, you know how to work it, girl."

I wink, point a blaster made out of fingers to show that I'm on his wavelength – but his instructions worry me. Does he suspect?

"I'm flying, Gassner," I say.

"Hey, how's Joe? I haven't seen him around."

The bastard sure knows how to land a cruel one. "Joe's just fine," I lie. I pray Allah give me strength to make minestrone of his meatball. But what the hell? "Ciao," I call, blow him a kiss and quit.

Drifting...

I was drifting monthsback when I found Joe Gomez. Drifting? It's a state of mind as well as a physical act. You can't have one without the other; they're sort of mutually inter-dependent. To drift, get high on whatever's-your-kick, fill your head with some sublime and unattainable goal, and hit the night. Ride the moving boulevard a-ways, alongside the safe-city civvies out for the thrill of slumming, and when their mundane minds become just *too* much, quit the boulevard and try out the mews and alleyways. Drift forever and lose track of time. There's something for everyone down there; was even something for me.

Back then I was a screwed up, neurotic wreck. My past was a time in my head I tried to forget about, and my present wasn't so strawberries-and-cream, either. A second-grade telepath indentured to a fifth-rate, one-man investigative Agency. I worked a twelve-hour shift and the work was hard: try probing a mind seething with evil sometime. I had another ten years of this hand-to-mouth, mind-to-mind existence ahead of me, and there were times when I thought I could take no more. If I survived the ten years I could leave the Agency, discard my ferronniere and let my telesense atrophy – but even then I'd always be aware that taken as a race we weren't up to much... So I had no hopes for the future and the only way I could take the present was to chew my 'gum and live from day to day. Even so, I neglected myself. I'd go days without eating; I was never fat, but after a stretch of working and drifting and starving I'd be famine-thin, wasted.

I suppose the drifting helped, though. It was part of the day to day routine. My goal? You'd laugh – but they say if you seek long enough, you'll find. And I found. My goal was *someone*.

I had no idea who. I sometimes kid myself I was looking for Joe all along, that I knew he existed out there among the millions and it was just a matter of time before I found him. But that's just old retrospect, playing tricks. Truth is, I was looking for a good and pure mind to prove to myself that we weren't all bad, that hope existed.

So I'd get high at the end of a shift, ride the boulevard and slip into the tributaries. On the prowl, drifting...

I was a familiar face down the lighted darktime quarter. I'd be given rat-and-sparrow kebabs by the Chinese food-stall owners who wanted to fatten me up. The touts, they left me alone after the first few weeks when I declined to buy. They hawked everything from themselves to pure slash, from spare parts for illicit surgery to the Goodbye Express itself – Pineal-z. The drug from the third planet of star Aldebaran that'd give you the trip of a lifetime and total you in the process. It freaked me, that hit. Onetime monthsback I was drinking shorts in a seedy slouch and through the wall I probed a jaded businessman who'd had his fill of everything and wanted out. He'd paid a cool half million for the pleasure of ending his life, and he went with an extravaganza. Subjectivewise he lived another eighty years and his pineal bloomed to show him the evolution of his kind. I tripped along with him until he died, then I staggered back to my pad. I was zonked for three days following, and for another week hallucinated Pithecanthropus and Neanderthal Man dancing the light fantastic on the boulevard. Only later did I get vague flashbacks, memories of the vast, impenetrable blackness that swallowed the oldster when the drug blew his head. It frightened me at first, this intangible nothingness I could neither experience nor understand. In time, a month maybe, I managed to push it away somewhere, forget.

Then I was back drifting again, seeking.

I'd black my connected-minds symbol and probe, discarding heads by the thousand one after the other as they each displayed the same flawed formulas. Some heads were better than others, but even the better ones were tainted with greed and selfishness and hate. And then there were the really bad ones, the heads that struck me at a distance with their freight of evil, that stood out in a crowd like cancer cells in lymph gland.

Then there were the shielded minds, in which *anything* might be lurking.

I found Joe Gomez in a bar called the Yin-Yang.

It's an underground dive with a street level entrance washed in the flutter of a defective fluorescent. Three figures were standing in the silver sometimes-light that night, and something about them caught my attention. They wore the fashionable greys of rich businessmen, and their minds were shielded. They were discussing something among themselves in a tone which suggested they had no wish to be overheard. And one of the guys had o-o tattooed on his cheek.

Now what the hell were three uptown executives doing whispering outside a slum bar at four o'clock in the morning? As sure as Allah is Allah not transacting business, I reasoned.

But I was wrong. They were.

I got close and listened in on their whispers. At the same time I became aware of an emanation from the subterranean Yin-Yang. The two connected. Casualwise, I slipped past the three execs and, once out of sight, jumped the steps two by two. The emanation was the sweet music of violin over din. My quest was almost over.

But not quite. I had to get him out, first.

The bar was a slouch. Felled junkies littered the various levels of the padded floor. I found the barman and asked him if the place had another entrance, and he indicated west.

Then I looked around and probed.

The guy with the harmonious brainvibes sat against the far wall, drinking beer. He wore the blue one-piece of an off-duty spacer, and I read with surprise that he was an Engineman. He was good-looking too in a dark, Spanish kind of way.

I glanced at the entrance. There was no sign of the executives. They were no doubt still debating whether this was the guy they intended to scrape. Obviously their telepath was a few grades below me; I knew immediately that the spacer was prime material for what they had in mind.

I projected an aura of authority and crossed the slouch. "Joe Gomez?"

He looked up, startled; surprised at being paged by a not-so-good-looking black girl. I realised that the telepath outside would be getting all this, too. So I slipped my shield from my tunic and palmed it onto his coverall. Then I grabbed his arm and blitzed him with a burst of life-or-death urgency.

As we hurried to the far door and up the steps I caught the tantalizing whiff of flux on his body. Then we were outside and swamped in the collective odours of a dozen ethnic fastfoods. "This way."

I ran him up the alley and under an arch, then down a parallel thruway and up an overpass. Crowds got in the way and we barged through, making good progress. Years of drifting had superimposed a routemap of the quarter on my cortex. The execs would be floundering now, cursing their lost opportunity. I'd grabbed the golden goose and I could hardly believe my luck. To be on the safe side I took him across the boulevard and up a towerpile into a cheap Mexican restaurant I used when I was eating.

Outside, the city extended in a never-ending, jewelled stretch. The million coruscating points of light might have indicated as many foci of evil that night – but we were away from it all up here and I had Joe Gomez. I could hardly control my shaking.

Then it came to me how close he'd been to annihilation, and I broke down. "You stupid, stupid bastard," I cried.

"Look, Sita – that's your name, isn't it?" He was bemused and embarrassed. He'd caught bits of me as I rushed him out, and he knew he owed me. "Who were those guys?"

"Who? Just your funeral directors, is who." My tears were tears of relief now. "They were pirates in the scrape-tape industry. I overheard them before I got your vibes."

"So? I could have been a star."

"Yeah, a dead star, kid. Not many ways you can be killed nowadays, but they would've killed you *dead*."

His tan disappeared and he looked sick. "But I thought the industry was legal? I've seen personatapes on sale in the marts–"

His naivety amazed me. "The personatape side of the thing is legal. They makes tapes of the famous, or how they think the famous might have been. But these pirates make personatapes of real people by squeezing fools like you *dry*. You're so good you gave me raptures, and they wanted that." And I was already wanting to snatch my shield away from him, wanting *more*...

He stared at his drink. He didn't seem very convinced.

"Listen, kid. You know what they'd've done to you if I hadn't happened along? They'd've killed you and taken your corpse to their workshop. They can scrape stiffs, and they're easier to handle – don't struggle. Then these guys, these pirates... they'd open your skull and go in deep and scrape the cerebellum, leaving your nervous system wrung out and fucked up. They'd get more than just emotions, they'd get everything. They'd rob you of your very self just to make a few fast creds, and then dump your body. And there'd be nothing no rep-surgeon could do to put you back together. You'd be dead. The only place you'd exist is on tape and as a ghost in the heads of non-telepaths who want the sensation of experiencing other states of being without having the operation."

I took a long drink then, angry with him. "And keep that shield. I want you to stay alive. Consider it a present."

"Thanks," he said.

"For chrissake!" I exploded. "Where the hell do you usually drop? Don't you know what a shield is for?"

"I work a line out of Lhasa, Kathmandu, Gorakpur... They're quiet cities. I never really needed a shield there. This is my first time here..." He avoided my eyes and gazed out at the city.

"Yeah, well – think on next time. This isn't no third world dive. This is for real. Mean City Central where you have to think to survive."

He nodded, sipped his drink.

I cooled. "Where you from, Joe?"

"Seville, Europe. You?"

"Chittagong, what was onetime Bangladesh. China now."

His gaze lingered on my tattoo. Then he saw the face on the back of my hand. "Your husband?"

I laughed. "Hey, Mr Innocent – you never seen one of these before?" I waved my hand around theatrically. "This guy's my boss. He *owns* me. I'm indentured to him for another ten years."

"I never realised..."

"No, well you wouldn't, would you?" I glared at him, bitter. Then I smiled. I had to remind myself that I had a Mr-Nice-Guy here, who was naive-for-real and wasn't playing me along.

I sighed, gave him history. "My parents sold me when I was four. They were poor and they needed the Rupees. I was one of six kids, and a girl, so I guess they didn't miss me... I checked out psi-positive when I was five and had the operation. I had no say in the matter, they just cut me and hey-presto I had the curse of *ability*. I was taken by an Agency, trained, and sold to Gassner when I was six. I've been reading for small cred, 'gum and a bed in a slum dwelling for nine years now."

Joe Gomez was shocked. "Can't you... I mean," he shrugged. "Get out?"

"Like I said, in ten years when my indenture runs its course. This makes sure I don't do anything stupid." I held up the miniature of Gassner, his face stilled now; it'd come to life when he contacted me. "With this he knows where I am at all times. There's nothing I can do about it."

We rapped for ages, ordered tostadas, drank. Beneath the jive-assed, streetwise exterior I was like a little girl on her first date. I was trembling, and my voice cracked falsetto with excitement.

Joe Gomez... He was short, dark, around twenty. He had a strong, handsome face, but his eyes were evasive and shy. It was what lived behind those eyes that I was interested in, though... He was pure, and I needed *pure*. I wanted to get into him, become one. I was nothing special to look at, but I was sure that if I let him take a look inside my head, gave him the experience... But at the same time I was scared shitless I might frighten him away.

We watched the dawn spread behind distant towerpiles.

My heart was hammering when I said tentatively, "Where you staying, Joe?"

"I just got in. I haven't fixed a place yet. Maybe you know somewhere?"

"I..." There was something in my mouth, preventing words. "You can always stay at my place. It's not much, but..." Sweet Allah, my eyes were brimming again.

"I don't know..."

"Give me the shield," I said.

"I get it. If I don't come with you, you want your present back, right?" He sounded hurt.

"Balls. I might be other things but I'm no cheat. I want to show you something."

He passed me the shield, a silver oval a little smaller then a joint case, and I put it out of range on a nearby table. His goodness swamped me, and I swooned in the glow. I pushed myself at him, invaded him, showed him what it was like to have someone inside his head... Then we staggered from the towerpile and rode the boulevard to the slums.

Joe was on a three-week furlough, and we spent every day together. We were inseparable, cute lovers like you see on the boulevard Sunday afternoons. The girl from Chittagong and the boy from Seville... I got better quick, saned-up and began enjoying life. I stopped drifting and phased out the 'gum. I didn't need them, now. Joe was my kick, and I overdosed.

We explored the city together. I saw life through his eyes, and what I saw was good. We tried personatapes. He'd be an Elizabethan dandy for a day, and I'd be Bo Ventura, latest hologram movie queen. Once we even sexed as Sir Richard Burton and Queen Victoria, just for the hell of it. We made straight love often, and sometimes we'd exchange bodies; I'd become him and he'd become me. I'd move into him, pushing into his central nervous system and transferring him to mine. I'd experiment with the novelty of a male body, in control of slabs of muscle new to me, and Joe would thrill to the sensation of vagina and breasts. At climax we'd be unable to hold on any longer and the rapture of returning, our disembodied personas twanging back to base, left us wiped out for hours.

Then one day towards the end of his furlough Joe pulled me out of bed and dressed me in my black skinsuit like a kid. We boarded a flier and mach'd uptown. "Where to?" I asked, sleepy 'gainst his shoulder.

"I'm a spacer–" he said, which I'd figured already. He was an Engineman, a fluxer whose shift was three months in a tank pushing a Satori Line bigship through the *nada*-continuum. "And I want to show you something."

We decanted atop the Satori Line towerpile that housed the space museum, and entered a triangular portal flanked by company militia. The chamber inside corresponded to the shape of the portal, a steel grey wedge, and we were the only visitors that day. By the entrance was the holographic sculpture of a man, vaguely familiar; the scientist who discovered the *nada*-continuum and opened the way for the starships.

Through Joe I had experienced everything that he'd experienced. His past was mine, his every sensation a shared event. I'd travelled with him to Timbuktu – and as far as Epsilon Indi. But there was one experience of his that defied my comprehension. When he entered the flux-tank of a bigship I could not go with him; I had no idea what it was to flux. Joe knew, of course, but he was unable to describe the sensation.

He likened it to a mystical experience, but when I pressed him he could draw no real analogues. To flux was an experience of the soul, he said, and not of the mind – which was perhaps why I floundered.

We walked down the ringing aisle of the space museum. At the far end, on the plinth and cordoned by a low-powered laser-guard, was a trapezoid of blackness framed in a stasis-brace. What we had here, according to the inscription, was a harnessed chunk of the *nada*-continuum.

It did nothing to impress a sleepy Bangladeshi, until she saw the expression on the face of her lover. Gomez was a goner; even transfer-sex had failed to wipe him like this. "Joe...?"

He came to his senses and glanced over his shoulder at the entrance. Then he vaulted over the laser-guard and lifted me quickly after him. "This is it, Sita. Take a look."

After a time the blackness became more than just an absence of light. It swirled and eddied in a mystical vortex like obsidian made fluid. I too became mesmerised, drawn towards a fathomless secret never to be revealed.

"What is it?" I asked, stupidly. I leaned forward. Joe held me back. He warned me that the interface could decapitate me as neat as any guillotine.

"It's the essence of nothing, Sita. That which underpins everything. It's Heaven and Nirvana and Enlightenment. The ultimate Zen state..."

His voice became inaudible, and then he said, "I've been there..." And I recalled something – the ineffable blackness I'd scanned a while back. My mind reached out for something just beyond its grasp, a mental spectre as elusive as the wind... Then the spell was broken.

Joe laughed, pulled himself away and smiled at me. He jumped back over the laser-guard and plucked me out. We held each other then, and merged. His period of furlough was coming to an end. Soon he would be leaving me, drawn away to another rendezvous with the *nada*-continuum. I should have been jealous, perhaps. But instead I was grateful to whatever it was that made him... *himself*.

Hand in hand we ran through the chamber like kids.

Allah, those three weeks...

They had to end, and they did.

And it happened that Joe died a fluxdeath pushing his boat through the Out-there beyond star Groombridge. That which had nourished him kicked back and killed him, with just three days to go before he came home to me.

I QUIT GASSNER'S and drop to the boulevard, my head full of Becky Kennedy and her loving parents. As I leave the towerpile a shadow latches on to me and tails, keeping a safe distance. I ride the boulevard to the coast.

Carnival town is a lighted parabola delineating the black bite of the bay. I choose myself a quiet jetty away from the sonic vibes and photon strobes, fold myself into the lotus position and wait.

Overhead, below a million burning stars, bigships drift in noiseless, clamped secure in phosphorescent stasis-grids. Ten kilometres out to sea the spaceport pontoon is a blazing inferno, with a constant flow of starships arriving and departing. Joe blasted out from here on his last trip, and for weeks after his departure the dull thunder of the ships, phasing out of this reality, brought tears to my eyes. Back then I came out here often, sat and contemplated the constellations, the stars where Joe might've been. He's back now, but I still like to stare into space and try to figure out just where the accident happened.

A noise along the jetty, the clapping of a sun-warped board, indicates my shadow has arrived. I sense his presence, towering over me. "Spider," I say. "Sit down. I've been expecting you." And I have – he's one of the few people I can rely on to help me.

Spider Lo is a first-grade telepath and he works for the biggest Agency in the West. He's about as thin as me, but twice as tall. He earned enough last year to buy himself a femur-extension, and I was the first to admit he looked really impressive riding the boulevard, especially in a crowd. He's a Chink, and I should hate him for that, but he's a gentle guy and we get along fine.

"Gassner sent me, Sita."

"That much I figured."

"He told me to make sure you did your stuff. To me, it doesn't look like you're doing that out here."

He hesitates, watching me. "I'll let you into a secret, Sita. Gassner's in big trouble. Business is bad and a few of the bigger Agencies are going for the take-over. They'd buy Gassner out for peanuts and employ him as a nothing button-pusher. As for you – you'd be taken on by whichever Agency buys. You'd be on longer shifts for less pay. You're a second-grader, remember..."

I let him mouth-off. His *secret* is no secret at all. He's telling me nothing I don't already know. I let my lazy posture describe apathy, and stare at the stars.

Spider tries again. "This case is worth two million to Gassner. It would mean solvency for him, and who knows even a rise for you. But you're blowing it."

"And won't Mr Gassner be angry with me," I say.

"Sita... this is the biggest case you've ever had to crack. You don't seem to be trying..."

Languid, I give him a look, long and cool. "Maybe I don't need to try," I say.

"Sita..." His Oriental features pantomime despair.

"I'm serious, Spider. Hasn't it occurred to you that maybe the reason I'm lazing around here is because I've got the case wrapped up?"

His eyes glint with quick respect, then suspicion.

"No shit," I say. "I know where Becky Kennedy's meat is hidden."

"You just this minute left the office, Sita."

I shrug. "How would you like to earn your Agency the two million riding on this case?" I ask him.

He tries a probe. I feel it prickle my head like a mental porcupine in a savage mood. But my shield is up to it.

"You don't have to probe, Spider. I'm honest – I'll tell you. Your Agency can pick up the creds from Kennedy when you find the body and deliver it to the resurrection ward–"

"But Gassner..." Understanding hits him.

"Yeah," I say. "You've got it."

Spider looks at me.

"Why you doing this, Sita? If Gassner folds, you get transferred, and that won't be a picnic for you."

"Listen, Spider. I'm getting out of it altogether. No more probing for this kid after tomorrow."

"You're not–" Alarm in his voice.

I laugh. "No, I'm not. I'm getting out and I want to see Gassner sink..." But there's an easier way than this to tell him.

I take my shield and toss it to him. He catches it, holds it for a second, then throws it back. That's all it takes for him to read what I'm planning. And he reads everything: my love for Joe and the reason I need big money, what I did yesterday and why I did it. He reads what I want him to do, and he slowly nods his head. "Very well, Sita. fine..." We finalise the arrangements, and then slap on it. We sit for a while, watching the starships and chatting, until Spider's handset calls him away on a case. He cranes himself upright and strides off down the jetty like someone on stilts.

I stay put a while. Above the city a hologram projection, like a stage in the sky, is beaming out world news. I watch the pictures but can't be bothered with the sub-titles. Only when the business review comes on do I take an interest. After five minutes the take-over bids are flashed up. Multi-Tec International today made bids for a dozen small-fry – one of them, I learn, Gassner's Investigative Agency. But the bid didn't make it and Gassner is still independent. I smile to myself. By the time I finish with Gassner he'll be wishing he never bought me, all those years ago.

I leave the coast and ride back into the city. I stop off at a call booth and get through to the Kennedys, using the teleprinter to make the demand. Then, instead of going straight to the Union towerpile, I make a detour to take in the cryogenic hive-complex, uptown. I ride the chute to the seventh level and squat beside Joe's pod. If I concentrate I can just make out his thoughts, deep down and indistinct. Even diluted, crystallised and fragmented by the freeze, his emotions are still as good and pure as always. I tell him that soon it'll all be over, and he responds with a distant, mental smile.

I'm tearful when I leave the hive and ride across town.

After I heard about Joe's death I began drifting again.

I got back on the 'gum and stopped eating and hit the darktime quarter. When I wasn't working I got high and drifted without sleep for nights, probing, seeking... It was impossible, of course. What I was seeking I had found and lost, and there could be no substitutes, however good. There were no more Joes, and it was no good telling myself that there had to be. It was too soon after his death and I was still too close to him to accept anyone else.

Then I got it into my head that Joe was still alive. I thought I could feel his brainvibes in the air, as if he existed somewhere in the world and was trying to get through to me. I concentrated and struggled to contact him, to prove to myself that he was still alive. Crazy, I know...

But I was right.

It was a month after the accident and I spent more and more time tripping on acid shorts and trying to forget. I reckoned that if maybe I could lose my identity, then the pain wouldn't be so bad.

Joe called a couple of nights later.

I was laid out on my bunk, coming down after a week of crazy, crazy nights drifting and tripping. My head was alive with vivid nightmares and Joe played a starring role.

When his face appeared on the vidscreen I knew it was a hallucination. "Sita!" it shouted. "It's me – Joe!"

I giggled. "I know you're dead, Joe. You died Out-there. You can't kid me."

"Sita..." His arms were braced on either side of the screen, and his head hung close. It looked like Joe, but there was something wrong with the geometry of the features. They were too clean-cut and perfect to be Joe's, even though they resembled his. Some effect of the acid, obviously...

"Sita, please – listen!" He was near to tears. "I know I died a fluxdeath. But they got me out in time. They saved me. They put me back together in a Soma-Sim and–"

"Where are you?" But I didn't believe. I was still hallucinating. Joe was dead, and what I saw on the screen was a phantom of my imagination.

"That's why I called. I need your help. I'm at the city sub-orb station. I just got in. I need your help..." He looked over the screen, then behind him. When he stared at me again I saw that he was swaying, holding the set for support.

I crawled across the bunk and sat on the edge. I could not bring myself to believe, however much I wanted to. If I rested all my hope on what turned out to be cruel illusion...

"Joe... What's wrong, Joe?"

"They're after me, Sita. The pirates. They almost had me. I got away. Please... come and get me." He grinned then, a wry quirk of the lips I knew so well and loved. "I can't move. They hit me and I can't move. I managed to get this far..."

I staggered around the room and collected my clothes. I struggled into the bare minimum required for decency and dropped to the street. I hailed a flier, gave the destination and collapsed in the back seat. I knew there'd be no Joe when I got there; already our dialogue was becoming dreamlike. It was too much to hope that I could save him a second time...

At the station I told the flier to wait and stumbled into the crowded foyer. I wasn't wearing my ferronniere and the absence of brainhowl was a relief. The call-booths were ranked at the far end beside a Somalian fast-food joint. I pushed through the crowd and collapsed against the first crystal pod. The caller inside gestured me away. I staggered from booth to booth, my desperation increasing when each one turned out to be empty. With three to go and still no sign of Joe I gave up and went berserk. I crashed against them one after the other, flailing at the doors with my fists. The last door remained stubbornly shut, as if pinned by a weight on the inside. I peered over the privacy screen and my heart went nova. Joe had slipped to the floor with his cyber-legs folded beneath him at crazy angles. He grinned when he saw me and reached out his arms...

I managed somehow to get him into the flier and back to my pad.

Once inside he collapsed on the bunk, the Joe Gomez I knew and loved, but *different*. The only part of him that had survived the fluxdeath was his brain, and the rest of him was a power-assisted Somatic-Simulation with all the sex bits and the latest Nikon optics. It was impossible to tell that the body was a Soma-Sim; the surgeons had been faithful to Joe's old appearance, if anything making him even more good looking than the original version.

I thought maybe I was still hallucinating...

"They were waiting at the port," he said. "They waited till I got in from the medic-base and they shot me, Sita. But I got away..." And he indicated his leg.

There was a hole in his thigh big enough to contain my fist. Charred strands of microcircuitry fuzzed the circumference, and the synthetic flesh had melted and congealed in dribbles like cold wax.

"It doesn't hurt," Joe reassured me, peering down. "I don't feel a thing. It's just that I can't walk..."

"We'll get you fixed up," I said.

"You've got a spare half million?"

"Surely the Line–?"

He laughed. "They took all my savings to put me in this."

"We'll find some way," I said. "Can't you go back–?"

His hand moved to touch the hole, with just the faintest whirr of servo-motors. "The Line's fired me, Sita. I'm in no condition to flux and I'm out of a job..." Tears were beyond the expertise of 21st-century cyberneticists, or Joe would have cried, then.

"Can you remember anything about the attack?" I asked.

"Not much. Three guys piled out of an air-car and called out to me. When I began to run, they opened fire–"

"Did you get the flier's plate?"

"I was too busy trying to survive, Sita."

I probed. I relived the attack and saw the same three guys I'd seen outside the Yin-Yang. The subconscious mind forgets nothing, and the quick glance Joe had taken at the air-car had lodged the plate code in his head. I memorised the code and came out. It was a slim lead, but perhaps a valuable one.

Joe reached out and pulled me to him. "You haven't said how good it is to have me back, Sita."

"No?" I opened up, and we merged. Beyond his relief at being with me I saw a dark shadow in the background, a sharp regret that he would never flux again. He was like a junkie deprived his fix, and the withdrawal symptoms were craving and melancholia. I shouldn't have felt jealous, but I did.

The following day I decided that my pad was not a safe place for Joe. Too many people had seen his arrival, and all it would take was for the scrape-tape pirate's telepath to send out a chance probe in the vicinity.

I had a contact in the cryogenic-hive complex uptown, and Joe agreed that this would be the best place for him until I came up with the creds to buy the services of a cyber-surgeon. I had a few ideas I wanted to think over during the next couple of days. I installed him in the hive, then left for Gassner's office.

I told my boss I was using the Batan II to check detail on the current case, and instead tapped into the city plate file. I found the number of the flier Joe had seen, and I was in luck. The flier was a company vehicle belonging to the Wringsby-Saunders Corporation. I looked them up and found they were into everything, but their biggest turnover was in the personatape market...

So I dropped to the boulevard and rode uptown.

The Wringsby-Saunders Corporation had a towerpile all to themselves, a hundred storey obelisk with a flashy WS entwined and rotating above the penthouse suit.

I marched in, exuding bravura.

I roamed. I was looking for company personnel with faces that matched those I carried around in my head. I took in every level and a couple of hours later found what I wanted. A tall executive left his office and strode along the corridor towards me. He wore silvered shades and an arrogant expression. He was shielded, of course – as he was on the last occasion I had encountered him. In the defective fluorescent lighting outside the Yin-Yang bar.

The glow-tag on the door of his office told me: Martin Kennedy. He was the marketing director of the personatape division, one of the top jobs in the Corporation. And not satisfied with a director's fat salary, Kennedy dirtied his fingers with illegal scrape-tape dealings. Some people...

Over the next few days I neglected my duties for Gassner and followed Kennedy. It was my intention to blackmail him; his superiors at Wringsby-Saunders would not be amused that one of their top executives was dealing in death...

Then something happened to make me change my mind. There was a better way of extracting what I wanted from Kennedy, one that did away with the risk to myself.

It came to me as I watched him arrive home one evening and meet his daughter in the drive. It was one of the few occasions when he was unshielded, and I learned that the only pure and unsullied emotion in Kennedy's head was the love he had for his daughter, Becky.

While Kennedy was unshielded I slipped him the sly, subliminal suggestion than Gassner's Investigative Agency was the best in town, specialising in murders, kidnappings, missing persons... The first place he'd think of when he found his daughter gone would be Gassner's.

I turned my attention to Becky and checked her movements. She had her own bodyguard who escorted her everywhere. Well, almost everywhere. He was a big, ugly bastard, but I wasn't going to let him stand in my way at this stage of the game.

I decided the best place to strike would be in the gym she used every Tuesday morning. I joined up for the classes and obeyed all the instructions like a good girl, despite the protests from my drug-wrecked body. I arrived early Tuesday morning and watched Becky at her callisthenics while her minder did the same, only with more interest in how she filled her leotard in all the erogenous-zones-to-be.

I was right behind them when they left the free-fall chamber. I'd taken the precaution of putting the chute out of action and barring the communicating doors. We were quite alone.

I hit the bodyguard with the neural-incapacitator and he dropped like a sack of wet sand. Then I did the same to Becky before she got a look at me. While the guy was still jerking his beef on the floor I dragged Becky along the corridor and into the service chute.

I'd prepared myself for this part of the operation all week. I'd told myself over and over that this was not murder, that before the three days had elapsed little Becky would be patched up and resurrected and as good as new. If not better. Inside a fortnight she'd be back working out at the gym, her death a thing of the past. Even so, as I pulled the trigger of the pistol I had to close my eyes and think of Joe... Then I photographed the corpse and concealed it behind a sliding panel. I'd done my homework and checked. The next chute inspection was due in a week.

I left the gym and mailed the developed print to the Kennedys. Then I made for the Supernova and drank acid shorts to help me forget.

Hours later, the call from Gassner came through.

I CROSS TOWN and head for the Union towerpile. "Bangladesh!" the cackle greets me. Old Pete the Beggar grins toothless along the sidewalk. I slip him ten and he lays 'gum on me. I'm high by the time I hit the foyer.

Spider Lo has done his stuff. He sits with Kennedy in the ground floor bar, done out in the deco of a bigship. I hoist myself onto a highstool, businesslike.

Kennedy gives me the inscrutable look through his silvered shades, but the empty glasses at his elbow belie his cool. "I'd like to know what's going on?" he asks me. "This... this gentleman apprehended me outside and claimed to be working with you on the case. I hope you've found my daughter–"

"Do you have the crystals?" I ask.

Kennedy hesitates, then lifts a valise onto the table. He opens it to reveal two sparkling crystals burning within the leatherette gloom. The substance locked inside them glints like powdered diamond. I take the valise.

"The Gassner Agency has been taken over," I tell Kennedy now. "As such, it no longer exists. Mr Lo here represents the Massingberd Agency. You will pay his Agency upon completion of the case."

"My daughter?"

"By the time I deliver the crystals, your daughter will be in the safe care of the city hospital."

Kennedy nods his understanding. Spider Lo pushes papers across the table and Kennedy signs. "Mr Lo will take you to the hospital, Mr Kennedy." I shake him formally by the hand, but his shield deflects my probe.

We move outside and Spider and I slap palms and go our separate ways. Little Becky Kennedy will be alive again in a short while. Thirty minutes ago Spider rushed a medic-squad to the gym to retrieve her corpse, and soon she'll be respiring normally in the resurrection ward, the attack edited from her memory, looking forward to whatever it is little girls look forward to nowadays. Her sub-orbital trip to Vienna, maybe.

I ride the boulevard, one last time. In case Kennedy suspected anything and put a watch on me, I dodge clever. I alight on 5th and take a devious detour through the downtown quarter, lose myself in crowds and backtrack numerously. Then I hire a flier and mach uptown to the cryogenic-hive.

After the formalities of payment and after-care instructions, I decant my shining knight from his sarcophagus and assist him to the flier. His head is hardly awake yet, barely thawed from the cryogenic state, and it's his power-assisted Soma-Sim that walks him from the ziggurat.

I think love at him to help the thaw.

I programme the destination of Rio de Janeiro into the flier, but before we set off there's the small matter of my indenture to sort out. I fly to the Satori Line towerpile, Joe immobile beside me. I leave the flier on the landing pad, drop to the twentieth level and enter the museum.

I have to wait a while before a rich family decide they've had their fill of wonder, and when they leave I leap over the laser-guard surrounding the shimmering shield of the *nada*-continuum.

I stand mesmerised, regardless of the danger should anyone enter and find me here. Before me is the ultimate, the primal state we all aspire to – the only thing ever to be wholly beyond my ability to grasp.

My contemplation is interrupted by a glow at the end of my arm. My hand tingles. Gassner's miniature portrait becomes animated. I hold up my arm, as if shielding my eyes from the *nada*-continuum, and stare at him. "What do you want, Gassner?"

"Sita!" he cries, and he uses my real name only in times of stress. His regular pallor is suffused now with the crimson of rage, and he's sweating. "Sita – where's Kennedy? I thought you–"

"I didn't crack the case, Gassner. Spider Lo got there first. Kennedy owes the Massingberd Agency, not you."

"Sita!" He's almost in tears. "Get back here!"

I smile. "I'm sorry, Gassner. I'm through. I've had enough and I'm getting out. Goodbye–"

He panics. He knows that without a telepath he's nothing. "You can't, Bangla–"

I can, and the *desh* is lost as I thrust my hand into the *nada*-continuum/reality interface. The satisfaction of getting rid of Gassner dilutes the pain of losing my hand; my tele-ability repels the frenzied communications shooting up my arm and keeps the agony below the tolerance threshold. The wrist is neatly severed when I stagger back, the stump cauterised and blackened. I jump the barrier and stumble through the chamber.

The hologram of the scientist stands beside the portal. Pedro Fernandez, discoverer of the *nada*-continuum and opener of the way. He seems to be smiling at me, and I know the smile. I give him a wink as I leave.

Joe touches my hand as I climb into the flier and take off. We bank over the city and head towards the ocean. I probe him. His head is slowly coming to life, warming as if to the sunlight that shines through the screen. I read Joe's need, his craving.

Above the city, canted at an angle, the hologram screen pours morning news over a waking world. Did the Gassner Agency surrender to the take-over bids that must surely come now? Come on, an ending like that would be just *too* storybook. I can only wait until we reach Rio and find out then.

Meantime, I hope.

Weakly, Joe says, "You get the crystals?"

I open the valise and shake them into his lap.

"Pineal-z," I tell him, and I open up and let him have the experience I had monthsback when I tripped on Pineal-z and lived.

"It's Pineal-z or me, kid," I tell him. "Enlightenment or love. Take your pick." And I withdraw, close up. I don't want to influence his decision and I don't want to eavesdrop on his infatuation with something I can never hope to understand.

Old Pete? Yeah, he kidded me not. He *was* someone famous, onetime. He was probably the most famous person in the world. He was Pedro Fernandez yearsback, discoverer of the *nada*-continuum and opener of the way.

I know for sure now that Old Pete is good, behind that shield of his...

I glance across at Joe. He's staring at the crystals in his hand, weighing the experience he had and lost against whatever I can give him. He drops the crystals back into the valise, looks at me. "We'll sell them when we get to Rio, Sita. Find a cyber-surgeon to fix my leg and get you a new paw."

Enlightenment, or love? Perhaps they're one and the same thing.

Tears fill my eyes as I fly us away from the city and into the sunrise, one-handed.

THE ART OF ACCEPTANCE

I CURLED IN the window and watched the crowds promenade down the lighted boulevard. It was spring again in Gay Paree and the streets were thronged with young lovers, poets and artists – my least favourite time of year.

Dan sat lotus on the battered, legless chesterfield. Leads fell from the lumbar-socket under his shirt, and a bootleg tantric-tape zipped ersatz kundalini up his spinal column. He'd told me to go home at midnight, but I liked being around him, and anyway I had to be on hand in case the fountain of pleasure hit jackpot and blew the chakra in his cerebellum. I'd told him he was playing Tibetan roulette with his meatball – bootleg tapes had scoured the skulls of many a novice – but Dan just laughed and said he was doing it all for me. Which he was, in a way, but I still didn't like it.

When I got bored I tidied the office, stacked Zen vids, cleared away *tankas* and Confucian self-improving tracts. Then I wrote *mahayanan* aphorisms backwards on his forehead, the only part of his face free from beard and hair, and inscribed his arms and palms with that old number, "He who has everything has little, he who has nothing has much," just to show him what I thought of all this transcendental malarky.

I was getting bored again when the building began to shake and flakes of paint snowed from the ceiling. The clanking downchute signalled the approach of a customer.

I yanked the jack from his socket and winced in anticipation of his wrath. He jerked once at the disconnection, then slumped. "Shit, Phuong–"

"Visitor," I said. I prised open his eye and peered in like a horse-doctor. "Jesus, you look wrecked."

He was all hair, blood-shot eyes and bad temper. I pulled him to the desk and sat him in the swivel chair, combing my fingers through his curls and arranging the collar of his sweat-soaked khaki shirt. The adage on his brow accused me, but there was no time to remove it. Footsteps sounded along the corridor. "Pull yourself together, Dan. We need the cash."

I switched on the desk-lamp, made sure my *cheongsam* was buttoned all the way up, and sat in the shadows beside the door.

She strode in without knocking. I like style – being possessed of none of it myself – and everything, from her entry to the way she crossed her legs and lighted a cigarillo, whispered sophistication.

"Leferve?" she enquired, blowing smoke.

"How can I be of service?" It was his usual line. I was pleased to see that her elegance left him unaffected; he was doing his best to disdain all things physical.

Even so, we needed this commission.

The woman re-lighted her cigarillo and fanned the offending smoke. It crossed my mind that all this was an act.

She was white, but throwback African genes gave her face the exaggerated length and beauty of the Masai. The lasered perfection of her features was familiar, too. I was sure, then, that I'd seen her somewhere before.

"You charge by the hour?"

"Five hundred dollars per."

She nodded. If she was aware of the ridiculous scrawl on his forehead she didn't lose her cool and show surprise. She wore a silver lamé mackintosh, belted at the waist, and when she leaned forward to deposit ash in the tray on the desk with a single tap of a long-nailed finger, the lapels buckled outwards to reveal tanned chest and the white sickle scars of a double mastectomy, the latest thing in body fashion.

"I want to hire you for one hour, for which I will pay you twenty-five thousand dollars."

"I'm not an assassin," Dan said.

"I assure you that I want no-one killed."

"Then what *do* you want?" He reached out to the chessboard on the desk and pushed white Bishop to Queen's four: *follow her*.

"That was a rash move, Leferve." She advanced a pawn, and smiled.

Dan toppled his king. "Now, perhaps you could supply me with a few details. Who are you, and what kind of work do you have in mind?"

She glanced around the office. "This is hardly the place to do business. Perhaps we can discuss these points later, over lunch."

Below the level of the desk, Dan gestured for me to go. He saw the writing on his arm and, instead of showing anger, he smiled to himself at this childish exhibition of my affection and concern.

I slipped from the office without the woman noticing me.

I TOOK THE downchute to the boulevard, ran through the rain and rode up the outside of the opposite towerpile to the flier rank. I found Claude and slipped in beside him. Claude had been an ex-spacer with the Satori Line, and in his retirement he piloted a taxi flier part-time. He sat back in the seat with his fingers laced behind his bulky occipital computer. "Action, Phuong?"

"When it shifts, follow that flier."

I pointed across the gap to the landing stage. The woman's flier was an ugly Soviet Zil, two tons of armoured, bullet-proof tank. No wonder the building had quaked when she landed. A uniformed chauffeur stood on the edge of the building and stared out at the lighted night.

Three minutes later the woman emerged and strode across the landing stage. The chauffeur hurried to open the door and the woman slipped quickly inside.

The Zil fired its 'aft jets, and I experienced the sudden pang of physical pain and mental torture that always hit me whenever I forgot to close my eyes. Even the *sound* of burners filled me with nausea.

I was fifteen when I took a short cut through a rank of fliers and the sudden ignition of twin Mitsubishi 500s roasted me alive. Only the skill of the surgeons and my parents' life-savings had saved my life and financed the reconstruction of my face so that it was as pretty as the rest of my body was hideous. I'd been rushing to meet a young Arab I thought I loved. He'd dropped me not long after.

The Zil lifted ponderously and inched out over the boulevard. The jets fired again and it banked with sudden speed into an air-lane, heading north.

"Easy does it, Claude."

He flipped switches and growled to his on-board computer, and we lifted. He steered barefoot and I was forced into the cushioned seat as we accelerated in pursuit.

Traffic was light, which had its advantages: although we had to keep our distance to remain inconspicuous, the Zil was easy to trace in the empty Paris sky. Lights spangled the city far below, but against the darkened dome our quarry's burners glowed red like devils' eyes.

Three minutes later the flier swooped from the air-lane and banked around the silvered bends of the Seine. Claude touched my hand and pointed to one o'clock. A small air-car flew alongside the Zil in a parallel lane. "Been following her since we took off," he told me.

The Zil decelerated and went down behind the high iron railings of a riverside mansion. "Passy," Claude commented. "Expensive. What now?"

The one-man flier, having followed the woman to base, banked and fired off across Paris.

"Move in, Claude. And when you've dropped me, follow that flier. I want everything you can get on it, okay?"

The mansion was a large square building as old as the revolution. Antiquity, though, was not its most notable feature. Even from a distance of five hundred metres I recognised the colony world flora that was fast becoming the latest sensation with the hopelessly rich.

"Now cut the jets and take us in low. I'm going to jump."

"Phuong–"

"Do as I say!"

He curled his lips and cut the flier across the corner of the extensive grounds at a height of ten metres. I swung the door open, picked my spot and jumped.

I landed bullseye in a fungoid growth like a giant marshmallow. I bounced, rolled to the edge and fell from a height of a couple of metres, landing on my backside and jarring my spine.

I was in a xeno-biological jungle. Through a lattice of vines and lianas I made out the lighted windows of the mansion. I picked myself up and began hacking a path through the alien salad. It was hard to imagine that I was on the banks of the Seine. I might have been an intrepid explorer trekking through the sweltering tropics of Delta Pavonis IV.

Then I came to the lawn before the mansion and saw the smallship, sitting inside a red-and-white striped, open-ended marquee. The ship was a rusty, ex-Indian cargo ferry, a vintage antique at home in the alien environment of the garden. I recognised its type from the days of my childhood, when I'd skipped college and spent hours at the Orly spaceport; the reversed swastikas and hooked Hindi script brought back a flood of memories. I knew the structural schematics of the ferry inside out, and I was tempted to fulfil an old ambition by boarding the ship through the dorsal escape chute.

Instead I sprinted across the lawn to a long verandah and climbed aboard. I crept along the wall of the mansion, came to a lighted window and peered inside. The room was empty. I moved along to the next window and found the woman.

She stood with her back against the far wall, holding a drink in a long-stemmed glass. She'd changed her mac for a gown, cut low to reveal the scars of her fashionable mutilation. It struck me as sacrilege, like the desecration of a work of art.

She was discussing the merits of various restaurants with someone on a vidscreen. I sat with my back against the brickwork and listened in for perhaps ten minutes, at the end of which I was none the wiser as to the identity of the woman – though I did know which restaurants to patronise next time I had five hundred dollars to blow.

I was thinking about quitting the scene when I noticed movement to my right. I looked up in time to see the shape of the uniformed chauffeur. I jumped up and ran, but he hit me with a neural incapacitator and I jerked once and blacked out.

When I came to my senses I found myself staring at a moving strip of parquet tiling, and felt a strong arm encircling my waist. The chauffeur's jackboots marched at the periphery of my vision and I realised I was being carried through the mansion.

I put up a feeble struggle, kicked out and yelled at him to put me down. We came to a large polished door and he used my head to push it open, then marched in with me under his arm like a prize.

"And... what *have* we got here?" the woman exclaimed.

"I found her on the verandah."

He stood me upright and gripped my elbow, and I played the idiot. I babbled in Kampuchean and made as if stuffing an invisible club sandwich into my mouth with both hands.

The woman glanced at the chauffeur. "I do believe the girl is hungry."

I nodded. "*Bouffe, merci, mademoiselle!*"

Then I saw the pix on the wall behind her.

There were perhaps a hundred of them, all depicting the same woman, close-ups and stills from old films and others of her accepting awards – small, golden figures with bald heads – framed and displayed in a monomaniacal exhibition of vanity. I thought I recognised the woman in those shots, though the face was subtly different, the planes of her cheeks altered by cosmetics to conform to some bygone ideal of beauty. Also – but this was ridiculous – the woman on the wall seemed *older* than the woman who stood before me.

She saw the scars on my neck that the collar failed to hide. She reached out, and I pulled my head away. Her lips described a *moue*, as if to calm a frightened animal, and she unfastened the top three buttons of my *cheongsam*.

She stared at me. I felt the weight of pity in her eyes that I came to understand only later – at the time I hated her for it. The usual reaction to my injuries was horror or derision, and I could handle that. But pity was rare, and I could not take pity from someone so beautiful.

She said in a whisper, "Take her away." And, before I could dive at her, the chauffeur dragged me from the silent room and frog-marched me through the mansion. I was holding back my tears as we hurried outside and through the grounds. He opened a pair of wrought iron gates, pushed me to the sidewalk and kicked me in the midriff. I gasped for breath and closed my eyes as his footsteps receded and the gate squeaked shut. Then, painfully, I pulled myself to my feet, fumbled with the buttons at my chest and limped back to the main drag.

I knew the woman. I'd seen her many, many times before.

That same face...

Her poise, the way she had of making her every movement a unique performance.

Stephanie Etteridge.

But that was impossible, of course.

* * *

Dan was out when I got back. I left the lights off, swung the Batan II terminal from the ceiling and dialled the catalogue of classic Etteridge movies. I sent out for a meal, sat back in the flickering luminescence of the screen and tried not to feel sorry for myself.

For the next hour I ate dim sum and noodles and stared at a soporific succession of dated entertainments. Even in the better films the acting was stylised, the form limited. At the end of every scene I found myself reaching for the participation-bar on the keyboard, only to be flashed the message that I was watching a pre-modern film and that viewer participation was impossible. So I sat back and fumed and watched the storyline go its unalterable way, like a familiar nightmare.

There was no doubting that, despite the limitations of the form, Stephanie Etteridge had something special. If I could suspend comparison between her movies and the holographic, computerised participation dramas of today, I had to admit that Etteridge had a certain star quality, a charismatic presence.

When I'd seen enough, I returned to the main menu and called up *The Life of Stephanie Etteridge*, a eulogistic documentary made only two years ago.

It was the usual life of a movie star; there was the regular quota of marriages and affairs, drug addictions and suicide attempts; low points when her performances were below standard and the fickle public switched allegiance for a time to some parvenu starlet with good looks and better publicity – and high points when she fought back from slash addiction, the death of a husband and universal unpopularity to carry off three successive Oscars in films the critics came to hail as classics.

And then the final tragedy.

The film industry died a death. In Geneva, a cartel of computer-wizards developed Inter-Active computer-simulated holographics, and actors, directors, script-writers were a thing of the past, superseded by the all-powerful Programmer. In one month the studios in Hollywood, Bombay, Rio and Sydney shut up shop and the stars found themselves redundant. A dozen or so mega-stars were paid retainers so that their personas could be used to give Joe Public familiar, reassuring faces to see them through the period of transition – until a whole new pantheon of computer-generated screen Gods was invented for mass worship. Etteridge was one of these tide-over stars, which was how I recognised her face; I'd seen many 'Etteridge' Inter-Active dramas as a kid. But it didn't take a degree in psychology to read between the lines of the documentary and realise that lending your face to a virtual character was no compensation for the denial of real stardom.

The documentary didn't dwell on the personal tragedy, of course; the last scene showed her marriage to an Italian surgeon, and while the credits rolled a voice-over reported that Stephanie Etteridge had made her last film in ten years ago and thereafter retired to a secluded villa in the South of France.

I was re-running that last film when Dan came back.

He'd washed and changed; he wore a smart, side-fastening blue suit with a high collar. I preferred him in casuals – but perhaps that was because I knew where he was going.

"You dining with that woman, Dan?" I asked.

He nodded. "The Gastrodome at twelve."

"I wish you wouldn't," I whispered, and I was unable to tell whether I was jealous, or scared at what the woman might want Dan to do.

"Like you said earlier, we need the dollars." He mussed my hair. "Did you find out who she is?"

I told him that I'd followed her to a mansion on the left bank, but I said nothing about my capture.

"There were tons of blown-up stills on the walls," I said, "all of the old film actress Stephanie Etteridge. I know you're going to call me dumb, but the resemblance is remarkable. Not only her face, but the way she moves. Look..."

I turned the screen to him while Etteridge played the spurned lover with a bravura performance of venom and spite.

"Recognise?"

He leaned close and whispered in my ear. "You're dumb."

"I know, I know. But you must admit, the resemblance..."

Dan nodded. "Okay, the woman does look like Etteridge. But that film's what...? Thirty years old? I'd say that Etteridge was about forty there. That'd make her seventy now... Are you trying to tell me that the woman we saw here today was that old?"

"But why all the pictures?"

He shrugged. "Beats me. Perhaps she's the daughter of the actress. Or a fan. Or some fruit-cake who thinks she's Etteridge. Have you accessed her? A hundred to one you'll find her dead."

So I turned back to the Batan and called up the information on Stephanie Katerina Etteridge. We scanned her life story in cold, documentary fact. Date of birth, education, professional status, the four marriages, her involvement with an American businessman jailed for an unspecified misdemeanour a matter of days before they were due to marry – though the documentary had said nothing about this. And her death...?

I threw the nearest thing to hand – a tape cartridge – at Dan. "You owe me!"

He fielded the cartridge and waved it. "Okay, so she's still alive – a crotchety old dame somewhere living on caviar and memories. She's over seventy, Phuong."

I turned away in a huff.

Dan readied the tape on the desk. He slipped a small mic into his pocket so that I'd be able to monitor his conversation with the woman over dinner.

"Catch you later."

I came out of my sulk. "Dan, take care. Okay?"

I ran to the door and tried to pull him to me, but he stiffened and kissed the top of my head as if I were a kid. Despite all the Zen he'd been pumping into his skull, he still could not accept me. From needing to show affection, my feelings polarised and I wanted suddenly to hit him, to hurt him as much as he hurt me. He murmured goodbye and took the downchute to the boulevard.

* * *

TWO YEARS AGO Dan had been an Engineman with the Canterbury Line, a spacer who mind-pushed bigships through the *nada*-continuum. Then the Keilor-Vincicoff Organisation developed the interfaces, and the bigships Lines went out of business, leaving thousands of Engineman and -women strung out and in need of the flux. Denied union with the bliss of the *nada*-continuum, Dan drank too much and got into Buddhism and to feed himself started a third rate investigative Agency based in Bondy. He advertised for an assistant to do the leg-work, and I got the job.

We got along fine for weeks, even though I was evasive and distant and didn't let him get too close. Then as I got to know him better I began to believe that we were both disabled, and that if I could accept the state of his head, then perhaps he could come to some acceptance of my body.

Then one night he asked me back to his place, and like a fool I nodded yes. The usual scene, as far as I could gather from the films I'd watched: soft light, music, wine... And after a bottle of chianti I found myself close to him. His fingers mimed the shape of my face, centimetres away; it was as if he had difficulty believing my beauty and was afraid to let his fingertips discover a lie. But it was no lie, just reconstructed osseous underlay and synthi-flesh done with the touch of an artist. We kissed. He fumbled my buttons and I went for his zip, meaning to get him with my mouth before he discovered my secret. I didn't make it. He touched me where my right breast should have been, then ripped open my bodice. He gagged and tipped me to the floor, strode to the window and stared out while I gathered my stuff and ran.

I stayed away for weeks, until he came for me and apologised. I returned to the office and we began again from the beginning, and it was as if we were closer, having shared our secrets – though never, of course, close enough.

* * *

Soon after that night at his place he began experimenting. He claimed that he was doing it for me. By embracing illegal skull-tapes, second-hand Buddhism and the *Bardo Thodol* rewritten for the modern era, he said he was attempting to come to some acceptance of my disfigurement – but I knew he was also doing it for himself.

Now I stared at the mystical junk that littered the desk and the chesterfield: the pamphlets, the mandalas, the meditation pins and bootleg tapes. In a rage I picked up a great drift of the stuff and threw it the length of the room. When the desk and chesterfield were cleared, and my anger was still not exhausted, I ran across the office, fell to my knees and pitched *tankas* and pins, magazines and effigies of Gautama through the window. I leaned out and laughed like a fool, then rushed down into the street and stomped on the useless relics and idols of mysticism, ground them into the sidewalk and kicked the debris into the storm drain. Then, as the rain poured down around me, I sat on the kerb and cried.

Hell, *real* love rarely lasted; so what chance had our corrupted version of attraction, what chance had the relationship between a screwed up Engineman attempting to rewire his head with bogus Buddhist tracts so that he could, in theory, ignore the physical, and someone whose body was no more than a puckered mass of raddled meat? It was unfair to both of us; it was unfair of myself to expect love and affection after so many years without hope, and it was unfair of me to keep Dan from other women who could offer him more than just companionship and a pretty face.

The tape was running when I returned to the office.

I lay on the chesterfield in the darkness and listened to the clink of glasses, the murmur of polite conversation. The Gastrodome was the de-commissioned astrodome of an old French bigship, amputated and welded atop the Eiffel tower. I'd been up there once, but the view had given me vertigo. Now I lay half asleep and listened to the dialogue that filled the room.

All I wanted was for Dan to refuse to work for the woman, so that he would be free from the danger of whatever it was she wanted him to do. Then, when he returned, I could tell him that I was leaving, and that this time there was nothing he could say to make me return.

"Tell me about when you worked for the Canterbury Line," the woman said. "Is it true that in flux you experience Nirvana?"

"Some Enginemen claim that."

"Did you?"

"Do we have to talk about this?" he said, and I knew that his hands would be trembling.

In my mind's eye I could see the woman giving an unconcerned shrug. "Very well, but I hope you don't mind discussing your occipital implant–"

Dan, "Why?" suspicious.

"Because I'm interested." Her tone was hard. "What kind is it, Leferve?"

"Standard Sony neo-cortical implant–"

"With a dozen chips in the pre-frontal lobe, sub-cortex, cerebellum, etc...?"

"You've done your homework," Dan said. "Why the interest?"

"When was the last time you fluxed?"

I cried out.

It took Dan aback, too. The silence stretched. Then: "Almost two years ago..."

"Would you consider doing it just one more time," she asked, "for twenty-five thousand dollars?"

I balled my fists and willed him to say no...

"I have a smallship I need taking on a short haul," she said.

There was a brief moment of silence, then Dan spoke.

"Insystem or interstellar?"

And I yelled, "Dan..."

"Neither," the woman said. "I want you to push the ship through the *nada*-continuum from here to Frankfurt."

Dan laughed. "You're mad..."

"I'm quite sane, I assure you. From A to B and back again. You'll be in the flux-tank for less than one hour."

"And the ship?"

"An ex-Indian Navy Hindustan-Tata with Rolls-Royce ion drive–"

"Crew?"

"None. Just you and me. The ship is pre-programmed with the co-ordinates. All it needs is someone to push it."

"And I'd be wasting my time asking what all this is about?"

The woman assented. "You'd be wasting your time. Can I take it that you want the job?"

Dan murmured something.

"Good," she said. "Here's my card. If you arrive at five, we'll phase out at six."

They left the restaurant and took the downchute to the landing stage. I sat in the darkness and stared at the wall, wishing that Dan had had the strength of will to turn his back on the flux. He craved union with the *nada*-continuum, but this gig would be just a quick fix after which his craving would be all the more intense.

I switched off the tape, then switched it on again. I couldn't face Dan and tell him that I was leaving – that way I'd end up screaming and shouting how much I hated him, which wasn't true. I'd leave a message to the effect that I needed a long break, and quit before he got back. I picked up the microphone.

Then the Batan chimed and Claude's big face filled the screen. "Phuong, I got the information on that flier."

"Yeah?" My thoughts were elsewhere.

"Belongs to a guy called Lassolini – Sam Lassolini."

I just shrugged.

Claude went on, "He's a surgeon, a big noise in European bio-engineering."

I remembered the documentary, and Etteridge's last marriage. "Hey, wasn't he married to–"

Claude nodded. "That's the guy. He hit the headlines a few years ago when the film star Stephanie Etteridge left him."

"You got his address, Claude?"

"Sure. De Gaul building, Montparnasse."

"Pick me up in five minutes."

I thought about it.

Now why would Sam Lassolini follow the Stephanie Etteridge look-alike to her mansion in Passy...?

There was only one way to find out.

THE DE GAUL building was the old city morgue, deserted and derelict but for the converted top floor, now a penthouse suite. Claude dropped me on the landing stage and I told him to wait. I took the downchute one floor and hiked along a corridor. I came to a pair of double doors and hit the chime. I felt suddenly conspicuous. I hadn't washed for two days, and I'd hardly had time to learn my lines.

A small Japanese butler opened the door.

"Lassolini residence?" I asked.

"The doctor sees no-one without an appointment."

"Then I'll make an appointment – for *now*."

I tried to push past him. When he barred my way I showed him my pistol and said that if he didn't sit down and keep quiet I'd blow a hole in his head. He sat down quickly, hands in the air.

I tiptoed down a passage and came to a vast ballroom with a chequerboard floor of marble and onyx tiles, and a dozen scintilating chandeliers. There was no sign of Lassolini; I would have called out, but the weight of the silence intimidated me.

I opened the first door on the right.

It took me about fifteen seconds to recognise the woman who this morning had visited the office, who I had followed to the mansion, and who, less than thirty minutes ago, had been dining with Dan.

She was hanging by the neck and her torso had been opened with something sharp from sternum to stomach; the contents of her abdomen had spilled, and the weight of her entrails anchored her to the floor.

I heard a sound behind me and turned. A tall, Latin guy looked down on me. He wore a white suit and too much gold. I did mental arithmetic and decided that he looked good for sixty.

"Sam Lassolini?" I asked.

He didn't deny it. "Who are you, and what do you want?"

I drew my pistol and aimed at his chest. Next to it I hung my identification. "Phuong Li Xian," I said. "I have the power of arrest." I indicated the woman. "Why did you do it, Lassolini?"

He looked past me at the the body and smiled. "If I may answer a question with a question: why your interest?"

I hesitated. "I'm working on her case."

He threw his head back and laughed.

My fist tightened on the pistol. "I don't see what's so funny."

He indicated another door along the hall. "Follow me."

He opened the door and entered the room. He turned to face me, his laughter mocking my shock.

Behind him, spread across the floor and the far wall, were the remains of what once might have been a human being. It was as if the wall and the floor had suddenly snapped shut to create a grotesque Rorschach blot of flesh and blood. The only part of the body that had survived the mutilation was the head. It sat beside Lassolini's right foot, staring at me.

It was the head of the same woman...

Lassolini left the room and strode to the next door. He paused on the threshold. "My dear..." I stumbled after him, amenable with shock.

Another atrocity. This time the woman had been lasered into bloody chunks and arranged on plinths around the room after the fashion of Dali.

"You're mad!" I cried.

"That did occur to me, my dear. Though what you see here is not the cause or symptom of it, but an attempt to cure myself. A catharsis, if you like."

"But... but which one is Stephanie Etteridge?"

"None of them is Stephanie," he said. "She is alive and well and living in Paris. And yet... all of them *were* Stephanie."

I took control of my shock, levelled the pistol and said with determination: "Look, Lassolini, I want answers. And if I don't get them..."

He bowed. "Very well, my dear. This way – and I assure you, no more horrors."

He strode down a long corridor. I had to run to keep up. We came to a pair of swing doors with circular portholes, and Lassolini pushed through. Another surprise: after the luxury of the ballroom, the stark and antiseptic utility of what looked like a hospital ward. Then I remembered that this place was once the city morgue.

We stopped at a line of horizontal silver tanks, and with an outstretched hand Lassolini invited me to inspect their contents.

I peered through the first frosted faceplate and made out the young, beautiful face of Stephanie Etteridge. In a daze I moved on to the next one, and the next: Etteridge, again, and again. Each tank contained a flawless replica of the actress.

I stared at him, and he smiled.

"Clones..." I murmured, and I experienced a curious vacuum within my chest.

"Perspicacious of you, my dear."

"But I thought the science was still in its experimental stages. I thought the Kilimanjiro Corporation had the rights..."

Lassolini laughed. "The science *is* still in its experimental stages," he said. "And I *am* the Kilimanjiro Corporation."

I gestured in the direction of the ritually slaughtered Etteridge clones. "But you still murdered human beings," I said. "Even clones are–"

Lassolini was shaking his head. "By no stretch of the imagination can they be considered human – as of yet. They are grown from DNA samples taken from the original Stephanie Etteridge, and their minds remain blank until the encoded identity of the subject is downloaded into them."

"So those...?"

"Merely so much dead meat. But it pleased me to sacrifice Stephanie, if only in effigy. These bodies were the ones I kept in supply for the time when she aged and required her youth again."

I looked into his youthful face. "So both you, *and* the Stephanie Etteridge I met, are clones?" I was beginning to understand.

He regarded me, as if calculating how much to divulge.

"We were married for five happy years," he said. "When her career came to an end, and she began to show signs of age, I promised her a new lease of life. Virtual immortality. Perhaps only this kept her with me, until my scientists perfected the technique of cloning, and the more difficult procedure of recording and downloading individual identity from one brain to another.

"She was nearly seventy when we downloaded her into the body of her twenty year old clone. Then... and then she left me, and nothing I could do or say would make her return. I had such plans! We could have toured the Expansion together in eternal youth." He seemed to deflate at the recollection of her betrayal.

"I considered hiring an assassin to kill the man she left me for, but as events transpired that proved unnecessary. She divorced me, and a matter of days before she was due to marry her lover he was arrested by the German police and charged with conspiring to sabotage a European military satellite. He was jailed for life."

He paused there and licked his lips. When he spoke next it was in barely a whisper. "You mentioned that you were on her 'case'?"

"That's right."

"Then... you're in contact with her?"

I was guarded. "I might be."

"*Then bring her to me!*" And I was shocked by the intensity of his emotion.

I glanced at the Etteridge clones, then back at the surgeon who had performed this miracle.

"I have a price," I said.

"Name it!"

With trembling fingers I fumbled with the buttons of my *cheongsam* and revealed my body.

CLAUDE WAS SNOOZING in his flier when I jumped aboard and yelled at him to take off. I checked my watch. It was five-forty, and Etteridge and Dan were due to phase-out at six. We burned across Paris towards Passy.

Ten minutes later we sailed in over the Seine. Claude slowed and we cut across the corner of the Etteridge estate. I opened the hatch and prepared to jump. "See you later, Claude."

His reply was lost as I dived.

This time I missed the marshmallow and fell through a bush with leaves like sabres. I picked myself up, bleeding from a dozen cuts, and limped through the jungle. It was three minutes to six when I emerged from the trees, and the smallship was still berthed inside the marquee. I ducked back into the vegetation and ran along the side of the tent. Once behind it I left the cover and dodged guy ropes.

I lifted the tarpaulin wall of the tent, squirmed through the gap and ran over to the dorsal escape chute. I palmed the sensor and waited for the hatch to cycle – ten seconds, though it seemed like as many minutes. I checked my watch: one minute to go. Then the hatch slid open and I jumped inside and curled in the darkness. Above me, the computerised locking system of the interior hatch rumbled away to itself and finally opened. I pulled myself into the carpeted, semi-lighted corridor. And I'd realised a childhood ambition: I was inside a smallship.

I could see along the corridor and into the bridge. Etteridge sat in a swivel-seat between the arms of a V-shaped instrument console, speaking to a soft-voiced computer. Beside her was the sen-dep tank, the hatch dogged and the alpha-numerics pulsing a countdown sequence. Dan was already in there.

I drew my pistol and started towards the bridge. If I could untank Dan before he fluxed–

Seconds later the 'ship phased into the *nada*-continuum.

The 'ship pitched, knocking me off my feet. I fell against a bulkhead, striking my head. I was out for only a matter of minutes, and when I came to my senses we were no longer flying through the *nada*-continuum.

I stared through the forward viewscreen and made out the concrete expanse of a penitentiary exercise yard. We were there for less than ten seconds. I heard the hatch wheeze open, and Stephanie's cries as a prisoner ran towards the ship and scrambled aboard. Laser bolts ricocheted from the concrete and hissed across the skin of the 'ship. Then the hatch slammed shut the 'ship slipped again from this reality.

I giggled like a lunatic. If only my younger self, the kid who'd haunted the Orly star terminal just to get a glimpse of phasing starships, could see me now: stowaway on the craziest jailbreak of all time.

Three minutes became as many hours; time elasticated – then snapped back to normal as we re-emerged in the real world of the red-and-white striped marquee on the lawn of the riverbank mansion.

Through the viewscreen I could see Claude, waiting for me in his flier.

I ran.

The Etteridge clone and the escapee were in each others' arms when I reached the bridge; they had time to look round and register surprise and shock before I raised my pistol and fired, sending them sprawling stunned across the deck.

I stood over the woman, smiling at the future she represented...

When I delivered Stephanie Etteridge, Lassolini would take from me the DNA which in four years, when cloned, would be a fully grown nineteen year-old replica of myself – with the difference that whereas now my body was a ninety percent mass of slurred flesh and scars, my new cloned body would be pristine, unflawed, and maybe even beautiful.

While Etteridge and her lover twitched on the deck, their motor neurone systems in temporary dysfunction, I untanked Dan. I hauled out the slide-bed, pulled the jacks from his occipital implant and helped him upright.

Of course, Lassolini had said nothing about what he intended to do with his ex-wife – and at the time I had hardly considered it, my mind full of the thought that in four years I would be whole again, an attractive human being, and the shame and regret would be a thing of the past.

Now I thought of Stephanie Etteridge in the clutches of Lassolini. I imagined her dismembered corpse providing the sick surgeon with his final cathartic tableau, a sadistic arrangement of her parts exhibited beneath the chandeliers of the ballroom in the ultimate act of revenge.

Etteridge crawled across the deck to the man she had saved. She clung to him, and all I could do was stare as the tears coursed down my cheeks.

What some people will do for love...

I PULLED DAN away from the tank. He was dazed and physically blitzed from his union with the infinite, his gaze still focused on some ineffable vision granted him in the *nada*-continuum.

"Phuong...?"

"Come on!" I cried, taking his weight as he stumbled legless across the bridge. I kicked open the hatch and we staggered from the smallship and out of the marquee. I had to be away from there, and fast, before I changed my mind.

Claude helped Dan into the flier. "I thought you said we were taking the woman?" he said.

"I'm leaving her!" I sobbed. "Just let's get out of here."

I sat beside Dan on the back seat and closed my eyes as the burners caught and we lifted from the lawn. We banked over the Seine and Dan fell against me, his body warm and flux-spiced from the tank.

As we sped across Paris, I thought of Etteridge and her lover – and the fact that she would never realise the fate she had been spared. I wished them happiness, and gained a vicarious joy I often experience when considering people more fortunate than myself.

I ASSISTED DAN into the darkened office and laid him out on the chesterfield. Then I sat on the edge of the cushion and stared at the tape on the desk, set up two hours ago to record my last farewell.

I picked up the microphone, switched it on and began in a whisper. "I've enjoyed working for you, Dan. We've had some good times. But I'm getting tired of Paris. I need to see more of the world. They say Brazil's got a lot going for it. I might even take a look at Luna or Mars. They're always wanting colonists..." And I stopped there and thought about wiping it and just walking out. Even nothing seemed better than this bland goodbye.

Then Dan cried out and his arm snared my waist. I looked into his eyes and read his need, his fear after his confrontation with the infinite. And something more...

His lips moved in a whisper, and although I was unable to make out the words, I thought I knew what he wanted.

I reached out and wiped the tape, then lay on the chesterfield beside Dan and listened to his breathing and the spring rain falling in the boulevard outside.

Elegy Perpetuum

It began one warm evening on the cantilevered, clover-leaf patio of the Oasis bar.

There were perhaps a dozen of us seated around the circular onyx table – fellow artists, agents and critics, enjoying wine and pleasant conversation. Beneath the polite chatter, however, there was the tacit understanding that this was the overture to the inevitable clash of opinions, not to say egos, of the two most distinguished artists present.

The artists' domes, hanging from great arching scimitar supports, glowed with the pale lustre of opals in the quick Saharan twilight. The oasis itself caught the sunset and turned it into a million coruscating scales, like silver lamé made liquid.

This was my first stay at Sapphire Oasis, and I was still somewhat out of my depth. I feared being seen as an artist of little originality, who had gained admittance to the exclusive colony through the patronage of the celebrated Primitivist, Ralph Standish. I did not want to be known as an imitator – though admittedly my early work did show his influence – a novice riding on the coat-tails of genius.

I sat next to the white-haired, leonine figure of Standish, one of the last of the old romantics. As if to dissociate himself totally from the Modernists, he affected the aspect of a Bohemian artist of old. He wore a shirt splashed with oils, though he rarely worked in that medium, and the beret by which he was known.

Seated across from him was Perry Bartholomew.

The Modernist – he struck me more as a businessman than an artist – was suave in an impeccably cut grey suit. He lounged in his seat and twirled the stem of his wine glass. He seemed always to wear an expression of rather superior amusement, as if he found everything that everyone said fallacious but not worth his effort to correct.

I had lost interest in the conversation – two critics were airing their views on the forthcoming contest. I turned my attention to the spectacular oval, perhaps a kilometre in length, formed by the illuminated domes. I was wondering whether I might slip away unnoticed, before Ralph and Bartholomew began their inevitable sniping, when for the first time that night the latter spoke up.

He cleared his throat, and this seemed to be taken by all present as a signal for silence. "In my experience," Bartholomew said, "contests and competitions to ascertain the merit of works of art can never be successful. Great art cannot be judged by consensus. Are you submitting anything, Standish?"

Ralph looked up, surprised that Bartholomew was addressing him. He suppressed a belch and stared into his tumbler of whisky. "I can't. I'm ineligible. I'm on the contest's organising committee."

"Ah..." Bartholomew said. "So you are responsible?" His eyes twinkled.

Ralph appeared irritated. "The Sapphire Oasis Summer Contest is a long-standing event, Perry. I see nothing wrong in friendly competition. The publicity will help everyone. Anyway, if you're so against the idea, why have you submitted a piece?"

The crowd around the table, swelled now by a party that had drifted up from the lawns below, watched the two men with the hushed anticipation of spectators at a duel.

"Why not?" Bartholomew asked. "Although I disagree in principle with the idea of the contest, I see no reason why I should not benefit by winning it."

Ralph laughed. “Your optimism amazes me, sir.”

Bartholomew inclined his head in gracious acknowledgement.

The resident physician, a man called Roberts, asked the artist if he would be willing to discuss his latest creation.

“By all means,” Bartholomew said. “It is perhaps my finest accomplishment, and has also the distinction of being totally original in form.” Just when he was becoming interesting, if pompous, he damned himself by continuing, “It should make me millions – which might just satisfy the demands of my wife.”

There was a round of polite laughter.

Ralph exchanged a glance with me and shook his head, despairing.

Perry Bartholomew’s separation from his wife, also an artist of international repute, had made big news a couple of years ago. Their ten year marriage had been a constant feature in the gossip columns, fraught as it was with acrimony and recriminations before the final split. He had, it was reported, taken it badly – even an arch-cynic like Bartholomew had a heart which could be hurt – unless it was his ego that had suffered. For a year he had lived as a recluse, emerging only when he moved to the Oasis for an extended period of work.

Tonight Bartholomew looked far from well. He was a handsome man in his early fifties, with a tanned face and dark hair greying fashionably at the temples – but now he looked drawn, his dark eyes tired.

Someone asked, “You said, ‘totally original in form’?” in a tone of incredulity which prompted a sharp response.

“Of course!” Bartholomew stared at the woman. “I am aware that this is a bold claim to make, but it is nevertheless true, as you will learn when I exhibit the piece. I have utilised a prototype continuum-frame to harness an electro-analogue of my psyche.”

There was an instant babble of comment. A critic said, “Can we have that again?” and scribbled it down when Bartholomew patiently repeated himself.

“But what exactly is it?” someone asked.

Bartholomew held up both hands. "You will find out tomorrow. I assure you that its originality of form will be more than matched by its content."

Roberts, from where he was leaning against the balustrade, asked, "I take it that this is an example of a work of art which you would contend is worth a human life?" He smiled to himself with the knowledge of what he was doing.

Bartholomew calculated his response. He was aware that all eyes were on him, aware that his reply would re-open the old argument between him and Ralph Standish – which was exactly what the onlookers were anticipating.

Bartholomew gave the slightest of nods. "Yes, Doctor. In my opinion my latest piece is of sufficient merit to be worth the sacrifice."

Ralph Standish frowned into his whisky, his lips pursed grimly. Bartholomew had made a similar declaration in the pages of a respected arts journal a couple of years ago, and Ralph had responded with a series of angry letters.

I willed him not to reply now, convinced that he would only be playing Bartholomew's childish game if he did so. But all eyes were on him, and he could not let the comment pass.

"Your views sicken me, Perry – but you know that. We've had this out many times before. I see no need to cover old ground."

"But why ever not, my friend? Surely you are able to defend your corner, or perhaps you fear losing the argument?"

Ralph made a sound that was part laugh, part grunt of indignation. "Losing it? I thought I'd won it years ago!"

Bartholomew smiled. "You merely stated your case with precision and eloquence, if I may say so. But you signally failed to convince me. Therefore you cannot claim victory."

Ralph was shaking his head. "What will it take to convince you that your philosophy is morally objectionable?"

"My dear Ralph, I might ask you the very same question." Perry Bartholomew smiled. He was enjoying himself. "So far as I am concerned, I occupy the moral high ground–"

"I cannot accept that art is more important that humanity," Ralph began.

"You," Bartholomew cut in, "are a traitor to your art."

"And you, a traitor to humanity."

"Ralph, Ralph," Bartholomew laughed, condescending. "I consider my view the height of humanity. I merely contend that a supreme work of art, which will bring insight and enlightenment to generations, is worth the life of some peasant in Asia or wherever. What was that old moral dilemma? 'Would you wish dead one Chinaman if by doing so you would gain unlimited wealth?' Well, in this case the unlimited wealth is in the form of a work of art for all humanity to appreciate in perpetuity."

Ralph was shaking his head. "I disagree," he said. "But why don't we throw the question open? What do you think? Anyone? Richard?"

I cleared my throat, nervous. I looked across at Bartholomew. "I side with Ralph," I said. "I also think your example of 'one Asian peasant' is spurious and misleading."

Bartholomew threw back his head and laughed. "Oh, you do, do you? But what should I expect from one of Ralph's disciples?"

"That's unfair, Perry," Ralph cut in. "Richard has a valid point."

"Perhaps," I said, "you might be less willing to expend a human life if that life was one closer to home. Your own, for instance?"

Bartholomew regarded me with startlingly blue eyes, unflinching. "I state categorically that my life is worth nothing beside the existence of a truly fine work of art."

"That," Ralph said, taking over the argument, "is letting Perry off the hook too easily." He swirled the contents of his tumbler, regarding Bartholomew across the table. "Would you be as willing to lay down the life of someone you loved?"

I was suddenly aware of a charged silence on the patio.

Everyone was watching Perry Bartholomew as he considered his wine glass, a slight smile of amusement playing on his lips. "Perhaps we should first of all conduct a semantic analysis of what you mean by the word 'love'?"

Ralph was red in the face by now. "You know damn well what I mean. But to counter your cynicism, I'll rephrase the question: would you lay down the life of someone close to you for a work of art?"

Bartholomew thought about this, a consummate performer playing the cynosure. "Would I?" he said at last. "That is a very interesting question. If I were to be true to my ideals, then by all means I should. Perhaps though, in my weakness, I would not..." He paused there, and I thought we had him. Then he continued, "But if I did not, if I chose the life of someone close to me over the existence of a work of art – then I would be morally wrong in doing so, prey to temporary and sentimental aberration."

Ralph massaged his eyes with thumb and forefinger in a weary gesture of despair. He looked up suddenly. "I pity you, Perry. I really do. Don't you realise, it's the thing that you call the 'sentimental aberration' that is at the very heart of each of us – that thing called love, which you claim not to know?"

Bartholomew merely stared at him, that superior smile on his lips. "I think we should have that semantic debate, after all."

"You can't apply your reductionist sciences to human emotion, damn you!"

"I think perhaps I could, and disprove for good the notion of love."

"You don't convince me, Perry – for all your cynicism." Ralph got to his feet. "But I can see that I'm wasting my time. If you'll excuse me, I'll bid you good night." He nodded at Bartholomew and left the patio with a quiet dignity that won the respect of everyone present.

Bartholomew gave a listless wave and watched him go, a twist of sardonic amusement in his expression. "Romantics!" he said with venom when Ralph was out of earshot.

The party broke up soon after that and I retired to my dome.

* * *

I WOKE LATE the following morning, breakfasted on the balcony of my dome overlooking the lawns, and then strolled around the oasis towards Ralph's dome. A couple of days earlier I'd finished the sculpture I had been working on, and I was still in that phase of contented self-satisfaction which follows creation.

I was passing beneath the pendant globe of Perry Bartholomew's dome when I heard his summons.

"Ah, Richard... Just the man. Do you think I might borrow your body for a minute or two?" He was leaning from an upper balcony, attired in a green silk dressing gown. "I require a little assistance in moving my exhibit."

After his arrogance last night, I was tempted to ignore him. The Oasis had attendants to do the manual labour, but at the moment they were busy with other artists' work on the concourse beside the water, ready for the judging of the competition tomorrow. I was about to call up to him that he'd have to wait until the attendants were free, when I recalled his overblown claims concerning his latest work of art. My curiosity was piqued.

"I'll be right up," I said.

I passed beneath the globe and entered the escalator shaft which carried me up to the central lounge. The door slid open and I paused on the threshold. "Enter, dear boy," Bartholomew called from another room. "I'm dressing. I'll be with you in a minute."

I stepped into a large, circular room covered with a luxurious, cream carpet more like a pelt, and equipped with sunken sofa-bunkers. Several of Bartholomew's abstract sculptures occupied prominent positions – hard, angular designs in grey metals, striking in their ugliness.

Bartholomew emerged on the far side of the room. "Good of you to help me, dear boy. The attendants are never around when one needs them."

He wore a white suit with a pink cravat, and seen at close quarters I was struck by how seedy, how ill the man appeared. He liked to project an image of foppish sophistication, but such a display from someone so evidently unwell seemed merely pathetic.

"I hope Ralph hasn't taken the huff over our disagreement last night?"

"I don't know," I said. "I haven't seen him today."

Bartholomew chuckled. "The man is a silly old goat," he said. "When will he learn?"

I was stung. I was about to respond that Ralph was a fine artist and a good man, then paused. "Learn what?" I asked, suspicious.

Bartholomew crossed to a pedestal arrayed with bottles and glasses. "Would you care for a drink, Richard?"

I told him that it was a little too early for me, frustrated by his calculated reticence. He was clearly playing another of his infuriating mind games. He poured himself a large brandy, turned and considered me.

"Learn," he said, "not to take so seriously my little digs. Our differences of opinion hardly matter."

"They matter to Ralph," I said. "He objects strongly to your philosophy. What should he do? Sit back and let your comments go unopposed?"

"But my dear boy, don't you think that I object to his philosophy? I assure you, I find his sentimentality just as sickening as he evidently finds my... my realism." He sighed. "It's a pity we can't still be friends. We were once very close, you know?"

I hesitated. Ralph rarely spoke of his friendship with Bartholomew. "What happened?"

"Oh, we encountered different circumstances, experienced divergent phenomena, and adopted our own philosophies to deal with them. Ralph was always an idealist, a romantic at heart. I was a realist, and the more I experienced, the more I came to see that my view of the world was the right one. Ralph has always had it too easy." He shrugged. "We've reached the stage now where our respective views are irreconcilable. I think he's a woolly-minded bleeding heart, and he no doubt thinks me a hard-nosed neo-fascist. But you know this – you probably think of me in the same way." He smiled, challengingly, across at me.

I murmured something to the contrary and avoided his gaze, wishing I had the strength to tell him what I really thought.

While he was speaking, I noticed a holo-cube on a polished wooden table in the centre of the room. It was large, perhaps half a metre square, and depicted a brown-limbed little girl in a bright blue dress, with masses of black hair and big eyes of lustrous obsidian. The contradiction between Bartholomew's ideals, and the display of such a romantic work of art, was not lost on me.

I crossed the room and paused beside the table. "It's quite beautiful," I said.

"I'm glad you like it. She is my daughter, Elegy."

"Your daughter?" I was taken aback, surprised first of all that he had a daughter, and then that he should choose to display her image in a holo-cube for all to see.

"The child," he said, "is incredibly intelligent. Precocious, in fact. She will go far." And, with that, any notion that Bartholomew had succumbed to paternal sentiment was erased. For him, the holo-cube of his daughter was merely a reminder of her intelligence quotient.

"She celebrates her eighth birthday tomorrow," he went on. "She is visiting me directly from her boarding school in Rome. You'll be able to debate world affairs with her, Richard."

I ignored the sarcasm. "I look forward to meeting her."

Bartholomew smiled. "But come, I'm keeping you. Please, this way."

We took a spiral staircase down to his studio. I recalled that he had described his work last night as utilising a continuum-frame, and I wondered what to expect. The large, circular chamber was filled with sunlight and the machinery of his art: large power tools, computers, slabs of steel and other raw materials.

He gestured across the room to his latest creation, standing against the far wall. It was a heavy, industrial-looking metal frame, hexagonal and perhaps three metres high – for all the world like the nut of a giant nut and bolt. It was not the dull, rusting frame, however, that was the work of art, but what the frame contained: an eerie, cobalt glow, shot through with white light, like fireworks exploding in slow motion. As I stared at it I convinced myself that I could make out vague shapes and forms, human figures and faces, surfacing from within the glow. But the images never remained long enough, or appeared with sufficient definition, for me to be sure. I might merely have been imagining the forms. The piece did, however, fill me with unease.

"The frame is an early prototype of the Keilor-Vincicoff interface," Bartholomew said. "I bought it for an absolute fortune when I realised it could be put to artistic use. What you see at its centre is a section of the *nada*-continuum, the timeless, spaceless form that underpins reality. Enginemen posit that the *nada*-continuum is Nirvana." He laughed. "I contend that it is nothing but a blank canvas, if you like, upon which we can project the contents of our psyches."

He indicated a computer keyboard set into the frame. "I programmed it directly from here–" tapping his head "–and it was the gruelling work of almost a year. It is totally original in form and content, and well worth the agony of creation."

"Is it titled?" I asked.

Bartholomew nodded. "*Experience*," he said.

I looked from what might have been a woman's face, screaming in terror, to the artist. "I'm impressed," I said.

He barked a laugh. "You Romantics! Unlike your work, this is not merely visual. It was created with the express intention of being participated in. Go ahead, pass through."

I stared again into its pulsing cobalt depths, veined with coruscating light, and stepped onto the plinth.

I glanced back at Bartholomew. "Are you quite sure?"

"Of course, my dear boy! Don't be afraid. I'll follow you in, if you wish."

I nodded uncertainly, wondering if I was doing the right thing. With reluctance, and not a little fear, I took one hesitant pace into the blue light. I was immediately enveloped in the glow, and without points of reference to guide my senses I experienced instant disorientation and nausea. I felt as though I were weightless and spinning out of control, head over heel.

More disconcerting than the physical discomfort, however, was the psychological. Whereas seen from outside the images in the glow were fleeting, nebulous, now they assailed me, or rather appeared in my mind's eye, full-blown and frightening. I beheld human forms bent and twisted in horrifying torques of torture – limbs elasticating to breaking-point, torsos wound like springs of flesh, faces stretched into caricatures of agony. These depredations were merely the physical counterpart of a prevailing mental anguish which permeated, at Bartholomew's perverted behest, this nightmare continuum. And beyond this, as the intellectual sub-text to the work of art, there invaded my head the ethos that humanity is driven by the subconscious devil of rapacity, power and reward – to the total exclusion of the attributes of selflessness, altruism and love.

Then, one pace later – though I seemed to have suffered the nightmare for hours – I was out of the frame and in the blessed sanity of the real world. As the horror of the experience gradually diminished, I took in my surroundings. I had assumed I would come out in the narrow gap between the frame and the wall – but to my amazement I found myself in the adjacent room. I turned and stared. Projecting from the wall – through which I had passed – was a horizontal column of blue light, extending perhaps halfway into the room. As I watched, Bartholomew stepped from the glowing bar of light – the artist *emerging* from his work – and smiled at me. "Well, Richard, what do you think?" He regarded me intently, a torturer's gleam in his eye.

To my shame I said, "It's incredible," when I should have had the courage to say, "If that's the state of your psyche, then I pity you." I only hoped that the agony I had experienced within the frame was a partial, or exaggerated, reflection of Bartholomew's state of mind.

"The depth of the beam can be increased from one metre to around fifteen. The devices are still used in shipyards and factories to transport heavy goods over short distances. I'll show you..." He stepped through the frame into the next room, and while he was gone I marvelled at how he could prattle on so matter-of-factly about the mechanics of something so monstrous.

Then I reminded myself that Bartholomew believed he had created here a work of lasting art.

Before me, the beam extended even further into the room, almost touching the far wall. Then it decreased in length to just one metre. He shortened it even further and, as if by magic, the wall suddenly appeared.

I returned to the studio, walking through the door this time rather than taking the malignant shortcut through the frame.

"We'll leave it at its original setting," Bartholomew said. "It's easier to move that way."

For the next thirty minutes we edged the frame onto a wheeled trolley and rolled it into the elevator. "We must handle it with the utmost care!" Bartholomew warned. "I know through bitter experience that the slightest jolt might eliminate the imprinted analogues. The aspects of my psyche programmed within it exist tremulously. If we should drop it now..."

We emerged into the sunlight, and I had never been so thankful to experience fresh air. We gingerly trolleyed the great frame along a tiled path to the concourse, Bartholomew flinching at the slightest jolt or wobble on the way. Part of me wanted nothing more than to topple the frame, but the moralist in me – or the coward – overruled the urge. At journey's end a couple of attendants helped us ease the frame to the ground. "Careful!" Bartholomew shouted. "It should be treated with the greatest respect. The slightest mishandling..."

By now, word was out that Perry Bartholomew was exhibiting his magnum opus, and a crowd had gathered before the frame like supplicants at the portals of a cathedral.

I took the opportunity, as Bartholomew prepared to make a speech, to slip away. Filled with a residuum of unease from my experience of *Experience*, I made my way around the oasis to Ralph Standish's dome.

I ENTERED WITHOUT knocking and made my way to the studio. I paused on the gallery that encircled the sunken working area. Ralph was standing in the centre of the room, holding his chin and contemplating the small figures playing out a drama of his own devising below me. The figures were perhaps half life-sized, at this distance very realistic, though seen at close quarters, as I had on earlier occasions, they were slightly blurred and ill-defined. I had been surprised to find Ralph dabbling in graphics when I joined him here last year – he usually spurned computer-generated art – but he had reassured me that though the method might be modern, the resultant work would be traditional.

He looked up and saw me. "Rich, come on down." He pressed a foot-pedal to kill the projectors hidden in the walls. The strutting figures flickered briefly and winked out of existence.

I descended the steps. "How are you this morning?" I asked. I was a little concerned about him after last night's run in with Bartholomew.

"Never better!" He beamed at me. He wore his old paint-stained shirt, splashed with the wine he squirted from a goat-skin at frequent intervals. "Last night did me the world of good."

"It did? I must admit, I was surprised when you invited Bartholomew to join us."

"I'd been avoiding him for the better part of the year," Ralph said. "Last night I thought I'd give him the benefit of the doubt, see if he was still as eager to expound his odious views."

"Well, you certainly found out."

"It made me feel wonderful, Rich. Made me even more convinced that my ideas are right. Not that I was ever in any doubt." He peered closely at me. "Talking about feeling wonderful, you're looking terrible."

I was surprised that it showed. "Well... Bartholomew just called me in to help him move his latest work of genius."

"You didn't actually enter the thing?"

"So you know about it?"

"He invited me across last month, before you arrived. I stepped into it then, though at the time it was still in its early stages."

"What did you think?"

"I was appalled, of course. The thing's an abomination. I dread to think what it's like now he's completed it." He directed a line of burgundy expertly into his mouth, pursed his lips around it and nodded. "To be honest, the whole episode's a tragedy. Quite apart from poisoning the minds of all who enter it, its creation has made him quite ill both physically and mentally. Did you notice, Rich, that the figures within the frame were all female?"

I recalled the twisted travesties of the human form I had experienced in the blue light. "Now you come to mention it..." I said. "Yes, I think they were."

Ralph nodded. "Did you also notice that they were all aspects of the same person – Electra Perpetuum, his wife?"

"They were? Christ, how he must hate her!"

Ralph perched himself on the arm of a chesterfield, watching me closely. "Do you want my honest opinion, Richard?" There was a light in his eyes, enthusiasm in his attitude.

I smiled. "Do I have any choice?"

Ralph was too occupied with his own thoughts to notice my affectionate sarcasm. "I think that although Perry might want to hate her, in fact he still loves her."

I snorted. "I'm not sure he knows the meaning of the word."

"Of course he does! He's human, dammit! He might have experienced tragedy and hardship over the years, which have no doubt hardened him, but in here–" Ralph thumped his chest "–in here he's like all the rest of us. He's a fallible human being."

"What makes you think he still loves Perpetuum?"

Ralph hesitated. "I was with him when he first met Electra," he told me. "That was ten years ago – at the time he was just getting over his disastrous relationship with the vid-star Bo Ventura. We were still quite close friends, back then. He was not quite the cynic he is now, but he was getting that way – I could see that from his criticism of my work, his views on art and life in general. When he started seeing Electra, I thought perhaps she might be good for him. She was – still is – his total opposite: warm, loving, generous to a fault. She lived life at a pace which honestly frightened me. I thought that Perry might be good for her, too – might slow her down a little, provide a calming influence... I saw them at intervals of perhaps a year over the next six or seven years. I was still on socialising terms with Perry, though things were getting pretty heated between us at the end. For the first few years, everything was fine between him and Electra..."

"And then?"

"Perry became ever more distant, withdrawn into himself and his thoughts. He alienated her with his philosophy, reducing everything to basic animal responses, where emotions like love had no place. Life to him became a vast, meaningless farce. When he published the articles attacking me and my work, Electra could stand no more."

Ralph paused briefly, then went on, "Anyway, she met someone else. I know it wasn't serious. She used this man as a means to escape from Perry. That was two years ago. I saw him shortly after the separation, and on the surface it was as if nothing at all had happened. He was still working hard, turning out his empty, minimalist sculptures. But about a month after Electra left, Perry went into hiding, became a recluse for a year. He saw no one, and I guessed that he didn't want to admit to the people who knew him that he'd been affected. He turned up here a year ago, and that... that *thing* is his first response to the end of his relationship with Electra."

"But it's a monument of his hate for Perpetuum," I said. "How can you possibly claim he still loves her?"

Ralph shook his head, emphatic. "I know the man, Richard. He's torn apart by a great contradiction at the heart of his life. He intellectually believes that such things as love, friendship, altruism do not exist. And yet he loves Electra, he loves his daughter, even though these feelings don't fit in with his reductionism. That work he calls *Experience* is, in my opinion, a response to the anguish of his separation from his wife. The only way he can overcome what he sees as the aberration of his feelings for Electra is by creating a work which he hopes will at once validate his cynicism and exorcise her from his mind."

"You almost sound sorry for him," I commented.

"Oh, I am, Richard. The man needs saving from himself."

I recalled the holo-cube of his daughter. As much as I found it hard to believe that Perry Bartholomew did indeed, as Ralph suggested, harbour human feelings in his heart, there was the memento of Elegy he kept on display in his lounge. I mentioned this. "I assumed it was merely to remind him of her intellect," I said.

"He purposefully gives that impression," Ralph said. "But believe me, he loves her. Why else would he agree to having her stay with him over her birthday?"

I was not totally convinced. "Because he wants to impress everyone with her genius?" I suggested.

Ralph smiled to himself. "We'll see," he said. "It should be quite an interesting few days."

He climbed from the chesterfield and moved to the balcony. I joined him. Across the sparkling expanse of the water, the concourse was thronged with a crowd of artists. Bartholomew's continuum-frame was the centre of attention. Ralph smiled to himself. "Will they ever learn?" he said.

I glanced at my watch. The sight of all the work arranged on the concourse reminded me that I had yet to exhibit my own piece. I would put the finishing touches to it that afternoon. "What are you doing this evening, Ralph?"

"Working, unfortunately. I have a few things I want to get ready for tomorrow."

We made arrangements to meet for breakfast the next day and I left for my dome. I took the long way around the oasis, so as to avoid the crowd and the malign aura that surrounded Perry Bartholomew's latest work of art.

Ralph was in good humour the following morning as we breakfasted on the patio overlooking the oasis. He buttered his toast lavishly, as if it were a palette, and gestured with it as he told me about a group of new artists whose work he admired. He was prone to mood swings, depending on how his work was progressing, and I could only assume that all was going well now.

Below us, on the concourse, a cover had been erected to protect the exhibits from the effects of the sun. People strolled down the aisles formed by the works, pausing occasionally to admire a piece more closely. Bartholomew's continuum-frame, huge and ungainly, looked out of place among the smaller crystals, sculptures and mobiles.

I was about to comment that the piece would be more at home in a breaker's yard when the artist himself rode up the escalator and crossed the patio. As he passed our table he inclined his head. "Gentlemen." He appeared rather frail this morning, his white suit hanging on his tall frame.

Ralph gestured, swallowed a bite of toast. "Perry, why not join us?"

Bartholomew paused, raised an eyebrow. "I think perhaps I might," he said. "Very kind of you."

He seated himself at the table and ordered breakfast – a single cup of black coffee. I felt uneasy in his presence. I recalled what

Ralph had said yesterday about saving Bartholomew from himself, but wished that Ralph had waited until I was elsewhere to indulge his missionary streak.

Bartholomew nodded towards the exhibition. "When does the fun begin, Ralph?"

"This afternoon, when the judges arrive."

Bartholomew nodded. He had the ability to make his every gesture regal. "And who might they be?"

"Ah... can't tell you that. Utmost secrecy. Competition rules..."

Bartholomew smiled and sipped his coffee. His attitude suggested that he thought the result of the contest a foregone conclusion. "I see Delgardo's showing a crystal. I rather like his work."

Ralph didn't, and was usually vocal about the fact. "He has a certain technical expertise," he said.

They continued with this vein of light banter, and I ceased to listen. I moved my chair back and propped my feet on the balustrade, enjoying the sun.

I was the first to notice them – two small figures hurrying around the oasis towards the patio. They almost ran up the escalator, and this exertion, in an environment where a leisurely stroll was *de rigueur*, caused me to sit up. The two men stepped from the escalator and crossed the patio. I recognised Roberts, the resident physician, and with him was a man in the uniform of a chauffeur: he walked with a limp and his jacket was scuffed and ripped.

They paused at our table.

Roberts cleared his throat. "Mr Bartholomew..."

The artist looked up, irritated at the interruption. "Yes? What is it?" His gaze took in the unlikely pair without any sign of consternation. At the sight of Roberts' diffidence and the chauffeur's bruised face, my stomach turned sickeningly.

"Mr Bartholomew... I'm afraid there's been an accident."

"Elegy?" Bartholomew's face was expressionless. "Where is she?"

"If you'd care to come with me," Roberts said.

Ralph took Bartholomew's elbow and we followed the doctor down the descending escalator, across the concourse and through the main gates of the Oasis.

"What happened?" Bartholomew demanded.

Beside us, the chauffeur was tearful, shaking from the delayed effects of shock. "I took the bend too fast... There was nothing I could do. I tried to..."

Outside the gates stood the open-top, two-seater Mercedes, its flanks buckled and scraped, the windshield mangled as if it had taken a roll. The hairs on the nape of my neck stood on end. I expected to find Elegy – the small, sun-browned girl I'd first seen yesterday in the holo-cube – lying dead or injured on the front seat.

To my relief the Mercedes was empty.

Bartholomew cleared his throat. "Where is she?" he asked.

"I'll drive this car back to the scene of the accident," Roberts said. He beckoned the chauffeur. "You'll have to direct me. Standish, you bring Perry in my pick-up." He indicated a small truck in the parking lot.

While Roberts and the chauffeur climbed into the Mercedes, we shepherded Bartholomew across the tarmac towards the truck. Outside the air-conditioned confines of the complex, the heat was merciless.

Ralph took the wheel and Bartholomew sat between us. We lurched from the car-park and along the straight, raised road after the battered Mercedes.

Bartholomew sat with his hands on his knees, staring into the shimmering heat haze ahead of us. I wanted to yell at him that he could show some sign of emotion, that we would fully understand.

"Why didn't the driver bring her back?" he said at last, as we bucketed over the uneven surface. "Even if she were dead, he should have returned with her body..."

In the driver's seat, Ralph gripped the wheel and stared grimly ahead. I said, "Roberts wouldn't be coming out here if she'd died..." I felt faint at the thought of what injuries Elegy might have sustained.

Ten minutes later the road began to climb into a range of low hills, no more than an outcropping of rocks and boulders, the only feature on the face of the flat, wind-sculpted desert. The surface of the road deteriorated and the truck lurched drunkenly from rut to pot hole and back again.

We rounded a bend. Ahead, the Mercedes had pulled into the side of the road. As Ralph eased the truck to a halt behind it, Roberts and the chauffeur climbed out, crossed the road and walked out onto a flat slab of rock. The chauffeur pointed to something below him.

"Christ," I said, unable to stop myself. "She's down there."

I jumped from the cab and ran across the road. The result of the Mercedes' prolonged skid was imprinted on the tarmac like double exclamation marks. Crystallised glass and flakes of paint littered the great anvil of rock across which the car had rolled.

Roberts was kneeling over a narrow fissure. The rock, perhaps the size of an Oasis dome, had split into two uneven sections. One section comprised the greater part, while the other was no more than a sliver, perhaps a metre thick.

I joined Roberts and the African and stared into the crevice. Ten metres down, wedged upright and illuminated by a bright shaft of sunlight, was Elegy Perpetuum. Her head was turned at an unnatural angle, clamped between the two great slabs. She was staring up at us with an expression that comprised both terror and entreaty.

Ralph and Bartholomew joined us.

Ralph, in a gesture of support, was gripping Bartholomew's arm just above the elbow. The latter stared into the fissure and, at the sight of his daughter, winced. It was his only concession to anguish, and seemed suitably in character.

Roberts was attempting to squirm down after the girl, and there was something faintly ludicrous, and at the same time terribly touching, about his futile efforts. He gave up at last and knelt, panting and staring down helplessly.

As my gaze adjusted to the sunlight and shadow in the well of the crevice, I made out greater detail. Elegy was wearing a red dress, and I saw that what I had at first taken to be torn strips of material hanging down her arms were in fact rivulets of blood. There was more blood on the slab of rock near the surface, splashed like patches of alien lichen.

"Elegy," Roberts called. "Can you hear me? Take deep breaths and try not to panic. We'll have you out in no time."

The girl stared up at us, blinked. If she'd heard, she gave no sign. She began to cry, a thin, pitiful whimpering reaching us from the depths.

Bartholomew knelt and peered down. He looked at Roberts. "Is there nothing you can do?" To his credit, there was a tremor in his voice.

"I contacted emergency services in Timbuktu as soon as I found out what had happened. They won't be here for another two, three hours." Roberts shook his head, went on under his breath, "But she might not last that long. She's bleeding badly and God knows what internal injuries she's received."

Bartholomew, down on one hand and knee like a dishevelled, ageing sprinter, just closed his eyes and kept them closed, in a gesture more demonstrative of despair than any amount of vocal bewailing.

Suddenly I could no longer bear to watch – either the little girl in agony, or Bartholomew in his own mental anguish. My redundancy, my utter inability to do a thing to help, only emphasised my fear that Bartholomew might resent my presence.

I strode over to the edge of the rock, taking measured breaths and trying to quell my shaking. Elegy's continual, plaintive whimpering, echoing eerily in the chasm, cut its way through the hot air and into our hearts.

There was a drop of perhaps ten metres to the shale-covered slope of the hillside. Elegy, pinned between the two planes, was positioned a little way above the surface of the hill. It occurred to me that if only we had the right tools to cut through the flake of rock...

I returned to the small group gathered around the dark crevice. "Are you sure there's nothing back at the Oasis? Drills, cutting tools – even a sledge hammer? The rock down there can't be more than a metre thick."

Roberts shook his head. "Don't you think I've considered that? We might have hammers, but we'd never smash through the rock before the emergency team arrives."

From down below, a pathetic voice called out, "Daddy!"

"Elegy, I'm here. We'll get you out soon. Try not to cry."

"I'm all bleeding!" she wailed. "My leg hurts."

As we watched, she choked, coughed, and blood bubbled over her lips and down her chin.

"Elegy..." Bartholomew pleaded, tears appearing in his eyes.

"We've got to do something," I said. "We can't just–"

Ralph was squatting beside Bartholomew, holding him. He looked up at me then and stared, and it was as if the idea occurred to both of us at the same time.

"Christ," he said, "the continuum-frame..."

I felt suddenly dizzy at the thought.

Ralph looked from me to Bartholomew. "It might just work, Perry..."

"We could position it down there on the hillside," I went on. "If we took the truck we could have it back here in twenty minutes."

I knelt beside Bartholomew, who was staring down at his daughter, his expression frozen as if he had heard not a word we had said. I said, "It's the only way to save her. We need the frame!"

He slowly turned his head and stared at me, stricken. Some subconscious part of me might have been aware of the incredible irony of what I was asking Bartholomew to sanction, but all I could think of at the time was the salvation of Elegy Perpetuum.

"It would never survive the journey," he said in almost a whisper. "Everything would be lost."

Roberts exploded. "Jesus! That's your daughter down there. If we don't get her out of that bloody hole she won't survive much longer!"

Bartholomew peered down the crevice at Elegy, who stared up at him mutely with massive, beseeching eyes and blood bubbling from between her lips. "You don't know what it cost me to create the piece," he said. "It's unique, irreplaceable. I could never do another quite like it..."

In rage I gripped his arm and shook him. "Elegy's unique, for chrissake! She's irreplaceable. Are you going to let her bleed to death?"

Something snapped within him, and his face registered a terrible capitulation. He closed his eyes and nodded. "Very well..." he said. "Very well, use the frame."

I hauled him to his feet and we hurried across the road. With Ralph's help I assisted Bartholomew into the back of the truck, where we stood side by side clutching the bulkhead. Roberts and the chauffeur climbed into the cab and started the vehicle, and we rumbled off down the road at breakneck speed, Bartholomew rocking impassively from side to side between us. He stared into the never-ending sky and said not a word as the desert sped by.

Ten minutes later we roared through the gates of the Oasis, manoeuvred through the concourse and backed up to the continuum-frame. We enlisted the aid of two attendants and for the next five minutes, with Bartholomew looking on and pleading with us to be careful, jacked the frame level with the back of the truck and dragged it aboard. Bartholomew insisted on travelling with it, as if his presence might ease its passage, and Ralph and I joined him in the back. We accelerated from the concourse and through the gates, leaving a posse of on-lookers gaping in amazement.

As the truck raced along the desert road and into the hills, Bartholomew clung to the great rusting frame and gazed into the radiance at its centre, its veined depths reflecting in his bright blue eyes. We lurched over pot-holes and the frame rocked back and forth. Bartholomew stared at me, mute appeal in his eyes. "It's going!" he called out. "I'm losing it!"

I stared into the swirling cobalt glow. As I watched, the marmoreal threads of white luminance began to fade. I could only assume that these threads were the physical manifestation of Bartholomew's sick, psychic contribution to the piece, the phenomena I had experienced as tortured flesh and acute mental anguish. Over a period of minutes the white light dissolved and the bright glow waned to sky blue, and Bartholomew simply closed his eyes as he had at the plight of his daughter.

Before we arrived at the scene of the accident, the truck turned off the road, crossed the desert and backed up to the great slab in which Elegy was imprisoned. We halted a metre away from the face of the rock and Bartholomew, like a man in a trance, touched the controls and extended the blue beam into the boulder.

Then we jumped from the truck and scrambled up the hillside. We gathered around the crevice, peering down to judge how near the beam was to the girl. I stood beside Bartholomew as he stared at his daughter, his expression of compassion tempered by terrible regret, and I felt an inexpressible pity for the man.

"We'll have you out in no time!" I called down to her.

She was staring up at us, blinking bravely. We were not so far off with the beam. It penetrated the rock one metre to her left; all that was required was for the beam to be shifted a little closer to the girl.

When I looked up, Ralph, Roberts and the chauffeur were no longer with us. I assumed they had returned to the frame. I took Bartholomew's arm in reassurance and turned my attention to the girl.

I stared down into the crevice...

I thought at first that my eyesight was at fault. I seemed to be looking through Elegy's crimson dress, through her round brown face and appealing eyes. As I watched, the girl became ever more indistinct, insubstantial – she seemed to be dematerialising before our very eyes. And then, along with all the blood, her image flickered briefly like a defective fluorescent and winked out of existence.

I had seen an identical vanishing act somewhere before – in Ralph's studio, just yesterday.

I looked at Bartholomew, and saw his face register at first shock, and then sudden understanding.

He stood and turned. "Standish..." he cried, more in despair than rage at the deception. "Standish!"

But by this time Ralph, along with the other flesh-and-blood actors in his little drama, had taken the Mercedes and were speeding along the road towards Sapphire Oasis.

Which was not quite the end of the affair.

I DROVE BARTHOLOMEW back in the truck, and we unloaded the continuum-frame and set it among the other works of art on the concourse. Evidently word had got back that something had happened in the desert. A crowd had gathered, and artists watched from the balconies of the domes overlooking the concourse.

Bartholomew noticed nothing. He busied himself with the keyboard set into the frame. "There still might be something in there I can salvage," he told me. "Something I can build on..."

I just smiled at him and began to walk away.

I was stopped in my tracks by a cry from a nearby dome.

"Daddy!"

Bartholomew turned and stared. Elegy Perpetuum, radiant in a bright blue dress and ribbons, walked quickly across the concourse towards her father, as upright as a little soldier. She ran the rest of the way and launched herself into his arms, and Bartholomew lifted her off the ground and hugged her to his chest.

She was followed by a tall, olive-skinned woman in a red trouser-suit. I recognised her face from a hundred art programmes and magazines – the burning eyes, the strong Berber features: Electra Perpetuum.

I was aware of someone at my side.

"Ralph!" I hissed. "How the hell did she get here?"

"I invited her, of course – to judge the contest." He smiled at me. "I've told her about everything that happened out there."

Electra paused at the centre of the concourse, three metres from Bartholomew. He lowered his daughter to the ground and the little girl ran back to her mother's side.

"I know what you did, Perry," Electra said in a voice choked with emotion. "But what I want to know is, do you think you made the right decision?"

I realised, as I watched Perry Bartholomew regard Electra and his daughter for what seemed like minutes, that what Ralph Standish had created before us was either the last act of a drama in the finest of romantic traditions – or a tragedy.

It seemed that everyone in the Oasis was willing Bartholomew to give the right reply. Beside me, Ralph clenched his fist and cursed him under his breath.

Bartholomew stared at Electra, seemingly seeing through her, as he considered his past and contemplated his future.

And then, with a dignity and courage I never expect to witness again, Perry Bartholomew stepped forward, took the hands of his wife and daughter and, between Electra and Elegy, moved from the concourse and left behind him the destitute monument of his continuum-frame.

ACKNOWLEDGEMENTS

"The Girl Who Died for Art and Lived"
first publised in *Interzone* 22, 1989

"The Phoenix Experiment"
first published in *The Lyre* 1, 1991.

"Big Trouble Upstairs"
first published in *Interzone* 26, 1988.

"Star of Epsilon"
first published in *REM* 1, 1991.

"The Time-Lapsed Man"
first published in *Interzone* 24, 1988.

"The Pineal-Zen Equation"
first published as "Krash-Bangg Joe and the Pineal-Zen Equation" *Interzone* 21, 1987.

"The Art of Acceptance"
first published in *Strange Plasma* 1, 1989.

"Elegy Perpetuum"
first published in *Interzone* 52, 1991.

Eric Brown would like to thank the editors of the above publications: David Pringle, Ian Sales, Nicholas Mahoney, Arthur Straker, Steve Pasechnick.

ABOUT THE AUTHOR

Eric Brown's first short story was published in *Interzone* in 1987, and he sold his first novel, *Meridian Days*, in 1992. He has won the British Science Fiction Award twice for his short stories and has published thirty-five books: SF novels, collections, books for teenagers and younger children, and he writes a monthly SF review column for *The Guardian*. His latest books include the novel *Cosmopath*, for Solaris Books. He is married to the writer and mediaevalist Finn Sinclair and they have a daughter, Freya.

His website can be found at: www.ericbrown.co.uk